A Special Kind of Treachery

ROBERT ADAM

CONTENTS

Preface

'Do we have the wisdom to achieve by construction and cooperation what Napoleon and Hitler failed to achieve by destruction and conquest?'

Edward Heath, 19 May 1971

'It is necessary, in the first place, to accept that in a certain sense the whole of our long negotiations were peripheral, accidental and secondary.'

Sir Con O'Neill, British lead negotiator, 27 July 1972

'Do not move an ancient boundary stone or encroach on the fields of the fatherless, for their Defender is strong; he will take up their case against you.'

Proverbs 23 v10-11

Prologue

Kramer picked me up from outside my hotel in the Fifteenth Arrondissement just before seven. It was a cold morning and seemed even colder because of where he was taking me. As I pushed open the heavy swing doors, something made me look up and then up again. High above the mansard roofs, just at the edge of vision, the ghost of the dying moon lingered on in a sky of the palest sapphire blue. A third of a million kilometres away, even the smallest craters on the rim of the crescent were crisply defined in the clear air. An object of awe, rather than portent - not that I was superstitious in that way. A momentary distraction from the fun and games Kramer had in store for me for the rest of the week.

Coming back down to earth, I crossed the chestnut tree-lined street to where he'd parked in front of a boulangerie, its windows fogged by the breath of customers queuing inside out of the cold. People going about their everyday business, people who could look forward to doing the same thing again tomorrow.

Kramer was also going about his business as he waited expectantly by the door of his gleaming Citroën DS - glossy black tribute to French automotive design, and his own personal homage to the General who'd loved the 'Goddess' too. Kramer's Gaullism and the smugness that went with it was something I'd had to get used to over the years. The more practical side of me wondered where he'd had the car polished to such a shine. I knew my unofficial boss hadn't done it himself, for Kramer was a senior member of the Commission in Brussels, with a top-floor office in the Berlaymont building and an apartment near the Royal Quarter. But he was much more than that, and he liked to remind me of it.

In nineteen forty, at the nadir of France's fortunes, he'd been one of de Gaulle's original *hommes de Londres*. As a junior diplomat, no older than I was now, Kramer had served the General from the very first day of his exile in the English capital, all the way until the liberation of metropolitan France. What exactly that service had entailed was only ever obliquely hinted at, and I'd often wondered what Carlton Gardens had asked of him in those first desperate few months following the capitulation.

But whatever de Gaulle had said to inspire Kramer back then, it had worked. Even during the bitter years of de Gaulle's second exile in the political wilderness after the war, Kramer's loyalty to the General had remained undimmed from deep within the French diplomatic service. But it was more than loyalty to a failed politician, it was faith. And an investment that would later handsomely pay off.

In the meantime, during the late forties and fifties, Kramer had seemingly reprised his wartime role as the most discreet of discreet fixers for the Quai d'Orsay. He'd been sent around the world to solve the problems that accredited diplomats couldn't be seen to touch. A bribe here, a little blackmail there, and sometimes... who knew what he'd done sometimes? He'd never admitted to it, but I was almost certain that at one point he'd been to Indochina, where the French intelligence agencies had taken over the local opium trade - until the CIA arrived.

But with the General's return to power thirteen years ago, he'd emerged from that demi-monde and become the consummate Brussels bureaucrat in his own right; on the surface merely another well-paid *fonctionnaire*, quietly dedicated to the Project. My best guess at Kramer's official status since nineteen forty was that he'd never actually appeared on the books of the SDECE, France's foreign intelligence service. That said, after having been in the business of international political intrigue for so long, I suspected Kramer had no need for any kind of formal recognition. But whatever his real relationship with Paris' secret services, I knew that during the two years I'd worked for him, they'd granted him any favour I'd known him to ask.

He came around to open the boot and I slung my gear into the narrow space between the wheel arches, next to two small canvas bags. Before I could close the lid, he quickly bent down to unzip my green holdall and slipped both his bags inside.

'One has your special equipment, the other something for Jimmy,' he explained with a half-smile. *'Allons-y!'*

We pulled out into the traffic stream, heading south-west out of the city. Despite the advancing clock, he drove smoothly and unhurriedly, humming a tune softly to himself. Neither the slow-moving *camionnettes* nor the mopeds that zipped past on our outside seemed to disturb him in the slightest.

I recognised this deliberate calmness. It usually spoke to a confidence in the imminent success of some scheme or other he had on the go. Right now it was a confidence I didn't share.

Once we'd crossed under the Boulevard Périphérique, he attempted conversation.

'All well at home?'

I grunted in reply. He changed the topic.

'Driving out here this morning reminds me of the war. All those journeys in the small hours to darkened airfields across East Anglia and the south coast of England to wish *bon courage* to our people.'

'You've never told me what you did for de Gaulle in London. Or at least, not in detail.'

He twisted round to check his blind quarter.

'Each year it becomes harder and harder to explain what it was like to people who weren't there.' With a flick of the indicator he changed lanes.

'We'd have a *petit verre* by the aircraft with the people crossing over that night, then they'd collect their parachutes, clamber up into the fuselage, and were gone.' A sombreness crept into his voice.

'Sometimes there'd be a backwards glance from the top of the ladder. Leaving a place of safety, I suppose. Sometimes never to return.'

I didn't rate his motivational technique. A gloomy tableau of mournful Frenchmen wasn't the picture I'd have painted to inspire someone.

He gave a soft sigh. 'There's nothing more evocative than the roar of aero-engines and the half-seen underside of a Lysander as it disappears into the darkness behind the moonlight,' he concluded wistfully.

I looked at him thoughtfully for a second. At his thinning hair, gold spectacles, and the lines around his eyes. 'Did you ever wish sometimes that you could have gone with them?' I asked.

He didn't have an answer to my question. Perhaps an explanation would have revealed more than he cared for.

We headed south-west for another twenty minutes. Kramer ignored the signs for the main entrance to the Vélizy-Villacoublay air base, instead taking the road which ran along its barbed wire northern perimeter. Past the concrete hangars at the far end of the airfield, he turned in at a secondary gate and stopped by a modest guardhouse, parking the car out of sight from the public road.

From the top of my own embarkation ladder, so to speak, I watched with a metallic taste in my mouth as he went to confer with the sentry. After a minute or so, he returned with a laminated vehicle pass which he tucked into the corner of the sharply curved windscreen of the DS.

'Just a few hundred metres further now.'

We drove down a service road, approaching the apron. A lone dark grey Transall transport aircraft sat there in the middle distance, blurred air behind the exhausts of its engines. As we came into the pilot's range of vision, he engaged the propellers and they slowly started to turn. The sickly-sweet scent of kerosene carried over to us in the cool morning air, becoming stronger as Kramer joined the taxiway proper and sped along it to the waiting aircraft.

'We're late,' I told him accusingly. 'They don't like wasting fuel.'

I thought back to the flights I'd taken with the Foreign Legion during the familiarisation course Kramer had insisted I go on in preparation for London. He'd pulled strings for me to join a group of NATO officers spending a fortnight observing the Legion at work. This particular jaunt had involved us shuttling between various bases in Provence, and as a bonus had even included a short trip to Chad, across the Mediterranean and over the desert to see the French Army in action on *Opération Bison*. But for me, the strangest experience of the whole time was having to wear a Bundeswehr lieutenant's uniform.

'Thomas, *arrête*,' said Kramer, bringing me back to the present. He'd clearly decided it was cover names only from now on.

As we approached the aircraft, the whine of the turbojets increased and the props began to spin faster and faster until they were a blurred, almost transparent disc. The tips of the blades appeared as a yellow outer ring - a warning that decapitation awaited the unwary.

Kramer brought the DS to a stop at the edge of the tarmac, hard by the grass. The aircraft's rear ramp was down and its loadmaster stood in the opening, urgently waving us on.

We got out and went round to the back of the car. Kramer handed me my bags.

'I meant what I said last year,' he said. 'This is the most important mission you'll ever undertake for France. If it's successful, you'll get Masson's job and the freedom to run the department as you see fit.'

'But it's not the most important, is it?'

I'd never get a better chance to put him under pressure. Or maybe, I thought wildly, to finally find that one irrefutable excuse not to go. Given the people I'd be mixing with, I didn't need a portent in the heavens to warn me that this little adventure would likely turn out quite differently to his blithe assurances. His answer needed to be quick because the plane was starting to rock back and forth on its brakes, the Air Force pilot straining to be released into his natural environment.

'It was urgent at the end of last year when you promised me the moon if I'd go to London. But the real action is happening back in Brussels right now. I should be working with Masson, spying on the delegations of all the accession countries.'

There was an impatient shout from the aircraft's loadmaster.

'We've already got O'Neill and the other British negotiators just where we want them. We've had them there since last year, before the talks even started,' said Kramer with a touch of irritation.

'As of today, England's accession is virtually in the bag. There's no secret that Masson can possibly find out for me in Brussels that compares to eliminating this one last outstanding risk.'

The loadmaster called out again. Then he unplugged his headset from the plane's intercom and started striding towards us.

Kramer glanced over at the crewman. He reached out and grasped my elbow, pulling me in towards him.

'We're in the final straight. Right now the prize is ours to lose. We have to shepherd the leaders through the final conference in Paris in eight weeks' time, and then we're done.' He spoke in a low voice, just loud enough to be heard above the noise of the engines.

'The preparations for May are nearly complete. We've carefully choreographed the illusion of an English win, a little theatre for their domestic consumption. After that, it's simply a question of them ratifying the treaty in their Parliament.'

'It sounds so easy.'

'Because it is,' he said, almost triumphantly. 'And there's no action I won't sanction to make sure it all comes off and our allies in England achieve their life's ambition. If this wasn't so important, I'd send Masson instead. *Voilà*.'

That wasn't quite true either. Neither of us would admit to his real reason for choosing me - at least, not out loud. Given what I was about to do, there was probably no one better qualified in any of the six EEC countries. Worse luck for me.

Chapter One

Reynolds enjoyed seeing the energy on display at airfields: the ground crew snaking out heavy fuel hoses, the aircraft handlers' arcane semaphore, the tug operators manoeuvring their out-sized charges precisely to the stand.

His own horizon since university was one limited to the walls of a succession of dreary offices at the Service's headquarters in Leconfield House and its outstations. A world of paper, of reading transcripts and writing reports, and of making considered judgements based on fragmentary information. A world of uncertainty and uncertain outcomes, unlike the world of aviation. In that world, if you made a mistake there were no half crashes or partial collisions with other aircraft.

For all Reynolds' time spent at the heart of the British security establishment, he'd only been to the government's de facto private airfield at Northolt once before today. One misty morning two years ago he'd waited by the same runway to collect a Soviet army intelligence officer who'd gone over to the Americans in Washington DC. After the CIA had put him through the wringer, the Service had requested his transfer for further debriefing in London.

Unlike this morning, that day there had been no time to stand and stare. Almost doubled over for fear of KGB snipers, the grey, careworn man had jogged the short distance from the US Air Force jet to the waiting car. Not that any of the automatic death sentences passed by Moscow Centre on defecting traitors had ever been carried out as far Reynolds knew.

He checked his watch and glanced over the roof of the pool car. Brierly stood leaning with his elbows on top of the Triumph as he scanned the sky from behind the open passenger door, an old-fashioned trilby pulled down low over his head.

He'd only met the senior man two days ago when Brierly had briefed Reynolds and his boss at Leconfield House. Despite the usual warnings about the need for secrecy, the assignment seemed simple enough. Now it was almost upon them.

All of a sudden, Brierly turned his head and Reynolds looked skywards too. A high-winged turboprop had emerged from the clouds and was descending the glide path, landing lights burning on the port and starboard undercarriage sponsons.

A few seconds later, the pilot brought the plane down to kiss the ground with the merest puff of smoke from its tyres. They watched the Transall disappear down the other end of the runway, before turning off and rolling at speed back along the taxiway to the apron where they'd parked.

The pilot applied the brakes and the aircraft slowed. Without stopping, he executed a smooth, controlled turn on the spot before finally coming to a halt, tail facing the Englishmen. Even as the pitch of the engines dropped, the rear ramp started to descend with a whine from the actuators.

Reynolds saw the heads of two men in the widening opening: the loadmaster in his khaki overalls and the one they had come to pick up, unsmiling as he stared out across the apron at the reception party.

As soon as the ramp hit the tarmac, the man was moving, an olive-green army kitbag hanging heavily from his shoulder and a black flight bag held by his side. When he'd approached to within a few feet, Reynolds noticed the crease of a scar running down from his left eye socket and a star-shaped lesion in the centre of each hand.

From that moment, in Reynolds' mind, the other man was 'the Assassin.' He thought the name might have been a character he vaguely remembered from The Threepenny Opera by Brecht. But wherever it came from, once a name had lodged in Reynolds' head, it stuck there for good.

Brierly went to intercept their visitor while Reynolds unlocked the boot. The man came round to the back of the car, slung in his bags and slammed the lid. A service number and the name 'Hofmann' in block letters had been written in black felt tip on one end of the olive-green bag - presumably to distinguish it from others when piled up in the back of an army truck.

The three of them stood by the car, staring awkwardly at each other until the Transall left in a renewed roar of its engines and the apron became quiet enough again for conversation.

Brierly spoke first and made the introductions.

'This is Reynolds. He's from our Secret Service. Our Sûreté, if you like. You'll be staying with him if we invite you back to London in a couple of weeks' time.'

The Assassin nodded noncommittally.

'This is Herr Hofmann,' said Brierly.

'You can call me John,' said Reynolds, acknowledging their similar ages. The Assassin nodded back but didn't offer his own first name. Arrogant devil, thought Reynolds. Trust the French to have sent over a West German to do their dirty work.

Brierly introduced himself. 'I'm a former colleague of Kramer's. He and I worked together during the first part of the war.'

'He told me in Brussels,' replied the Assassin. There was an underlying cadence to his voice which Reynolds couldn't place - perhaps the influence of the Legion which softened the accents of legionnaires who came from all corners of Europe and beyond.

'During these next two days you're on probation while we decide if we want to use you on this job,' said Brierly. He gave a quick look at his watch. 'Time to go.'

There was a fraction of a second's hesitation on the West German's part before Reynolds reached for the handle and opened the rear passenger door for him. Brierly joined the Assassin in the back and Reynolds took his place behind the wheel.

They moved off, Reynolds driving them in silence around the perimeter track to the main gate while Brierly quizzed their visitor.

'What did Kramer say about my work with him during the war?' he asked.

The Assassin shrugged.

'No details. Simply that you and he were collaborators.'

Brierly gave a slight cough. 'We wouldn't typically use that word in this context. Kramer helped me recruit agents from among the French servicemen who'd escaped to England in nineteen forty.'

The Assassin would have preferred Brierly to have just told him plainly that he'd made a mistake in English. 'How easy was it to convince Frenchmen to go back and fight?' he asked.

Brierly paused for the briefest of seconds before replying. 'Kramer was very persuasive. My organisation trained them, then he and I sent them over.'

'Who were you with? The Special Operations Executive? The SOE?'

Reynolds' ears pricked up at the Assassin's question.

'I was. Kramer wasn't. But the French embassy sometimes used SOE agents for their own political tasks.'

'How many survived?' asked the Assassin in a neutral voice. Reynolds looked in the rear-view mirror to try to catch his expression.

'We had enough success to make it worthwhile.'

'And since the war?'

'I stopped doing that kind of thing a long time ago.'

The Assassin stared at Brierly until the ex-SOE man felt the need to give his story an ending.

'The war was a special time. Special in every way. For those of us in our twenties, it was the high point of our lives up until then. But afterwards there was no point in hanging around the peacetime organisations, trying to relive our glory days.'

'What did you do instead?'

'I turned my political warfare skills to good use. I found a new calling as a lobbyist - a kind of policy adviser, you might say.'

Up in the front, Reynolds raised an eyebrow at this as they approached the sentry barrier. Once out of the main gate, he turned right and joined Western Avenue by the Polish Air Force memorial. The arterial road became the Westway and soon they were driving through Notting Hill and across the top of Hyde Park to Mayfair.

Compared to Paris' wide boulevards and grand Baron Haussmann-style apartment buildings, London's streets felt provincial in scale to the Assassin. But he was struck by the extent of Hyde Park which seemed to carry on and on, a couple of kilometres at least by his reckoning, almost the same length as the Bois de la Cambre in Brussels.

Some things he was expecting. There were the same red buses, black taxis and red phone boxes that he'd seen previously in pictures of London. And there were red post boxes too, curiously of the same size and shape as the green ones in Dublin the year before.

On the pavements, younger people in donkey jackets and jeans pushed past men in suits and well-dressed women in smart coats. To his puzzlement, once he even saw a man wearing a bowler hat and striped trousers coming out of a hotel on the Bayswater Road, a furled umbrella in his hand.

Going by what he'd seen so far, London certainly seemed busy, but unlike the first time he'd been to Rome, the busyness seemed purposeful. That day last summer she'd sat icily in the back of the taxi with her boyfriend, as they weaved in and out past overladen trucks, three-wheeled vans and tiny Fiats on the way in from Fiumicino. No one did happy-go-lucky chaos like the Italians.

When they pulled up at the entrance to the Dorchester, Reynolds expected the Assassin to be impressed or at least appreciative of the Service's choice of accommodation. Instead, he was impassive, as if having top-hatted flunkeys guarding his hotel from the riff-raff was a usual experience. Reynolds couldn't say the same. Looking back at his own childhood, he realised his parents must have pinched themselves for years to keep him at school. It was a sacrifice that neither side had ever explicitly acknowledged.

Brierly cleared his throat and turned to the Assassin. 'Our first meeting isn't until noon so you'll have a couple of hours to freshen up. I'll call you from reception when we come to collect you.'

'Give me three hours,' he replied peremptorily. 'I need to make a call.'

Brierly's eyes narrowed for an instant. 'If you insist. Half-eleven, then.'

Both men got out of the car. The Assassin took his bags from the boot and without a backwards glance disappeared into the hotel, brushing off the waiting porters. Brierly came round to sit next to Reynolds in the front.

Reynolds put the car into gear and drove round the corner into Stanhope Gate. In a few short seconds they'd reached its other end. Brierly rapped the dashboard a couple of times, then pointed to an empty spot by the side of the street.

'Drop me off there.'

Reynolds slotted in between a Ford Cortina in the new curved body style and a large Mercedes.

'Well? What do you think of our latter-day Beau Geste?' asked Brierly.

'We've scarcely met him. I prefer not to rush to judgement.'

'Sometimes you have to,' said Brierly sharply. 'What do they teach you in your Service these days?'

Reynolds gave himself a moment before venturing an answer. 'Arriving by military transport was pretentious. Hofmann could easily have flown into Heathrow.'

'Is that it?' asked Brierly. 'How about the fact that he doesn't really want to be here? Didn't you pick up any clues at all?'

Reynolds stood his ground. 'What about the paratroop-carrying aircraft? If the French wanted to fly him in privately, a small air force liaison jet would have made more sense.'

Brierly pursed his lips.

'What are you trying to say? My old wartime colleague is playing some kind of game with us?'

Reynolds gave a slight shrug.

'When Hofmann comes to lodge with you, I want you to keep a close eye on him. Let me know immediately if something seems wrong - right?'

'What mischief do you think the French might be getting up to?'

Brierly glanced out of the passenger side window.

'I don't know. I'll meet you outside the Dorchester at half-eleven. Don't be late.'

-

In his room on the third floor, the Assassin quickly unpacked his black flight bag. When he was done, he unzipped the army kitbag to do a final inventory of its contents. Slipping an A-Z out from the inside pocket, he stood there consulting it for a minute, tracing a route through the maze of streets with his forefinger.

There was no point in staying angry with Kramer. For all the pressure put on him, ultimately, he'd agreed to come. His immediate objective was to get through the next two days and then home to Brussels for whatever awaited him there. The bitterest fights didn't always involve knives and fists. The sooner this was all over, the better for everyone concerned.

Checking his watch, he reclosed the kitbag and swung it over his shoulder. Once out of the room, he went down by the service stairs rather than using the lift and walked straight out through the back of the hotel, ignoring the strange looks from the staff members coming the other way. Heading north past blocks of substantial Georgian and Victorian red brick buildings, he took a couple of random turns and doubled back at least once before making his way east towards Soho.

Just beyond Piccadilly, the streets became narrower and soon took on a sleazy aspect. Some of them seemed to be almost continuous rows of bookshops, massage parlours, and cinemas showing blue movies. Even mid-morning, the doors to the walk-ups were open and he saw the occasional customer duck inside off the pavement.

He fetched up in front of a club just behind Brewer Street, nestling between a snack bar and a sauna. Above its metal-clad door hung a small neon sign in the form of a three-leafed clover, unlit at this time of day. He pounded the door until someone inside slid back the cover of the viewing slit.

'I'm here to see the boss. *Le patron*,' he announced to a pair of suspicious eyes.

'Who are you?'

'Je suis Thomas.'

The eyes disappeared for half a minute, then a heavily-built man unbolted and squinted at the Assassin's cheek. A second, even bigger bouncer stood behind him, with a scar of his own, running left to right across the bridge of his nose.

'Show me your paws,' said the first man. He reached out and grabbed both of the Assassin's wrists at the same time, twisting them to inspect the front and back of each hand.

'*Vaffanculo*,' growled the Assassin, as he snatched them back. Last year in Italy he'd learned a whole new list of descriptive curses.

With a jerk of the bouncer's head, he was summoned inside. He looked coldly at the man, quickly pushing past before he got any ideas about checking inside the kitbag.

The second bouncer took the Assassin across the seating area by the bar, its floor still sticky from the previous night's entertainment, then upstairs to a dimly-lit corridor on the first floor. A well-worn, almost threadbare runner down its middle led to a door at the far end. His escort knocked twice.

'*C'est qui?*' asked a voice from inside. The bouncer told him through the closed door.

'*Entri.*'

Jimmy Malta's office was windowless, but perhaps in compensation for the lack of a view, both floor and walls were carpeted in zebra-print. After a second or two, the Assassin saw a man of around Kramer's age, sitting behind a polished ebony desk at the rear of the room. Unlike Kramer, his carefully styled hair was still thick and innocent of any grey. Jimmy ignored the interruption to his work, carrying on for a few seconds longer as he inspected a thick ledger, making swift notes in its margins. He looked up to stare at the Assassin.

'*Lascia ci,*' he said with a nod to the bouncer. Jimmy closed the book and came around the desk.

'You just got in?' he asked the Assassin in English, as soon as the other man had left the room.

'About an hour ago.'

'Kramer sent a package with you?'

'I have it here.' The Assassin touched the shoulder strap of his kitbag.

Jimmy nodded again. 'Take a seat.' He pointed to a settee and chairs ranged around a low table over by one of the monochrome walls. 'Just a moment,' he said, as he returned behind his desk.

More ebony furniture stood against the opposite wall, a sideboard with rows of bottles and upturned glasses on coasters ranged along its top. The Assassin placed the bag by the side of a chair and sank into soft crimson plush.

'Why "Malta"?' he called across the room, as the nightclub owner set two glasses down on the desk and poured a measure into each from a brown glass bottle.

Jimmy looked up, waiting a deliberate second or two before replying. The Assassin had met similar men in Italy last year. Now he remembered what dealing with them was like.

'When I came to London to join my cousins just before the war, people overheard us speaking Corsican and assumed we were Maltese,' he said, screwing down the cap of the bottle. 'The name stuck, for me anyway.' He shrugged. 'Confusion is useful sometimes.'

'I get it,' said the Assassin, thinking just then of his own new persona, specially created over the past few weeks for this mission.

'How did Kramer end up working with Germans?' asked Jimmy. 'I thought he hated them?'

'Senior bureaucrats in Brussels don't care which nationalities they employ.'

Jimmy carried the glasses over to the sideboard and opened the door to a concealed fridge.

'So who's he really working for over there?' he asked. He took out a bottle of iced water to top up the yellow spirit in the glasses, turning the liquid cloudy.

'Officially - only the EEC. Who was he with when you first met him?'

Jimmy turned round to face the Assassin, a glass in each hand. 'It was the early part of the war. But he came to me in confidence. And a secret is still a secret, even after thirty years.'

He brought over the drinks and sat down on the settee. 'Kramer said he wanted me to store a bag for you. What's in it?'

'Your package, among other things.'

'Show me the other things.'

The Assassin paused for half a heartbeat. It wasn't in his nature to make concessions to anyone.

'You sure this room is private? No one's going to interrupt us?'

Jimmy nodded. 'There's an electric lock on the door. It opens from my desk.'

The Assassin unzipped the holdall and laid two pistols on the table.

'Makarov 9mm and silencer. Browning Hi-Power - also 9mm but with a different cartridge. I have ammunition for both. Not to be mixed up.'

Jimmy took a handkerchief from his breast pocket and picked up the Makarov. He hefted it in his hand.

'Why bring a Soviet gun?'

'Confusion can be useful. You said so yourself.'

Jimmy replaced the Makarov and picked up the Browning, still using his handkerchief.

'Ever used them before?'

'What do you mean by "used"?' The Assassin didn't wait for an answer. 'The Browning, yes. Not the other one.'

'Not yet, you mean?' Jimmy put the Browning back down on the table.

'Not if I can help it.'

'Did Kramer tell you to bring them?'

'They're only with me for insurance. I got caught out last December.'

'But you learned your lesson?'

The Assassin cocked his head in ironic agreement.

'Okay. They'll go into my safe. What else have you got there?' The undercurrent of hostility in Jimmy's tone had faded now to one of mere curiosity.

The Assassin put the guns back into the holdall. He took out one of the canvas bags Kramer had given him that morning and passed it across the table. Jimmy leant forward expectantly and fumbled with the buckles. Inside was a brick-sized package wrapped several times in black plastic. Taking a switchblade from the pocket of his jacket, Jimmy flicked it open and pierced the wrapping. He wiggled the knife inside the package for a second or two, before bringing the blade up to his mouth, carefully touching the white powder on its sharp edge with his tongue.

'Okay. C'est bon.'

'No wonder Kramer wanted me to fly military this morning.'

'You must have guessed?'

The Assassin shrugged. 'Kramer keeps his cards close to his chest.'

Jimmy eased back into his chair and crossed one leg over his knee. He took a sip of the pastis and the Assassin took his chance to get the measure of the man on whom he would be relying for his logistical arrangements.

'So can I ask? How did a boy from Marseille come to London with nothing and end up with all this?' He motioned with his hand around the room.

For the first time the Corsican broke into something approaching a faint grin. 'My eldest cousin and I had a good war. We started off as housebreakers during the blackouts of the Blitz. Then we stole supplies from the Free French forces using a network of corrupt quartermaster sergeants. By 'forty-four I was running my own troupe of Piccadilly commandos.'

He swirled his glass.

'The real Maltese controlled almost all prostitution back then, but just before D-Day there were over a million Americans in England. More than enough to go round.'

'You had a busy war.'

'On the night of VE Day one of the Messina girls tried to turn fifty tricks. She missed her target by one.'

'Maybe she was in love with her pimp?'

Jimmy raised an eyebrow. 'Then she was deceiving herself. The brothers were making ten thousand pounds a week just after the war - that would be about thirty thousand in today's money.'

'So how does Kramer fit into your story of wartime London?'

Now Jimmy gazed at the opposite wall, his eyes fixed somewhere in the middle distance.

'He walked into our old bar in Greek Street one night during the Blitz, just as the All Clear sounded. The Luftwaffe never shut us down for long. A bomb had fallen in the next street and there was broken glass all over the pavement. None in our windows either. I can still remember the crunch underfoot that night as he came in through the front door. He ordered a brandy and said he had to speak to a clan member there and then. Maybe it was all a reaction to the air raid. He wanted information on the Marseilles waterfront. Trying to sound out where our people stood with regards to Vichy. Who his agents could trust.'

'So he was with the BCRA?'

Jimmy shrugged. The Assassin swirled his glass, savouring the cool fragrance. It spoke of Provence and fields of summer lavender.

'Tell me about these English people that I'm meant to be working with. Did you know Brierly during the war?'

'Not that I remember. I told you, it's been thirty years. According to what Kramer told me at the time, there were a lot of oddballs drifting in and out of the picture just after Dunkirk. Lots of newly-created secret organisations too, all fighting each other to the death for personnel and budget.'

'Like gang warfare between spies?'

Jimmy looked narrowly at the Assassin.

'I wouldn't know. Our family always kept out of trouble by paying off whoever was on top at the time: Billy Hill, Jack Spot, the Richardson gang, the Kray twins before they got banged up.'

'Have you had competition from other wholesalers over the years?'

Jimmy took a sip of pastis, looking at the Assassin over the rim of his glass. He slowly shook his head.

'Some. But we're very cautious, very discreet. We know not to be greedy. The Triads next door in Chinatown have their eye on our routes from Saigon though. We'll see what happens there when the Americans leave.'

'Didn't the SDECE sell you out to the Bureau of Narcotics over the transatlantic trade?'

Jimmy looked reprovingly at the Assassin again.

'Ignorance is dangerous. Whatever Kramer might have told you, the English end of our operations is still going strong. I should know.'

'And what do the English think?'

'The deal with the local London bosses is that they leave us alone as long as we stick to running just the one club as our cover and don't take too much of their passing trade.'

Jimmy uncrossed his legs and set his drink on the table.

'But that's enough questions about my business.'

'How about the guy they're taking me to see later today? Smythe?' asked the Assassin. 'Kramer says you'll be hosting an event for him?'

'He keeps himself to himself. Works with people who organise sex parties.'

'I thought he spied on the attendees in some way?'

'You can't find out about the scene unless you're part of it.'

'Is Smythe trustworthy?'

'He's a *flic* who hangs around Soho, so he's as trustworthy as someone in his position can ever be. West End Central nick is the most corrupt in the country.'

The Assassin looked down at his glass and gave it another idle swirl, letting the silence open up.

'Maybe I'm being harsh,' continued Jimmy. 'He arranged a party here once before, about a year ago. A regular one.'

'What's a "regular" party?'

'Adults only, for a start. And where the majority of the guests are genuine swingers as opposed to tarts hired to pad out the numbers. Otherwise it's just prostitution and I've been out of that game for decades.'

'Which part of the police is Smythe connected to?'

Jimmy shook his head.

'It's never been clear. He's not part of Obscene Publications or the Flying Squad, so he's not working for the Syndicate.'

'What's the Syndicate?'

'The people who run Soho: pimping, porn, and the protection that goes with it. The chief superintendents of the two squads that I mentioned are on the payroll. Remember I told you the Messinas were making the equivalent of thirty thousand a week at the end of the war? Today the Syndicate brings in at least triple that.'

'Growth industry then? Do they sell drugs as well?'

'Do they need to?'

The Assassin frowned to himself as he did some quick mental arithmetic. 'That's an obscene amount of money. No wonder the police don't want to miss out.'

'The heads of those two squads need to remember the tale of the goose that laid the golden egg.'

The Assassin nodded in solemn agreement. He bent down to close up the kitbag, fastening the two zip handles together with a miniature padlock.

'I'll need access day or night.'

'Someone is always here.' Jimmy picked up his glass again and finished the last of his pastis. 'Are we done now?'

The Assassin stretched his legs, as if he was about to get up.

'One last question. You've been in England a long time. What are the people here like?'

'The ones who come to Soho? They prove that with the lights off, people are all the same under the skin.'

'I meant the English in general.'

'From your tone it sounds that you don't like them very much,' said Jimmy.

The Assassin shrugged.

'They can be stoical in the way that Russians are meant to be. I saw some of that during the war. But they're suspicious of authority too. It comes out in their sense of humour. Macmillan was constantly being humiliated by the TV comedians towards the end.'

'Were there riots here in 'sixty-eight like in Paris?'

'Some unrest. But nothing compared to France. No rumours of a coup. They're not radical in the way we are. They've never had cause to overthrow their government.'

'Lucky them,' said the Assassin.

He got to his feet. 'Keep my things safe.'

The Assassin chose to wait for Brierly downstairs in the foyer of the Dorchester rather than in the room as instructed. Along with not making concessions, he had an instinctive aversion to being told what to do.

He sat watching the comings and goings in the lobby for a while. The whole world seemed to have arrived in London this March. Amongst others, the Dorchester was playing host today to American executives, Japanese businessmen, and keffiyeh-wearing Arabs in dark chalk stripe suits.

At half-past eleven he looked up as Brierly appeared through the revolving doors, right on cue.

'You seem keen to get started,' said the Englishman laconically.

'How far are we going?' asked the Assassin.

'Just south of the river. We're meeting Smythe at his house.'

Reynolds was parked on the hotel's forecourt, waiting in a brown Vauxhall Viva this time. He tapped a finger impatiently on the steering wheel as he kept half an eye on the doormen, who didn't look like they'd tolerate anything less than a Rolls taking up the space for long. The others got in and he started the engine, swinging round to turn left onto Park Lane heading south.

When he looked back in the rear-view mirror a little later, Reynolds saw the Assassin peering out at the grimy streets around Victoria station and wondered how London looked to someone used to the cities of the West German economic miracle.

They crossed the iron-grey Thames by Vauxhall Bridge, just as a deeply-laden collier chugged underneath on its way to the power station at Fulham. After twenty minutes, they'd arrived in Stockwell where a circle of four short terraces of older houses curved around a central green.

'Nice area,' said the Assassin, the first casual opinion he'd volunteered so far that day.

Reynolds watched from the car as his passengers trooped up the steps to one of the end houses and knocked. He settled down for a long wait.

The door was opened by Smythe himself. He had a sardonic set to his mouth and a hard stare for the Assassin. Their host was a much younger man than Brierly, under forty thought the Assassin. Smythe stood back to admit his visitors, flicking his eyes between them as they stepped inside.

They followed him through to a large dining room just off the hallway. Two original rooms had been knocked together into one which ran from the front to the back of the house. Not much of the rest of the interior seemed to have survived the new decade either. Chimney breasts had been blocked up, mantelpieces were gone, and the staircase had ranch rails for bannisters. Smythe sat them down around a long rosewood teak table with a view over the rear garden.

Brierly made the introductions.

'This is Detective Chief Inspector Smythe, but he goes by plain "Mister" these days.' Then to Smythe, he added, 'This is the West German. You can call him "Thomas."'

'First or last name?' asked Smythe.

'First.'

'Right. To business,' said Brierly. 'Today is the only time the three of us will meet together.' He turned to the Assassin. 'If this operation goes ahead, your main day-to-day contact will be Smythe.'

'And what does Mr. Smythe do, day-to-day?'

'I catch nonces.'

'Smythe works for the Metropolitan Police,' said Brierly.

'You mean the London city police?'

'Yes. Apart from the parks and the City proper. Have you ever had dealings with the law?' asked Smythe, eyeing the Assassin's facial scar.

'No,' he replied tersely. 'What's the "City proper"?'

'The financial district,' replied Brierly, paying back the Assassin's shortness in kind.

'And what are "nonces"?' he asked, wading through a sea of idioms. It was going to be a long few weeks at this rate he thought.

'Pederasts,' said Brierly. 'Child abusers - as in the sexual sense, rather than battered babies. They're trying to give themselves a new name now: "paedophiles." They think it will make them more acceptable to society.'

'What's the age of consent here?' asked the Assassin, his expression carefully blank.

'Sixteen. Twenty-one for queers,' replied Smythe.

'And do you catch many of the sexual abuser types?'

Smythe took a new pack of John Player Specials from his jacket pocket and reached for the ashtray in the middle of the table. Breaking the cellophane wrapper he offered a cigarette to each of the others. Both declined. The Assassin was trying to keep a promise.

'Abuse is almost impossible to prove. Few juries are prepared to believe the testimony of a borstal boy over the word of men with status in society.'

'So how do you prove abuse on the occasions when it is possible?'

Smythe took his time over lighting up before replying. Even his gold lighter was showy, patterned with a knurled roller at one corner for ignition.

'Sometimes the abusers get careless. Take things too far, so that it's hard to deny the evidence. Sometimes they pick on the wrong child - one who's protected in some way.'

Brierly glanced briefly at Smythe, then flicked his gaze back to the Assassin.

'If it's so hard to get accusations against real child abusers to stick,' asked the Assassin, 'why will anyone take seriously allegations against a high-profile figure who's in the public eye almost every hour of the day?'

'The top man has had rumours around him for years. Mainly the obvious one. But he's very private about his relationships. No one has produced any definitive evidence either way,' replied Brierly.

'You know how these things work,' said Smythe.

The Assassin wasn't sure that he did. 'Politically speaking, he's survived this far,' he said. 'If there are rumours, they certainly haven't held him back from high office.'

'We're not taking any risks,' said Brierly.

'Who's "we"?' asked the Assassin.

Smythe and Brierly looked at one another again.

'Interested people within the Conservative Party,' replied Brierly. 'And the people at the institute I work for.'

Smythe exhaled a long stream of smoke, then tapped his cigarette on the ashtray. 'Sometimes,' he said, 'no matter how much you tell yourself the rumours are ridiculous, sometimes they're not.'

The Assassin raised his eyebrows. 'You really think there's a chance in this case?'

'There's always a chance,' replied Brierly. 'But no matter how small it might be, nothing can be allowed to derail our accession to the EEC. There's too much at stake for Europe - this kind of opportunity only comes around once in a thousand years.'

It wasn't a comparison period the Assassin would have chosen.

Smythe tapped some more ash off the end of his cigarette, silently watching Brierly as the lobbyist continued to argue with the Assassin.

'You and I need to convince Kramer that the British premiership is secure and that we're a reliable partner of France. The talks are at a very delicate stage right now.'

The Assassin made no answer to this. He wondered just how close Brierly was to the negotiations, given what Kramer had told him as he got on the plane that morning. He took out a pocket notebook.

'I know the plan in outline,' he said. 'What are the details?'

Brierly got up and went over to the window at the front of the house to check that Reynolds was still waiting in the car.

'Three men,' said Smythe, drawing on his cigarette. 'All connected in some way to Heath. Through the government, the Conservative Party, or else socially. All of them nonces known to the police to different degrees.'

'How did they get onto your radar? And then onto mine?'

'I keep a watching brief on the scene,' said Smythe. 'All the filth that bubbles up from that particular cesspool - the gossip, the smears, and the outright lies. But when these three charmers started dropping harder hints about the Prime Minister, I put the word out and Mr. Brierley showed an interest. Then he told your Mr. Kramer and now you're here.'

The Assassin frowned. 'Are our three targets acting in concert? What kind of hints are we talking about?'

'The usual mixture of the half-believable and the wildly implausible,' said Smythe. 'How they have a letter written by him to one of his fellow students at Oxford. Records of payments to his personal office from foreign governments. Suggestions that he conspired to have the former chairman of the Conservative Party removed in a smear campaign of his own.'

'Have they made any actual threat of blackmail?' asked the Assassin, still dubious.

'We believe there's a high chance of it,' said Brierly, still watching Reynolds' car.

'How can you ever know that? Blackmail is a big step. And once you start, you have to see it through to the end. They must know the dangers of taking on a Prime Minister.'

'Because he's Prime Minister is precisely why they might do it. Especially just now given what's going on in Brussels. They might judge it's the perfect time to demand a big payoff to stay quiet.'

'People's personal circumstances change all the time,' added Smythe. 'Businesses go bust, ex-wives demand bigger alimony payments. Who knows when they might suddenly need to make a lot of money quickly?'

The Assassin frowned again. 'So you're saying that this effort is entirely pre-emptive? Wasn't there a blackmail attempt on Heath reported last year? A plot by the Czech intelligence service?' he asked.

Brierly snapped round from his position by the window. 'Where did you hear that?' he asked suspiciously. 'It's not a secret within certain circles at Westminster, but it's not public knowledge either.'

'You just said it's not a secret. It came from the Czech ŠtB officer who defected a couple of years ago, Josef Frolik.'

Brierly stared at the Assassin. 'What did you hear exactly?'

'Frolik claimed that the Czechs sent a male organist over to England to play at a couple of concerts which Heath attended. Then the man in question extended a return invitation for Heath to play in Prague. The plan was for Heath to be seduced and photographed in the act.'

Smythe snorted. 'That would have been a sight for sore eyes. Can you imagine it? The frigid old git would scarcely have known where to look, let alone where to put it.'

'Careful who you're calling "old,"' said Brierly sharply.

The Assassin gave them both a frustrated glance.

'What's the relationship between the two of you and the Secret Service?' he asked with a nod towards the street where Reynolds was waiting.

Brierly came to sit back down. He half-reached for the pack of Players which Smythe had left on the table, but then thought better of it.

'This operation is highly compartmentalised. Reynolds and his direct boss, Masterson, know that you're here to get into their Service's file of suspected enemy operatives, but they don't know why. They've no need to know and they should know better than to ask. Their instructions come from high up within the intelligence community and then higher up again.'

It wasn't the answer the Assassin had been looking for, but he let it pass.

'These higher up people,' he asked, 'would they be the same as the ones in the Conservative Party whom you mentioned earlier or are they people at your institute?'

'They're just a group of concerned citizens from across Europe,' replied Brierly smoothly. 'The same as Kramer and I.'

The Assassin glanced across the table. Smythe looked sceptical but was trying not to show it.

'Listen up,' said Brierly. 'Just because Reynolds and his boss have been warned by their lords and masters not to dig, it doesn't mean that the pair of them won't try to weasel out of you what it is you're up to here. You need to be on your guard against their natural curiosity. Trust no one.'

It was a philosophy the Assassin already subscribed to. 'So what's my cover story when I'm with the three targets?'

'Amongst ourselves, we've taken to calling them the "Marks." But it's up to you what story you choose. My suggestion is that you're a West German over here on business who represents British exporters in mainland Europe, and that you're looking for amusement in the evenings.'

Smythe smirked at this. Brierly carried on. 'But for the third Mark, that is the actual cover story I'd use. He owns a manufacturing business. To get his attention, you could offer to find him business partners in the Eastern bloc.'

'And it's as simple as that? I get photographed in the company of the Marks so that if required, you can tell your tame journalists there's a suspicion they were working for the other side all along? Maybe leak a photo or a list of my meetings with them?'

'You've got the idea,' said Brierly.

'And will a single photo in each case be enough?'

Smythe spoke up. 'Seven years ago the Sunday Mirror acquired a photograph of a Conservative politician and one of the Kray twins sitting together on a sofa. With one picture and some carefully placed rumours they spun a story that they were queer for each other.'

'The Secret Service ended up getting involved in that affair,' added Brierly. 'So yes, our tabloids can make a scandal out of almost anything. The Mirror didn't even need to print the picture in the end.'

'I can see the headline now,' said Smythe. '"The Playboys and the East German Spy."' He tapped more of his ash into the tray. 'I wonder what they would have made of the story about the Czechs and Heath?'

'The Mirror had to pay Lord Boothby forty thousand pounds in damages, so they would have thought twice about reprinting any stories that might have appeared in Red Justice.'

The Assassin gave the lobbyist the briefest of looks, wondering how many people knew the title of the Czech Communist Party newspaper, let alone translated it.

'Really? For the West German press, paying damages is just a cost of doing business. Ask Axel Springer.'

This time he appeared to have caught them out with a local reference.

'For the Marks' threats to be credible,' he continued, 'they must have been prepared to leak their material on Heath to the press, surely? What if they intended to get someone like Springer to publish it overseas, beyond the reach of your laws?'

'The Boothby story was published by Stern in West Germany. But now we're getting into imponderables,' said Brierly. 'What I can tell you is that back in 'sixty-nine no one in Whitehall took seriously the suggestion that Heath was at risk of blackmail from homosexual communists. I'm sure even the left-wing papers on Fleet Street would think the same, titillating as the story might be.'

'It could be a thing of beauty,' admitted the Assassin. 'If the Marks go through with their threats, release Frolik's story about the Czechs which presumably you've been sitting on until now, and use the photographs of them with me to claim the communist bloc is attempting a new smear of Heath.'

Smythe drew on his cigarette. Brierly glanced quizzically, first at the policeman, then at the Assassin. 'I didn't want the risk of trying to bump them off. An assassination. Neither did you, as I understand from Kramer.'

'Was it you who gave him that idea?' said the Assassin coldly. 'Not that he needed the encouragement. Do either you or Kramer know how messy that kind of thing can be?'

'You speak from experience, "Thomas"?' asked Smythe with a speculative look.

Anger flashed in the depths of the Assassin's eyes.

'You can only get rid of so many people that way before you're found out,' he replied sharply. He gave himself a moment. 'Take the subtle approach and you can keep going until you've neutralised them all.'

Brierly gave a ghost of a smile. 'During the war Kramer was always impetuous. Assassination as a first resort. I'm not entirely sure he's mellowed over the years.'

'Desperate times called for desperate measures. Isn't that what you would say over here?' asked the Assassin, his voice under control again.

'You weren't even alive at the time. And if you had been, we'd have been on opposite sides. If I was going to say anything, it's that you remind me of the younger, less mature Kramer.'

The Assassin was impassive. Let Brierly think what he wanted, the best illusions were those which people created for themselves.

'That's a compliment, if you must know,' said Kramer's former colleague. 'Don't take it the other way. Tonight, you and I are going for dinner with a couple of people at my club. People in your line of work who take a professional interest in our French counterparts.'

'What sort of club? An English *Herrenklub*?'

'Yes. At least, I think that's what it's called in German.'

'Do I need to dress up?' asked the Assassin, knowing how much the upper classes in most countries loved their ceremony.

'No, you're a guest. A lounge suit will suffice. A business suit and tie. Reynolds will drive you back now and I'll pick you up from the hotel at seven.'

'And tomorrow?'

'Tomorrow, Smythe is going to take you to Hampshire to continue your education.'

The policeman gave him a sly look from under lidded eyes.

Chapter Two

Piccadilly, London - Thursday, 25th March 1971

Brierly's club had once been a grand townhouse on Piccadilly. Flambeaux burned in sconces on either side of the door and a succession of black cars and black taxis pulled up to the portico.

Brierly and the Assassin came on foot, having walked the short distance from the Dorchester. That had surprised him. Nobody at Kramer's level in the Commission would have thought twice about being driven here.

The other men arriving were all wearing tuxedos or dress uniforms and the women were in ballgowns and furs. Brierly was wearing a bow tie and dinner jacket too, but no row of miniature medals as the Assassin had seen on the chests of some of the other civilians.

'There's a regimental association dinner taking place here tonight. We're blending in,' explained Brierly.

'I'm not,' said the Assassin, giving him the evil eye. For a fleeting moment he felt like turning on his heel, just to teach the other man a lesson. Brierly ignored him, marching on ahead past the doormen to shrug off his coat by the cloakroom counter.

A large oil hung in the foyer. British infantry in red tunics, white cross-belts and dark-coloured kilts were formed into a square, standing and kneeling with fixed bayonets, holding off a cavalry charge. During the Napoleonic Wars, thought the Assassin. The British hadn't fought in Western Europe for a hundred years afterwards, missing out on such delights as Solferino and Sedan.

'We're dining upstairs in a private room,' said Brierly, leading the way across the marble floor to a staircase with an ornate wrought iron balustrade.

Up in the room, the table was set for six - gleaming cutlery laid on heavy linen. Someone was already sitting there, a man of about

Brierly's age with broad streaks of silver in an otherwise black mane of hair. He reminded the Assassin of a badger.

The new man stood up and came forward to greet them.

'This is Clive Fryatt,' announced Brierly. 'He works at the Foreign Office.'

Fryatt gave the Assassin a curt shake of the hand. 'There's champagne if you want it,' he said, indicating the ice bucket standing over on a side table. He returned to his own seat and took a sip from a glass that was already half empty.

'Brierly tells me you served in the French Foreign Legion?'

The Assassin had rehearsed his lines with Kramer long before tonight, but even so he took his time as he poured champagne for Brierly and himself.

'I joined when I was nineteen. I completed the full five years.'

'Were you in trouble with the police in West Germany?' asked Fryatt. 'Isn't that the usual reason why young men from overseas enter the service of France?'

The Assassin looked coldly at the Foreign Office man.

'I did my compulsory fifteen months in the Bundeswehr. But afterwards I wanted to be more than a peacetime soldier. It was around the time of the mercenaries in the Congo,' he added by way of explanation.

'I thought conscription was eighteen months in West Germany?' asked Brierly, instantly suspicious.

'Nineteen sixty-three was the year of the transition from twelve to eighteen months. So my year class served fifteen.'

'And did you? See service in Africa with the Legion?' asked Fryatt.

'I was in Chad with them.'

The Assassin had only spent two days there out of his familiarisation course last month, but the Englishmen didn't need to know that.

'And then you were recruited by Kramer into the SDECE?'

'No. Immediately after the Legion I ended up in Internal Affairs at the EEC. As muscle. That's where I met Kramer. Last year he asked me to do a special job for him away from Brussels. Things progressed from there.'

'Special like this job, eh?'

'No. Much trickier,' replied the Assassin, taking a sip of champagne. The description hardly began to do it justice. And it had been the spring of 'sixty-nine, not last year. But they didn't need to know the truth about that either.

'Well let's see how tricky this job turns out to be,' said Fryatt. 'So after five years in the Legion, is your loyalty still to France these days?'

'My loyalty is to Kramer. But we're all close to one another at the Commission. We have a higher calling.'

Dissimulation came as easily to the Assassin as it seemed to for Brierly. He'd had no other choice over the months and years since his and Kramer's paths first crossed.

'And what calling is that?' asked Fryatt with a cynical edge to his voice.

'European unity. Although some people take it more seriously than others,' he added.

Both Englishmen looked closely at the Assassin, but he appeared to be saying all of this quite genuinely.

'What do you mean, "more seriously"?' asked Brierly.

'Different people have different views on the final form it will take.'

'And just how far does Kramer want it to go?'

'He's dedicated thirteen years of his life to the Project,' replied the Assassin guardedly. 'But we've never really discussed the end state. He doesn't think much of the idea in some quarters that it's the European Parliament which one day should become the government of the Community.'

'I should hope not,' said Fryatt. 'As far as I'm concerned, the whole point of joining the EEC is to keep the plebs well away from power. Let them have their Potemkin village of a parliament, but for God's sake don't give it any real responsibilities.'

'I know some people who'd agree with you,' said the Assassin with a trace of bitterness.

'A hard line on European federation doesn't sound much like the Kramer I knew,' said Brierly. 'Either in London during the war or afterwards.'

'Read his speeches,' replied the Assassin. 'Maybe he's changed over the years.'

He turned to Fryatt. 'What's the view of the Foreign Office towards accession?'

Fryatt rang a silver push-button bell in the centre of the table before replying.

'We're almost entirely in favour of it, of course. But Heath doesn't want to know. He came up with the strategy for the negotiations all by himself. And to all intents and purposes he's also running the only talks that count, the ones with France and West Germany. He's created a special "Europe Unit" within the Cabinet Office to cut us out of the loop.'

'I can't imagine that's won him many friends amongst the diplomats,' said the Assassin.

'He wants all the glory for himself. He's gone as far as setting up his own secret communications channels with Pompidou. Ones that even the French Foreign Ministry aren't privy to.'

Brierly grunted. 'That's somewhat unfair to Heath,' he said. 'Two years ago your man in Paris held private talks with de Gaulle about changing the EEC into a looser confederation. No wonder he's wary of trusting you.'

For the briefest of seconds, the Assassin saw a flash of anger from Fryatt directed at his colleague.

'He's your man, Christopher Soames, not ours. What Wilson was doing when he appointed a failed Conservative MP as ambassador to France was beyond all of us,' said Fryatt with a sneer.

'Soames is Churchill's son-in-law. It wasn't that far-fetched an idea,' replied Brierly equally superciliously.

There was a lull for a moment. The Assassin probed to see what other confidences were on offer. 'Despite what you said in front of the policeman earlier today about the negotiations being at a delicate stage, from what I've heard, it sounds like the deal has already been done. The only question is who gets the credit.'

Fryatt touched his cutlery briefly to make sure the knives and forks were parallel to each other. 'What do you do for Kramer day-to-day in Brussels?' he asked by way of reply.

The Assassin glanced away from the table for a moment to a painting hanging on the wall. A bewhiskered Victorian colonial administrator wearing a cravat stood with one hand tucked into his frock coat. In the picture's background, an elephant stood next to a dilapidated vine-covered stone temple. Past glories, but not forgotten - not in this club at least.

'This and that,' he said, with a final look at the snake lurking in the tree above the administrator's head. 'He calls me in as he needs me. My main job is still with Internal Affairs.'

Further questions were interrupted by the arrival of the waiter with the menu cards.

'What do you recommend?' asked the Assassin after a perfunctory look.

'They do the turbot well at this club,' said Brierly. 'And I generally start with the medallions. They get in salt-marsh lamb from Romney on the South Coast.'

'I'll have the same.'

The waiter began to clear away the extra cutlery set at the Assassin's place.

'What's that?' he asked, pointing to one of the pieces.

'A marrow spoon,' said Fryatt, with the faintest of curls on his lip. The Assassin's face was carefully blank.

Once the waiter had gone, Fryatt started up again. 'So what's the real story with you and Kramer and the SDECE?'

'I have a temporary contract with them for the duration of this job. But I'm still employed by the EEC in the meantime.'

Fryatt looked at the Assassin over the rim of his wine glass. 'That sounds lucrative. Kramer looking out for your financial interests, is he? Who's doing your regular job in Brussels whilst you're gone?'

'Officially I'm on secondment to the Police Nationale in Lyons, investigating CAP fraud. It's far enough away from Brussels so that I don't get any unexpected visits from friends at the weekend.'

Brierly pursed his lips at the evasion. 'The CAP. It's a running sore for the Commission. Didn't a man die during the farmers' protests in Brussels a couple of days ago? The papers were saying there were fifty thousand of them in the city centre.'

'Can you blame the farmers?' asked the Assassin, happy to move onto neutral ground. 'The Agricultural Commissioner wants to cut the number of farms in half across the entire EEC.'

'I know what the Mansholt Plan is,' said Brierly in an irritated voice. 'So what are you saying? You think he shouldn't be trying to make European agriculture more efficient?'

'I'm not paid to think in Internal Affairs.'

No one contradicted him.

'What's it like working in Brussels?' asked Fryatt.

'It's my first office job after six years in different uniforms so I've had nothing to compare it with.'

'How come you speak English like a professional?' asked Fryatt again.

'School. And from practising with English speakers at the Berlaymont and when on holiday.'

'Where on holiday?'

The Assassin tried to hide his frustration. He had his own questions waiting to be asked. 'Here and there. There always seem to be English or American tourists wherever I go.'

'You do realise that there's no point in being cagey with us?' said Fryatt. 'Any of those little personal details we can get from Kramer?'

'Don't forget that you've only got these two days to convince us about your suitability for this job,' said Brierly.

'So why is Smythe taking me to Hampshire tomorrow?' he asked brusquely.

The other two looked at one another. 'You're going to meet someone who used to be involved in the abuse of children but got caught,' said Brierly.

'A prisoner?'

'Not exactly. It was suggested he retreated from public life. So he did. Into a monastery.'

'Did he mean it? His change of heart?' asked the Assassin.

'Why do you ask?' said Fryatt.

The Assassin looked troubled.

'You can judge for yourself tomorrow,' said Brierly. 'Almost no one knows more about the abuse scene. Not even our policeman friend.'

'So tell me again, why am I going?'

'We only intend putting you in the company of each Mark once,' said Fryatt. 'You need to know enough about their extra-curricular activities to be convincing when you meet them.'

'What do you mean, "convincing"?' asked the Assassin warily.

'So that they don't immediately suspect you of being an agent provocateur,' replied Fryatt.

The Assassin took another sip of champagne. 'When it comes down to it, how worried are you really about these Heath rumours? Could he conceivably be part of that world?'

'I've told you already,' said Brierly. 'He's very secretive about his private life - both before and after he became Prime Minister. It's only natural that people try to guess.'

'But truthfully, what do you think?'

'The only person he loves is himself,' said Fryatt. 'My bet is that if he gets off at all, it's when standing in front of a mirror.'

He drained his glass and there was a moment's silence while the Assassin deciphered these words.

'That's sick,' he concluded.

'Not as sick as taking out his urges on children,' said Fryatt. 'Not that he's tempted in that way, I'm sure.'

He looked pointedly at the Assassin before speaking again.

'How about this for a story? In nineteen fifty-nine, Heath was shepherding the Obscene Publications Bill through Parliament on behalf of Macmillan, the Prime Minister at the time. Just at that moment, a Conservative MP who owned a publishing house decided it was the perfect opportunity for some free publicity and brought *Lolita* to the British market.'

'The pervert novel written by the Russian author Nabokov,' explained Brierly.

'I've heard of it.'

'Anyway,' continued Fryatt. 'Heath went to Nicolson - that's the MP - and asked him to stop the presses until the bill had been passed. Nicolson asked Heath if he'd actually read the book, and if so, what he thought of it. Heath said 'yes' to the first question, but can you guess his answer to the second?'

Fryatt paused in anticipation but no one took the bait.

'It was "rather boring". I mean, what kind of a mind draws that conclusion from a story of how a twelve-year-old is drugged and then screwed by her own stepfather in a motel?'

'One who's seen worse than that?' suggested the Assassin.

Brierly clapped his hands in disapproval. 'Repeating those stories just encourages the speculation. Heath's marital status is what it is. But if the government is going to get through the next year intact, all of us need to be ready to defend him, whatever we might actually believe about him.'

The waiter returned with the entrées and a white-jacketed sommelier in tow. The wine was uncorked and there was an exchange of opinions with Fryatt.

Once the serving staff were gone, the Assassin revisited Brierly's statement about the stability of the government.

'Just how important is Heath to accession? After all, according to what Kramer's told me, the real talks are virtually at an end. If he's forced to resign for some reason, even in the next few weeks, surely that's not going to stop a deal being signed? Not after ten years of on-off negotiations?'

'There is no deal, not yet anyway. And even then, it's still got to go through Parliament,' replied Brierly. 'Hypothetically speaking, if the government fell, all bets would be off.'

'Why would it matter? Haven't both main parties applied to join the EEC at different times in the last decade?'

'Enough of what we call the "Establishment" - the nexus of government, public institutions and business interests - have come around to the idea of Europe over the past ten years. But the general populace isn't so enthused. If we lose momentum now, we may never get it back,' said Brierly.

The Assassin thought about this for a moment, while he took a sip of the red. It was perfectly balanced, just on the right side of astringent.

'It's not only a question of momentum,' he said. 'You need to complete accession before there's any real progress on initiatives like the Mansholt or the Werner Plan. You don't want to frighten the voters.'

'The Werner Plan will be awkward for us, I admit,' said Brierly. 'But we're preparing a smokescreen to disguise it.'

'How are you going to explain away the move to a single currency by nineteen eighty? Centralised EEC control of national budgets, taxes and public spending?'

'Use some common sense,' said Fryatt. 'People aren't interested in the boring details of exchange rate convergence and fiscal transfer mechanisms - either now or in the future. Anyway, there's more immediate problems: labour disputes, unrest in Ireland, inflation. All things which might distract public opinion from something that's supposedly been urgent for a decade.'

'And in any case,' said Brierly. 'we're not really lying about the plans for federation. It's more a case of the Establishment protecting the public from too much truth.'

The Assassin gave him a frosty look, even if his own life of deception made it a hypocritical one.

'The truth about just how weak Britain is on the world stage,' continued Fryatt. 'And about how much of our remaining freedom of action we'll have to give away to secure accession.'

'Is that what the English nomenklatura think? That you're so weak you have no choice but to join the EEC? Economically speaking, England's not West Germany but you're hardly in crisis.'

'We tend to say "the UK" these days, rather than "England,"' said Brierly.

'We say "*Angleterre*" in French. Sometimes "*Grossbritannien*" in German. We don't use the other term.'

Fryatt pursed his lips. 'Whatever. We utterly indebted ourselves fighting Hitler. By the end of the war we'd borrowed so much that our National Debt was over twice the size of the entire economy.'

'What's the level today?'

'Sixty percent.'

'So it's gone down a lot?' he said. 'What's West Germany's figure?'

'Twenty percent.'

The Assassin put his head to one side. 'I never realised the difference was so large. But yours isn't a small economy.' The Assassin counted quickly on his fingers. 'Either fifth- or sixth-biggest in the world?'

'We're the sixth,' said Fryatt. 'Which makes us smaller than France, let alone West Germany. And we supposedly won the war.'

Brierly was more philosophical. 'Our national income per head is only four-fifths that of France. But for Heath, the need to catch up economically isn't as important as the belief that Europe should unite under one flag.'

'What economic need? Asked the Assassin. 'Your debt levels are coming down, aren't they?'

'You're from West Germany. You must know just how fast your economy expanded after the war. We had a quarter of the global market for manufactured goods twenty years ago. Now it's half of that,' said Fryatt.

'People back home talk about the *Wirtschaftswunder,* but I came of age in the 'sixties. I've only ever known a successful economy.'

'If we don't join now, the gap between Britain and the rest of Europe will only get wider,' said Brierly. 'But you're missing a fundamental point. We shouldn't be seeing this as a competition between Britain and the Six at all. The driving principle behind the

EEC is that we put national rivalries behind us. Everyone wants peace in Europe. Even if Britain didn't start the war, we suffered because of it. Heath saw that first-hand.'

The Assassin finished the last morsel of salt-marsh lamb on his Wedgewood plate.

Fryatt spoke up. 'But don't get the idea that accession is only Heath's ambition. Macmillan was the first to force Britain to confront political reality,' he added. 'He had personal reasons too. He was badly wounded in the First World War. Bullets hit just as hard during that failure of European diplomacy as in Hitler's war.'

'It was Macmillan back in 'sixty-one who made the original decision to join,' said Brierly. 'He had an early taste of European federation as Churchill's political representative in the Mediterranean. He effectively ran the occupation government in Italy for a time. And he knew Jean Monnet when they were both in Algiers, where the Allies had their Mediterranean headquarters and Monnet was Armaments Minister in de Gaulle's government-in-exile. Supermac was well groomed.'

'Who groomed Heath?' the Assassin asked them both.

'Macmillan made Heath the lead negotiator for our first accession attempt,' said Brierly. 'He's been trying to pull this off for the past ten years.'

'You said earlier that the ordinary people aren't so enthused. What do they think about joining the EEC?'

'They're not expected to have an opinion, even if they could understand the issues. You said yourself a couple of minutes ago, entry to the Common Market is the policy of both political parties. It's already been decided for them.'

Fryatt reached over to top up the Assassin's wine glass.

'The voters can only cope with simple explanations. That's why they're voters instead of being in government.'

The waiter returned to clear their plates and bring side dishes for the main courses. They watched in silence as he laid out steaming tureens of vegetables in the middle of the table.

'Which countries have you been posted to by the Foreign Office?' the Assassin asked Fryatt, once the waiter was gone.

Fryatt brushed his hand lightly through his black-and-silver mane.

'Too many to mention. Wherever I'm sent. Just like you.' He looked at the Assassin for a moment. 'I was in the Trucial States from late 'sixty-seven until 'sixty-nine. Helping to broker the terms of our departure.'

'The "Trucial States"?'

'The oil states in the Persian Gulf,' said Brierly. 'We have suzerainty over them until the end of this year - we run their foreign affairs.'

'In addition to knowing best how to negotiate our entry to the EEC with France, Heath also believes himself to be an Arab expert,' said Fryatt. 'With hindsight, he thinks he knew all along how Suez would unfold. And he would have maintained a British presence East of Suez if he'd become Prime Minister in the sixties - before Wilson abandoned our bases in the Gulf.'

'But it hasn't stopped him giving it a good go anyway,' said Brierly.

'He's been running his own secret war in Oman since July of last year,' said Fryatt.

'Who's taking bullets for him there?'

'Special forces under the cover of a training team.'

'The Soviets are next door, in South Yemen,' said the Assassin. 'Some of their satellites have specialists in the country advising the secret police and the army.'

'Speaking of next door. The former Sultan of Oman is staying in a suite at the Dorchester a few floors above you.'

'Former?'

'His son took over the sultanate in July of last year. Deposed his own father in a coup and sent him into exile. That truly is Realpolitik.'

The waiter returned with the main courses. Brierly ordered a second bottle of the white.

'Did you work with Kramer at any point during the latter part of the war?' the Assassin asked him.

'No. As I told you on the way in from Northolt this morning, we were only together in the agent recruitment business for the first couple of years. In 'forty-two Kramer went to Algiers just after the Torch landings to prepare for the move from London of the French government-in-exile. He might well have met Macmillan in Algeria. He almost certainly would have spent time there with Monnet.'

'He's never mentioned it.' The Assassin wondered how much Brierly really knew of what his boss had got up to in Algeria. Last year Kramer had started dropping hints about who'd really been behind the assassination in Algiers of Admiral Darlan, one of de Gaulle's rivals for leadership of the Free French. The Assassin supposed that eventually everyone had a need to confess.

'Did you leave England at all during the war? The UK, I mean?' he asked Brierly.

'Kramer went east. I went west, to Washington.'

'Did you come across Kim Philby out there? I believe he was in SOE for a time, just like you.'

'Don't forget your manners, Herr Hofmann,' said Fryatt sharply.

'The government and the intelligence services are sick to their back teeth of sex and spy scandals,' said Brierly in a more measured tone. 'There's been far too many during the past decade. The story about Lord Boothby and Ronnie Kray? It was the year after Profumo, which made it in some ways even more traumatic for the Conservative Party. They lost the election to Labour only three months later.'

'Forget nineteen sixty-four. There was a spy for the Czechs in court only yesterday,' muttered Fryatt. 'Former RAF sergeant. A naturalised Briton, originally from Czechoslovakia.'

'How many scandals have there been in recent years then?' asked the Assassin.

Fryatt began to count with his fingers. 'The Admiralty spy John Vassall in 'sixty-two. Profumo and Keeler the following year. The Conservative MP photographed *in flagrante* with an Intourist guide in Moscow in 'sixty-five. The Labour MPs exposed by the Czech defector, Frolik, last year. And those are only some of the ones we know about.'

The Assassin raised his eyebrows. 'I'd heard about the Czech attempt to entrap Heath. I didn't know they had actually been successful in recruiting agents inside your Parliament.'

'Oh yes,' said Fryatt. 'They got Stonehouse, the former Labour Minister for Aviation, in the same way that the KGB caught the Tory MP, Anthony Courtney, in 'sixty-five. Stonehouse brazened it out when he was confronted by MI5 though. Insufficient evidence. But we know he's guilty. Going to those lengths wasn't always necessary. One of the Czechs' other informants was the Labour MP Will Owen. He was given the informal name "Greedy Bastard" by their residency. Went to trial last year.'

'But Profumo was the biggest fish, yes? That's what Kramer told me.'

Brierly rested his cutlery on the edges of his plate and turned towards the Assassin.

'It was convoluted,' he said, looking at the other man closely. 'But this evening is meant for us to build trust with one another.'

The Assassin nodded.

Brierly continued. 'So let me give you the inside story there. The short, unvarnished one.'

The Assassin offered the bottle around the table. Fryatt placed a hand over his glass.

Brierly began. 'Profumo was a defence minister under Macmillan. He went to a sex party at a large house in the country called Cliveden in the summer of 'sixty-one. While he was there, he began a liaison with one of the call girls, or maybe she was just a good-time girl. Christine Keeler was her name. She lived in London with another girl at the house of an osteopath, a back doctor called Ward.'

'Okay,' said the Assassin.

'But Ward was being used by the Secret Service,' said Brierly.

'Our equivalent of your domestic intelligence agency, the Bundesverfassungsschutz. Popularly known in this country as "MI5",' explained Fryatt.

'I know what they're called.'

Brierly tutted at the interruption. 'Originally, they'd asked Ward to get close to the Soviet Naval Attaché. Whether or not the girls he lived with were to be used as bait for Ivanov, you can decide for yourself. But whatever happened, Keeler caught the eye of both Ivanov and Profumo.'

'So MI5 ended up entrapping their own man? Was that before or after Keeler had become involved with the Soviet attaché?'

'After.'

'How did they get themselves and Profumo out of that one?'

'Not particularly well. They framed Ward and sent him for trial on a procurement charge - pimping, in other words. And they made sure he committed suicide before the trial finished. They couldn't do anything for Profumo though. Not after he was caught lying to Parliament.'

'What a mess.'

'Indeed. Maybe now you get a sense of why this operation has to be so compartmentalised. We wouldn't go to these lengths with you unless it was absolutely essential. Forget the Americans in Vietnam and their so-called "collateral damage", even the KGB couldn't have engineered the removal of Profumo.'

'Ultimately it led to the resignation of Macmillan as party leader too,' added Fryatt. He stabbed a roast potato.

'The Conservative Party will never allow themselves to be put in a Profumo or Boothby situation ever again,' said Brierly tonelessly. The Assassin couldn't decide if he was trying to convey a sense of menace or hide one.

'Between the Czechs and MI5 it doesn't sound like there's a lot left in Britain for the KGB to do,' he suggested. 'How active are the East Germans here?'

'The aim in spying is not to get caught, which leads me to suspect that the Stasi are devious bastards because there's hardly a sniff of what they might be getting up to,' said Fryatt.

'Germany is the best at everything,' replied the Assassin matter-of-factly. 'But they're hardly serious players in the UK? Just the usual cultural friendship societies? They can't do much without diplomatic recognition and an embassy.'

'It's coming, thanks to détente. Perhaps in a couple of years. Once West Germany normalises relations with Berlin, then we'll follow,' said Brierly. 'The East Germans are certainly acting as if they'll be recognised. They've just acquired a property in Belgrave Square for their Foreign Trade Office. We assume it's for a future embassy building.'

'Same square as the West German embassy is on. The cheeky sods,' added Fryatt.

'But East Berlin needs to be careful until then,' said Brierly. 'We won't be so keen to grant them recognition if they're caught misbehaving.'

'But they won't be,' said the Assassin. 'MI5 knows that my impersonation of one of their people is just that. It was the deal Kramer made with you. He was very insistent about it. None of us want to cause a diplomatic incident because we've been caught fabricating a false smear by a Warsaw Pact country.'

Fryatt shook his head in disagreement. 'It's not a real risk. If something does eventually leak out in a garbled way and a Soviet satellite takes some flak, it will further tarnish the Kremlin's image. Two for the price of one,' he added breezily.

'"Flak"? As in the German term?' asked the Assassin uncertainly.

'Our air force spent some time over there during the war. Picked up the lingo,' replied Brierly drily. Then his expression darkened. 'My youngest brother was shot down during a raid on Hanover in 'forty-three. They never found his body.'

The Assassin composed his face.

'So for obvious reasons,' continued Brierly, 'if we're going to implicate any Warsaw Pact country in wrongdoing, our first choice will always be the East German republic.'

'I understand,' said the Assassin.

'How much preparation has Kramer given you for this role?' asked Brierly. 'Has he briefed you on how the Stasi operates?'

'He's learned quite a bit about them over the years,' replied the Assassin in a calculated voice.

'Well, you need to sound like a West German who quietly sympathises with the East, so that if pressed, the three Marks will admit they had suspicions all along,' said Fryatt.

'Kramer told me to act myself and let you worry about putting two and two together for the Marks. He said to keep it simple and not over-plan or over-embellish.'

'But it couldn't hurt if you were to make the odd vaguely positive comment about East Germany. Or defend them to a degree if the worst excesses of the regime come up in conversation.'

'It's going to be tricky to get that one right,' said the Assassin. 'Almost nobody in West Germany is neutral, even vaguely, when it comes to having an opinion on the puppet state in the east.'

Fryatt looked shrewdly at the Assassin.

'Yes,' said Brierly. 'But people here won't know those nuances.'

'What's your personal opinion on East Germany?' asked Fryatt. 'You're from Hamburg, right? Kramer gave us the impression you had family on the other side of the border.'

There was a moment's pause from the Assassin 'I had a grandmother who lived in the Soviet occupation zone but she died in the fifties. There's something else you haven't mentioned though.'

'What's that?'

'When I raise MI5's suspicions with my visits to the East German Foreign Trade Office, the East Germans will be suspicious too. The Stasi are completely paranoid. They wouldn't be so stupid as to have their own people permanently staffing Belgrave Square but their caution will rub off on the actual trade officials.'

'So? What are you trying to say?'

'I may only get one or two meetings out of them. I need to be discovered by Reynolds quickly when the time comes.'

'Nothing like an optimistic German to dampen the party mood, eh?' said Fryatt.

'I'm just trying to be realistic.'

'Then you'll just have to do a good job at convincing them,' said Brierly. 'Kramer told us you're the best he had. Prove it to us as well.'

'I hope you're a damn sight more cheerful when it comes to partying with the Marks,' said Fryatt.

The Assassin frowned.

'How far are you prepared to go there?'

'What do you mean?' asked the Assassin suspiciously.

'You'll take drugs if you're offered? Dance with the strippers? Screw them to show the Marks that you're one of the boys?'

'I don't bang girls in front of other people.'

'No one said you'd have to. Jesus. What sort of parties do you go to in Brussels?' said Fryatt contemptuously.

The Assassin didn't give an answer to that.

'Dessert?' Brierly asked Fryatt.

'No. I want a cigar. Let's go to the bar.'

Brierly led them back downstairs, to an almost empty anteroom next to the bar. They found a low table with padded leather armchairs set around it, well away from the hubbub in the other room. In the far corner, two men were speaking earnestly in low voices.

Fryatt took their orders and went back through to the bar. When he returned with their drinks, he had someone in tow.

'This is Cornelius De Wyck, a chum of mine. He spent some time in the same outfit as you.'

'Hello,' said the new man in an even more fruity accent than the other pair. He reached out a hand to the Assassin.

'And this is our West German friend, Herr Hofmann. Or perhaps Monsieur Hofmann. He's just spent five years in the Legion.'

'Oh really?' The new man sunk down into the squeaking leather, raising his eyebrows for the briefest of moments. He had a Dutch first and last name but sounded completely English to the Assassin.

'Which regiment were you with?' asked the English-Dutchman.

'La Troisième. So you were in the Legion too?' asked the Assassin.

'It was the back end of the fifties. I was trying to impress a girl.'

'You saw the end of the war in Algeria?'

'I saw a few things, for sure. When did you get out?'

'At the end of 'sixty-nine.'

'Did you know the Adjudant-chef who ran the second company of the GILE?' asked De Wyck. 'He would still have been there when you were in.'

The Assassin looked back at him evenly. 'Which one? Müller?'

'Giant of a man. Impossible to miss.'

The Assassin shrugged. 'Are you really English with a name like De Wyck?' he asked, deflecting.

'Don't be so bloody cheeky. We've been in Somerset since William's time. How far back can you trace your family tree?'

The Assassin switched to French and rattled something off in reply. The pair of them fired back and forth like this for three or four minutes while Brierly and Fryatt occasionally glanced at each other.

'That's enough for now, Hofmann,' said Brierly. 'No one likes a show-off.'

De Wyck didn't look so friendly just then either. '*Peut-être*,' he said finally to the Assassin. Then to the others, 'Well, well. Got people to see. Must dash.'

He got to his feet and returned to the bar. Through the open door of the anteroom, the Assassin saw him go up to a group of men and women sitting on high stools. He clapped a man on the shoulder and ran his hand down the bare back of one of the women. She giggled and shrugged him off.

The Assassin turned to Brierly.

'What time are we leaving tomorrow?'

'Smythe will pick you up at ten. You can have lunch on the way there, have your meeting, and then he'll make sure you're back in London in plenty of time for your flight.'

'The night is still young,' said Fryatt 'Why don't you do some of your own research at one of the clubs frequented by single men alone in London? Head north towards Oxford Circus or east to Soho.'

'What? Dressed like this?' asked the Assassin.

'You'll fit right in with the other freaks. I need a moment with Brierly. You go on. The cloakroom is that way to the left of the bar.'

The Assassin slowly made his way back to the Dorchester. From what he'd heard so far today, on the surface the task didn't seem so complicated: meet the Marks, get photographed doing so, go home for good. But life was never that simple, in either the affairs of men or of nations.

The suspicions he'd had back in Brussels hadn't been assuaged, that he'd end up doing more with the three Marks than merely being seen in their company with a cigar and whiskey. And once he was in MI5's book of suspects, he wondered who else Brierly and Kramer might decide he could usefully smear whilst he was in England.

One thing was for sure, Fryatt, whoever he really was, definitely did not enjoy the reminders of the spy scandals of the past decade. No wonder the Assassin was on probation today and tomorrow. They'd given him enough examples of what happened when the British state and the members of its Establishment had been caught out before. Not that Brierly and Fryatt had needed to. The whole of the intelligence world knew of the disaster zone which was MI5 and MI6.

Chapter Three

The Assassin had already been waiting for Smythe on the steps in front of the Dorchester for ten minutes at least. The temperature wasn't any warmer than yesterday but the early clouds had cleared and on the other side of Park Lane, the sun lit up the green grass of Hyde Park through the bare trees.

At dinner last night when Fryatt listed the spies who'd operated under the noses of the Secret Service for years, he hadn't chosen to mention the Cambridge spy ring - the so-called ideological spies who'd been at the very heart of the British intelligence establishment from the thirties into the fifties.

Kim Philby was the best-known, celebrated in the USSR, abhorred in the West. He'd helped the KGB's predecessor recruit the others in the ring whilst still at university. But when Kramer had briefed the Assassin back in Brussels, it was the history student, Guy Burgess, whom he used as his example of how deeply the British state's institutions had been penetrated.

After Cambridge, Burgess had begun his long journey of infiltration with a job at the BBC. During the war he'd parleyed his experience at Broadcasting House to get a transfer to the propaganda department of MI6 where he'd managed to secure a job for Philby too. Department D had later been transferred to the SOE. But while SOE had kept Philby on, Burgess didn't last and went back to the BBC where he ran political programming. The revolving doors turned once more and he joined the Foreign Office press department. There, he had almost unlimited access to top secret policy documents, such as Britain's negotiating position at the Yalta conference and the contingency plans that had been made for a possible war with the USSR following the defeat of Germany. His service to Britain was rewarded by being made personal assistant to a Labour Foreign Office minister and the flow of information from the very top of the British government continued into the Cold War proper.

And that was only Burgess. Philby had used his SOE job as a springboard to return to MI6 where he'd ended up as head of the anti-Soviet section during the war and the Balkans controller for MI6 afterwards, exposing a string of agents later picked up by the Albanian security service. Then he got the plum - head of the MI6 station in Washington, which allowed him to expose CIA spies within the rest of the Soviet bloc too. Not bad, thought the Assassin, for someone who'd started his professional career as a freelance journalist.

In nineteen fifty, Philby was joined at the British embassy in Washington by Burgess, who'd been promoted within the Foreign Office in the almost automatic way that the Establishment looked after its own. But that move had also marked the start of their downfall, triggered when Philby sent Burgess back to England to order a third Soviet spy, Donald Maclean, to defect just before he was exposed by the CIA.

Maclean had spent time at the embassy in Washington too, but during the war when he'd become Secretary of the joint American-British committee on atomic policy. However, the pressure of his double life meant that he'd steadily become more and more mentally unstable over the years.

By 'fifty-one Burgess was in no fit state to carry on for much longer either. His drinking was becoming worse and his erratic personal behaviour in America increasingly difficult for the British embassy to defend. Instead of merely arranging Maclean's escape to Moscow, when he returned to England, Burgess decided to join him. It was the end for Philby's career in MI6 too, and not before time as far as the US was concerned.

Betrayal of trust between the allies scarcely began to describe it. Apart from the string of CIA spies betrayed by Philby and then shot, Maclean had also betrayed the US at the strategic level. In nineteen fifty he was head of the Foreign Office's American desk and leaked the joint British and American deliberations over the use of the Bomb against the Chinese during the Korean War.

Twenty years later, the poison still hadn't been drawn. Not least because there were rumours of further, undiscovered Cambridge spies. Only a decade ago, the KGB defector Golitsyn had claimed there had been at least five spies in the network, not three. Neither MI5 nor MI6 had been able to put the allegations completely to rest. Not in public anyway.

In defence of the British though, it wasn't clear that the other Western intelligence agencies were much better. By the early sixties the French SDECE had been penetrated from top to bottom by the KGB. And as for West German intelligence, that had effectively been an open book to the Stasi for years.

All of this had taken its toll elsewhere. Last year the Assassin had been told that the CIA's head of counter-intelligence was a clinical paranoid. No wonder, he thought, given Angleton's experience of his western allies, let alone of his own fellow Americans who'd betrayed the atom bomb programme to Stalin during the war. Even if most of those were second generation immigrants from the Russian Empire.

The Assassin continued to wait outside the main door of the Dorchester. Smythe eventually arrived, twenty minutes late. He rolled down the driver's window and greeted the Assassin with an embarrassed grin. His car was a British make, a dark green Jaguar saloon with a flowing sculpted front end which looked somewhat dated compared to a squared-off BMW. The man himself was wearing a camel hair coat over a dark lounge suit, which to the Assassin made him look like a prosperous gangster. Someone who wouldn't be out of place at Jimmy's Club Trèfle.

'Vauxhall Bridge was jammed solid,' he explained. 'Let's go. We'll have the meeting first, then go for a quick lunch afterwards.'

'*Kein Problem.*'

The Assassin got in and Smythe pulled out into Park Lane. 'If we'd been doing this trip in a few weeks, we could easily have made up time,' he said. 'They're about to open a new motorway from Sunbury down to Hampshire. End of May, I heard.'

The Assassin was expecting the same interrogation on the journey as the previous night at the *Herrenklub*. But after some further complaints at the traffic and the other drivers, Smythe flicked the radio on, happy to leave his passenger in peace for the rest of the journey, which apparently meant being forced to listen to the inane burblings of Neil Diamond and Perry Como. Even George Harrison was better when he came on to sing 'My Sweet Lord.' Up to about the fourth verse the Assassin thought he'd heard 'Hallelujah' being sung in the refrain, but then started doubting himself when he recognised the name 'Hare Krishna.'

Eventually, the Assassin felt that politeness demanded some effort on his behalf. After forty minutes they hit a stretch of road with trees on either side and he asked if they'd already left London.

'It depends on what you mean. We've only just reached Richmond Park. After this we're back into the suburbs again.'

'I didn't realise how big the city is.'

'By population it was bigger at one point. But it's been going down since the war as they ship people out to the new towns.'

'How old were you when it ended?' asked the Assassin.

'Twelve.' Smythe looked at him neutrally. 'There's more cheerful things to talk about though. You like football, boxing, the gee-gees?'

Anecdotes about the bets on horses which Smythe had won at improbable odds led to tales about the pre-war racetrack gangs who controlled bookmaking at the meetings and how the Flying Squad had shut them down, mainly through brute physical force.

The robbery squad seemed to be a particular fascination of Smythe's. He claimed to have worked for a couple of years with one of the undercover officers who'd played the part of a drugged security guard in 'forty-eight when the Squad had foiled a bullion raid at Heathrow. The extended brawl with truncheons on one side and bolt cutters and starter handles on the other had been one of the stories that inspired him to join the Met, or so he said.

The war was never far from the surface though. When the conversation moved on to football, the name of Bert Trautmann came up - the former Manchester City goalkeeper and holder of the Iron Cross who'd played the last fifteen minutes of the 'fifty-six FA Cup Final with a broken neck. After a further digression on whether imported Löwenbräu lager qualified as beer - the Assassin was prepared to be dubious about anything that came out of Bavaria - he brought the discussion back to the task in hand.

'How did you first meet Brierly?' he asked Smythe. 'You said yesterday that when the three Marks started their threats, you put the word out and Brierly found you.'

'Did he tell you last night what he does?'

'No, not specifically. So far on this trip he's said that he's a political lobbyist, an adviser who works for an institute of some kind.'

'What do you think he means by that?'

'He writes papers, runs seminars, tries to persuade influential people in favour of EEC membership.'

'I think it's a cover for something else,' said Smythe. 'Or maybe he's combining two things at the same time.'

The Assassin gave Smythe a quick look. 'Do you know the other guy I was with last night?' he asked. 'Fryatt?'

Now it was Smythe's turn to glance across to the other seat. 'Yes, I work with him, so to speak. He's the liaison between his organisation and my part of the police.'

There was a wariness now in the Assassin's eyes. It sounded like Brierly's operation was less compartmentalised than he'd implied.

'What does the Foreign Office have to do with the sex party scene in London?' he asked. 'Isn't that more the thing for Reynolds' employer?'

'The world is changing, Thomas. Fifteen years ago people were still taking the boat to America. Nowadays, thanks to the jetliner, everywhere's closer to everywhere else.'

'I suppose so.'

'The Foreign Office's customers come to them these days,' said Smythe, warming to his theme. 'They come to London for work and for play and for a good time away from their wives. Why wouldn't Fryatt's people want to know if American industrialists and Arab oil sheikhs take their fun here in ways that would leave them compromised?'

'You said yesterday that you help to catch pederasts. How does photographing Japanese businessmen at parties help with that? Entrapping foreign visitors makes Fryatt's outfit no better than the KGB.'

'I just keep my ear to the ground. On behalf of everyone. My bosses make any political decisions.'

'Have you gone permanently undercover in some way? Is that why you're no longer known by your police rank?'

'Do you get a kick out of annoying people with your questions? Don't forget, you're still on probation until we get back to London this afternoon.'

'Okay.'

Smythe relented a little. 'To answer your first question about how I met Brierly - Fryatt knows people. He collects useful men in the way that you probably used to collect chewing gum cards as a lad. If you get those in West Germany, that is.'

The Assassin decided the time wasn't right for probing Fryatt's real role at the Foreign Office either. 'Last night they told me a little about the person we're visiting today,' he said. 'Was it your idea to take me down here to see him?'

'Brierly and the other stuck-ups talk about child abuse as if it's just another Soho perversion - something theoretical that doesn't actually happen in real life.'

'I'm not so sure. Brierly and Fryatt told me quite openly at dinner that this man was an abuser. A pederast who got caught.'

'He's called Voaden. He moved down here a couple of years ago after the details of a party too outrageous even by Mayfair standards were picked up on by the gossip journalists. No names were made public but the people who mattered knew who'd been involved.'

'What happened? He did something criminal? Or it just got out of hand?'

Smythe turned to look at the Assassin, raising his eyebrows for a second. Then he went back to giving his full attention to the A3.

'Both?' asked the Assassin. 'But whatever it was, it didn't matter, because presumably there was no trial?'

Smythe nodded grimly. 'The daughter of a judge overdosed on drugs. She was found dead the following morning, slumped in a corner. Her heart had given out, but no one realised and they partied on for another three or four hours afterwards. The post-mortem wasn't conclusive.'

The Assassin shook his head. 'For real? No one saw her out cold and thought they'd take advantage of her while she was unconscious?'

Smythe gave the Assassin a sharp, disapproving look.

'That was the way it happened,' he said frostily.

'In that case they couldn't have easily pinned it on Voaden? I'm guessing he wasn't the only source of drugs at the party?'

'It no longer mattered. By that point some people were looking for any excuse to bury him.'

'Because he'd eventually compromised more and more people over the years?'

'It's what the Establishment does. A quiet word and no unpleasantness. Only the really unlucky ones like Stephen Ward and Christine Keeler actually go to trial.'

As they weaved their way through Guildford, the Assassin turned this over in his head.

'Germans have always been somewhat in awe of English ruthlessness. Hitler was fixated with the idea that the only way the English could have ruled India with so few people was by using harsh repression - which turned out unlucky for the Ukraine. And before him, the Kaiser had a deep inferiority complex towards his English grandmother and cousins.'

'It's a bit cheeky of you to bring up those two characters. Anyway, what's all that got to do with today's world?'

'Maybe you're not so ruthless these days as you like foreigners to believe. You couldn't even make up your minds about Kim Philby - about whether he was a traitor or not. You investigated him for a decade after he quit MI6, unwilling to admit the truth. It was only when he eventually fled to Russia eight years ago that you finally decided he'd worked for the KGB all along.'

'What are you trying to say? That the old conquering spirit is no longer there? We've laid down the white man's burden? We're full of doubts about our place in the world?'

'You tell me.'

Through glimpses between the trees outside the car window, the Assassin could see the ground falling away steeply from the road as they traversed a long ridge. Smythe tapped his fingers on the driving wheel.

'The youth of today have cast aside notions of Empire faster than last season's fashion. In my father's time, bright middle-class boys with a taste for adventure could go overseas to make their career in the Indian Army or the colonial police forces. Now their ambitions are limited to light office work, an Austin-Healey in the garage, and a colour television in their centrally-heated lounge.'

'There must be some people here who still have a sense of purpose? How about the socialists? How about the students on the campuses?'

'I wouldn't know. I never went to university.'

'Nor did I. But I was told by someone who lectures at one of the universities in Brussels that the Marxists have a plan to take over first academia, then the media, then all of politics.'

'Students are so stoned they can hardly tie their shoelaces half the time.'

'The "Long March Through the Institutions" he calls it. Dreamt up by a German socialist, Rudi Dutschke.'

'Dutschke? You've heard of him in Brussels, have you? Back in January he was front page news here. A nine days' wonder. Heath had him deported for breaking his conditions of residency, not to engage in political activity.'

Smythe shook his head disgustedly.

'Students and lecturers at Cambridge went on strike over it. Not that anyone would have noticed.'

'Maybe Heath is smarter than he looks,' said the Assassin reflectively. 'By the way, what do you think about joining the EEC?'

'Truthfully? Don't tell the others, but I'm neutral. I think it makes sense to do more trade with Europe, but I think that nutters like Brierly who talk about a United States of Europe are as out of touch with reality as the Communist Party of Great Britain.'

'But in all seriousness,' said the Assassin, 'much as it's a delicate topic, a form of political union between the UK and West Germany can't be a bad thing, no?'

'It's a delicate topic for obvious reasons. Which is why if Heath talks about it at all, it's only in general terms. Something that might happen a very long way in the future.'

'But people know that's where the EEC's headed? How about the single currency by nineteen eighty?' asked the Assassin.

'I hadn't heard about that one. But aren't you listening? Collectively, we hate the Germans. And we're not that much fonder of the French either. We never have been and never will be. If Heath pushes us too far down that path there'll be trouble.'

'Why do you think the English are so different to the French and the Germans?'

'They each produced a European dictator. We couldn't. It's not in our nature. No identity cards or police permits here. Personal liberty is a mark of being British.'

The Assassin grunted. 'Try living with half-a-million Soviet soldiers on the other side of your border and then maybe you'll take security more seriously.'

'There's no point in living if you can't be free.'

Smythe pulled off the main road and drove down a long tree-lined avenue. At its end was a grand house built in the Gothic style, although the square crenellated turrets at its corners spoke more to a crude pastiche of influences. The Assassin wondered if the wealthy man who'd built it had also fancied himself as an amateur architect.

'We're here,' said Smythe. 'These are the people who know how to look after themselves. The Church makes up its own rules for life.'

'The Catholic Church?'

'This is an Anglican monastery,' said Smythe, lifting one finger from the steering wheel to point at a painted sign by the side of the drive.

'I never knew there was such a thing as Protestant monks,' said the Assassin.

Smythe shrugged. He swung the car round to park on a tarmac forecourt which had been laid where a garden once had been, going by the now-dry ornamental fountain marooned in the middle of the cars.

The Assassin stared as a monk wearing an ankle-length habit got out of a Volkswagen.

'Before we go in, have you been told the names of the three Marks by anyone? Either here or in Brussels?' asked Smythe.

The Assassin shook his head.

'Good. Be careful what you say to Voaden. Back in the day, he knew a lot of people who were active on the scene. He might well still be in touch with them. I'll make the introductions and explain why you're here. Let's go.'

Smythe had clearly been here before. Without a backwards glance he locked the car, bounded up the steps to the monastery's front entrance, and pushed open the heavy double-leaved door.

The Assassin followed, taking in the freestanding crucifix at the end of the hall and hanging on the wall behind it, a painting of Mary in a blue robe, surmounted by a crown of golden stars. Smythe marched down a side corridor smelling of beeswax polish and rapped loudly on a panelled door.

'Come in,' called someone from inside.

A monk was sitting in a wing-backed chair by the window reading a newspaper. There was a sink in a tiny alcove by the door, and a neatly made bed against the wall. He got up and gave Smythe a wry look.

'Hello Smythe.'

'Hello pervert.'

'Not anymore. Well, not much anyway. Definitely not during Lent.'

The Assassin looked puzzled. Smythe carried on.

'I've brought someone to see you. An overseas colleague from Belgium. He wants the benefit of your insight into the mind of the nonce.'

'Who is he? Psychology student?'

'Never you mind Voaden. Just answer his questions.'

'Does he want you here when he asks them?' said Voaden with a glance at the Assassin.

'Wherever you feel most comfortable talking,' replied the Assassin.

'We can go to the herb garden.'

'I'll be here,' said Smythe. 'Looking at your collection of dirty magazines of intergenerational love.'

'You do that Chief Inspector. If you use them, keep them clean. They're worth a fiver each.'

The monk took the Assassin down the corridor and out the back of the building into a walled garden. The earth in the beds was mostly bare with a few straggly plants here and there which had clung on through the winter - sad-looking lavender and rosemary with blackened tips.

Voaden gathered the skirts of his habit and sat down on a stone bench covered with lichen.

'You're welcome to sit. I don't bite,' he said to the Assassin.

'Where's the herbs?' the Assassin asked, still standing.

'Mostly still in the greenhouse. We're starting afresh this year with some of the perennials. Lemon balm and other mints. Sage too, I believe. Come June it will look very different. Anyway, I always like coming out here. Even in the gloomy seasons it seems to hold the promise of sunnier days.'

'How did you end up in this place?' asked the Assassin, coming over to sit down at the opposite end of the bench.

'I did a deal with Smythe. I retired from public life, and they said that in exchange, public life would retire from me.'

The Assassin's mouth moved silently as he worked this one out. He was already uncertain about whether the monk's claim of celibacy during Lent was serious or a joke in poor taste.

'Why did you choose a monastery?' he eventually asked. 'Did you change your ways?'

'Is that what you think I did?' Voaden gave the Assassin a cool look. 'Suggestions that I'd seen the light was certainly a convenient excuse to my network for going on permanent retreat.'

The Assassin seemed disappointed. 'How many people knew you then?' he asked.

'Everyone darling. Too many people.'

'What did you get up to with them?'

'Everything darling. My parties were notorious. Boys, girls, older ones, younger ones, younger ones still.'

'Who came?'

'No corner of the Establishment was left uncorrupted.'

'What made them do it? The child abuse. Weren't regular prostitutes and drugs enough for them?'

Voaden gave him a secret smile. He leant forward and placed a hand on the Assassin's knee, who immediately stiffened.

'What made them do it? You sound like they were led astray by a wicked uncle.'

He moistened his lips with the tip of his tongue.

'Darling, it's the ultimate high. The nearest you can come to playing God without actually killing someone.'

Clouds were moving fast across the sky, casting the two men alternately into sunlight and shadow. Voaden looked closely at the Assassin. 'You've tasted something of that forbidden fruit?'

'I've never abused a child,' he replied curtly.

'Oh darling. Maybe one day.' Voaden shook his head regretfully.

'It's just another experience, right?' suggested the Assassin unconvincingly. 'After you've done everything else that high-class whores have to offer, or tried the latest hallucinogen from the West Coast?'

'There's nothing quite like it, the heightened feeling of power and dominance you get from watching their fearful faces anticipate what's coming next. They know they're helpless and they know exactly what you're about to do.'

The Assassin could have sworn that Voaden gave a low moan as he said this.

'And for obvious reasons, the smaller they are, the greater their feeling of pain. And the greater your pleasure. It's better than any drug yet invented, and it's completely addictive.'

The Assassin's lips were set in a straight line. 'Like any other rape, I suppose? That feeling of power and control?' he asked.

'Amateur psychiatrist, are you? There's less physical risk with children. Although some men's pleasure is heightened when they fight back. Mine was.'

The Assassin looked away for a long second.

'Don't the men ever stop to think that it might be wrong?' he asked in a flat, artificial voice.

'Stop? Just as with any drug-taking, the bolder among us like to test themselves, to push the boundaries with younger and younger partners.'

'Where did you find your victims?' asked the Assassin grimly. 'Which parent allows their child to be corrupted in that way?'

Inside his jacket pocket he clenched his hand into fist.

Voaden shook his head. 'Doesn't your question contain its own answer? Think of the places where parentless children live together, watched over by those whose low public salaries or whose similar inclinations turn them into willing helpers.'

'You mean jails for minors and orphanages?' asked the Assassin.

'Anywhere we could get them from, darling. Sometimes it was guardians or foster parents looking for extra income.'

Assassin nodded to himself slowly. 'Drugs are lucrative, this is no different I suppose?'

'It's rarely mentioned when people discuss that special kind of love. But it has to be paid for. And paid for handsomely. Nothing in this life comes for free. Five pounds for a magazine is a day's wage for the average man.'

The Assassin took his hands out of his pockets and folded his arms.

'Who are the customers then? Men with unhappy marriages? Men who prefer not to get married?'

'For some it's a step-by-step thing. As I said, they take younger and younger partners. And at a certain point, they're so young, that boy or girl, who can tell or even cares? For others on the wrong side of middle age it's a chance to feel young again by feeling someone young.'

'And when even sex with the children isn't enough? What then? The true ultimate drug?'

Voaden licked his lips and fingered the knots on the cord of his habit.

'Of course it's been known to happen. But killing a child has an entirely different set of consequences in society to the death of an adult. Ask the Moors Murderers.'

The Assassin hadn't heard of them. 'How do people work themselves up into that kind of frenzy?' he asked. 'They feel a need to punish the unclean?'

'That sounds religious,' said Voaden.

'You're the one wearing a monk's dress.'

'I suppose you're right. I do believe in a spiritual world though.' His face went dark.

'There was another reason why I chose to come to a monastery, but I don't care to dwell on it.' He gave a shiver.

The Assassin followed Voaden's eyes across the garden to a statue of a saint, crucifix held high above his head in a clenched fist.

'What?' he asked, realisation dawning. 'You thought it would be amusing to put on rituals at your parties with black candles and pig's blood?'

Voaden worked the knots of the cord faster with his fingers.

'Sometimes when you invoke the spirit of Aleister Crowley you get more than you bargained for.'

'I don't know of him, but I get the gist. Stupid of you to dabble in those things.'

A lone bumblebee made its way across the square of ground, investigating the early flowers planted around its edge.

'Is Heath involved with children?' asked the Assassin.

'Heath? As in Edward Heath? How did he come into the picture?' asked Voaden suspiciously.

'Just answer the question.'

Voaden shrugged. 'Someone who's in love with himself as much as Ted might well choose to indulge in heightened pleasures. He's somewhat of an epicure, attracted to the finer things in life.'

'What do you mean?'

'Paintings by known artists, expensive wine, concert music by the very best performers. But my guess is that he'd only partake if it was his own initiative. Stubbornness can be both a virtue and a vice.'

'If he doesn't like women and doesn't like men, could he satisfy himself in other ways?'

'Don't try to place a construct on the facts in the public domain, such as they are.'

'And the private facts? What's your professional opinion of Heath?'

'I've just given it. He's capable of it. We all are.'

The Assassin shook his head solemnly. 'Never.'

Voaden raised an eyebrow. 'I've heard that said before. But I was very good at corrupting people, darling.'

'It sounds like you took pride in your work.'

'I selected the choicest playmates for myself and for others. Ever so carefully and ever so discreetly. I organised parties, scouted out private venues, vetted invitations. I went to a lot of trouble to find the ripest fruit and places where we could enjoy it undisturbed.'

'But it was all for nothing in the end? You got caught.'

'I got too close to too many powerful people. No one wanted another society scandal. The choice was permanent retreat or permanent disgrace, but darker outcomes were hinted at.'

The Assassin was impassive.

'You don't look surprised,' said Voaden. 'You called it the true ultimate drug earlier. Are you speaking from personal experience?'

The Assassin shook his head slowly in refusal at the question.

'Have you come to England for another fix of death?' asked Voaden more urgently now. 'Is it me you've been sent to dispose of?'

'Is it death you deserve?' The Assassin let the question hang for a moment. 'All of us deserve it.'

He got up from the bench and walked over to inspect a carved stone face cemented into the wall. Then he turned around and looked Voaden full in the eye.

'Don't concern yourself. I've said "no" to any new temptation in that area. At some point you have to. Otherwise, no matter how you much resist, it will take control and tip you over the edge of the world into the darkness of the void.'

Voaden smiled back. 'Strong words indeed. But the journey up to the edge is so exciting. And without knowing where it ends, how else can you feel alive?'

'Could you have left it all behind if you hadn't been made to? Did you get tired of the parties, toward the end?'

'Once you've tried everything, nothing is left. But I hadn't tried it all by the time I stopped. Then again, the very act of stopping is itself an act of control. And better to have control, even of a life that's mostly celibate than to have no life at all.'

The Assassin crossed his arms and looked down at the ground.

Voaden smirked. 'Anyway, it's a pleasant enough retirement. There's no real work. I just need to go through the motions of the prayers and the odd service when my migraine isn't playing up.'

'Do some men never get tired of pushing the boundaries of decency? Never reach their limit?'

'Of course.'

'And in the other direction. Are some men celibate forever? Is Heath?'

Voaden gave the Assassin a calculating look.

'All men have natural instincts one way or another. But they can be suppressed, trained out. And other ones trained in. That's why we take them young. Whatever they taste first, that's generally what they come back to seek out.'

'So are you suggesting that however Heath was formed during childhood, he won't have changed from it? Such as having an aversion to sex?'

'Those sound like leading questions.'

The Assassin came to sit back down on the stone bench, further away from Voaden this time. 'How can you tell if men are inclined to pederasty but are keeping it hidden?' he asked. 'What are the signs?'

Voaden shook his head slowly. 'Without stating the obvious, are you investigating someone in particular in England? Or is it someone back home, wherever it is you come from?'

'I'm not investigating anyone,' replied the Assassin. 'Not yet, anyway. But there's no such thing as having too much background information.'

Voaden gave a short sigh. 'You want to recognise signs of men's suppressed inclinations? Apart from obvious, superficial things like lingering looks? I suggest a displaced interest in child welfare. A desire to be a father figure to children.' Voaden licked his lips. 'I could tell you so many stories. Prominent people I've known. People in the public eye. People unable to control their urges.'

'But not Heath?'

'Let's go back inside. It's getting chilly sitting out here.'

In Voaden's room, Smythe was flicking through the newspaper which the monk had been reading when they arrived.

'Find anything interesting?' asked Voaden.

'It's The Times. Just a story about West Pakistan invading East Pakistan.'

There was a single short knock at the door. A curly-headed priest appeared in the opening. At least, the Assassin assumed he was more than a mere monk because of the black apron he was wearing over his habit.

'Company I see, Brother Clement. We have choir practice now. All of your little friends have come this afternoon and your favourites are keen for extra tuition afterwards.'

The priest opened the door fully and stared hard at Voaden's visitors. His vestments were tailored to his trim figure and he had an arrogance about him that grated. With a disdainful parting look he turned around in a swirl of his robes and left.

As they pulled out of the drive the Assassin asked Smythe about the final scene in Voaden's room.

'So he's supposedly retired, but he still gives into temptation?'

'I think you're being generous. These people feel they're entitled to take whatever they want, whenever they want. I fucking hate them.'

'Why doesn't the Anglican Church discipline the pair of them? Why do they let Voaden get away with it?'

Smythe rolled his window down a crack, before sticking a cigarette in his mouth and thumbing the roller on his lighter.

'He seems to have learned nothing,' said the Assassin more insistently. 'He deserves to be behind bars.'

'How many nonces do you think I've helped to put away?'

The Assassin shrugged. 'You said yesterday it was hard to get convictions.'

'None. That's how many.'

'It doesn't say a lot for your society. Or your state church.'

'And you think West Germany is any better?'

The Assassin pulled a face. 'I just expected more from your country.'

Smythe said nothing to this.

'Why do you keep on going then, if your job is so thankless?' asked the Assassin.

'Because even if I can't touch the big guys, from time to time the people in charge decide to snap up some of the smaller fry. Just to send a message to everyone that we're watching. And we are able to rescue some of the kids from time to time. Although they're not innocents. Not by any means. Not after years of taking it up the bum from strange men.'

The Assassin didn't challenge him on whether it was the children's choice to stop being innocent in the first place.

'So what did you think?' asked Smythe. 'Are you any keener to go after our three perverts, now that you've heard what the old lecher had to say?'

'But we're not really going after them, are we? At least not over their own child abuse. Although who knows what the blackmail material on Heath might contain?'

'They're going to get the shock of their lives when MI5 get their hands on them, whenever that time comes. The threat of losing their directorships and whatever other comfortable sinecures they've acquired over the years will dampen their enthusiasms for sure, let alone the risk of being ostracized by their social class. The message will soon get out to their networks too.'

'It's hardly a prison camp in Siberia.'

'It might as well be for some of these people,' replied Smythe.

The Assassin murmured something to himself which the policeman couldn't catch. 'What did you say?' he asked.

'*Zersetzung*,' replied the Assassin, but he didn't explain what it meant. 'How did Voaden end up this way?' he asked Smythe instead. 'What was the path that led him to this place?'

'His path? You sound like a Victorian moralist trying to find a scientific basis for criminality. You're forgetting that I'm a policeman. There's often neither rhyme nor reason to these things. People just are the way they are.'

'But black candles and pentagrams? That speaks to a disturbed mind.'

Smythe shrugged, both hands still on the wheel.

'You asked me how he started? These public school types...' He tailed off for a moment.

'Apparently in every school there's a school tart. Often one of the younger boys who'll perform for rewards, I don't know... pocket money, answers to homework questions, getting someone picked for a sports team.'

The Assassin shrugged back. 'What's your point?'

'This may come as no surprise to you, but Voaden was one. A tart at age twelve. But just as every tart has a pimp, so he had one too. An older boy who made Voaden provide his favours to the others.'

Smythe looked across to make sure the Assassin was paying attention.

'Do you know who Voaden's pimp was?'

The Assassin shook his head.

'His own brother. That's who. They were at the same school.'

There was a look of disappointment on Smythe's face at the Assassin's apparent lack of reaction.

'You secretly like all this stuff, don't you Smythe?' he said. 'The enjoyment that comes from watching someone else's horror? *Schadenfreude?*'

'Don't come over all hoity-toity with me. I'm just telling you how twisted these people can be. Despite what the so-called "paedophiles" claim, it's not all spaced-out free love, world peace and the Age of Aquarius.'

They pulled off the A31 by the Hog's Head Hotel for lunch. Instead of going inside, Smythe waited for a gap in the traffic and led the Assassin across the road to the Little Chef opposite.

'This will be quicker,' he said. The Assassin would prefer to have risked the delay, but presumably Smythe knew better.

Once they were inside and sat down at the table, Smythe handed him a menu.

'What's a "steaklet"?' asked the Assassin, pointing to the entry for the Chef's Grill.

'Work it out for yourself. I'm having the gammon.'

'Fifty-two and a half pence. You're not holding back.'

'Ten and a half bob in real money. Anyway, you can't go wrong with chips.'

'You mean "French Fried Potatoes"?' said the Assassin.

'Don't be a snob.'

Smythe lit another cigarette while they waited for their order to be taken.

'When I was speaking with Voaden he mentioned the Moors Murderers. Who were they?' asked the Assassin.

Smythe glanced around the restaurant. 'Keep your voice down. There's kids here.'

'So who were they?'

'Boyfriend and girlfriend who went on a killing spree up North near Manchester. But they did more to the children than killing them.' As Smythe said this, there was a strange light in his eye.

'I can guess. Was it bad?'

'Very. Real sick stuff. But they got caught in the end. It would have been the death penalty for them, if the nonces in Parliament hadn't got rid of capital punishment the year before they went to trial.'

'Where are they now?'

'In jail on multiple life sentences. Three victims, with suspicions that there's more bodies out there. Maybe in a few years' time they'll bargain for parole by revealing the locations of the graves.'

'Did the case cause any of Voaden's customers to stop and think?'

Smythe shook his head and drew his lips into a thin line. 'If anything, I wouldn't be surprised if it gave them ideas, made them jealous. The thought of kidnap and then, you know. They did it to both boys and girls. Took photographs and recorded one of them on tape begging to be allowed to go home. He strangled them all.'

The odd look was back in Smythe's face. The Assassin raised an eyebrow, but then he himself had described it to Voaden as the ultimate drug.

Smythe drew heavily on his cigarette, gazing out of the window at the passing cars until the food arrived. Somehow, after all the things they'd just discussed, neither of them had any desire for renewed conversation.

They ate in silence and when they returned to the car, the Assassin carried on sitting with his own thoughts until London.

Smythe dropped the Assassin back at the Dorchester.

'I'll see you in a few weeks if we decide to have you back. What are you getting up to until your flight leaves?'

'I have shopping to do.'

Back in his room, the Assassin packed his black flight bag. He checked out and headed for Piccadilly Circus. Giant advertising hoardings vied for the attention of the passers-by: Lamb's Navy Rum,

Coca-Cola, Cinzano, Player's Gold Leaf, Wrigley's Gum. He did a complete circuit of the tourist traps around the junction and its famous fountain in the centre before turning into Regent Street. After walking under an arcade of arches, he crossed the road to a large shop he'd seen the previous day on his way back to the Dorchester from Club Trèfle.

Red and white striped awnings over the pavement shaded displays of toys behind the plate glass. He hesitated before walking inside.

On the first floor he bought a child's rag doll, a rabbit wearing a pink gingham dress. On the second floor he bought a painted wooden soldier with detachable arms and legs.

Both purchases were stuffed deep into his bag. He hailed a taxi at the top of Regent Street and told the driver to go to Heathrow Airport, Terminal Two.

Chapter Four

Just over a month later, the Assassin arrived back in England on a dull Wednesday morning. The nine o'clock Sabena flight from Brussels was on time and once he'd gone through customs at Terminal Two, he made his way to the Skyway Hotel on Bath Road, just outside the airport's northern perimeter.

In the end, the two-week break before the Assassin was meant to return to England became four weeks and then started pushing five. He suspected that Kramer and Brierly's attention had been elsewhere; the scene-setting for the Heath-Pompidou summit in late May was his best guess. The delay didn't do anything for his suspicions as to the true importance of the mission.

According to Kramer, the meeting at the Elysée Palace was to be the prelude to the successful conclusion of the negotiations, ensuring that all the right people got the credit and giving momentum to the ratification process. But just before the two leaders met, their representatives, O'Neill and Jobert, planned to simulate a deadlock in the talks with a surprise resolution which would mean the summit taking place in an atmosphere of impending triumph rather than crisis.

The latest scheme, just before the Assassin left Brussels, was that the final ministerial meeting before the summit would be artificially dragged out until the midnight announcement of a negotiating breakthrough. When the Assassin asked what kind of breakthrough, Kramer smirked. In exchange for the British opening up all of their market sectors to EEC goods from the very first day of membership, they would get a temporary concession to allow them to carry on importing New Zealand butter for a time. When the Assassin asked about the Werner Plan, Kramer's smirk merely deepened.

Part of the Assassin wondered if Kramer and the Commission were going too far. But he supposed they had no choice. They'd sold supranationalism to the member states by claiming it only worked if the collective transfer of powers to Brussels was done on a permanent basis - the one-way street of *engrenage*. So when new countries applied to join, you couldn't allow even the odd exception when it came to giving up their powers too. Once you'd done that for one country, before you knew it, the rest would be trying to reverse the wrong way down the street too.

He idly wondered too, if arriving by military transport in March had been a mistake - an unsubtle reminder to Brierly of the balance of power in the accession negotiations, if they could even be called that. More a case of the British being given time to digest the terms they were signing up to. Or going by Brierly's hints about smokescreens at dinner in the *Herrenklub*, being given time to explain them away.

According to Kramer there would be no more humiliating retreat than that over fishing, where the British had claimed they would force the Six to change the principle of equal access to each other's fishing grounds. But ultimately Kramer didn't seem bothered about O'Neill's ability to wriggle out of that one either.

The Assassin checked into the hotel and went up to his room to unpack.

From the window, a row of mouldering concrete buildings blocked the view of the runway but did nothing to block the aircraft noise. The hotel itself was smart enough. But regardless of how much they'd spent on bold striped carpets, gold paintwork, and table sculptures in the lobby, no amount of American interior design could compensate for the hotel's location.

Just as the Assassin finished hanging up his suits, Smythe rang from reception, and a couple of minutes later he appeared framed in the doorway, large as life.

'Good flight?' asked the policeman, striding over to take the only chair.

The Assassin leant back against the windowsill, keeping one eye on the narrow slice of runway visible in the gaps between the buildings opposite.

'Shouldn't we be at your office in Scotland Yard or wherever, if we're doing a briefing?' he asked.

Smythe folded his arms and gave him a sardonic look. 'I never do any of my private business there. Some of the people I deal with can't be seen within a mile of a police station. Others know the nicks of central London only too well, from the side of the cell doors where people are wearing the blue serge uniforms.'

'How official is your status within the police?' asked the Assassin. 'If you walked into West End Central this morning would the Obscene Publications Squad be pleased to see you?'

'"West End Central", "Obscene Publications"? It sounds like you've been speaking with Jimmy Malta at some point. Don't play the smart alec with me.'

'I've no idea who you really are.'

'Nor do we,' said Smythe. 'So shut up and let's talk tactics instead. What did your Monsieur Kramer tell you about the three Marks when you saw him again in Brussels?'

'He gave me names but no real details. I've no idea how sociable they are or how easy it's going to be to get photographed in their company.'

'Don't worry on that score. They can be sociable enough in the right setting, but you'll have to work for it.'

The Assassin glanced out of the window and caught his breath as a white-and-blue Pan-Am jumbo came into land. It was the first time he'd ever seen one. There had been pictures of course, but he hadn't anticipated the sheer size of the Boeing in real life. He turned back to see Smythe staring at him.

'Shouldn't we be trying to do more than merely take photographs?' he asked the policeman. 'Don't we at least need to try to recover the material they claim to have on Heath?'

'Patience. That comes later, after you've gone back to Belgium. At the right time we'll arrest them and get MI5 to interview them. As I said before, they'll crack soon enough under the threat of being made pariahs to their social class.'

Smythe got up to fetch the ashtray from the bedside table. He sat down again at the desk and lit up.

'Do you have any files, any background on these people?' asked the Assassin. 'Something I can study before I meet them?' He pulled out a notebook from his jacket.

Smythe drew on his cigarette.

'The first Mark is called Annersley. Long-time member of the Conservative Party with links to the Monday Club set.'

The Assassin looked at him expectantly.

'Right wing pressure group. On the more distant end of the spectrum. Supports Rhodesian independence on Smith's terms. That kind of thing.'

The Assassin smiled politely but without any real understanding.

'So how do I get to meet him? Go to their club and give a talk on all the wartime fascist commandos that I've met in Spain and Italy recently?'

'And have you?' asked Smythe sceptically.

'How do Annersley and I get together?' asked the Assassin, avoiding the question.

'We'll put on a private party at Club Trèfle - Jimmy Malta's club. I'll pass the word around and persuade Annersley to come when he's next in London.'

'How long will all that take to arrange? And what am I meant to be doing in the meantime?'

'After you've made contact with the East German Foreign Trade Office and got Reynolds to put you under MI5 surveillance, then you're free to do whatever you like - within reason.'

'I'll go mad waiting around for days in Reynolds' flat.'

'As far as I'm concerned, you're getting paid to have a holiday in London. Get to know the locals. Brush up on your English. Lose your accent.' Smythe tapped his cigarette on the ashtray.

'And the second Mark? Same plan for him? Another party at Club Trèfle?'

'Who? Barker? Basically, yes. He's a senior trade union official who's made several trips behind the Iron Curtain.'

'Someone already on the intelligence services radar, then?'

'I doubt he's under any kind of surveillance. This isn't the Soviet Union. To moderate left-wingers he's already a potential Communist informer. Being seen with you will be the final nail in the coffin as regards his credibility with the mainstream - if it ever leaks out that is.'

'One Mark from the right, one from the left. Isn't that what they call a cliché?'

'We didn't choose them that way, they chose themselves. But it can't hurt that they each have their own personal networks. As I just said, before long we're going to give these three beauties the fright of their comfortable lives. Brierly and I are going to send a message to every point of the political compass not to play games with Heath's reputation.'

'It still sounds like they've been set up for it,' said the Assassin with narrowed eyes.

'I don't know everything that's been discussed between Brierly and Kramer. But I know when not to ask. You should take a leaf out of my book.'

'When do we get to Barker?'

'Relax. It's almost summer and with any luck the miniskirts will be out again soon. The Beatles are no more and it's a new era for rock music on both sides of the Atlantic. I'm sure you'll find plenty to do, and plenty of girls to do as well.'

'This is serious, Smythe. Kramer's been given the blessing for this mission from the highest authorities in France.'

Smythe looked amusedly at the Assassin. 'Grow your hair longer and don't be so Prussian about life.'

The Assassin pursed his lips. 'I need to be finished by the start of June. I can't wait around here forever. How about the third man, Grieves? When can I get started on him?'

'He's a wheeler-dealer who's bought up a number of electrical engineering businesses over the years. Apparently he's always on the lookout for new opportunities to diversify, or so I've been told. As Brierly said last time, you'll pretend to be a consultant helping Western companies gain access to Eastern bloc markets. You should use the same story with the players at the East German trade office. One set of lies is easier to remember than two.'

The Assassin scribbled some notes. 'And what do you and Brierly know about the people in Belgrave Square? Does anyone suspect them of being anything more than trade officials?'

Smythe clicked his fingers. 'Doesn't matter. Whoever you meet will be desperate to do business with us,' he said with a casual confidence. 'They'll do anything to try to overtake the West.'

The Assassin chose not to offer his opinion on that.

'To get you and Annersley in Club Trèfle together won't be straightforward, you know. I need Jimmy to put on a limited-invitation party and get him to put out his feelers far enough in advance so that there's some genuine guests as cover. Then we need to borrow a few girls from other Soho clubs who are happy to relax with our punters after their own jobs are done for the day, and who aren't fussy about getting paid in anything more than drugs. Then ahead of the party, I have to set up the lighting and the concealed cameras, and afterwards I need to develop the film and make copies of the prints.'

'Do these parties make money?'

'If people buy drink and drugs at them, yes.'

'And if the parties are more intimate? You charge an entrance fee?'

'Nothing in life comes for free.'

The Assassin was reminded of a similar phrase used by Voaden last month in Hampshire. 'What do they charge for parties where you can abuse children?' he asked.

Smythe cocked his head to one side. 'Don't get too involved in my world, Thomas - it's not wholesome. I say it for your own protection. Physically, morally, even spiritually - if you're that way inclined.'

'But I am involved in your world.'

'You're literally only going to make conversation with the three Marks in various settings and get photographed doing so. By the way, Annersley bats for both teams.'

'What do you mean?'

'You'll find out when you meet him.'

The Assassin looked suspiciously at Smythe.

'What did Jimmy say about me?' asked the policeman. 'Assuming you spoke to him, that is.'

The Assassin glanced out of the window again before replying. A Laker Airways 707 burst above the roofline of the buildings, trailing dirty smoke from its turbojets as it clawed its way into the air.

'I met him the day before you and I went to Hampshire. Kramer wanted me to get to know Jimmy in case I'd be coming back here. But all that he said about the police was that the ones who covered Soho were easily bought off. He didn't give me the names of any officers.'

'On the way back from meeting Voaden, I told you a straight story about how many successful prosecutions of serious abusers my evidence gathering has led to. Jimmy's given you a clue as to why.'

'So how do you intend to turn that around? Would you cross the line for a good cause?'

'Just because the odds are stacked against us,' said Smythe, 'it doesn't stop me collecting anything I come across which might incriminate these people. I'm building up my dossiers all the time. But who knows? You being here might change the odds of a conviction.'

'How do you mean?'

'This whole spooky charade with you and Brierly is the best chance I've had to nail them in almost four years. The three Marks have given people a reason to act which can't be ignored.'

'How long have you been doing this job for then?' asked the Assassin, puzzled.

'After the Profumo Affair, the Met realised they needed to keep their own permanent watching brief on the scene. The higher-ups wanted to make sure they had early warning of problems, in case friends of the police like wealthy crooks and informers needed to be kept out of trouble.'

'But Profumo was in the early sixties. Was there someone before you, or have you been doing this job all that time?' asked the Assassin, half in horror.

'That's not for you to know.'

'Who else is spying on the sex party scene, if the Met wanted their own people to do it?'

'I can't speak for every institution of the British Establishment, but MI5 sponsor "Eve's", a cabaret club in Regent Street, next to Soho. Popular with foreign diplomats, High Court judges, and most notoriously with the Bishop of Southwell, who had to resign on grounds of ill health and his partiality to their topless dancers.'

'The Metropolitan Police already has a Vice Squad, doesn't it? Isn't that what Obscene Publications is part of? Why not use them for early warning of misbehaviour?'

Smythe stubbed out his cigarette and got up to stretch. He looked down his nose at the Assassin.

'Okay, I get it,' said the Assassin with a touch of impatience. 'Vice is as corrupt as the other squads which cover Soho. But by some miracle they might at least have some basic moral standards and draw the line at tolerating child abuse. Or at least, tolerating child abuse amongst senior police officers. Is that what it was? When they needed someone more ruthless, they called you?'

'Not such a German knucklehead after all, are you?'

The Assassin gave a slight shrug. 'Do you work on your own, then?' he asked. 'Don't you ever find it hard to remember what side you're meant to be on, if you're running around collecting evidence on one hand and stopping your bosses in the police and their friends from getting into trouble with the other?'

'How about you?' Smythe jabbed a finger at the Assassin's chest. 'I said earlier that no one knows who you are, or what it is exactly that you do for Kramer, or even how many there are of you. If you're working without supervision, who's checking your moral compass?'

'I know what's right and what's wrong. Even if I don't always do it,' said the Assassin defiantly.

'That's a good one,' said Smythe sarcastically. 'I'll have to remember it in case I ever get confused as to which side I'm on.' He patted his pockets.

'Your cigarettes are on the desk,' said the Assassin, pointing to Smythe's pack of John Players which he'd left there.

From just outside the room, they heard voices in the corridor - a man and a woman laughing together. There was a sharp bang as the door to the neighbouring room slammed shut.

'Are you off now then?' asked the Assassin. 'What do you do during the day when you're not arranging parties? You maintain your card index of abusers at one of your special department's secret locations?'

'One day I'm going to end up punching you.' Smythe opened and closed his fists a couple of times.

'Call it professional courtesy,' said the Assassin. 'Go on, you know you want to. How often do you get the chance to talk to someone else about your job?'

Smythe stared at the Assassin for a second or two. 'I have plenty to keep me busy. Meeting people, picking up gossip. Then meeting my superiors in the Met to pass on what I've learned. Creating evidence where it's needed to fill in gaps in a story. The job I'm doing with you is my bread and butter.'

Flicking his wrist to check the time, he sat down again.

'I can do it in my sleep.' He tilted the chair back against the desk and lit another cigarette.

'Don't you ever get bored of doing the same thing year in, year out, with no prospect of promotion because you know too much to be allowed back into the real police?'

Smythe didn't reply. Instead he sat up straight as if listening to something.

'Fuck me.' He stood, picked up an empty water glass from the desk, and held it to the wall of the adjacent room which the couple had just gone into. The Assassin looked distastefully at Smythe's back.

'Tell me this instead then,' he asked, as Smythe placed a hand flat against the wall, fingers splayed out. 'Will we do any permanent good for even one of the children who've been abused by these three? You said that we might scare off some of these *putain* bastards for a while. But what then?'

Smythe waited a few seconds before turning round, looking troubled now.

'Have you heard of the "Flee at once, all is discovered" telegram? Probably not, being foreign.'

'Tell me.'

'A hundred years ago someone supposedly sent that message to every bishop in the Church of England. Six words were enough to get several of them to pack their bags and run for the next boat to Calais. Or so the story goes.'

'The modern Bishop of Southwell was in good company then?'

Smythe held up a finger and turned to lean in close to the wall.

'Jesus. They're really going at it now.'

He replaced the glass on the desk.

'Twitch a couple of strands of the web and the current crop of sinners will go scurrying in all directions. They've been left pretty much alone since Profumo, so when the music stops, they could well turn against each other. We might start a chain of accusations and denouncements that makes a whole monastery of Voadens ride off into the sunset.'

The Assassin shook his head.

'You're only telling yourself that. We're fighting human nature here. People who have an urge to satisfy the crudest of instincts for power and control. And we're fighting other people who are more than happy to make money from it.'

'Always the optimist, eh? What's your idea for how these people can be persuaded to stop? Apart from locking them up and throwing away the key?'

The Assassin put his head to one side. He opened his mouth, wanting to say that there was no power within themselves that could make them change, but then shut it again.

'We've got work to do,' he said instead. 'I'm going to call the trade office in Belgrave Square today and try to get a meeting for tomorrow.'

'Aren't you meant to be moving into Reynolds' flat?'

'Friday. I'm staying here tonight and tomorrow.'

'You know that you can only move as fast as I can set up these meetings with the Marks?' said Smythe.

'Try me.'

Chapter Five

Fitzrovia, London - Friday, 30th April 1971

Two days had passed. The Assassin had wasted no time and called Belgrave Square as soon as Smythe had left the hotel. But to his faint disgust, the policeman's claim about their desperation to talk seemed to have been correct, for he'd been given an appointment with a trade advisor the following day.

Twenty-four hours after his meeting with Herr Uhlmann, he was still struck by the surrealness of Brierly and Kramer's plan. Yesterday he'd gone there in the knowledge that after some judicious hints from Reynolds to his fellow MI5 officers, they'd eventually tag him as someone linked to the Stasi, if not as a direct collaborator, then perhaps as a person of interest.

But even before his name crossed someone's desk at Leconfield House, the London officers of the Stasi's foreign intelligence department, the HVA, would already have been assessing him, as they did for all such casual callers - suspicious that they might be agent provocateurs sent to trail their coats by MI5. But little did Kramer's English partners or the London HVA know that the surrealness went a level deeper than that.

Since arriving in London, the Assassin had spent the bulk of his free time wandering the streets, from World's End in Chelsea to the Angel in Islington.

Every town had its different quarters, but London was unlike any other place he'd been to. The whole city buzzed with its own unique energy - "Swinging London" was what they'd called it in the sixties. Sleepy Brussels it was not. Even the exuberant excesses of the Reeperbahn back home in Hamburg were constrained to a few streets in the Saint Pauli district.

At the *Herrenklub*, Fryatt and Brierly claimed the country was depressed at having been excluded from the EEC for ten years and having a GDP per head of only eighty percent of France's. But Londoners didn't seem so bothered as they thronged the department stores, cinemas, and theatres of the West End. Compared to Paris, restaurants left something to be desired, but if you had money, or even better, an unlimited expense account, the city could provide.

After a couple of days of jumping on and off the open rear platforms of the red double-decker buses he was starting to feel like a real Londoner. He was even learning which cars to ride on the Underground for a quick exit at the bigger stations and had begun to call it "the Tube."

Each day so far, he'd allowed himself one activity a normal London tourist would do. Today it was a drink in the bar above the revolving restaurant at the top of the Post Office Tower. He sat with a gin and tonic as he and his fellow patrons swept the city skyline twice every three quarters of an hour. To the west, the buildings typically rose five or six stories at most. The Dorchester's eight floors stood out, along with the other hotels along Park Lane, bookended by the Hilton, a whole twenty-eight floors high. The City in the east was different. There were more tower blocks than in the West End, but from this perspective, Saint Paul's Cathedral seemed to be almost as tall as them. To the north was a range of green hills in the direction of East Anglia, where Kramer had been during the war.

In the late afternoon he returned to left luggage at the West London Air Terminal on Cromwell Road to pick up his bags, and by half-past six he was ringing the bell of Reynolds' flat in Earl's Court.

Reynolds buzzed him in, and the Assassin climbed to the third floor. He knocked and was admitted to a modest flat. Reynolds' place was tidy, but in a proper sense - not in the way that most bachelors would quickly shove the mess under chairs and in cupboards.

'You're staying in here,' said Reynolds, once the customary civilities were over. He showed the Assassin to a box room that faced a windowless angle of the house next door. As a bonus, the room also benefited from a partial view of a forlorn backyard and the row of dustbins lined up along its rear wall.

'Ever had a lodger before?' asked the Assassin.

'No. I had the idea of sharing when I first got the place. But then with the work I do it was easier to avoid explanations to a housemate.'

The Assassin frowned. 'Won't it look suspicious to counter-intelligence at MI5 if the very first lodger you take in after changing your mind supposedly turns out to work for the Stasi? They'll wonder if you're being targeted because you've been careless with your cover.'

'My boss and I have worked out a story. I put a classified advertisement in The Times for a flat share a couple of weeks ago. If anyone asks, I'll say I decided to start saving to get a bigger place and I went with you because you were happy to pay cash up front.'

'I suppose I am then?' said the Assassin with a half-smile. 'All the details have to check out, don't they?'

But he didn't go on to ask how much Reynolds wanted, and just then the Englishman was too embarrassed to ask.

'The kitchen is through here,' said Reynolds instead. 'Tins are in this cupboard. Take what you want. Or if you'd prefer your own stuff, there's shops on Earl's Court Road.'

'Thanks. At most, I'll only be here a couple of weeks or so.'

Reynolds attempted some warmth. 'It'll be an experience for sure. How many MI5 officers end up with lodgers from the SDECE?'

The Assassin gave him a faint smile in return. Reynolds led them back out into the hall.

'The bathroom is through here. Make sure you open the window when you shower. The freeholder lives in the flat below. Widow of a headmaster. She has an obsession with black mould.'

'Any other house rules?'

'She doesn't approve of loud music. Or drugs.'

'I'm sure she'll have no cause to complain.'

They returned to the kitchen.

'You want a drink of something?' asked Reynolds. 'I have a bottle of wine in the fridge and cans of beer.'

'No tea? Isn't that what you drink most of in England?'

'Now you're making fun.' Reynolds opened the Frigidaire and handed the Assassin a can of Ind Coope and a glass.

'Let's go through to the lounge,' he said.

They took their cans and went to sit on opposite sides of the low table that stood in front of the TV - the Assassin on the sofa and Reynolds on the chair.

'You have an ashtray?' asked the Assassin. 'Can I smoke in the flat?'

'Here. Use this.' Reynolds took a saucer from underneath a terracotta pot containing a sickly rubber plant standing in the middle of the table. He slid it across to the Assassin.

'No. Not now, thanks. I only asked in case I ever needed to.'

'Are you trying to stop?'

'It's been suggested to me. Do you ever have people over to stay? A girlfriend at the weekend?'

Reynolds shook his head. 'No. I'm not quite at that stage yet.'

'Okay.' The Assassin opened a penknife to pierce his beer can. 'The ring pull snapped,' he explained.

'Sorry,' said Reynolds, 'There's an old churchkey in the kitchen drawer.'

'So your boss is in on this too?' asked the Assassin. 'Who else within your organisation?'

Reynolds looked back at him warily.

'Are you having second thoughts about this?' he asked. 'That you and your boss are somehow betraying your other colleagues?'

'No matter how reasonable these unofficial arrangements might appear to be,' replied Reynolds, 'or even how logically they're presented, if they go wrong there's all sorts of consequences. Informal agreements are worse than no protection at all when scapegoats are required.'

'But there's no risk to MI5. Adding a person of interest to your file who isn't actually working for the other side can't hurt. Worse would be to have an illegal operating in the UK, but not on your radar.'

'So you say. But then you never know. Having your name on our list might lead an investigator down a false path one day or suggest a connection that doesn't exist.'

'What does your boss think about it all?'

'He's ambitious. He'll do anything which he thinks will help his career.'

'Has someone promised him something out of this operation?'

Reynolds pulled a face. 'As I said, he'll try anything for advancement, no matter how speculative.'

'What's he like to work for? Tough boss?'

Reynolds slowly poured his beer into the glass, unsure of how much more he should say.

'If there's any one thing that drives him it's his hatred of MI6. He hates them almost as much as the IRA.'

The Assassin looked at Reynolds sceptically. 'Seems obsessive. What did MI6 do to him? Blow up his best friend?'

'It's personal to Masterson,' replied Reynolds, glancing once more at the Assassin's scars.

'I won't tell anyone, I promise. I just like to know how people think.'

Reynolds looked dubious but he explained anyway, not wanting a confrontation on their first evening together.

'All throughout university he was desperate to be recruited by MI6. He made sure he was in the tutorial groups of suspected recruiters. He joined the right societies - he even joined the OTC. The army unit for students,' Reynolds explained, as he saw the Assassin's mouth start to form the question.

'But it was all to no avail - even though he had family friends whom he thought were connected with Century House. Then one day he did get a call, but it was for an interview to join the Secret Service, not MI6.'

'Despite his disappointment he took the job anyway?'

'I suspect he saw it as a foot in the door of the intelligence community. After all,' said Reynolds with a wry smile, 'there are some precedents for a transfer to MI6.'

'What? Like Richard White, the former director of MI5?'

'That was never meant to get into the public domain,' said Reynolds. Then, more bitterly, 'Bloody journalists. MI5 and MI6 don't even officially exist. And it's "Sir Richard" by the way.'

'West Germany is progressive. We don't have titles. East Germany even more so.'

Reynolds looked darkly at the Assassin for a moment. But he seemed to have imparted this in a spirit of information rather than insult.

'Anyway, joining MI5 didn't make Masterson happy. He's consumed with a desire to prove himself. I wouldn't be surprised if he wants to make it all the way to Director, if only to lobby the politicians to have MI6 shut down.'

The Assassin pursed his lips for half-a-second before replying. No wonder the KGB and the Stasi ran both foreign and domestic intelligence under one roof. 'It's the way these things go inside government organisations,' he informed his new flatmate again.

'What's your boss in Brussels like?' asked Reynolds.

'French. He works to his own rule book. Most of my time is spent trying to work out what it is he wants me to do.'

'What happens after this assignment? Will you go back full time to EEC Internal Affairs?'

'We'll see. Maybe the SDECE will give me another contract.'

'Why did you leave the Legion? Didn't you enjoy soldiering?'

'It was an important part of my life at the time, but it's over now.' It certainly was, all two weeks of it.

Reynolds looked pensive. 'My father was a major in the Army. Royal Engineers. He joined at age fourteen - as a boy soldier. He only retired last year.'

'What are the "Engineers"? Motor mechanics?'

'No. I think you call them "Pioneers" in your army.'

'Where did he serve during the war?'

'In Burma. Fighting the Japanese.'

'What does he think of Germans?'

'He hates them less than the Japs. He bloody hates the Japs by the way, but he's never really explained why. What did your people do in the war?'

The Assassin paused for a moment. He opened his mouth to speak then thought better of it.

'You don't want to talk about it?' asked Reynolds solemnly. 'Was your father involved in things he shouldn't have been?'

To Reynolds' surprise, the Assassin's face reddened momentarily.

'It's easier if we don't discuss it. I never knew him. I was born in nineteen forty-five.'

'I'm sorry.'

'I'm sorry too,' the Assassin replied, more grimly now. He took a sip of the watery beer and recrossed his legs.

'It will get easier you know,' said Reynolds. 'As the war fades into the past. Joining the EEC will help too. We'll be part of a joint political enterprise with France and West Germany for the first time.'

'Don't forget Italy,' said the Assassin.

'Yes, Italy too. We've been at war with everyone in Europe, I think. Except Portugal, Belgium and maybe Luxembourg. And Norway and Switzerland, I suppose.'

The Assassin changed the topic from all the wars that England had won.

'Do you have to report to your boss how much rent I pay you?'

'No. I just need to be able to show I received something if I'm asked. But that's unlikely.'

'What did you put in the newspaper advertisement?'

'Fifteen pounds per week. I wanted to make sure no one actually took me up on it.'

'I'll pay for three months up front.'

Reynolds looked at him shrewdly. 'What if you're not here that long?'

'Tell them you asked for a non-refundable deposit.'

Before Reynolds could protest, the Assassin reached into his wallet to find the money and quickly press it on him. As he took out a fistful of tenners, a black and white passport photo fell onto the table between them.

The Assassin cursed under his breath. Reynolds bent down to retrieve it before his lodger could make a move.

'Nice looking girl. Who is it?' He kept hold of the photo as he eyed up the Assassin.

'It's a prop,' said the Assassin after half-a-second's delay. 'Part of my German disguise.' He reached out and Reynolds reluctantly handed it over.

The Assassin gave Reynolds a wink, too quickly to be convincing. 'It's a regulation going back to Napoleon that the French intelligence services should only have pretty girls on file,' he said.

'What if your girlfriend sees it?'

'I never said I had one.' Then he relented. 'She doesn't know what I do.'

'Have you had many girlfriends?'

'I only left the Legion a year ago. I didn't have much opportunity before that. There's been a few since then,' he added tonelessly. 'Belgian, Irish, German, Swiss.'

'You get around.'

The Assassin was taken aback by Reynolds' envious look. If Reynolds had ever met the obsessive politics student from Gent whom the Assassin had only got rid of with extreme difficulty, he might have thought differently.

'Brussels is an international city,' he said. 'Lots of people on secondment from their national governments. Living on their own and looking for company in the evening. And you?'

Reynolds shrugged. 'Just the one long-term female friend.'

'Why don't you say "girlfriend"? We've only got one word in German for both: "*Freundin*."'

Reynolds replied somewhat embarrassedly. 'I fell into it. We had a few dates and then it became expected of me.'

The Assassin frowned.

'I go over to her parents for Sunday lunch every couple of weeks or so. She and they have come to see me as a regular thing.'

'But you don't?'

'She's not someone I could take to the club, or take to meet my work colleagues.'

'Why?'

'They're of a different class. Social class.'

The Assassin looked at him blankly. Reynolds ploughed on with his explanation, without really knowing why.

'I mean, it's not as if our family is rich. At least, not rich in comparison to the families of some officers in the Service. I went to Dover, not the best-known public school. My parents had to scrimp a bit. Save money,' he explained. 'My father got a grant for my education from the Army.'

'Where does your girlfriend live?'

Reynolds paused, unwilling to go on. But some quality in the Assassin's voice compelled him.

'The East End. Her father works for a shipping company at one of the docks. He's a clerk of some kind.'

'I understand,' said the Assassin, thinking back to the women in their ballgowns and furs at the *Herrenklub*.

'But if you like her, then what's the problem? Don't you need to tell her one way or another at some point?'

Now Reynolds looked even more embarrassed than before.

'Excuse me,' said the Assassin. He got up and took his bags through to the bedroom.

By the time he returned to the lounge, Reynolds had switched on the television. A Western was playing. Two cowboys were facing one another down the middle of a dusty street, hands trembling over pistols slung by their sides, ready for the draw.

Reynolds looked up guiltily.

'I just let it run in the background. "Europa" is on at eight on BBC Two.'

'What programme is that?'

'It's a series of clips from foreign broadcasters with English commentary added on top. Sometimes they show footage from Moscow Television.'

Reynolds was on edge. Now that the preliminaries were over, he realised he resented the intrusion into his private life. He'd made himself an unchallenging routine here in Earl's Court and he liked it.

'Will your flat be watched at any point?' asked the Assassin.

'After I make my report on you to my boss, someone might occasionally swing by after I leave for work in the morning. Just to see where you spend your days.'

The Assassin glanced out of the window at the street below.

'Have you eaten already?' he asked Reynolds.

'I eat lunch most days in the staff restaurant. I usually take a sandwich in the evening.'

'I have an expense allowance. If you like, we can eat out tonight if you know of somewhere discreet.'

'No, you go ahead. There's a place on the Old Brompton Road I go to sometimes. I'll draw you a sketch map of how to get there.'

The Assassin acknowledged him with a nod.

'What are you doing tomorrow?' asked Reynolds. 'Have you been given the weekend off?'

'Brierly's arranged a trip into the country. Someone else they want me to meet.'

As the Assassin made his way downstairs to go and find the restaurant, he began to get a sense of why Heath might be content to remain a bachelor. Especially if he liked his comfort and his domestic arrangements just so.

But he began to feel sorry for the Prime Minister too, isolated at the pinnacle of his power. Unlike even Reynolds and himself these next couple of weeks, Heath didn't have the option of going home at night to talk to another person. To be distracted even for one evening from whatever was troubling him just then - which for the leaders of nations, was presumably all the time.

Chapter Six

Brierly pulled up a little way down the street from Reynolds' flat just before ten the following morning. Smythe drove a Jaguar that was a cross between a sports car and a luxury saloon, Brierly's choice was a sensible Morris 1800 whose large cabin windows and overall proportions vaguely recalled Kramer's Citroën DS.

The Assassin got in and slammed the door.

'Easy,' said Brierly. 'This isn't a Mercedes.'

'Sorry, I forgot.'

Brierly glanced across with a slight frown. The Assassin didn't appear to notice.

'So what's this meeting about?' he asked. 'Why did you say we'd be away all day?'

Brierly checked the traffic and pulled out behind a dark green Bedford panel van. The Assassin gave it an odd look. At the end of Park Lane, Brierly crossed the junction and took the Edgware Road heading for the A1.

'I'm taking you to East Anglia as a favour to an old friend. You're also going to meet someone who I'll be using to stay in contact with you going forwards.'

'Not Smythe?'

Brierly pursed his lips. 'No, not Smythe.'

'How is this trip doing someone a favour?' asked the Assassin.

'We're indulging an old man. A mentor of mine. I told him what you were doing over here and he wanted to meet you.' Brierly glanced in the mirror as they waited at the lights by Aberdeen Place, where the Regent's Canal crossed under the road.

'He's one of the early British federalists. But if he wants to feel like he's still part of the project, then I'm happy to oblige. You ought to find his stories interesting.'

'How early is "early"?'

'The First World War. He saw the light in France in nineteen seventeen.'

'Fond of Germans, is he?'

'I'm sure he doesn't hate you collectively.' Brierly glanced across at his passenger again. 'Maybe the one who bayoneted him in a shell hole as he lay there wounded, he might still hate personally.'

'Why is he keen to see me, then?'

'Because you're Kramer's man and he has a fondness for him.'

'Really? He knew Kramer during the war?'

Brierly tapped forefinger on the Morris' spindly steering wheel.

'Edward Devilliers was close to people at the Free French headquarters in Carlton Gardens. He was desperate to get the ear of de Gaulle for a time. Kramer indulged him, gave him the appointments he asked for.'

The Assassin was dubious, wondering what game Kramer had been playing back then and on whose behalf.

'The highlight of his war was advising Jean Monnet in the summer of nineteen forty,' said Brierly with a hint of overweening pride. 'When Monnet was asked to help draft Churchill's offer of political union with France, just as the panzers were knocking on Paris' door.'

'First I've heard of it. What did the French say to that idea?'

'The French Prime Minister backed it. He needed something he could use to persuade the French cabinet not to make a separate peace with Hitler.'

'We all know how that turned out.'

'It was an offer, a grand gesture intended for effect - not a fully negotiated treaty. But afterwards Devilliers kept on promoting the idea to the Free French government in London, trying to maintain the momentum and persuade de Gaulle that England's intentions around unification that summer had been honourable.'

'And Churchill and his cabinet just agreed to unite their country with France? Without any kind of debate?'

'At the time nothing seemed unreasonable in the fight against Hitler. Even an alliance with Stalin.'

'Did Devilliers have an official position back then? Who was he working for?'

'It was his own initiative, after the original authors of the unification proposal moved on to other things. No one else was prepared to put their heads above the parapet.'

'But who was Devilliers?' asked the Assassin more insistently.

'An economist at Cambridge who hung around the brighter stars of Keynes and Salter. He occasionally got invited down to the private meetings which Keynes held with influential academics and politicians at his house outside Brighton.'

'And Keynes and Salter?'

'Keynes was also an economist, famous both here and in America. He was the Treasury's representative at the Versailles conference after the First World War. But he fell out with the other members of the British delegation and was cut out of the negotiations. He ended up opposing the final terms of the Treaty, unsurprisingly enough.'

'*Diktat*,' murmured the Assassin. 'And Salter?'

'Civil servant turned academic. Close ally of Jean Monnet from when they worked together on the Allied shipping council during the Great War and then at the League of Nations afterwards.'

The Assassin wound down the window a crack. They were driving through Cricklewood now, following a Number 32. An advertisement for Navy Cut was displayed in the panel above its rear window.

'Monnet didn't stay in the League for long,' said the Assassin. 'He was only there a couple of years.'

Brierly changed up a gear to overtake the bus. 'He left in frustration at what he saw as its impotence, but Salter persevered. He proposed that the structures of the League should be used as a template for the government of a future European state.'

'After Monnet left the League, he became an investment banker in America and China,' said the Assassin.

'Did Kramer tell you that?'

'I do my own research from time to time,' replied the Assassin curtly. 'What are you really saying? Monnet gave up, but the dream of European federation was kept alive in England?'

'It was Salter who was the first to realise that European unification would never work unless it was organised on a supranational basis. No more joint decision-making by individual governments acting in concert. In his plan, the European state would be run by a Secretariat. Staffed by its own civil servants to avoid the danger of national allegiances. Just like the European Commission today, or so you claimed to Fryatt and me in the club. Effectively, Salter sketched out the design for what later became the EEC - almost thirty years ahead of time.'

'But no one's heard of Salter these days. People only know of Monnet.'

'Yet they were colleagues for years. During both world wars too. Along with Devilliers, Salter also helped draft Monnet's joint proposal with Vansittart for Franco-British union.'

'Is Salter still alive?' asked the Assassin.

'He's in his nineties, I believe.'

'Monnet is over eighty. I didn't realise how much the wider European movement owed to the English.'

'Before the war there was a mass organisation in Britain called the Federal Union. They had over a hundred thousand members at one point and its publications were distributed throughout Europe. Their ideas made it into Spinelli's wartime manifesto on European unification.'

The Assassin raised an eyebrow at the mention of the name.

'I said to you once before,' continued Brierly, 'France isn't the only one to have suffered at Germany's hands. Devilliers has been working towards this moment for decades, ever since he left that dressing station in Arras to return to Blighty. After all the ups and downs and false starts over the past decades, our accession to the EEC will be his life's crowning achievement.'

As they crossed under the North Circular, they saw signs for Wembley. The Assassin asked which tube line the stadium was on.

'I don't believe it is on one. Why do you ask? Are you a fan of association football?'

'What other type of football is there?'

Brierly tutted but didn't enlighten him. 'Before you ask,' he said instead, 'No, I didn't watch that match here five years ago.'

'You did well. But we paid you back in Mexico last year,' was all the Assassin said in reply. Brierly was silent.

'Have you ever been to a Cup Final?' asked the Assassin, still trying to make conversation. 'I read in the Daily Express that it's next Saturday: Liverpool versus Arsenal.'

'Why on earth would I come into town on a weekend for a soccer match? I've never been to one in my entire life and I'm not going to begin now. I've never read the Express either, come to that. Ask Reynolds to go with you, if you want some company. Nannying you is his job for the next few weeks.'

'Perhaps I shall,' replied the Assassin.

After passing through Hendon they joined the A1.

'We have to go north for a while, then east. There's plans for a motorway direct to Cambridge by the end of the decade,' said Brierly. 'Before you start on the superiority of your autobahns.'

'I wasn't going to say anything.'

'Kramer's been up this way a few times,' said Brierly. 'We came here a lot during the war. Did he tell you?'

'He mentioned something about going to meet people at the airfield before they departed on missions.'

'During the war you could hardly drive ten miles in any direction across Cambridgeshire, Norfolk and Suffolk without hitting an airfield. Flat country and near to enemy territory.'

'Ten miles apart doesn't sound close. Sixteen kilometres.'

'Four minutes flying time. It could have meant life or death for a wounded crew member.'

'Bomber airfields?'

'Yes. Amongst others.'

'Your brother was based in this area?'

'He was with 115 Squadron, flying Lancasters. They were stationed at Little Snoring. He joined at age nineteen and was killed at twenty.'

'It must have been hard on your family.'

Brierly glanced across at the Assassin. 'My parents were never the same again. But we weren't the only ones to suffer a loss.'

'I know of a family in West Germany whose eldest son was a fighter pilot. He was shot down after a daylight raid on Essen in 'forty-four. American fighters got him as he came into land.'

'Do they still resent the Allies today?'

'No. They resent the German electorate for giving Hitler his opening. Even though he didn't actually win the final election. Not by fair means anyway.'

'And your own family's history during the war?'

'I don't talk about it.'

They slowed to a crawl outside Stevenage.

'Did Kramer take you to the airport in Paris?' asked Brierly.

'Yes.'

'Did he offer you a brandy?'

'No.'

'After the first few agents he sent over were all captured or killed he stopped. Out of superstition. It worked, though. He stopped toasting them and they stopped dying.'

'He hardly ever talks about the war. Nothing operational anyway. Only anecdotes about having to live with the English in London. And he only told me those because it was the day after de Gaulle died and he was drunk. He held a wake for his French friends in Brussels and invited me to join them.'

Brierly grunted. 'If you don't know anything about Kramer's war, then you don't know him.'

The Assassin looked out of the window as they started moving faster again.

'Do you trust him?' asked Brierly. 'Kramer, that is?'

'Why? Don't you?' the Assassin replied.

'You've no idea of the depth of hatred which he could justifiably have of you and your kind. After what the Gestapo and the Vichy's Sûreté did to his people.'

'He's never mentioned it. He might not love Germany, but he doesn't dislike me.'

'Of course not,' retorted Brierly. 'You served France for five years in the Foreign Legion.'

'I'm as much French as West German.'

'Indeed.'

They left the A1 before Baldock, heading for Royston to pick up the Old North Road where the A10 became the A14.

'We could have taken the train from King's Cross once but the line to Somersham was closed to passengers a couple of years ago.'

'Why?'

'Modernisation. Sweep away the old, in with the new.'

'Is that your metaphor for why England - the UK - wants to join the EEC?'

'It's the argument which some people use.'

'What's your personal reason for wanting Britain to join?'

'Isn't it obvious? I want to make sure another war never happens again.'

'What if a future European state goes rogue? Attacks Russia or America.'

'Stop being facetious.'

But the Assassin wasn't joking. 'Who are you to know the future? A war between the Soviets and the Americans isn't so far-fetched. They're fighting one another in Vietnam right now, even as we speak. It's just that no one's describing it that way.'

'You're fantasising. They're not confronting each other directly. That's why it's called the Cold War.'

'Even so, putting wars to one side, what's your guarantee that the EEC will always behave as you want it to?'

'What are you hinting at?'

'How do you know that Britain will always see eye to eye with France and West Germany?'

'Oh, that question.'

'It's only natural that each country should seek to turn EEC membership to its national advantage.'

'Why? Does West Germany want to run Europe? Or do you think we want to take over Brussels after accession?' asked Brierly. 'Start telling Paris and Bonn what to do? That's dead-end thinking.'

'How do you see a ten-country EEC working for you then?' asked the Assassin, half in fascination, half in faint pity.

'You're looking at it from the wrong angle. An EEC of ten rather than six will be able to promote our national interests better than we currently do on our own. British sovereignty won't be eroded or diluted in any way by joining the EEC.'

'Don't take me for a fool. I work there. That argument is sophistry and you and I both know it. Nor will it survive a real examination, either by the press or by Heath's political opponents.'

'That's what you think, is it? Heath's done a good job so far of squaring many different circles.'

The Assassin cocked his head.

'How does he explain away the explicit inclusion of the idea of ever-closer union in the Treaty of Rome, if you're selling a story that your national sovereignty won't be diluted?'

'He told Parliament before the election last year that there was no detailed blueprint for a federal Europe. He also told them that the members of the Community who favour a federal system are prepared to give up those ambitions to make it easier for Britain to join.'

The Assassin shook his head.

'Those are both lies. There's been any number of blueprints over the years. I've met Altiero Spinelli privately in Brussels. He and I have discussed his wartime manifesto face to face. I'll say it again. One day Heath will be found out. It only takes a journalist to write to the British office of the European Movement to get a copy of Spinelli's work.'

Brierly pursed his lips in anger for a moment.

'In the years to come no one's going to remember all of the things Heath said in the run up to accession. And afterwards we won't let him push for political union faster than we judge British public opinion will accept.'

'How long do you think Heath is going to be in power? And who are "we"? People in Britain? Or are you part of a bigger European network?'

'Like-minded believers in European unity who instinctively know what the EEC should become. But if you're fishing for some kind of secret cabal such as the Freemasons, you'll be disappointed,' he added quickly.

The Assassin was tempted to ask Brierly why he thought even the like-minded English would have a say when it came to setting the pace of unification after accession, but forbore from doing so. Even if they were allowed into the inner circles at the Commission, they'd find it difficult to maintain an independent point of view there for long.

Silence descended inside the car and the miles rolled by.

After Huntingdon they headed east across prairie-like fields. Where it was exposed, the loam was coal-black, blacker than any the Assassin had ever seen before. Further and further they headed off the beaten track, along narrow lanes and through tiny villages dominated by over-sized churches. Even this far from London, the countryside had an air of quiet prosperity. All thanks to the fertile soil he supposed.

Eventually they arrived at a large house built in grey brick, square and squat with Georgian windows and a smear of virulent green lichen across one gable end.

Two cars were already drawn up on the gravel drive. A flame-red Mini Cooper and a black DS just like Kramer's, but with British plates and the steering wheel on the wrong side.

An old man in a tweed jacket and corduroys came out to greet them. His white hair was still thick and his grip surprisingly strong.

'Welcome. Do come in. I'll ask Mrs. King to bring tea.'

The Assassin followed Brierly and the other man into a large downstairs drawing room. It had a fireplace with an ornately-carved wooden surround, thick carpet of some hard-wearing stuff, and old paintings on the walls next to the occasional photograph. Chairs and settees were ranged around the sides of the room, facing the warmth. There was a young woman in the room too, sitting in a window seat as she looked out over the fields. She got lightly to her feet to greet the newcomers, pulling her long golden brown hair round behind her neck as she did so.

'This is Miss Warrington-Williams,' said Devilliers.

'Please, call me Selene,' she said, looking appraisingly at the Assassin.

The Assassin took a good look at her too. He thought she'd judged her appearance well. A dress cut to the new midi length slightly below the knee, in a subdued floral pattern which suited her willowy figure. No visible makeup, not that she needed it, apart from pale lipstick almost the same shade as her natural colour. Understated, but still there. All-in-all, the suggestion that an offer might be made at some point in the future, but not a promise.

'Thomas,' said the Assassin, reciprocating.

'She works for me,' said Devilliers. 'She works for Brierly too.'

The Assassin waited.

'I'm in Number Ten,' she said. 'Oh, it sounds grand but I'm just one of the galley slaves.'

'Miss Warrington-Williams works in administration. She keeps an eye on things for us there. Servants' gossip,' said Brierly.

'Take a seat,' said Devilliers, pointing to a settee with embroidered antimacassars. They all sat. Going by the stack of books on the side table next to Devilliers' chair, he was in his usual place. One where he spent a lot of time.

'So you're Kramer's young man?' he said, turning a beady eye on the Assassin. 'Once upon a time he was a young man too, running around on behalf of other people. Now he has followers of his own, it seems.'

'Brierly said you met Kramer during the war. It's hard to imagine that he was my age once.'

'Yes. He was a busy little bee. We all were, working every waking hour in those dark days after the invasion of France.'

Devilliers gazed into the fireplace and the pile of coals glowing in the grate. For a moment, he seemed to have forgotten that the others were there.

The Assassin looked at Brierly who gave him a discreet nod.

'He helped you make the case to de Gaulle for European federation after the war's end?' asked the Assassin in a slightly louder voice.

Devilliers looked up from his reverie. 'Yes. But I'm not sure how much the General understood of what Kramer and I were proposing. Maybe it would have been better coming solely from a Frenchman. De Gaulle was a disappointment to us in the end.'

The Assassin blinked quickly, wondering again just how helpful Kramer had been all those years ago when he was presenting Devilliers' arguments.

'During the war did Spinelli's name ever come up?' he asked Devilliers, changing tack.

'Who? The Italian federalist?'

'Yes.'

The old man growled. 'Stubborn old fool. He managed to split the Union of European Federalists in the late fifties. All because unification through the EEC was too gradualist for his liking. A purist, not a pragmatist.'

'He's made his peace with Brussels since. He's there now, working as the Commissioner for Industrial Policy.'

'What's your interest in him?'

'He's one of the key figures in the movement. I thought perhaps you might have worked with him at some point since the war.'

'No. We had enough to keep us occupied here, making the arguments to our own politicians.'

The Assassin bit back a comment on what Spinelli had achieved in his own country. Stubborn he might be, but he'd successfully persuaded the leader of the Christian Democrats, Italy's quasi-permanent ruling party, to write support for federation into the country's post-war constitution.

There was another pause in the conversation. The Assassin wondered if he was going to have to provide the entertainment for the whole of the afternoon.

'He wrote a manifesto on European unification when he was sent into internal exile by the Fascists. He looks forward to the final victory over the nation-state.'

Selene turned to look at the Assassin with a faint air of amusement.

'We try not to use that kind of language in Britain, Hofmann,' said Brierly. 'Even when we speak amongst ourselves. No point in loose talk which might inflame the gutter press if it got out.'

'Take a leaf from Heath's book,' said Devilliers. 'The other day he said we're building a common home where we'll sing "merry songs of peace" to one another.'

The Assassin wouldn't have put Heath down for a psychedelic.

'Even dressed up in flowery language, the extinction of national identities is still the plan,' he insisted.

'It was Shakespeare's flowery language, as you call it,' said Devilliers. 'But it's the right plan for Europe. The only way we'll finally bring peace to the Continent.'

'It's the only way we'll bring peace to the world too,' said Brierly, a sudden urgency in his voice. 'Mankind's only hope of salvation from nuclear war is ultimately to have a supreme authority which runs the planet. The United Nations won't cut it. It's nothing more than a warmed-up League of Nations. And I guarantee it will prove equally ineffective if the Cold War ever looks like it's about to turn hot.'

The Assassin looked at him solemnly. 'What are you saying? That supranationalism is the perfect system of government?'

'The EEC points the way. I'm convinced it's the answer to the ills of the world.'

Beneath Brierly's bluff exterior there was a lurking fanatic - verging on an outright blasphemous one at that. Maybe Smythe hadn't been too far off the mark when he'd described Brierly as a 'nutter.'

'By implication then, anyone standing in the way of the EEC is also one of those ills?' he countered.

'People are allowed to have different opinions,' said Brierly loftily.

'Given the magnitude of your claims, your logic would suggest not.'

The Assassin was troubled. The worst authoritarians were often those who sounded the most reasonable on the surface.

Devilliers had been listening to their exchange.

'I carry the scars from the first time this century when we Europeans fell out amongst ourselves,' he said, briefly tapping his chest. 'So does Macmillan. He was two years in hospital after they took him out of his own shell hole.'

The Assassin looked around the room. An officer's sword hung above the door they'd come in by.

'There were twenty-one years between the world wars,' he said. 'It's been twenty-six since the end of the last one. How long do you think this is all going to take? For something that you're saying is existential? Something that's going to save us from nuclear war no less?'

Devilliers glowered now. Selene looked coolly at the Assassin.

The awkwardness was broken by a knock at the door as Devilliers' housekeeper arrived with a tea trolley. She served Devilliers and left the trolley by the fire for the others to help themselves.

'Lunch will be in a quarter of an hour,' said Devilliers. 'Mrs. King is putting out a cold collation.'

The Assassin was intrigued as to what kind of dish it was.

Once she'd left, Brierly picked up again.

'You asked how long building the new Europe was going to take? But you do know that Rome wasn't built in a day?'

'Everyone knows that, even Spinelli,' said the Assassin. 'He's reconciled himself to the idea that federation needs to take place in stages.'

'Which stages?' asked Devilliers.

'For now he's happy enough to be a technocrat without a popular mandate. But he hasn't given up on his belief that the parliament in Strasbourg should one day become the supreme democratic government of all Europe.'

'What's Kramer's view on that?' asked Brierly.

'What's Heath's?' replied the Assassin. 'Do the members of the political parties here really understand where he's taking the country? Does his Conservative Party understand that by seeking EEC membership they're arguing for their own parliament's eventual replacement? What do the British socialists think?'

'"Labour" is what we call them,' said Selene in a voice carefully calculated to avoid condescension.

'Heath makes no secret of the political aspect of the EEC,' said Brierly. 'He's sold it to the right-wing of the Party as the restoration of our rightful place as a leader of the Western world.'

'You just told me in the car on the way here that that's dead-end thinking,'

'But it sounds highly attractive to the Right after two decades of falling behind France and West Germany economically, on top of losing an empire. To the wider public he's sold it merely as some common-sense initiatives in a few areas of mutual concern beyond trade. Such as speaking with one voice to the Soviet bloc.'

'So he supports de Gaulle's grand concept of a European superpower, standing apart from the USA and the USSR? Which logically leads back to the Werner Plan and its timetable for full monetary and economic union by nineteen eighty.'

'I told you when we discussed it at dinner in March, Werner's proposals won't get a mention before accession. The line that Heath and the Foreign Secretary are taking with the press is that any new supranational political institutions will only evolve gradually over a long period of time. And by the way, he never explains the meaning of the term "supranational" either, let alone use it. I should have said earlier, that word is also banned among us.'

'Nine years until monetary union seems a long time, but it's not.'

'He's told people that he'll veto any further progression towards a federal state if he disagrees with it.'

'But that's just more of the sophistry we discussed on the way here,' said the Assassin. 'Because everyone in this room knows that he enthusiastically agrees with both full federation and a common currency. His tricks with words will eventually catch him out.'

'A policy veto is a fact which the anti-marketeers can't deny,' said Brierly.

'But a year into the accession process, does anyone in this room believe there are any circumstances in which Heath would use a veto against ever-closer union? And even if he did, you know that the logic of the Luxembourg Compromise arrangement isn't watertight? It's not guaranteed to deliver a veto as an outcome.'

A gap opened up in the flow of conversation again. The Assassin had assumed the others knew about the hidden workings of the gentleman's agreement which allowed West Germany and France to square the circle of national veto rights in 'sixty-six. But maybe not.

'On the surface the Compromise gives the illusion that individual countries can block policies in particular areas of national concern but underneath, the supranational basis of the EEC treaties remains unchanged. And it's those which are the fallback if the Compromise is ever set to one side,' he said.

'You're worrying unnecessarily,' said Devilliers finally. 'Heath has thought longer about how to sell accession to the public than any politician in Britain today. And we've been gently guiding him from behind the scenes all the way.'

'Heath is our creation,' said Brierly in a cold, controlled voice. 'We've nurtured him for decades, well before he knew it himself. He still doesn't fully realise what other people have been doing for him over the years.'

'For decades, you say? That's a bold claim,' said the Assassin.

'He came to the attention of the right people early on. His very first speech in the House of Commons, back in nineteen fifty, was all about the Schuman Plan. He spent a quarter of an hour praising the West German government's political ambitions for the European Coal and Steel Community.'

Selene took her chance to jump in.

'In a so-called "maiden" speech the convention is that the speaker only talks about their constituency, not policy.'

'A vacancy in the Whips' Office came up a few months later,' said Brierly. 'His political mentor, Lord Swinton, who used to work for Reynolds' outfit, told him to seize the opportunity to become part of the Party machinery. So he did. He stayed there for nine years, a veritable *éminence grise.*'

'And the Party repaid him for his service,' Selene continued. 'Looked after him at elections, brought him fully into Cabinet when his time as a Whip was done.'

'It was certainly lucky for the EEC that a federalist like Heath became leader of your right-wing party to carry on Macmillan's work.'

Brierly winced. 'Heath has always said that soft-right and soft-left have more in common than what divides.'

'That's the premise of the "One Nation" faction within the Conservative party which he claims to have started,' said Selene.

'Why do you say "claims"?' asked the Assassin.

'He claims a lot of things,' she replied. 'Not all of them true.'

Devilliers looked at the Assassin. 'Why do you say it was lucky he became leader? I just as good as told you earlier, we did everything and more to make sure it happened. We maintain our preferred list of potential candidates for years in advance.'

'You both make it sound just like the Freemasons after all,' said Assassin, with half an eye on Brierly. 'They like to dabble in political intrigue in other countries in Europe.'

'Don't indulge yourself with clichés from Pravda,' said Devilliers.

The Assassin's momentary faraway look was replaced by one of slight contempt for the older man. Last year he'd learned better, even if he couldn't tell the others in the room how he'd found out.

'Sometimes the rumours aren't rumours,' he said coldly.

'No freemasons are involved here Hofmann,' said Brierly, equally frostily. 'Just people who've been inspired over the years by Monnet and Salter.'

'People who've put in years and years of the necessary work to do what needed to be done,' said Selene.

'What do you mean?' he asked.

'Well for one thing, back in 'sixty-five at the start of the leadership campaign to replace Alec Douglas-Home, only ten percent of Conservative MPs supported Heath.'

'Who was counting?'

'The Daily Telegraph ran a poll,' replied Brierly on her behalf. 'So we pulled out all the stops. A group of younger men ran his campaign. People like the MP Peter Walker and the journalist Nigel Lawson. His prominent parliamentary supporters from the right of the Party were packed off to the shires, away from Fleet Street and the risk of embarrassment. Every waverer was intensively canvassed. Lawson even made sure that Heath attended church the weekend before the contest to swing the Church of England vote within the parliamentary party.'

The Assassin raised an eyebrow.

'Then after he won the Conservative leadership, we started work to prepare him for the premiership.'

'There wasn't time before the 'sixty-six election, though,' said Selene. 'To make him more human it was decided he should be seen to take up an outdoors hobby. Organ music raised too many of its own questions.'

'I had to touch my wife's brother to help pay for that damn yacht,' said Brierly bitterly. 'And then again for its replacement earlier this year. And I got shanghaied into contributing towards the annual running costs too. More fool me.'

The Assassin glanced around the room. Devilliers was sitting out the lecture for the time being. Selene didn't seem to find the yacht comment odd either.

'The senior figures in the Party even tried to get him to take a wife,' said Brierly.

Selene suppressed a snort at this.

The Assassin's other eyebrow joined the first.

'No one tried very hard. He had a female friend from before the war, but she got tired of waiting to be asked,' explained Brierly.

'He was quite a good-looking man in his day,' said Selene. 'Quite the charmer at Oxford too, or so they say. He's lost weight again since taking up yachting.'

'Anyway, we smoothed out enough of his personal awkwardness to get us the win we needed in the election last year,' said Brierly. 'At least the money I paid out for that bloody boat was worth it in the end.'

There was silence around the room for a few seconds.

'You've gone to a lot of effort over this, haven't you?' said the Assassin. 'You must really want it.'

'We're deadly serious,' said Devilliers, speaking up again. He gave the Assassin a piercing look. 'These are questions of national destiny. And the destiny of an entire continent too. We're not going to let our plans be derailed at the last minute by mean, small-minded men.'

The Assassin crossed his legs and took a sip of the tea.

'Don't you want milk with that?' asked Selene, noticing his cup for the first time.

'It's fine,' he replied.

Devilliers snapped his fingers at the distraction. 'Keynes and Salter drank from this same tea set. You stand on the shoulders of giants.'

'Did you ever meet Monnet?' the Assassin asked the two older men.

'Yes, I did,' replied Brierly. 'When I went out to Washington in 'forty-two. Monnet was there at the same time, working for the British Purchasing Commission. That was just before he went to Algeria to serve in de Gaulle's government.'

'What was he doing in America working for the British?'

'He helped us renegotiate orders for war matériel from US manufacturers which had originally been placed by the French Third Republic.'

'What was he like in person?'

'When you met him, you knew you were in the company of the cleverest man in Europe. In decades to come his name will be placed alongside that of Julius Caesar.'

The Assassin noted that Brierly didn't reference Napoleon. Or anyone else.

'You met Salter too?' he asked him again.

'I didn't,' replied Brierly. 'Devilliers did.'

Devilliers nodded gravely.

'So between the wars, while Monnet was off making money in China, Salter drew up the blueprint for the EEC? But you didn't even try to join the European Coal and Steel Community?' asked the Assassin.

'It's not that surprising,' said Devilliers. 'In nineteen fifty-two when the ECSC formally came into being we'd only just nationalised the coal and steel industry. To place decisions like cutting or expanding production capacity into the hands of the bureaucrats in Brussels and Luxembourg was the wrong time, politically. Unfortunately for us.'

'"The Durham miners won't wear it," is what Herbert Morrison apparently told the press,' said Selene. 'He was speaking about the miners' trade union,' she added, sensing another question from the Assassin.

'And what do the trade unions think about the EEC today? Do they realise what freedom of movement might mean for them over the long term?' he asked.

'We've got an article about it coming out in The Times next week,' said Brierly. 'It's not going to trouble them particularly, not least because West Germany is a more attractive destination for Italian workers right now.'

'And I'm sure the unions can co-opt any new foreign workers who might arrive here into their movement,' said Devilliers.

'The power of the British trade unions has only grown since the war,' said Brierly. 'And they're becoming ever more militant. Heath gave the impression before the last election that he was going to tackle the worst of their excesses. At least, that's what some members of the Party took away from the pre-election policy conference.'

'But only a month after he took power, he had to ask the Queen to declare a state of emergency because of the national dock strike,' added Selene. 'On top of running the accession negotiations he's expended significant political capital on passing the Industrial Relations Bill which is meant to ban informal strikes. It had its Third Reading this March.'

'There's significant ongoing opposition to the Bill from the left,' said Brierly. 'It's our one area of concern for the government's future. He risks triggering a real trial of strength with the unions at some point. The rumblings of the volcano are there to be heard.'

'It's not just the dockers either,' said Selene. 'The first-ever national postal strike took place earlier this year.'

Brierly got up to replace his cup on the trolley. 'It only finished a couple of weeks before you first arrived.'

'If you'd tried to send any postcards home, they would have got caught up in the seven-week backlog,' said Selene in a neutral voice.

The Assassin stared at her. People didn't get personal information from him that easily.

'Is there a strand of thought within the Conservative Party that wants to take on the trade unions?' he asked. 'To deliberately start a fight to the death?'

'This is Britain. We don't operate that way. At least, not so directly,' said Brierly.

'So is there a happy combination of interests across different parts of the Establishment then? To remake Britain's place in the world by joining the EEC and at the same time use freedom of movement to threaten the workers by importing strike breakers?'

Selene replied. 'Heath isn't an enemy of the unions. Or at least, not of the union leaders. He needs them to take control of the rank-and-file members and stop the unofficial strikes. He gets on well with Feather at a personal level.'

'Who's Feather?'

Selene looked at Brierly who motioned to her to carry on.

'Leader of the Trades Union Congress - the overarching body for the trade unions in Britain. One evening before the election, Heath had him over for dinner at his private rooms in the Albany. He played Feather the "Red Flag" on his Charlemagne Prize piano afterwards.'

'But what if Heath's relations with the trade union leaders go sour, there's industrial unrest and they bring down the government ahead of accession? And before you say it's not possible, look at Italy where they've had constant violent protests since 'sixty-nine and the cabinet changes every six months when the coalition parties fall out.'

'We keep on telling you,' said Devilliers. 'We've been working on this for decades. We're not going to let anything or anyone derail us, not even Heath himself. He'll have to fight his battles with the unions later. Accession comes first.'

He clapped his hands. 'I believe Mrs. King is ready for us now.'

Devilliers led them through to a dining room where plates and a selection of cold meats and pies had been set out. 'Collation' seemed to be no more than a collection of dishes, as the Assassin now realised. Selene scarcely gave them a glance, going straight to the sticks of celery and dip.

Once they'd all filled their plates to their satisfaction, Devilliers started quizzing the Assassin in earnest. The conversation before lunch must only have been the warm-up. 'How long have you worked with Kramer?' he asked.

'Just over a year.' To get a cover story about five years in the Foreign Legion to fit with the age on the Assassin's passport, he and Kramer had needed to adjust some of the real-life dates.

'So you've known him for hardly twelve months? What have you done during that time to gain his trust?'

'He found me in Internal Affairs. He needed some people checking out, some missing material chasing down. I did what he asked, and then some more. Since the autumn of last year we've been watching people within the delegations of the applicant countries, making sure they're not subject to any hostile interference from outside the Six.'

'Yes, but have you been in any pressured situations?' asked Devilliers. 'Beyond merely watching people, what special tasks have you undertaken to earn this level of trust?'

The Assassin shrugged.

'Brierly must have told you something about what he and Kramer did in the war,' Devilliers continued. 'They weren't running Thomas Cook tours to France, they were playing with men and women's lives.'

Just then Brierly glanced at a photograph above the dresser. A group of men in flying suits, posing by the nose of a four-engined aircraft with black undersides.

The Assassin hesitated. 'I was in the Foreign Legion for five years. He knows I'll do whatever it takes to get this job done. I've been across Europe for him and I haven't let him down yet.'

'How do we know you're committed enough to see this thing through to the end?'

'What exactly do you imagine I've been sent here to do?' asked the Assassin in confusion.

Devilliers didn't answer.

'Has Kramer offered you any kind of personal incentive?' asked Brierly.

The Assassin sensed it was time to give them something. 'If I do this job for him and do it well, Kramer's promised me a promotion to run a secret department which investigates external threats to the EEC. A kind of counter-intelligence unit if you like. Very private, with a big expense budget and a small, select number of staff. It's only been recently set up. I'll be its second-ever boss.'

'So the start of your own growing empire, then?' asked Devilliers. 'That's some plum which Kramer's dangling in front of you.'

'Jobs for my friends,' the Assassin replied with an involuntary glance at Selene.

Devilliers stood up to carve more slices of beef, seemingly satisfied for the time being.

'Try this. It comes from the farm of an old acquaintance in Herefordshire.'

The Assassin decided there had been enough personal questions for the time being. 'In your opinion, Herr Devilliers, what do the voters really think about joining the EEC?'

Devilliers transferred a slice to his plate and pushed the carving board in the Assassin's direction.

'We don't plan on asking them. Or letting them have a say. For all of the sensitivities about the political nature of the EEC that we touched on before lunch. That's why we need to get the negotiations wrapped up quickly and rammed through Parliament without excessive scrutiny.'

The Assassin shook his head dubiously at this.

'The polling shows that most voters are against joining the EEC for the time being,' said Brierly. 'Before the election last year, Gallup reported sixty percent. It's hardly changed since then. In fact, there's a poll coming out in tomorrow's Sunday Times which says that sixty-five percent are opposed. On the other hand, Fleet Street is unanimous in its support for the Common Market.'

'Seems like ratification could still be challenging if the MPs listen to their voters.'

'Perhaps. But with the press behind us, we'll simply get them to paint any public figure who opposes joining as being a backwards-looking reactionary. We'll drown out dissent with a clamour of received wisdom that Europe is a good thing.'

'Most Conservative MPs are performing seals,' said Selene. 'They'll clap for whoever tosses them a fish. "Inside Common Market good, outside Common Market bad."'

'Heath isn't one for taking much notice of the polls anyway,' added Devilliers. 'The pollsters got their prediction for the election last year very wrong.'

'They had Heath ten points behind. But then he won a thirty-seat majority,' said Selene. 'In the end, people were ready for a change after five and a half years of Wilson. Heath was the modern, technocratic candidate.'

'And that's despite Heath only being four months younger than Wilson,' said Brierly smugly.

Selene continued. 'He had a sophisticated TV campaign too, which may have caught Labour and the polling firms by surprise. It was also the first time that eighteen-year-olds could vote.'

From her knowledge of the details, she sounded to the Assassin like she was more than a mere galley slave.

'But we do have some opposition within the Conservative Party,' said Brierly. 'Even though opening accession negotiations was part of the election manifesto which the MPs stood on. That's where Selene's young man comes in. He's in the Whips' Office, just as Heath used to be.'

'You've used that term a couple of times now. You're going to have to explain it to me,' said the Assassin.

'It's the office which organises the Parliamentary votes,' she said. 'Makes sure the government's MPs vote for the bills - the laws that it proposes.'

'Okay.'

'Heath was one. A deputy Whip and then the boss, the Chief Whip. He knew all the MPs' little secrets, the real reasons why they claimed they'd missed a late-night vote.'

'Okay. A late-night vote,' the Assassin repeated uncertainly.

'Because they were with their mistresses instead of sitting in Parliament,' explained Selene. 'They'd get a phone call threatening that their wives would be told if they didn't put their trousers back on and get back to the House to vote.'

'Okay.' The Assassin said more confidently, having finally caught the gist of what she was saying.

'He loved all the secrecy as a Whip,' she continued. 'He even started a card index on the MPs in which he recorded their psychological strengths and weaknesses. He was promoted to Chief Whip after only six years as an MP and he revelled in the power it gave him.'

'It sounds almost like Heath was running his own secret police force,' he said.

'There's a Westminster story about a black book where the Whips record the sexual misdemeanours of MPs. But it's not just a story, I've seen it,' she said.

'Where do they get those kinds of personal details from?'

'Other MPs who come to them with reports of their rivals' peccadilloes.'

'I can believe it,' said the Assassin. 'I can believe it only too well.'

He looked at Brierly shrewdly for an instant. No wonder he had Selene working for him in Number Ten. But there was something else from earlier that was still niggling at him.

'Setting aside the expense, how does Heath find the time to go yachting?' he asked the room.

'You'd need to ask him. It was his choice to take up sailing, about five or six years ago,' said Brierly. 'We encouraged him in it and covered his expenses. It even helped him lose weight for the TV cameras, as Selene said earlier. Of course, given his personality, he's now become somewhat monomaniacal about it all.'

'He's taken up ocean racing. Got himself a professional crew too,' said Selene.

'Any success?'

'He won a race in Australia back at the end of 'sixty-nine. Sydney to Hobart, competing in a field of eighty or so. His yacht back then, the first *Morning Cloud,* was the smallest one taking part. He's planning to enter the America's Cup later this year,' she added, becoming more animated as she told her story.

'How much has all that cost his backers so far? He had his boat transported all the way from England to Australia, you say?'

'I'm sure everything was accounted for properly,' sniffed Devilliers.

'Even the overseas donations?' asked the Assassin. 'Am I here to protect the French government's financial investment?'

'It was all from private individuals,' said Brierly. 'I know that only too well. Heath never pays for any of his professional expenses if he can help it. And that's despite his backers making him a Name at Lloyds.'

The Assassin let the last statement go without requiring an explanation. 'If your brother-in-law could afford a contribution, couldn't your wife have funded yours?' he asked instead.

Devilliers frowned. 'That's rather an impertinent question, Hofmann. I don't know how things are done in France or in Germany. Here we don't talk about money.'

They finished their meal, then returned to the drawing room for coffee.

'So Hofmann,' asked Devilliers. 'What do you think of the plan which Brierly and Kramer have cooked up? Your honest opinion please.'

'I think we're playing a dangerous game. Creating a fictional Eastern bloc agent could set all sorts of alarm bells ringing that you didn't intend to. Even if your partners in MI5 and the police have led you to believe they've got everything under control.'

'Dangerous in what way?'

'Everyone in Europe knows your security services are riddled with traitors. What if the other side hears about our play and claims that MI5 are conducting a smear against your own citizens?'

'The intelligence services have put the leaks to a stop and found all three of the Cambridge spies,' replied Brierly. 'But precisely because people are still nervous about Establishment treachery is why the smear will work so well.'

'We're the experts here,' added Devilliers.

'What do you think, Selene?' asked the Assassin.

She looked at him for a second before answering. 'A KGB connection sounds bad enough. An East German communist link would be even more ruinous for their reputations.'

'What if the other side comes after me to teach MI5 a lesson not to use agent provocateurs? They're extremely security conscious. Extremely protective of their people overseas.'

Brierly looked at him with contempt. 'I thought Legionnaires had a backbone. Anyway, we already discussed this in March. As far as we know, there are no Stasi agents operating in Britain.'

'I understand your wariness, Hofmann. But that's the plan which Kramer, Brierly, and I settled on at the start of this year,' said Devilliers.

So he was still an active player after all, thought the Assassin. Or at the very least, an occasional one.

'Having said all that, you make a point,' said Brierly. 'After this first week, I'd always intended that any contact you had with us would be minimal. Our policeman friend will brief you on the day-to-day work. But Selene will be your liaison in London if you need to get in touch with me.'

'We're to meet up every couple of weeks,' she explained. 'So I can report back.'

'Why don't you take a turn in the garden with Miss Warrington-Williams,' suggested Devilliers. 'So you can discuss your arrangements with her in private.'

Yes, said the Assassin to himself. And so that you and Brierly can discuss me in private too.

Going by her preparations for a visit to the garden, today wasn't Selene's first time at Devilliers' place. Returning to the hall, she took a long black woollen coat from the peg and wrapped it tightly around herself before leading him outside through the kitchen at the rear.

The front of the property where Brierly and the Assassin had parked was sheltered by trees, but the back was swept by an icy wind. A bedraggled rhododendron bush with spotted leaves sat forlornly in the middle of the lawn.

She marched down the length of the grounds and into a small walled garden at the bottom. 'That's better,' she said, sitting down out of the blast on a warped bench.

The Assassin hovered, unwilling to sit beside her and unsure that the slats would take their combined weight anyway. Instead, he stamped his feet a couple of times to keep the blood flowing.

'They say that the wind in the Fens comes straight down from the Arctic through the gap between Scotland and Norway,' she informed him.

'It feels that way.'

'How long has Brierly said you're going to be here?' she asked, looking up at him.

'He hasn't given me a definite end date. But I'm out of here in June. I have other business I need to attend to.'

'I don't think you get a choice in the matter. There's nothing more important to Brierly and Devilliers than this, nor will there ever be. And for your Monsieur Kramer too, from what I understand.'

'Think about it. I can't spend months running around London dropping hints as to how misunderstood East Germany is. This thing has to be done quickly and quietly, if at all.'

'Do you speak from experience?'

'It's just common sense. Amateurs like to waste time. They imagine they're playing some kind of intellectual chess game against the other side. Real professionals are straight in and out and don't make a fuss about it.'

'Does your girlfriend agree with that approach?'

The Assassin looked at her stony-faced for a fraction of a second.

'Do you have a cigarette?' she asked. 'I'm still freezing.'

He dug into his pocket for the pack he carried in case he had nicotine cravings and shook one out for her. She took it and put it between her lips, still unlit. He offered her his lighter, clicking it twice to get it going. She leant towards him, bending down to cup the flame, almost touching his hands with hers as she did so, even though the air was virtually still in the shelter of the walls.

He watched as she leant back, took the glowing cigarette out of her mouth, then tucked her coat and dress more tightly under her knees with her free hand.

'You want to sit?' she asked.

'No. I'm fine.' There was a moment's pause. 'Is your boyfriend in the Whips' Office part of this?'

She gave him a speculative look. 'Why do you ask?'

'These three people that we're smearing - are any of them close to Conservative MPs? MPs who might need a warning to support Heath in the accession vote?'

She took a drag before answering.

'They're always connected to each other in some way. Through school, university, Army regiment, the Party. Frederick might know. But he's not my boyfriend. Just someone I sleep with from time to time.'

'Do your friends inside know that? They seem to think you have the ear of one of Heath's private enforcers.'

'They know what they need to know.' She smoothed the coat over her knees again.

'So how much real opposition is there within the Conservative Party to accession?'

'Fred's boss says the split is four-fifths in favour of joining. But that still leaves over sixty potential rebels and the Party's majority is only thirty. They're talking about a "fierce campaign of conversion" for the doubters.'

'How's that going to work?'

'I'll tell you some other time,' she said. 'But they can ponder the fate of the former chairman of the Conservative Party, whom Heath had kicked out about three or four years ago for being opposed to the Common Market.'

The Assassin looked away from her and gazed past the wrought-iron gate at the back of the walled garden. Beyond Devilliers' property was a large field of bright green winter wheat.

Suddenly he straightened up, walked over to the gate, and peered between the bars.

'What was through that way?' he asked, turning back to look at Selene.

She got up off the bench and came over to stand close by his side.

'What do you mean?'

'Those buildings over there.' He pointed to a row of huts in the middle distance with semi-circular roofs, standing next to a rusting iron tank perched on top of a brick tower.

'What are they?' he asked. 'Part of an abandoned barracks?'

'It's the old airfield. Look.' She pointed to the far side of the expanse of open ground.

Now the Assassin could just see a control tower, gap-toothed where windows once had been. Nearer still, the line of a concrete runway gradually resolved itself behind the long feathery tufts of the young wheat plants, running for several hundred metres across his field of vision.

He gripped the bars of the gate, looking for a second or two longer before he turned back to Selene.

'What arrangements shall we make for our meetings in London?' he asked. 'I've no idea when I'll next have news for you. It all depends on how fast Brierly's police contact is able to arrange an event where I can meet the Marks.'

'You mean Smythe?'

'I didn't know if you knew his name.'

'He gives me the creeps,' she said.

'I think I know what you mean.'

'Let's meet next Saturday, whether you've got news or not. My flat's in Chelsea. Here, I'll write the address for you. We can go for lunch nearby.'

It was the day of the Cup Final but the Assassin decided not to mention it.

She took a slim black notebook from her coat. 'You have a pen?'

He handed her his Pelikan. She knelt down before him on one knee to scribble the address, then ripped out the page and got back up to hand it over. He folded the paper and tucked it into his wallet.

'What you said back there about the other side finding out. How would that happen, practically speaking?' she asked.

'Because we don't know who they might already be blackmailing. How about the trade union official who's been to the East? What happens when Smythe tells him he's been seen with a spy from a Soviet satellite? If any of the Marks happen to be working for the KGB and go complaining about us to their controllers then we'll all be exposed.'

'So why are you going along with this then?'

'I'm not the one dealing with any fallout. Not personally anyway. I really am in and out of here in the next six weeks, if that's how long it takes.'

'I suppose you have a point.'

'We should go back inside.'

'Have you made your arrangements, Hofmann?' asked Devilliers, looking up when they re-entered the room.

'Yes.'

'Any last questions before you head back to London?'

'I have a couple more, if you have time.'

The Assassin went to stand by the fireplace, facing the others. Selene sat on the couch opposite Devilliers. Brierly gave her a shrewd look.

'I understand that a group of people, thoughtful people like Macmillan who have a personal connection to Monnet, have been inspired over time by a vision of a United States of Europe. Sometimes they've nurtured their ambition for decades. But how did eighty percent of the ruling party in Britain, a country which has stood apart from the rest of the world for so long, suddenly come to believe in Monnet and Salter's dream too?'

Brierly opened his mouth to speak but the Assassin carried on.

'Let me finish. Germany and Italy only came into existence a hundred years ago. We both unified from many constituent parts. Under Napoleon, France built an empire from Spain in the west to Poland in the east. The notion of becoming part of a larger entity isn't completely alien to us. But no one's invaded England for almost a thousand years. Why give up your independence now?'

Brierly looked at Devilliers and then at Selene. 'I told you already. Nobody wants another European war.'

'Again. For us, unifying into a larger European nation isn't a new idea. But there's no chance that Germany will go to war with France again. None. Not after what happened last time. Not after what Germany did to the Jews.'

An uncomfortable silence opened up.

'And in any case, there is no such thing as a single "Germany" anymore. 'Even if for some unknown reason, Bonn decided one day it wanted to fight the rest of Europe, the Soviets and the Americans would have something to say about it first. Why is Britain buying this Grimms' fairy tale?'

'Did Kramer ask you to quiz us?' said Devilliers. 'Is he having second thoughts about helping me?'

'No. Not at all. He wants to see Britain's accession as much as you do.'

But not for the reasons you think, thought the Assassin to himself.

'What are you implying, then?' asked Brierly sharply. 'You've come all this way to say that you're having personal doubts and want to back out?'

'I've told you my own selfish career reasons for being in England. I simply want to leave here today with some sense that all this effort we're putting in for Heath will be worth it. That his pro-EEC power base in the wider Conservative Party isn't much weaker than you've led Kramer to believe. What if a big enough section of the party, or even the wider establishment, wakes up to the true meaning of federation and changes its mind over the EEC? What if Heath gets deposed in a palace coup?'

'Miss Warrington-Williams can give you the inside story direct from Number Ten,' said Brierly drily. 'The Conservatives are the oldest political party in Europe: Chartism, Socialism, Marxism - they've seen them all off. Fighting for survival and suppressing internal dissent is ingrained in the party's psyche. Resistance within the Party to the Common Market has been progressively ground down over the past ten years. Any new opposition, if it ever comes to much, will melt faster than a snowflake in the Sahara.'

Selene wasn't worried either. 'The Conservatives won't change their minds over Europe,' she said. 'The figure of eighty percent that I gave you in the garden tells you all you need to know. The consensus in the Party is strongly in favour of joining.'

'Regardless of that,' said Brierly. 'The MPs look to Fleet Street as a guide to the Establishment's thinking, and ultimately of public opinion too. People will come round to accepting accession if only from fear of looking foolish if they don't. If Heath does lose the next election, it won't be over this.'

The Assassin was unconvinced but nodded along anyway.

'It's the way things work in England,' said Devilliers. 'As long as Heath is in charge, the Party will police itself and crush any rebels. Loyalty to the leader is prized above all else and treachery is remembered for decades to come.'

'The Conservative Party's entire raison d'être is for the Conservative Party to be in power,' said Selene. 'They're utterly single-minded in that respect.'

'It sounds more like the Communist Party of the Soviet Union,' said the Assassin, but not in a joking way. 'Speaking of the Cold War, here's my very last question. What does America think of Heath and of the UK's accession to the EEC?'

'Think? In nineteen sixty-one they gave approval for it,' said Devilliers. 'Macmillan told Kennedy he was applying three days before he told Parliament.'

'Monnet went to work early on the Americans. Back in 'forty-five, when he was in Washington advising on the Marshall Plan he made friends with an up and coming lawyer called George Ball, politically connected to the Democrats,' said Brierly.

'I didn't know Monnet worked on the Marshall Plan,' said the Assassin.

'Monnet appointed Ball as his American lawyer when he ran the European Coal and Steel Community in the early fifties. Ball stayed close to the Democrat party machine, and in 'sixty-one he was appointed by JFK as his deputy Secretary of State - that's their foreign minister - with special responsibility for European affairs.' Brierly was on a roll now.

'Ball became one of Kennedy's most trusted advisers as well as being Monnet's inside man in Washington. So when Macmillan went to Kennedy to get his support for joining the EEC, Monnet and Ball had already prepared the ground. Macmillan's cousin's blessing was a foregone conclusion.'

'Cousin?' asked the Assassin, perplexed.

'In a way. Macmillan's nephew is married to Kennedy's sister.'

The Assassin had to admit defeat. 'Cutting all the strings that Monnet's been pulling over the years will take more than sixty dissident Conservative MPs,' he said finally.

For the journey back to London, Brierly gave the Assassin the choice of going all the way with Selene or travelling with him as far as Cambridge, then taking a train to King's Cross. After a slight hesitation he accepted Brierly's offer.

'I'd have thought you'd rather have gone with the girl,' said Brierly with the faintest of smirks.

'It's my last chance to speak with you, if you really meant what you said back there about us not meeting again.'

'What more do you want to know? We've just spent all afternoon talking.'

'Tell me something more about Kramer's activities during the war. You said I didn't really know him.'

'There's not much left to say. Or at least, not anything that I can tell you under the Official Secrets Act.'

'What was he like back then - as a person? Nationalistic? Full of hate for the Germans? Full of hate for Pétain? Or was he a foreign playboy diplomat in London who used his interesting-sounding job to chat up girls and get them into bed?'

'You've really no conception of what life was like in wartime London, do you? Anything went back then. People lived for the moment. There was a blind eye to homosexuality for one thing. All those public schoolboy officers placed in charge of impressionable men? The Grenadier Guards doing what they're known for best?'

The Assassin changed tack. 'How did you get back in contact with Kramer after all this time?'

Brierly gave an impatient sigh. 'We've been in touch with the main movers in Brussels since the very start of the Coal and Steel Community in 'fifty-two. There's no one at the Commission that we won't speak to. Not if they can help us shift public opinion in the UK - either directly or indirectly. Kramer's hardly an unknown figure there.'

'So you've been watching him for some time?'

'We watch lots of people. But this is really none of your business. It feels like you're spying on your own boss.'

'Did Heath ever stop watching people after he finished in the Whips' Office? It must have been hard to have been responsible for compiling the black book of secrets and then to suddenly be cut off from your prime source of intelligence. Especially if you were trying to climb the greasy pole and you were only supported by one in ten of the MPs going into the party leadership election.'

'Nothing gets past you, does it? Kramer chose his Sorcerer's Apprentice for a reason.'

'It's not just an institute or some kind of think tank you work for, is it? There's no way you're going to allow Britain's destiny in Europe to depend solely on a few conferences, discussion papers, and the odd guest article in a newspaper.'

'What do you think I do?'

The Assassin shrugged.

'I'm not going to insult you by spelling it out. And I'm not going to embarrass myself by asking if your institute is a cover for a secret committee somewhere within the Conservative Party.'

'Selene told you enough back there about the nature of the Party to work it out for yourself.'

The Assassin grunted. 'And what's Miss Warrington-Williams' real role in all of this?'

Brierly turned and looked down his nose at the Assassin. 'There's pretty much no boundary we won't cross to drive EEC accession over the finish line.'

'Just make sure you don't ask the same of me.'

Half an hour later, the Assassin's train pulled into the single long through platform at Cambridge. He boarded and pushed his way to the front to find a seat for a quick getaway at King's Cross.

His mission still hadn't properly started yet. He supposed that following this afternoon's interviews, if Devilliers and Brierly were to have second thoughts, there was always the chance of them sending him back to Kramer.

He was having second thoughts too. Ignoring the planned theatre around the accession talks, getting an agreement between the governments on the treaty was the straightforward part. But no matter how strong the consensus in the Conservative Party was in favour of EEC membership, questions were bound to be raised about the details of what they were signing up to. Things like monetary union weren't going to be as easily explained away as Brierly imagined. If twenty percent of MPs were already unsure about a 'Common Market', how many more would be dubious about an explicit 'United States of Europe'?

Perhaps his mission was more important than he'd realised. For despite all of Heath's personal faults, maybe only he had the strength of conviction to carry the party, the self-belief to sustain the fantasy of a British Prime Minister leading the way in a new Europe.

And late in the day as it might be, what did he himself think of enlargement? The EEC was what it was, and Brussels insiders didn't pretend otherwise. But the employment of multiple layers of equivocation, half-truths and outright lies by Heath to promote it didn't sit easily with him - even though he was guilty of doing the same things in his everyday job.

But when all was said and done, if European union was the future which British politicians wanted, who was he to stop them?

Chapter Seven

On Tuesday morning, the Assassin was back in Jimmy Malta's upstairs office with the zebra print walls. This time he was with Smythe in tow, the nightclub owner and the policeman making a pair in their dark suits, white shirts, and narrow ties as they blended in with the décor.

Jimmy stood by the ebony sideboard to pour drinks while the others waited at the low table for him to bring them over.

'So you two know each other already?' asked Smythe. 'You met each other when Thomas was last in London?'

'I made a courtesy call on Kramer's behalf,' replied the Assassin. 'For old times' sake. He and Jimmy knew each other in London during the war.'

'Did Jimmy tell you how he knows me?'

The Assassin looked at the Corsican who gave him a nod. 'You asked him to put on a party here last year.'

'We put it on together,' said Smythe. 'Jimmy has a side line in supplying music, entertainers, and stimulants for private events.'

'What was your contribution, then?' asked the Assassin.

'I supplied the guests.'

Jimmy crossed the room carrying a tray with three scotches. 'My girls can provide whatever theme the organiser wants, as long as our fixed costs get paid upfront.'

'Did you make much money from the party last year?' asked the Assassin.

'Tut, tut, Thomas. You know better than to ask that question to gentlemen of honour,' said Smythe.

Jimmy sat down and waved his hand around the four points of the compass. 'When you walk through Soho, what do you see most of?'

'Bookshops and cinemas.'

'There's your answer then. Compared to the Syndicate's activities, our occasional parties hardly register. Just as we promised them.'

'People say that capital is attracted to the investments with the highest return,' said Smythe. 'If it's popular, it's profitable.'

The Assassin wouldn't have put him down for a speculator. Perhaps Smythe had paid for his house and its swanky contents by playing the stock market, although somehow the Assassin doubted it.

'I thought that competition drove down prices?' he replied. 'And porn doesn't seem like it's something that's difficult to get into?'

'It's a question of distribution more than production,' said Smythe. 'The Soho bookshops sell a mixture of legal and illegal material. The payoffs to the Obscene Publications Squad happen for a reason.'

'Presumably to warn the Syndicate of raids so they can hide the hard stuff?' said the Assassin.

'You're sure you've never dealt with the police before?'

'What do you think happens after the raids?' asked Jimmy.

'The police sell on any material that does get confiscated? Back to the people they originally tipped off, as a kind of additional contribution to their protection racket?' The Assassin looked at them both over the rim of his glass.

'You'd be right at home in West End Central,' said Smythe. 'How did you guess?'

'I grew up in Hamburg,' said the Assassin quickly. 'Everyone knows what goes on in port cities.'

'One of Obscene Publications' favoured purveyors of smut is a crook called Mason, who has unrestricted access to the wire-mesh evidence vaults at Holborn nick. Drives up there to pick through the best, or if you like the worst, of the material taken from people who forgot to pay off the Dirty Squad, as they're also known by. Talk about "Cash and Carry"....'

'Evidence equals paperwork,' said the Assassin. 'All policemen hate paperwork.'

Smythe frowned at the Assassin again.

'Smythe,' said Jimmy, shifting gear. 'What kind of party are we laying on for the end of next week?'

'Nothing too kinky. No performers who look younger than sixteen. Nothing crazy on the drugs scene either. Weed and cocaine but no needles. Việt Grove but without the sordidness.'

'For how many?'

'About thirty guests and entertainers. I'll take the same room as last time, with the peepholes along one wall. We need to set it up so that there's clear angles for the cameras.' Smythe winked at the Assassin. 'We're making top-quality Kraut smudges and rollers. Under the counter stuff.'

'Stills and movies,' said Jimmy.

'Can't you just leave the ciné-camera running and record the whole room at once?' asked the Assassin.

'The lighting won't be good enough. I need to be there to make sure we don't waste our chance.'

'How about a staged shot?'

'How do you mean?' asked Smythe.

'A private room where our man and I go with a couple of girls.'

'Getting into the mood, are we Hofmann? Looking forward to free drugs and nookie away from your girlfriend? Or boyfriend? Everyone knows the reputation of Germans. All those black leather uniforms and discipline.'

The Assassin gave him an inoffensive smile. 'And yet ironically in Germany, we call it the "British disease."'

'The room I have in mind has alcoves with hangings,' said Jimmy. 'There's enough privacy for people to get relaxed if they want to. But I'm not hosting a full-blown orgy. I don't need my club getting that kind of reputation.'

'Good enough for you Hofmann?' asked Smythe. 'I heard that you like to screw in private.'

'I'll do what needs to be done.'

'Good lad. I'm sure you will.'

'You take drugs?' Jimmy asked the Assassin.

'I've never done anything stronger than weed.'

'You have lived a sheltered life, Thomas, haven't you?' said Smythe.

'Parts of it, yes.'

'If you need to keep a clear head on the night, I can tell you where to go for herbal cigarettes,' said Jimmy. 'And if you think you'll have to snort something, bring milk powder.'

'Just play your part in front of our man,' said Smythe. 'You've got virtually nothing to do, it's all been set up for you. If I'd had my way when this was being planned last year, I'd have had them accidentally bashed too hard on the head, no questions asked.'

'Who said "no"?' asked Jimmy curiously. 'And by the way, that was never happening anywhere near my club. Not unless someone wanted to be taken by one of my boys on a trip out into Epping Forest with a spade.'

'Kramer refused to consider it,' said Smythe. Then he added slyly. 'Thomas too, I believe.'

The Assassin frowned at Smythe. 'We're not meant to be discussing those details. Either here or anywhere else.'

Smythe frowned back at him. 'Okay. Enough chit chat. What more do you need from us now, Jimmy?'

'Nothing. Kramer said the French embassy would take care of the costs. I just need you to point out whoever your target is on the night. One of the girls will make sure he doesn't leave before Thomas gets to him.'

'Any chance of getting the second target to come to the same party?' asked the Assassin. 'Just to speed things up?'

'No. I want to keep the two approaches separate. The less coincidences the better. It's a suspicious, secretive world that they live in.'

'Like Kramer and Jimmy's world during the war,' said the Assassin.

'Don't be shallow,' said Smythe. 'People got tortured and killed by Nazis in that one.'

Jimmy nodded silently, lost in his thoughts.

-

That lunchtime, the Assassin and Reynolds had agreed to meet at a pub on Knightsbridge opposite Harrods, but Reynolds was late. Almost bursting through the door, he hurried over to the table where the Assassin was waiting.

'Sorry. We had a flap on at the office. You're lucky I was able to get away. Masterson covered for me.'

'It happens,' said the Assassin evenly. 'You still have time to eat?'

'I'm cooking an omelette this evening, if you want to join me. When's your meeting at Belgrave Square?'

'In thirty minutes. We've got time for a couple of pints.'

Reynolds drank more slowly than the Assassin, but got tipsy faster.

'I'm not used to beer in the middle of the day,' he admitted after a pint and a half, replacing his glass on the table.

'How does it feel to know you're going to denounce me as soon as you get back to your office?'

'Don't sound so melodramatic,' replied Reynolds. 'No one's dragging you off to the basement of the Lubyanka.'

'By the way, where do your people watch the Foreign Trade Office from on the square?'

Reynolds frowned. 'I never said that we did. I was instructed to follow you down there and note the time that you go in.'

'So any surveillance is intermittent? Or is that what you want people to think?'

'If I report you going there, and if we do have someone else in the area, the time has to match with whatever they might record.'

'I think the flower kiosk on the corner is the most likely place,' ventured the Assassin.

Reynolds shrugged. 'What story are you using with your contact?' he asked.

'He's got a name.'

'Who is he then?'

'He's called Uhlmann. He sounds like a Saxon from his accent. Dresden at a guess.'

'Dresden,' said Reynolds reflectively.

'It's on the Elbe. Just like Hamburg. Connected in other ways too.'

The Assassin looked closely at his flatmate. The Englishman glanced away and the Assassin took some small comfort from his embarrassment.

They parted ways at the corner of Knightsbridge and Wilton Place. Reynolds walked on for a few yards, then doubled back to see the Assassin passing the construction site for the new Berkeley Hotel, being built where the Krays' infamous Esmeralda's Barn gambling club had once stood.

He carried on following the Assassin at a distance, watching him stride down the road towards Belgrave Square and then on into Number Thirty-Four. Once his flatmate had disappeared from view, Reynolds took a discreet look at the nondescript flower kiosk across the street, but he didn't recognise anyone inside.

That evening, the Assassin got back to the flat almost two hours after Reynolds. For some reason, the Englishman wasn't in the best of moods.

'Where have you been all day?' he asked the Assassin. 'I thought we were going to eat together?'

'Sorry. I misunderstood. After my meeting I walked up to Highgate.'

'You walked there from Belgrave Square? That must have taken hours.'

'It's the best way to get to know the city. I didn't have anything else to do for the rest of the day.'

'You could have at least taken the bus. What was Highgate's attraction? Karl Marx's tomb?' Reynolds was quicker on the draw than the Assassin had given him credit for.

'Of course. The Communist Party of Great Britain commissioned it but Berlin paid the bill. For East German citizens it's a kind of place of pilgrimage.'

'You could have been back here helping write up my contact report.'

'It's a significant monument for West Germany too, you know. That evil bastard destroyed my country.'

Reynolds was taken aback by the Assassin's vehemence. 'He wrote a book. He didn't start either of your world wars.'

'Without a hostile Communist regime in Russia exporting revolution, Hitler would never have been able to use the threat of the Red menace to get into power. And if any genuine Germans need another reason to hate him, Marx's Soviet heirs smashed Germany into pieces and stole our territories in the East.'

'There's only two parts, East and West Germany.'

'There's thousands of square kilometres of our country, hundreds of kilometres to the east of Berlin that the Poles and the Russians both took parts of.'

'Steady there.'

'You think I'm not serious? Don't talk to me in that sneering tone. You're lucky I didn't take a hammer to the statue. I assume the bust is three metres off the ground for good reason.'

'You wouldn't have been the first to have had a go,' said Reynolds, attempting to humour his flatmate. 'Some neo-fascists set off a bomb under it last year.'

He paused. 'If you've been away with the Foreign Legion for the past five years, how come you know about Berlin paying for the tomb, if that's what really happened?'

'You want help with your report or not?

There was silence for a heartbeat. Reynolds raised his hands in a placatory gesture. 'What should I put in it? What else would have reasonably triggered my suspicions, apart from unexpectedly seeing you go into the East German Foreign Trade Office?'

The Assassin ran his hand through his hair and stood up. Pacing over to the window, he gazed at the back of the flats surrounding Earl's Court Square.

'What am I meant to be? A newly-arrived East German illegal resident, or a West German who works for them?'

'Let's make you East German. It sounds more threatening.'

'It sounds less convincing. An MI5 officer wouldn't get that lucky from taking in a random lodger. And in any case, a real Stasi agent would give nothing away. Even in late night drunken conversation.'

'You seem very certain about their level of professionalism.'

'Everybody in West Germany knows it.'

'We're only creating a sufficient illusion of suspicion here,' said Reynolds. 'Not trying to prove something in court. I just need to ring enough alarm bells to get someone to tail you and take photographs when you finally go out in public with Uhlmann.'

'I know.' The Assassin looked up at the ceiling for inspiration.

'Okay. How about this? You can say I was vague about the details of my childhood growing up in West Germany. The small things, like the games we played, the sports clubs I joined. Even the subjects in the school curriculum and the foreign books that we studied in literature class.'

'What else?'

'You don't speak German, otherwise I'd say to put in something about dialect words.'

'I need more.'

'Obsessive about keeping receipts. For claiming expenses.'

'Really?'

'They're always careful when it comes to spending hard currency. Don't get me wrong - they'll happily splash out if they feel it's worth it. But in the lower ranks at least, they know they're accountable.'

'How do you know all these details? You did a crash course on the Stasi with the SDECE before coming here?'

'How much does MI5 know about the Ministry? It doesn't sound like a lot.'

Reynolds pursed his lips. 'On its own, I don't know that this will be enough to get the right level of attention. How about mentioning your visit to Highgate?'

'Don't be ridiculous. Berlin's foreign trade office after lunch and Marx's tomb in the afternoon? This isn't a comic opera. You want to be taken seriously at work?'

'Okay.'

Reynolds got typing and let the Assassin read the result.

'Looks fine to me. Let me know how it's received by the people in your office.'

'The behaviour you described - with the carefulness over expenses and the evasiveness about the details of their childhood - it reminds me of someone I met at a reception given by the West German embassy last year.'

'Really? You have a file on him? You want me to check him out?'

'It's just a thought.'

'I'm serious. I could find a pretext to get close to him. As I told you earlier, I've nothing else to do all day. Ask your boss and I'll happily take a look at your list of German suspects, both East and West.'

Chapter Eight

Twenty-four hours had passed since Reynolds submitted his contact report on the Assassin.

The friction between them hadn't only been on the evening of the Assassin's excursion to Highgate, every one of the first few days of their enforced Anglo-German domesticity had been awkward. The pair of them had little in common apart from a professional connection, and Reynolds' natural discomfort at having any kind of stranger in his flat had only become more acute. Ahead of the weekend, he'd resolved to make a fresh start and had bought in bacon, eggs and an extra loaf of bread with the vague intent of offering Saturday brunch.

To his relief, the previous evening the Assassin had taken himself off to the pub. This morning, emerging from the bathroom, Reynolds asked the Assassin which one he'd been to. The West German was non-committal, merely saying he'd got into a darts game somewhere on the Shepherd's Bush Road and had gone on to a couple more establishments with the new acquaintances he'd made there.

The session must have been a heavy one, because before breakfast the Assassin went out in running gear for the very first time. He didn't bother asking Reynolds where the nearest park was and didn't say when he'd be back either.

If the Assassin's offhandedness was Reynolds' motivation, the West German's absence was his opportunity. To Reynolds' shame, it was also the chance he'd been waiting for.

Ever since it had fallen out of the Assassin's wallet, he'd been burning for a second look at the photograph of the girl. Overcoming his ingrained abhorrence at prying into the affairs of people he actually knew - even if only superficially - he crept into the Assassin's room, guessing he had at least half-an-hour to spare. The wallet sat there, staring up at him accusingly from the top of the bedside table. Somehow, reading the transcripts of private conversations at his desk in Leconfield House seemed less intrusive than what he was about to do.

Unwillingly and yet willingly at the same time, he slowly picked up the wallet. Opening it, he checked each pouch for the photo without success. Now caution went to the wind and he became frantic, checking again and feeling the lining for hidden compartments. He pulled out the Assassin's money and a loose bundle of business cards, some with East German addresses. Finally, rechecking the contents for a third time, he found what he was looking for, folded inside a red Irish twenty-pound note.

The girl was just as striking as he'd remembered. He couldn't believe the snap was a prop. No one would want to keep it in their wallet to be reminded that she wasn't their real girlfriend. But the photograph wasn't just passport-sized, it looked like it really had come from one. And as he ran his fingers over the glossy surface, to his surprise he could feel the indentations made by a stamp.

Reynolds held the photo up to the light, tilting it this way and that to try to read the words embossed on the image. Then he frowned, for he recognised the letters that made up a fragment of the name 'Deutsche Demokratische Republik.'

Nonplussed for the present, he carefully replaced the photograph and the wallet's other contents, then put it back down on the table as near as he could remember to where he found it.

In the end, his momentary panic was for nothing because the Assassin didn't return before he had to leave for work.

That morning, Reynolds decided to get off the tube at Green Park, one of his three options for Leconfield House. The Service's employees had always been expected to vary their route into work where possible, but these days there was an added frisson to their precautions thanks to the rumours going around the office about a new IRA bombing campaign in England. The last one had started in January of 'thirty-nine, a few months before the Second World War and had lasted until the spring of nineteen forty.

But if the Irish chose to bomb Leconfield House this time, then good luck to them thought Reynolds in his more cynical moments. Perhaps in an attempt to make it blend in with the rest of the government estate, the building had had minimal amounts spent on its outwards cosmetic appearance over the years. Inside, it wasn't much better. Reynolds and a couple of the other Assistant Officers on his floor had placed bets on when the strip of peeling paint shaped like South America hanging off the ceiling of their tea room would finally succumb to gravity.

It would be the closest to South America that Reynolds was ever likely to get during his career. By contrast, his father had served all over the Empire: from Bermuda to the Sudan. When he himself had joined the Service in the late sixties, there was still the chance of an overseas posting to an MI5 station in one of the former colonies where the British provided intelligence training and advice to the police forces of the newly independent countries. But three years ago, all of MI5's overseas stations had been brought under joint control with Century House, and in the British intelligence world, 'joint' all too often seemed to be Latin for 'MI6'.

Just after eleven, Reynolds knocked on the open door of Masterson's office. His boss looked up as he entered.

'What is it?'

'I need to talk about Hofmann.'

'Close the door for a minute, will you?'

Reynolds did as he was asked.

'So,' said Masterson. 'What's he done now? We only spoke about him on Monday.'

'I'm really not sure he's all that he claims to be.'

Masterson gave a frustrated sigh. 'Of course he's not. Who did you think the French were sending to us? If the boot was on the other foot, I wouldn't be telling anyone what he really did for me in Brussels.'

'Something about him is troubling me,' insisted Reynolds. 'It's nothing much, but sometimes one mistake is all it takes.'

He explained about the photograph of the girl.

'Hofmann said it was part of his disguise?' asked Masterson. 'Maybe it's his real girlfriend and they've applied an East German stamp to the photo?'

'That's a lot of effort to go to for something that might never be seen. And for something he didn't want me to see.'

'Yes, but not something he tried to hide particularly well. And if he really didn't want you to see it again, he'd have got rid of it, surely?'

'Maybe it's of sentimental value. A girlfriend in East Germany that he doesn't get to see very often?' suggested Reynolds. Now that he'd started, he had to carry on. The portrait of the Queen on the wall behind Masterson's head gave him a look that seemed to say she approved of his sense of duty.

'Why would his girlfriend destroy a passport merely so he could have a photograph of her?' replied Masterson. 'And even if she no longer needed the passport, why that photo?'

Reynolds shrugged. 'What if he helped her to defect from East Germany and he kept it as some kind of souvenir?'

'You're fantasising. How long is this game going to go on for? I've got work to do.'

Reynolds' face wore a stubborn look.

'Okay. Guess again,' said Masterson resignedly.

'Why would an ex-Legionnaire, who only came to Brussels and to Kramer's attention a year ago, find himself mixed up with an East German girl? From the time I've spent with him so far, I think there's a deeper link to Berlin that's not clear. He's very informed for someone who supposedly hasn't been in any part of Germany since age nineteen.'

'Is that the best you have?' asked Masterson.

'Do you know what he asked me the other evening? In so many words he said he was bored and that he'd happily spend time going through our files of East and West German suspects. Just so he could give us his own assessment of whether they might be Stasi agents.'

'Did he indeed?' said Masterson, more alert now. 'That's either very generous or very bloody cheeky of him.'

'Doesn't it sound suspicious to you? What if he secretly has a woman on the wrong side of the Wall? Then he's open to blackmail from the Normannenstrasse.'

Masterson rubbed his hands over his face. 'Give me a moment to think. This is not the news I need.'

But now Reynolds had the bit between his teeth.

'What if the people giving us our directions from higher up have been tricked too? What if, beyond all reason, Hofmann does have a hidden East German connection that even his boss in Brussels doesn't know about?' he asked.

Masterson looked up impatiently. 'Well, keep an eye on him then. You're his babysitter for the next few weeks.'

Reynolds studied the ceiling for inspiration. 'Or what if he deliberately wants us to think that he works for the Stasi?'

Masterson covered his head with his hands again, resting his elbows on the desk.

'Why on earth would he do that?' he asked in a muffled voice.

'I'm not really sure. Maybe Kramer wants to cause mischief between us and MI6?'

Masterson shook his head. He put his hands on the edge of the desk and pushed back his chair. 'Why are you bringing up that lot?'

Reynolds looked at him warily. 'I was trying to guess where your instructions about getting Hofmann into our book of suspects came from.'

Masterson frowned and shook his head slowly. 'You think it was Century House? "From the top" is all that you need to know. Has Hofmann given you any clue as to what he's doing here in Britain?'

'Not to me.'

'That's what I expected,' replied Masterson. But he didn't look that disappointed.

Reynolds tried another throw of the dice. 'The same morning that I picked up Hofmann from Northolt, Brierly told me to come straight to him if I ever suspected our guest was working to a different agenda.'

'Did he indeed? That was very bloody cheeky of him too. It feels like everyone's keeping secrets from me these days.'

'It seemed ridiculous, so I didn't mention it.'

'Really? Or were you planning to open a private channel to Brierly and his people behind my back?'

Reynolds shook his head and frowned. 'That's equally ridiculous.' He bit back a comment about secret policemen and their instinctive paranoia.

'And have you gone to Brierly about this?'

'Of course not. I only saw Hofmann's pin-up properly this morning.'

'Well, don't. We'll deal with this ourselves, if I think it's necessary. Without interference from the other place.'

Masterson pushed back his chair some more. Crossing his legs, he put his feet up on the desk.

'You're forgetting that if by some fluke he is working for East Berlin, either formally or informally, then he's an enemy operative that's gone into our files. Maybe there's some double game being played that neither of us know about,' he said, attempting to inject a more collegiate tone into his voice.

Reynolds shook his head in frustration. 'Isn't that the same thinking that led to no one putting up their hands about Philby? People had their suspicions, but they assumed that leaving him in place must have been intentional on someone's part? No one wanted to rock the boat.'

Masterson shrugged. 'Then as I said, carry on keeping an eye on him.'

'If Hofmann does have a dirty little secret from his past,' said Reynolds, 'it would embarrass the French, and that can never be a bad thing. It could also hurt MI6 if they're involved somewhere in the background,' he added, venturing onto thinner ice.

Masterson looked shrewdly at Reynolds. 'I'll decide on the right course of action as regards our colleagues from south of the River, if it ever comes to that. And as regards our foreign allies too. Don't interfere in things you know nothing about.'

'So beyond keeping an eye on him, what else can I do to make sure Hofmann doesn't spring any nasty surprises on us?' asked Reynolds, finally washing his hands of responsibility.

'Send him the message that if he tries to double-cross us, we'll find ways to make life difficult for him on both sides of the Wall.'

'I need to wait on the right opportunity for that kind of conversation.'

'Don't wait too long,' said Masterson coldly. 'You're the one I'm going to blame if he catches us out.'

Chapter Nine

Selene's flat was in a red brick Victorian mansion block behind the King's Road. The Assassin rang and waited on the pavement by the bottom of the stone steps up into the building.

Today she was wearing Saturday casuals too, which for her were faded blue jeans under an Indian-print dress - the opposite end of the fashion scale to when he'd seen her last in East Anglia. She hadn't completely dressed down though, because she was also wearing plain silver rings on the first three fingers of each hand and on both thumbs.

'You look like a mobster,' she said, skipping down the steps towards him. He shrugged off his black leather jacket and swung it over his shoulder. The day was too warm for it anyway.

'Have you met many?' he asked. 'The Mafia men I know wear tailored silk suits from Milan.'

'Ha ha. Very funny.'

'So where are we going?'

'To a little place around the corner from Sloane Square. The proprietor has a soft spot for me.'

'Does he know you already have a boyfriend?'

'I go to a different restaurant with each man.'

She really did seem to know the owner for she got a kiss on the cheek and was shown to an out-of-the-way table right at the back of the restaurant, behind a bamboo screen. Dark green plastic vine leaves had been threaded through the lattice to give the occupants even more privacy. They sat and she passed him a well-thumbed menu.

'Try the spaghetti alla carbonara,' she instructed. 'Do you want a bottle of wine?'

'What do you normally have?'

'Oh, just a carafe of the house red. It's not bad.'

Their orders were taken by the proprietor himself. He'd been hovering near the back, presumably knowing from before that she liked to get going quickly.

'How are your preparations coming along?' she asked, once the man had gone.

'I had a second meeting with the official at the East German Foreign Trade Office whom I'm to be photographed with next week. Reynolds has gone through the motions of reporting his suspicions of me to his boss.'

'What's your contact like on a personal level?'

'Wary. As I expected.'

'You're coming to them with proposals for new investments and trade. Why would he be wary?'

'Because East Germany is a small nation squeezed between powerful ones. And if there's ever going to be a final settlement between the superpowers, the two Germanies are most likely where it will happen.'

'It'll be a final settlement for the rest of the world too,' she said.

'In a way you can't blame the Communist bloc for trying to start fires in every other continent.'

'What? Even Antarctica?'

But the Assassin wasn't in the mood. 'They're only trying to take the fight to the Americans as far away from their home countries as they can.'

'What are you saying? That the Kremlin is even more fearful of us than we are of them?'

'Put yourself in their shoes. Washington wasn't almost encircled by an invading army thirty years ago. That's why the people at the trade office are suspicious. Anyone who walks in the door trying to set up partnerships with companies in East Germany might be a foreign agent. Someone seeking out discontented managers of state enterprises with a view to espionage or subversion.'

'They're paranoid.'

'No, it's what I said to you and Brierly in East Anglia. They're extremely security conscious. They take the intelligence game way more seriously than the West.'

She took a breadstick from the basket in the middle of the table and snapped off a piece.

'So what else have you been up to, apart from being sweetness and light to your estranged countrymen?'

'Smythe and I met the owner of Club Trèfle to discuss the arrangements for a private party where I'm to meet the first Mark.'

Selene rolled her eyes. 'Club Trèfle? You know that's a suit in cards? Club Clubs?'

'It's owned by a Frenchman.'

'Corny name. Not the corniest establishment up Soho way though,' she said.

'True. But not the most salubrious, either.'

'Are you a prude? Then you're the wrong man for this task.'

'Why? How would you have done things if you'd been in charge?' he asked.

'If Kramer had sent a German girl, I'd just have told her to take each of the Marks to bed. Put Smythe behind a two-way mirror with a movie camera and it would all have been over in a week. Bang, bang, bang. Job done.'

'I was all Kramer had available. No one volunteered for the job.'

'Isn't there anyone else working with you in Brussels?'

'In the Internal Affairs department? Of course. Germans, Dutch, French. The odd Italian from time to time. All the languages are covered.'

'Couldn't one of them have done this assignment?'

The Assassin silently shook his head.

'What happens when Britain joins the EEC?' she asked. 'Will there be jobs set aside for us at the Commission?'

'I'm sure Heath's negotiating it as we speak. I don't think he intends to be a passive member.'

Selene sniggered. The Assassin ignored her, unsure what the joke was.

'What's it like working for him in Number Ten?' he asked instead.

'I started twenty years too late. Once upon a time Heath was quite clubbable.'

'Clubbable?'

'Exhibited bonhomie. Was friendly, personable. He drove a roadster before he became MP but traded it in for a boring saloon afterwards. Mobilised an army of volunteers to campaign for him at his first election too - literally so, because some of them came from the Territorial Army unit he commanded at the time.'

She lit a cigarette, blowing the smoke out of the side of her mouth before continuing.

'But then something changed. Or perhaps with political success came arrogance. As I said, he was made a Whip at a very early stage in his parliamentary career. All those secrets he kept on behalf of the Party, all that power he had over the junior MPs - the "backbenchers" as we call them. It can't have helped him stay on an even keel.'

'That's not surprising,' said the Assassin. Then he frowned. 'Was Heath in the Army?'

'All of his generation were. That's to say, in one or other of the services. Or in government work related to the war effort. Heath was an officer in an anti-aircraft regiment. Went over shortly after D-Day and fought his way through France and the Low Countries, ending up in Germany. After the war, he joined the Territorials - what we call the Army reserve.'

'Did the war affect him much?'

She gave an ironic laugh. 'I'm not sure that it did. It probably simply reinforced his view that unreconstructed Germans are frightful and that European federation is a good thing.'

'Nothing's going to distract him from that goal, is it?'

'It's the degree of coldness which is shocking. Whatever he was like in his younger days, it feels like he's ended up at a place where he's incapable of human emotion. He's impatient with people, has no real interest in them, or understanding of what motivates them. And he expects other people to act towards him in the same unemotional way - and towards one another too.'

The Assassin took a sip of the rough red and tried to ignore the smell of her cigarette smoke. 'It sounds as if he's got some kind of psychological complex.'

'Before the election last year he took advice from PR people. How to dress, how to talk. Even, I kid you not, when to laugh. But as soon as he won, he ditched them all. It was like once he became Prime Minister, he'd ticked that box and had no further need of anyone's help.'

She paused for breath and took another drag on her menthol filter. Heath's social ineptness obviously exercised her.

'But he doesn't understand that people need to be continually sold to. Which includes people in his own party too. He despises the local Conservative activists by the way, truly despises them. He's lower-middle class at most, but he's become the most dreadful snob over the years.'

'But he managed to get the Party members to vote him into leadership? Brierly talked in East Anglia about how Heath was encouraged to go to church the Sunday before the vote to win their support.'

'It's the MPs who vote for the leader, not the members.'

The Assassin was puzzled. 'So the delegates to the Party congress tell the MPs how to vote?' he asked.

'I don't understand your question.'

'In West Germany the local cadres of the CDU and the SDP return delegates to the party congress which then votes on the party leader. But you're saying that the ordinary Conservative members have no say in who leads their party? None at all?'

'Now you understand why Heath despises them.'

'Now I begin to understand why a British political party might adopt a policy of EEC membership without popular support.'

'It's not as black and white as you're implying. The MPs take soundings from their local associations, so the ordinary members have a degree of influence, even if it's only an indirect one. But it's not much,' she admitted. 'Not when there's a leadership vote pending and the candidates can bribe wavering MPs with positions in government or the Shadow Cabinet.'

'It all sounds very nineteenth century,' said the Assassin, with a wondering look in his eye. I don't know how the British will find Brussels when they get there.'

'Perhaps it does sound that way to you,' she said. 'But it's how we work over here.'

'Maybe Heath doesn't know how things are done in Brussels. What happens if it all goes wrong for him, the Party realises what he's signing up to, and turns against accession?'

She shook her head in a very definite manner, loose strands of chestnut hair waving back and forth in front of her face. 'That won't happen. But I admit that the leadership being in the gift of the MPs means that no leader is ever completely secure, even if they're popular with the actual grassroots members. Maybe that's why Heath despises the backbenchers.'

'But if Heath's fate rests with them, isn't his arrogance like some kind of self-inflicted curse? Like Doctor Faustus or Macbeth?'

Now she curled the ends of her hair around the fingers of her free hand.

'There's constant murmuring in the background which becomes louder from time to time. Despite the fact that he won the election when all the pundits said it was impossible.'

'Didn't the win just reinforce his arrogance, his self-belief that he's always right?'

'Of course it did. But sometimes it feels like everything is conspiring against him. Even the way he conducts government business hurts him - the way he makes policy decisions. He takes ages to weigh things up, so comes across as being indecisive.'

The Assassin topped up their wine glasses from the carafe.'

'But after he does come down on one side or the other,' she continued, 'he's incapable of changing his mind in response to actual events. And when other Cabinet members do suggest an alteration of course, he treats them as if they're mentally defective. Especially when it comes to European issues, which he thinks he's the only one capable of understanding.'

'Maybe he doesn't have a complex. Maybe it's just a blend of arrogance and stupidity.'

'Maybe you're right. He's always had a need to over-plan everything. Dates back to his time in the Army during the war I expect.'

'I guess he'll leave nothing to chance when it comes to the parliamentary vote on accession, then? Your boyfriend in the Whip's Office will be busy when the Bill goes for a vote?'

She gave him a reproving look.

'We told you back in East Anglia. Heath was a Whip for nine years. If anyone knows how to force a Bill through Parliament by fair means or foul, it's him.'

'And what foul means does he have to hand? Apart from his card index and the Whips' black book? Is that why Smythe has spent the last few years taking photographs at parties?'

'I think the idea that Heath or the Conservative Party could be behind Smythe is stretching it. I imagine Ted would run a mile from that kind of suggestion. The topic disgusts him.'

'Don't dismiss the idea entirely,' said the Assassin. 'Devilliers has spent decades campaigning behind the scenes for British membership of the EEC, or so he says. Why wouldn't he lay in some extra insurance for the final push?'

Their orders arrived. Selene stubbed out her cigarette and the conversation took a more informal turn as they quizzed each other about their families while they ate.

The Assassin said he was an only child, but that was the only real personal detail he gave. He was happy to tell her anecdotes about growing up in Hamburg and how it had even more canals than Venice and then all the tourist spots in London that he'd been to so far. But she found it impossible to get any meaningful information out of him. From time to time he claimed a lack of understanding of English, but she suspected it was feigned.

She was more open. She told him something of her early life in Shropshire, growing up in the countryside. As she described him, her father was a farmer, but she'd been to gymkhanas from an early age, so the Assassin suspected that Mr. Warrington-Williams owned more than a couple of hectares. However, as the minutes went by, she still didn't say much about either of her parents. The Assassin began to get the sense that growing up he'd had more attention from one parent than she had from two.

'Did you go away to a residential school?' he asked, knowing from Kramer it was what the wealthy English did for their children.

'You mean like a ladies' college? No, no,' she laughed softly. 'I went to the grammar in the town. That's where my friends went.'

'And your brothers and sisters?'

'I'm an only child.'

The Assassin nodded to himself. 'Did you go to university? Maybe not, if you're working in administration,' he said, chasing the last of his tortellini around his plate.

She laughed again. 'I read economics at Cambridge. I even passed my degree - but only just.'

The Assassin gave her a concerned look.

'Nine men for every woman,' she said, smirking. 'More than nine for every attractive girl.'

'Lots of parties then?'

'More fun than writing essays.'

'When did you leave?' he asked.

'Nineteen sixty-eight.'

'Were there student protests in Cambridge that year?'

'None to speak of. Why do you ask? Is that your idea of what students get up to?'

'I know someone in Brussels who was part of a sit-in at one of the universities there. It was more than a sit-in though. The way he told the story, more like an occupation of enemy territory.'

'That didn't happen in Cambridge. At least, not during my time.'

'So you studied the same subject as Devilliers? Is that how you came to work for him and Brierly?'

She gave a hollow groan.

'God. Is everything an interrogation with you? What other, more interesting ways do you have of making me talk?'

The Assassin smiled politely at yet another reference in English he didn't get. He sometimes suspected that his regular drinking companions down the pub only tolerated his company for the chance to mock him in plain view of everyone else. He didn't mind. It was better than staying in the flat with an edgy Reynolds, watching him try and fail for an entire evening to conceal his discomfort at the Assassin's presence.

'I only know Devilliers through Brierly,' she said. 'After university, I decided that I did want to get into politics after all, so my father pointed me in Brierly's direction.'

'Are you a member of the Conservative Party, then?'

'No. Not yet.'

She looked at him reflectively and her eyes narrowed. 'We thought it best when I took the job in Number Ten that I should be a neutral.'

The Assassin looked back at her, equally shrewdly.

'You can't stay in administration forever.'

She gave him a faint smile. To the Assassin it seemed to be directed half at herself too.

The waiter came back with the dessert card, but Selene waved him away, lighting up again instead. The Assassin asked for coffee and the bill.

'How seriously do you take the threats from the three Marks?' he asked.

'I'm not sure. People spreading rumours and personal smears is par for the course in politics.'

She took a long drag on her cigarette. Tilting her chin, she exhaled straight up at the ceiling, where an ancient fan was slowly beating the smoky air to complaints from its worn bearings.

'I know why we're putting on a show for these three,' she said. 'But there's a question of priorities that's being ignored.'

The Assassin frowned.

'An entirely separate issue. One that Brierly and Devilliers seem to have blithely forgotten.'

'Which is?'

'The moral one. Why are we spending all this effort just to smear child abusers? If we're confident we know who they are and what they're getting up to, we should be trying to expose them. Any risk of some temporary, passing discomfort to Heath doesn't count by comparison. It's wrong to simply brush this stuff under the carpet. That wasn't part of the agreement when I went to work at Number Ten.'

'You're not just a typist, are you?'

'I never said that I was. And I bet you don't just audit expense claims either, or whatever it is you supposedly do at Internal Affairs in Brussels.'

'I'm just acting out a part over here in London. But even if we wanted to, these people aren't easy to catch. Not if they have protection all the way to the top of the Establishment pyramid.'

'Now you're sounding like Smythe.'

'But of course I find it abhorrent too,' he added quickly.

'What would it take to make you act? To intervene instead of watching them do the business?'

The Assassin frowned at the insinuation of him being a participant in something degrading, even if only a passive one.

'Who did the three Marks first make these threats to, by the way?' he asked.

'Brierly heard about them from Fryatt. That's as much as I know. Well?'

'I don't know what you want me to say. If I can somehow help these children - whoever they are - I will. Even Smythe hasn't been in the game so long that he's given up trying to protect at least some of them when he can.'

But even as the Assassin said these words, he realised how weak they sounded when spoken out loud. For the time being though, it seemed to be good enough for Selene. They settled up and left the restaurant.

As they walked back up the King's Road, she asked him what his plans were for the rest of the afternoon.

'Nothing in particular. I had some idea of going to the Cup Final but it starts in less than an hour. I suppose coming from Hamburg, I should support Liverpool.'

'You can come back to mine if you like and watch it on TV. I have a bottle of wine in the fridge. Or beer, if you'd prefer.'

'No. It's not that important.'

'And this evening? Do you have any plans?'

'Not as yet. I'll probably find a pub and play darts with the regulars again.'

'I'm going to a party in Fulham with some girlfriends from work. You're welcome to come along.'

'Thanks for the offer, but I need to keep a low profile. It wouldn't do for you to come under suspicion because you'd been seen out in public with an East German of ill-repute.'

'There's still something we need to do though.'

She didn't explain what she meant, and as they walked along, the Assassin's antennae, which were sensitive even at the best of times, started to twitch once again.

They kept on walking and found themselves back at the bottom of the steps into Selene's building. She turned and looked him full in the eye.

'This is me. Don't you want to come up anyway? Let's go to bed together. Afternoon sex is the best kind of sex.'

Her face was quite open. Guileless, he would even have said. The Assassin was silent for a long couple of seconds. The other pedestrians on the pavement gave them a wide berth, as if they could sense his discomfort.

'Is this a test of some kind?' he asked neutrally.

'No. I just think we should get it out of the way sooner rather than later. I think Brierly's expecting me to sleep with you.'

The Assassin shook his head. 'Why? So that he can put me under an obligation? Do you always do whatever Brierly asks of you sexually?' he added more sharply,

'Jesus, no. Fuck you. Not everything in life has to be a cold-hearted transaction.'

They both looked round as the driver of a bright yellow MGB honked his horn. The man waved a hand through the window at a girl in hotpants walking past who gave him a wave back.

'Is this how you seduce all your male friends?' he asked solemnly.

'Forget it. I was only offering,' She took a step back from him and crossed her arms. 'Anyway, real men don't need to be seduced. They want it all the time.'

The Assassin slowly cocked his head to one side then the other, as if weighing up his response.

'Even if they do,' he said finally, 'it doesn't make them available.'

He pursed his lips. 'You're better than that,' he continued. 'You owe it to yourself.'

For a moment it looked like she was about to snap out a retort. She uncrossed her arms and let them fall to her sides.

'I said forget it,' she said, her cheeks flushed.

'Don't waste yourself on me. Find someone for a proper relationship.'

'I didn't ask you for a sermon. Look. I'm sorry if I embarrassed you. I said forget it.' But she had a look of disappointment on her face, as if she'd missed dessert for the second time that day.

'Okay. *C'est rien.* We won't mention it again. I'll see you next week.'

'*Au revoir.*' She turned and climbed the steps. With a final half wave after unlocking the door she disappeared inside.

The Assassin spent the rest of the afternoon in a pub near Victoria Station which had a TV in the saloon bar. Liverpool lost two-one to Arsenal, three goals in under twenty minutes during extra time. If he'd gone up to her flat, he'd have had time to see them all.

Chapter Ten

The Assassin had left his previous meeting at the foreign trade office with a bundle of brochures and a list of addresses of state-run combines who might be of interest as trading partners for the fictional British firms he claimed to represent. He told Herr Uhlmann that he'd return with a selection of the East German firms his clients wished to meet and finished the meeting with a suggestion that they go for lunch the next time the Assassin was in London.

At the start of the week, he and Reynolds had come up with a list of suitable restaurants which would allow for easy observation of the diners, and on Wednesday lunchtime all three players found themselves in the Grill Room at the Savoy.

Reynolds was sitting a couple of tables away with a girl from Registry who spoke German. He'd brought her along, both as his cover, and also to hear what the two Germans actually said as opposed to what the Assassin might claim later that evening when they reconvened in the flat.

Unfortunately, although Clare Markham-Regis had assured him she knew the language when he'd asked her, she kept frowning and leaning towards the two actual Germans to try to hear over the background noise of the restaurant. He tapped her foot under the table. According to the Assassin there was no point in making Uhlmann any more suspicious than he already was.

At the German table, on their third meeting Uhlmann was slowly warming up to Reynolds' flatmate. Or at least, he was becoming happier to go with the flow of the conversation and get a free lunch at the Savoy Grill out of it.

The first two times they'd met, the Assassin had repeated the story that he represented his British clients in his spare time when not working at the Agricultural Directorate in Brussels. It was only a slight variation on the one that Brierly had suggested he use with the third Mark, and that Smythe said he should reuse with the trade office.

In his conversations with Uhlmann so far, the Assassin had successfully brushed off the suggestion that the firms he'd invented take a stand at the Leipzig Trade Fair. He'd also been insistent that if they ever did, it would be through him and not Berlin's preferred British broker, a Communist businessman called Denis Hayes - a description which sounded like a paradox to the Assassin's ears. According to Uhlmann, one of Hayes' other ventures was running Berolina Travel, which tried to sell the delights of the Republic to British tourists in competition with package holidays to Spain. The Assassin had a shrewd idea as to which one got the vote of the British public. He wondered what other purpose Berolina served East Germany. Probably as a front to facilitate travel by regime officials to the West.

Once the Assassin's remaining business questions had been dealt with before the main course, Uhlmann fired off some of his own.

'What's Brussels like?' the trade adviser asked casually.

The Assassin considered this for a second. 'The city? Or the EEC?'

'Your organisation.'

The Assassin was wary of general questions. They were like being taken on a journey without being told where you were going.

'It's a place of opportunity. It's growing all the time, both in terms of staff and numbers of offices. Soon there'll be a whole new diplomatic and administrative quarter centred around the Berlaymont.'

'How many people are there today?'

'Over four thousand. Even more after the accession of the new countries.' The concept of economies of scale was alien to Kramer's fellow bureaucrats.

'Will the English be welcome in Brussels?'

'Things will change. Right now the Six naturally divide into four and two. How the alliances work out later will depend on how compliant the British are.'

'And will they be, in your opinion?'

Now the Assassin was on surer ground. He expected that whatever he said to Uhlmann would be typed up from memory later that evening. Not that anything in the report would actually help East Germany in the areas that mattered for the long-term survival of the regime, such as providing the cars, colour televisions and centrally heated homes which Smythe claimed the British middle classes also coveted.

The Assassin shrugged. 'I don't know what the British are trying to achieve through EEC membership. I don't think they really know themselves, let alone be able to explain it in concrete terms to anyone else. Hoping for "merry songs of peace," as Heath apparently said the other day.'

'Does anyone originally from our country work there?'

The Assassin paused. Uhlmann hadn't even tried to finesse his clumsy implied question about who at the Berlaymont had family in the East and hence might be open to blackmail. He shook his head. 'Not on my floor. We have Dutch, French, Belgians. A few Italians,' he said, repeating the list he'd given to Selene on Saturday.

He glanced away from the other man.

'It's a strange place,' he added by way of diversion. 'Not a true centre of power, not yet anyway. Maybe more one of influence.

'How do you mean?'

'Because when it comes to creating industrial policies that favour one particular nation's manufacturers and food producers over those of its rivals, the people who work in the Berlaymont are much more than boring bureaucrats.'

Uhlmann looked blank. The Assassin took a sip of wine and spoke to save the other man the embarrassment of having to ask for an explanation.

'The officials at the Commission draft European laws, the Council rubber-stamps them, and then they get handed down to the member states. The national governments transcribe them into local legislation and pass them off as the work of their own parliaments. It's the hidden hand of the Commission across six, soon to be ten countries.'

'So what kind of people work there?'

'All sorts. Semi-retired politicians looking to boost their pensions without too much, or even any work. True believers in federation, like the former prisoner of the Italian fascists whom I know. Everyday careerists too, of course. Because they know that if they wait long enough, the EEC's powers will only grow and their own powers of patronage with it.'

147

'You need to be patient to achieve anything worthwhile in life,' said Uhlmann. He savoured his Beaujolais for a moment, while the Assassin did some probing of his own.

'How long have you been in London, Herr Uhlmann?'

'I was posted here just before we moved to our new premises in Belgrave Square.'

'Berlin expects to get diplomatic recognition from the British in the near future?'

Uhlmann shrugged. 'It's looking that way. But while we wait, we can't afford to upset their Foreign Office.'

'I'm sure the new First Secretary of your Party wouldn't thank you.'

Uhlmann removed his spectacles to stare at the Assassin. 'He won't thank anyone stirring up trouble for us in London, either.'

'That's not why I'm in England.'

'You realise that if any of your British clients want a high-level invitation to Berlin, I or one of my colleagues will need to check them out? Maybe visit their premises?'

'Of course. That won't be a problem,' replied the Assassin. 'Anything you want, I can arrange. And if they need anything in terms of licences or permits, I'm sure other arrangements can be made too,' he said matter-of-factly.

Uhlmann gave him a frosty look.

'You're a cocky one.'

'No one else is looking out for me.'

'War orphan, you said the other day?'

'I had my mother,' replied the Assassin, equally coolly.

'Did she warn you what would happen to your moral principles if you got sucked into working for greedy capitalists?' asked Uhlmann.

The Assassin raised an eyebrow. 'Don't assume her politics. Or mine.'

'Why? Secret socialist, are you?'

The Assassin's face went blank. 'You sound like you're jealous. You go to all that effort to help Western businessmen make money from the Republic, and what compensation do you get?'

'Who said I…?'

The Assassin gave a single 'tut' under his breath at this and shook his head ever so slightly.

Uhlmann stared at him, and the Assassin stared back. The colour slowly drained from Uhlmann's face as the silence stretched out between them.

'What are they saying?' Reynolds asked his colleague from Registry.

'I can't tell. But the older one doesn't look very happy.'

Reynolds had already worked that out for himself. Uhlmann had his head down now, giving his full attention to the food on his plate as he carefully cut it up into tiny forkfuls.

The Assassin was reflective too. He made a comment to the other man which neither of the MI5 operatives could catch. They saw Uhlmann nod slightly, but whatever had taken place earlier between the two had changed the mood.

Now the Assassin leant across the table towards Uhlmann. He pointed with his pen at a document of some kind he'd just laid down between them. They no longer came across as recent acquaintances out for a business lunch.

Reynolds looked around desperately for a waiter. A vague idea had come to him, almost subconsciously, that he needed to record the scene being played out at the other table.

After a minute or two, he eventually caught the eye of one of the staff.

'Excuse me. Can you take a photo of my friend and myself? It's for a special occasion.'

The waiter gave him a disdainful look but took the proffered Instamatic anyway, standing back to get both Reynolds and Miss Markham-Regis into the shot. At this angle, the camera was bound to capture the Germans in the background. For verisimilitude Reynolds leant across the table to take his colleague's hand. She turned to look him in the eye but didn't pull away.

Across the road from the Savoy, an MI5 photographer was loitering on the far side of the Strand, pretending to be a tourist. He or she should already have snapped the two Germans together on their way into the restaurant. But as Reynolds watched the pair conferring out of the corner of his eye, the sense came to him even more strongly than before, that his own photograph might be useful at some point.

But as to exactly when that might be, let alone why, he was no clearer than after he'd spoken with Masterson a week ago. When it came to navigating the intentions of the British, the French, and possibly the East German intelligence agencies, right now he was at sea without a compass.

Chapter Eleven

Jimmy Malta had promised Smythe he'd transport his guests to the radical end of Notting Hill and give them a spaced-out Việt Grove experience they wouldn't forget. He hadn't let his clients down.

The Assassin arrived deliberately late, just after midnight when the party was well underway. The music was loud and the lights had been turned down low for privacy. The walls of the party room tonight were hung with tie-dye sheets and stylistic images from the Kama Sutra. Joss sticks burned in holders and one of Jimmy's girls had even found some Black Power and anti-Vietnam war posters to add to the ambiance. Of course, the real mood was being provided by the off-duty showgirls in their groovy King's Road gear and the piles of spliffs and twists of cocaine served from behind the bar. For those that preferred tablets, there were Methedrine and other pills too.

The Assassin was also dressed to kill. He wore an open-fronted shirt with wide lapels and a gold medallion he'd bought from a stall in the Portobello Road that afternoon. Pointed winklepicker shoes completed his discomfort.

Reynolds had raised an eyebrow when his flatmate had emerged from the bedroom into the lounge. He'd even clicked his tongue when he noticed the jewellery, like a parent cautioning an unruly teenager.

'It's not your sort of party,' the Assassin had told him. It wasn't his sort of party either, but it was the job.

The Assassin had a surprise when he saw Jimmy himself up at the bar. He headed over to the background beat of the Jimi Hendrix Experience. A very much more alive Jimmy Malta nodded back at him, snapping his fingers at the barman for a vermouth.

'I didn't expect to see you here in person tonight,' said the Assassin.

'I wanted to make sure our friend wasn't stocking the bar with his own supplies.'

'Where's the other guy?'

'*Côté droit, alcôve centrale.*'

The Assassin turned round to look down the length of the room. There were drugs and girls, but he couldn't quite see what was happening in the alcoves because of the hangings separating the huddles of sofas. Things didn't seem to have reached too wild a stage yet.

He lit a joint handed to him by Jimmy along with the drink, and slowly made his way down the room, swaying along whenever one of the good-time girls came up to him.

Peering into Annersley's alcove he saw his target surrounded by other young people occupying all the available seats. They seemed to be having a good time, and a couple of the heavy petters looked like they were about to take things a stage further. Annersley seemed happy enough to watch for now, as he sat back in his seat, cigar in hand.

It was time to go. The Assassin finished his drink in one, put the empty glass on a side table, and took a puff of weed. Walking up to where Annersley was sitting, he stood there for a second until the Mark looked up. Their eyes met, and the Assassin reached down to grab the hand of one of the girls sitting next to his target, pulling her to her feet. He sat in the seat she'd unwillingly vacated and dragged her back down to sit on his knee.

'Oi, mister.'

'If you don't like it, get lost.'

She grumbled some more, but didn't move. Rather, she started to get comfortable, draping her arm around the Assassin's neck. He pushed her off and deliberately turned to Annersley. With a backwards look of disgust over her shoulder, the girl left.

'You're a feisty one,' said Annersley in a slow drawl. 'Who did you come to see? Me or her?'

'I like meeting new people. She was boring.'

'She was boring or all women are boring?' he asked, raising an eyebrow.

'I only came to England to meet fascinating people.'

Annersley half-turned in his seat towards the Assassin. 'And are you fascinating? Which exotic part of the world did you fly in from tonight, my ageing chicken?'

'Belgium.'

Annersley snorted.

'But it was too wild. So I joined the French Foreign Legion for a quieter life.'

'Did you now?' Annersley gave the Assassin a lascivious look. 'Communal bathhouses? Sweaty young men sponging each other down after a day spent marching around in the hot desert?'

He briefly laid the palm of his hand on the Assassin's chest. As if in response, the girl on Annersley's far side put her hand on the Englishman's crotch. He reached down and grabbed her wrist.

'None of that. Go and get me something from the bar.' He slapped her rump as she got up.

When she was gone, Annersley moved back slightly to take a better look at the Assassin.

'And who invited you here tonight?'

'Jimmy. He wanted me to meet someone called Smythe, but he's not here.'

'Then there must have been some confusion. Smythe is an impresario, not a party goer.'

'Maybe that's why Jimmy suggested it. So I get invited to Smythe's parties.'

'Looking for work after the Legion are you?'

'I get by,' the Assassin replied with a grin.

'I bet you do.'

Annersley leant over with a pointed finger to trace the scar running down the Assassin's cheek from his eye socket.

'Who did this to you?'

A shadow passed momentarily over the Assassin's face. He stubbed out the half-smoked joint in the ashtray on the table in front of them.

'Some men. I was asking for it, I suppose.'

'Tell me everything. Did you fight back?'

The Assassin's eyes narrowed and the scar on his cheek whitened slightly.

'They tied me down to a table.'

'How many were there?'

'Lots.'

'Old ones, young ones? Rough men?'

'Some might have been teenagers. I couldn't see properly. It was dark.'

'And your hands, dear boy?'

Annersley took both the Assassin's hands in his.

'I was stabbed.'

'That must have hurt.' Annersley placed a thumb on the scar in the middle of each of the Assassin's hands and massaged them slowly.

'It did, like hell.'

'And did they take their time over it?'

For a fleeting moment it looked like the Assassin was going to be sick. He slowly waggled his right hand. 'I asked the one who did this not to. He did it anyway.'

'I bet you liked the feel of his powerful blade. I bet you did, really.'

'It was an experience for sure.'

'So what are you doing these days, apart from looking for boyfriends in London?'

'I live with a man in a flat on Warwick Road.'

'Do you now?'

Annersley reached across to the ashtray for the discarded joint and relit it for himself. He slowly sucked the end as if trying to savour the Assassin's taste, before exhaling a long stream of smoke.

'And you, whoever you're called, what would you really like to do in life, apart from having a new man each night?'

The Assassin shook out a couple of cigarettes from a pack of Marlboros. He'd kept his promise not to smoke for as long as he could.

'My name's Tom.'

He offered one to Annersley. The older man shook his head and looked up as the girl he'd sent to the bar returned with a twist of cocaine. He patted the empty seat beside him and she sat down.

'Scram, the rest of you,' he said to the other two couples in the alcove. They stopped what they were doing and left to murmured complaints.

'I didn't come here to discuss my philosophy of life,' said the Assassin.

'No, you came to find a better offer than the boy in Warwick Road. But you'll have to work for it.' Annersley stubbed out the joint again. Then he reached round to caress the line of the girl's cheek, running a finger down the side of her neck and finishing up under her breast.

She grasped Annersley's wandering finger and laid his hand on her lap, smoothing it flat. Undoing the twist of cocaine, she tapped the white powder into his palm. He gave himself a moment, then bent down and snorted it up in one go. He smacked his lips and opened his eyes wide for a second.

The Assassin regrouped. 'And are you a better offer? What is it that you do?'

'I know people. People in business and people in politics.' Annersley gave him a sideways glance. 'Ones who would be shocked to see me here. Which is why I come, of course. Forbidden fruit is the sweetest, as is the thrill from the risk of getting caught.'

'You mean the thrill from balancing on the edge of oblivion,' said the Assassin slowly.

Annersley blinked hard again. 'You've been close to the edge before, haven't you? And not just with the knifework. What happened? You got caught holding hands with your boyfriend in the barracks and the other Legionnaires thought they'd teach you a lesson?'

'Something like that.' The Assassin gave a faint grin for the first time since he'd started telling his story, even if there was no real warmth in it.

'I'll have that cigarette now, if you're still offering,' said Annersley.

The Assassin reached back into his jacket for the pack and offered it to the Mark.

'What else did you try in the fleshpots of Marseilles when you were there on leave?' asked the older man as he took a cigarette.

'Not everything.' The Assassin clicked his lighter and gave Annersley a speculative look. 'I drew the line at the houses offering Moroccan boys.'

'Did you indeed? Whyever did you deny yourself that experience? Do you know the sense of sweetness some men experience when giving that kind of love to a child? The sense of dependency a younger boy can come to have on an older lover over time? Stronger in some cases than even the parental bond?'

The Assassin put his left hand into the outside pocket of his leather jacket. He gave himself a moment.

'No. I didn't know that. Is that why the boys choose to sell themselves? They're looking for love?' The Assassin took a drag on his Marlboro, tilting his head to exhale straight up at the ceiling, just as he'd seen Selene do the other day. 'And how would you know about that kind of thing?'

Annersley looked at the Assassin shrewdly while he took a long drag himself, the tip of his cigarette glowing bright. 'Don't dismiss out of hand what you've never tried.'

Silence descended for a short time. They watched a couple in the middle of the floor, their arms draped around each other's necks, hip to hip, grinding slowly in rhythm to the music.

'What kind of politics are you into?' asked the Assassin. 'Women's liberation? Civil rights? Marxism-Leninism?'

Annersley dragged his eyes away from the pair on the dancefloor.

'No, you naughty scamp. My ambition is for Britain to regain its place in the world.'

'And what is your place these days? All your colonies are gone.'

'There's more than one way to exert power.'

'Is that why you're joining the EEC, then?'

Annersley took another drag and looked warily at the Assassin. 'That's an odd question to ask. At a quarter past one on a Sunday morning in Soho.'

'It's the only item of British news we get in Belgium. All that people talk about is whether you'll create trouble when you join, and how much you're going to annoy the French.'

'That's because your own country is so fucking boring.'

'So why join us in the EEC then?'

'We're not just going to join it, we're going to run it.'

'Is that what your leader thinks?'

'I wouldn't be surprised. I've met him, you know.'

'Who? Edward Heath?'

'I was at a meeting where he gave a speech on Africa. That's my special area of interest.'

'What did he say?'

'After the meeting, a few of us met him privately. He told us that once Europe is united, we can get back into the geopolitical great game.'

'Really?'

'We're going to be a force in the world again. In Africa, we'll put all of the colonial baggage behind us and have a fresh start there too.'

'You're a supporter of Heath, then? You like him as a person?' asked the Assassin.

'He has his moments,' replied Annersley.

'What's your fascination with Africa?'

'It's unfinished business for the West. Even today, it remains a poorly-explored treasure trove of natural resources. A continent of opportunity for investors prepared to take risks.'

'Do you advise on investments there? Advise the people you know in business and in politics?'

Annersley shrugged. 'Despite independence, Europe's former colonies need our capital and expertise just as much as before. Anyway, why do you ask? How big was your leaving gratuity from the Legion?'

'You'd be surprised at its size.'

Annersley gave the Assassin another shrewd look and laid a hand on his knee. 'Do you want to continue this conversation elsewhere?'

'I need another drink first.'

'I need to piss,' said Annersley. 'Don't run away.'

The Assassin left it a minute, then went back up to the bar.

'Well?' he asked Jimmy, now on serving duties and in the middle of pouring a scotch and two Babychams for the man next to him.

'You're done here tonight. Smythe spoke to me on the internal line.' The Corsican nodded to a phone on the shelf below the counter. 'He says to come and see him at his house on Monday morning.'

'Okay.'

The Assassin thought for a moment, then made his way back to the alcove. Annersley was already sitting there, waiting for him expectantly.

'I have to go,' announced the Assassin, still standing. 'I told the man who's letting me stay with him that I'd be back before three. I think he might get jealous if I don't. I can't afford to live anywhere else if he kicks me out.'

'I'm sure you could find a sympathetic landlord without too much trouble. Sit down for a minute.'

The Assassin shook his head. 'Maybe you can tell me all about Africa some other time,' he suggested with a greasy smile.

'How will I find you?' asked Annersley.

'Leave a message with Jimmy.'

'Maybe I will. Do you have a second name?'

'Hofmann.'

'Well Tom Hofmann, I have an idea or two for some things we can do together. To get to know one another better.'

'I'll look forward to it.' The Assassin cocked his head to one side. 'I have one last question for you. Is Heath a queer too?'

Annersley got to his feet and stepped up close to the Assassin, almost touching him. 'Is that something else you talk about in Belgium?' he asked with an intense stare.

'No. It's just something I wonder about, the more stories I hear about him.'

Annersley stepped closer and took the lapels of the Assassin coat in his hands. 'He may well be. But he may not know it.'

'How do you mean?'

'Just what I said.'

'What if one day he realises who he is?' asked the Assassin.

'It would explain a lot,' replied the Mark. 'He might be less irritable, embrace his nature. Why do you ask? Planning to make a pass at him, are you?' He smoothed the Assassin lapels and took a step back.

The Assassin shook his head. 'When would I get the opportunity to do that? And why would I want to get friendly with someone like Heath in the first place?'

Annersley gave him a faint look of amusement. 'You tell me. Maybe powerful politicians turn you on? It's a strange old world we live in, while we still can.

'What do you mean?'

'Forget conventional perspectives, Tom. Forget thinking that you have to satisfy your landlord in lieu of rent. Step out, take risks, seize life. Seize everything that's on offer and everything that's not.'

'At whose expense though? You can't take from people who don't want to give. And I've never forced myself on anyone, of any age.'

Annersley gave the Assassin a sly smile.

'That's their loss.'

Chapter Twelve

As he'd been instructed by Jimmy, on Monday morning the Assassin made his way over to Smythe's house in Stockwell.

He gave a couple of sharp raps on the door, wondering what kind of mood he would find the policeman in. It was a while before Smythe opened up and when he did, it was with a curt nod. Instead of the dining room where they'd met with Brierly back in March, the Assassin was taken down a narrow staircase into a gloomy basement room.

The walls of the room had been painted white to make the most of any light that might leak in through the pavement-level window past the heavy red velvet curtains. Two recliner chairs upholstered in cream velour faced an end wall which was clear of pictures or any other decoration. There was a drinks cabinet directly opposite the door, and next to that, another cabinet with a smoked glass sliding front. Behind it sat a large hi-fi with more knobs than the Assassin had ever seen before in a private dwelling. Today, the red curtains were half-drawn and Smythe had switched on a couple of standard lamps with orange shades which gave off a sickly artificial light.

The overall effect was slightly sleazy. It resembled a tiny lounge bar, or possibly a private film viewing room, like the ones you might find in a blue cinema on Hamburg's Reeperbahn or in Soho. The Assassin wouldn't have been surprised to see a projector and a rack of skin movies on the table between the two chairs.

The Assassin stood standing in the doorway, unsure if Smythe had a favourite chair out of the two, and generally uncomfortable with the whole set up.

'Take a seat,' said Smythe, pointing, as he poured himself a whiskey.

'When Kramer said this job was undercover, I didn't think he meant underground,' said the Assassin. 'Do you even have your own office somewhere?' he asked, still leaning against the door jamb. 'When we were at the hotel out by Heathrow, you never said either way'

'This is where I do my top secret business.'

Smythe had already poured himself a drink and now he offered the Assassin one too. Reluctantly, he accepted a Bell's. It was only ten o'clock.

'Fuck me Hofmann. I thought you were going to bore Annersley to death. I was expecting to find him in the toilets with slashed wrists rather than have to go back in there and talk to you some more.'

Smythe took a seat in one of the armchairs. The Assassin remained standing. He had no intention of coming to sit next to another man. Not after his experience at the party just past.

'How long were you watching us for?'

'I was snapping away the whole time, for reasons that I'll explain later. There wasn't even the compensation of some spicy background shots because the party didn't get going properly until after you left.'

The Assassin shook his head in silent disapproval.

'What did you talk to him about?' asked Smythe. 'You weren't actually trying to chat him up, were you?'

'He couldn't stop telling me about men in the bathhouse.' The Assassin sipped his drink.

'Then you're lucky that was all he wanted to do. Anyway, whatever you said to him, he wants to meet you again.'

'When did you hear that?' asked the Assassin.

'I made sure I bumped into him when he was leaving to ask how he'd enjoyed the party. He mentioned you specifically. Said you were into some seriously kinky stuff and wanted to go even further.'

The Assassin didn't volunteer what Annersley might have meant by that.

'I saw him stroking your facial scar,' said Smythe.

'I made up a story about how it happened.'

'Well, now he's invited you and me to a private party down in Devon. And best of all, the second Mark is going to be there too.'

'Is that a suspicious coincidence or simply a reflection of the number of players on the scene?'

'Listen Thomas, this is the real thing. There'll be minors there, they're being brought down from London and elsewhere to entertain the guests.'

'How do you know those kinds of details? Did Annersley tell you?'

Smythe looked darkly at the Assassin. 'Because I know the owner of the house where the party's being held. He asked me a while back if I'd help run things for him on the night.'

'Did you have all this planned out before or after we put on the event at Jimmy's?'

'I knew something was on the cards for next month. The exact date only gets told to people closer to the time.'

'So when is it?'

'I don't know myself yet.' Smythe took a pocket diary from his jacket and checked an entry.

'What do you actually do?' asked the Assassin, 'when you say you help "run things on the night". Do you procure the children?'

'Jesus. What did Annersley slip into your drink at the party? Don't be sick. No. I take care of security.'

'Which means?'

'I'm a glorified bouncer. I check the guest list, turn anyone away who's not invited. Collect payment beforehand - for those that are paying their own way. I also check that the venue is physically secure and intervene inside if things get out of hand between the punters. With my fists, if necessary.'

'Why do they use you?'

'Because having a tame policeman around reassures the organisers. Makes them think they're immune from prosecution because the Met wouldn't want the scandal. Some of the guests have a high profile within their chosen professions. Almost household names in some cases.'

The Assassin couldn't believe that Smythe wouldn't be taking a healthy cut for providing his services. Especially if he was collecting the cash on the night.

'I suppose so. How indulgent are the police towards society celebrities?'

'Where do you want me to start? When Wilson was in power up until last year, everyone saw how police worked hand in glove with the Labour Party to look after their own. One of Wilson's cabinet ministers, an MP called Jim Callaghan, used to be the Police

Federation's parliamentary adviser. Well in with senior officers and very persuasive when it comes to making charge sheets and the notebooks of overenthusiastic constables magically disappear.'

'How many of the Labour MPs did they have to protect?'

'I don't know. Your namesake, Tom Driberg, was and is the most notorious. Openly homosexual back when it was still illegal and still addicted to cottaging and rough trade today. We think he does it on purpose to dare the Establishment to make an example of him.'

'Did you say "Driberg"?' the Assassin asked.

'Yes. Why? Do you know of him?'

'No… no particular reason. His name sounds German, that's all. What's "rough trade" and the other one?'

'"Cottaging" is sex with male prostitutes in public toilets. "Rough trade" is when dainty queers take it in the rear from working class men - like a kind of submission fetish.'

'If people know that men like Driberg are politically protected by the police, then does you being at these parties encourage them to get up to more extreme abuse than they would otherwise have done?'

Smythe shook his head slowly. 'I can't solve the problems of the world. If I thought too much about what I do, I'd go mad.'

The Assassin watched him as he said this, wondering again how Smythe came to find himself trapped in a job that seemed to bring so little satisfaction. People might also say the same thing about him, of course.

'Who can solve the world's problems, humanly speaking?' he asked.

'What other kind of speaking is there?' replied Smythe with a sarcastic look.

'How far does the moral decay within your Establishment go then, if they're protecting people like Driberg?'

'That's a strange line of attack. What prompted your question? Because we legalised homosexuality?'

'I don't know. You tell me. You legalised abortion too.'

'Jesus, Thomas. Don't come over all Mary Whitehouse on me. Anyway, after your titillation of Annersley on Saturday night, you've got nothing to be proud about.'

The two men stared at each other. Smythe looked down at his glass and took a drink.

He eyed the Assassin again. 'Even as an observer I have to be on my guard the whole time,' he said more quietly. 'No one is left untainted by abuse. Even if you don't take part, then from having to watch.'

The Assassin took a sip of his own drink. 'Do they have regular prostitutes as well as minors at these parties?' he asked. 'Like the ones that came on Saturday night? Are you ever tempted to bang them when they're out of their mind on drugs?'

'I think you're keener on that kind of thing than you let on,' said Smythe. Then he shrugged. 'I'm only human too. I need to make the odd demonstration from time to time to maintain the trust of the organisers. If there's tarts at the party next month, you can have a go at them yourself, as much as you like. Consider it a perk of the job.'

Now Smythe became solemn. His sarcastic asides were all used up. 'Don't get me wrong, Thomas. I told you back when we met at the hotel, I'm glad that you've come to England. I've a feeling in my bones that some good is finally going to come out of all the years I've spent watching these people.'

The Assassin was unconvinced that any of the abusers on the scene would take much notice of the smears that had been planned for the three Marks, but didn't say so out loud.

'Do you have the photos from the club on Saturday night?' he asked instead.

'That's the other thing. Here.' Smythe reached for a brown envelope lying on the low table between them. He opened it and fanned out a sheaf of both colour and black and white photos on the table's mirrored surface.

The quality wasn't great. The Assassin could see immediately that the ambient light had been too low for the camera to work without a flash. Smythe seemed to have tried several exposure times, but none of the prints were clear.

'This one might do,' said the Assassin. It showed Annersley holding the Assassin's hands as he inspected his scars. But even in that shot Annersley could claim he'd been with someone else.

'This is why I was snapping the whole time you were there,' said Smythe. 'I suspected they wouldn't turn out right when they were developed.'

'Didn't you check the light levels before the party?' asked the Assassin in frustration.

'Of course I did. But someone dimmed the wall lights halfway through, just before you arrived. The room was smoky, too. You'll have to go to Devon to finish the job on Annersley, whether the second Mark turns up there or not.'

The Assassin threw his hands into the air. 'Fine. I suppose. I guess there's no choice, not now we've started down the path with Annersley. But I can't be seen in the company of any minors.'

'Don't worry, I'll think of something that won't involve your member on display where it shouldn't be.'

So that was why Selene had sniggered when he'd used the word. 'When will you know the date of the party?'

'If Annersley's already mentioning it in conversation, then it won't be much longer. Give it a week or so.'

'More delays,' said the Assassin impatiently. 'I want this next episode over and done with quickly.'

'How far have you got with the Foreign Trade Office?' asked Smythe.

'I'm finished with them for now. MI5 photographed me with my contact at the Savoy last week. I'll hear in a couple of days' time if I've made it onto their list of persons of interest.'

'Then you should get working on the third Mark, Grieves. I'll get Brierly to set up a meeting with his lawyer, Mr. Jackett.'

'Why him?'

'That's what Brierly and I decided. Grieves is different from the other two, not so easy to get hold of - either socially or otherwise. If you're going to approach him with a proposition about doing business in the East, it needs the blessing of his lawyer first.'

'Where do I go to meet Jackett?'

'He's got an office in the City somewhere. I'll phone you with the details once I've been given a time.'

'What's going to happen to the negatives from Saturday night?' asked the Assassin.

'Here. You might as well have them.'

Chapter Thirteen

The Assassin had first seen the Square Mile from the top of the Post Office Tower, with its clusters of high-rise blocks dotted amongst older buildings. During his wanderings down at street level over the weeks that had followed, he'd been struck even more starkly by the mix of old and new. Steel and concrete offices built in the past fifteen years contrasted with classical buildings reminiscent of imperial Paris or Berlin. A reminder that even though England was smaller by population compared to West Germany, and smaller by size compared to France, until recently its capital city had been the capital of an empire too. But although the British colonies were no more, going by the names of the banks over the doors of the buildings, London's reach across the globe seemed hardly to have diminished.

The denizens of the City still possessed the restless energy of the old merchant adventurers, too. At rush hour, pinstriped bankers, insurance brokers, lawyers, clerks and accountants thronged the exits from Bank station under the watchful eye of the Duke of Wellington, sitting on his horse in front of the Royal Exchange.

The whole place even smelt of money. From the cigar emporiums to the bespoke tailors, it stood apart from the rest of London, an island immune to the industrial unrest the Assassin had read about elsewhere - unrest that sometimes seemed to be triggered for the most trivial of reasons. Only on Monday, British Leyland workers had come out on strike because the previous weekend workers from another trade had had the audacity to move car bodies from the paint shop, even though it wasn't in their job description.

He wondered how the outlook of the English on the rest of the world outside Europe would change after accession. A couple of days ago, he and Reynolds had spent a rare evening in together, watching the BBC Panorama interview with Pompidou ahead of tomorrow's summit with Heath. The triumphal summit, following the thirteen-hour-long ministerial meeting eight days previously, which had concluded with a choreographed breakthrough at dawn when Britain agreed to open its markets from day one of membership - just as Kramer had predicted.

The British capitulation was complete before the wheels of Heath's Hawker Siddeley executive jet had even grazed the tarmac at Orly. In nineteen forty France had signed away its future in a railway carriage in the Compiègne Forest. A little more than a quarter of a century later, Britain would be doing the same, but to the sound of clashing rifle butts as its Prime Minister was saluted on his way into the Elysée Palace.

Playing his role in the theatre put on for the BBC viewers, the French president had been insistent with the presenter that Britain's only geopolitical option was 'Europe.' The 'open sea' belonged to the past.

Just after three o'clock on Wednesday afternoon, the Assassin took the District Line from Earl's Court to Blackfriars. The openings in the tunnel roofs at certain stations puzzled him again, as they did every time he rode the line.

The lawyer's office itself was in an older plain-fronted building in the narrow streets behind Ludgate Hill. Going by the chipped tiles in the entrance hall and the bank of tarnished brass buttons for the various tenants, even within the City, wealth was sometimes distributed unevenly too. The Assassin rang for Jackett & Partners, and after a few seconds there was a click as the interior door unlocked.

He pushed it open and climbed a set of grimy stone stairs all the way to the top floor where the door to Jackett's office was ajar. Through the crack, he could see a secretary slowly typing in front of a dusty window as she gently cooked in the glasshouse heat from the twenty-degree temperature outside.

The Assassin knocked to announce himself and a small, ferret-like man with a darting expression came over to open up.

'Yes?'

'I have an appointment in two minutes with Mr. Jackett.'

'That's me,' said Grieves' lawyer. Looking around the single-room office, the Assassin suspected that the 'Partners' in the title of Jackett's practice might have been added as an embellishment. Or else they'd all left him over the years.

The pair briefly shook hands, and the Assassin was shown to a chair facing a corner desk. Out the window to the east, the dome of Saint Paul's rose above the line of the roofs.

'My apologies for the lack of space,' said the lawyer. 'I'm afraid you'll have to take us as you find us.'

'It's not a problem,' replied the Assassin, suddenly wondering again just how important smearing the three Marks would turn out to be on Britain's path to accession. Even as they took their seats, the pencils and notepaper were being laid out in the President's office on the first floor of the Elysée for the summit the next day.

'So,' said the lawyer. 'I understand there's a Mr. Brierly who suggested that you and Mr. Grieves should meet. You have a business proposition for him?'

'You weren't approached by Brierly directly?'

'He had someone he knew call me to set up the meeting. Something to do with exports to East Germany?'

'Who was the intermediary?' asked the Assassin, puzzled.

'No one you'd know. Someone I've done work for before.'

New doubts began to niggle the Assassin.

'I screen everyone who comes to Mr. Grieves looking for money,' said Jackett. 'He's a successful businessman. He receives several approaches for investment each month.'

Looking around the tiny office, the Assassin's scepticism remained. 'Some of the details are for his ears only.'

'He trusts me implicitly.'

The Assassin hesitated.

'I'm a busy man,' said the lawyer. 'I'm seeing you today as a favour. You've got ten minutes.'

The Assassin waited a second or two before starting his pitch, ignoring the heaps of paper on Jackett's desk and the open cardboard boxes of files underneath.

'I work for the EEC in Brussels. In the course of my job, I've made useful contacts on the other side of the Iron Curtain. The communist countries are always on the lookout for opportunities to do profitable business with the West.'

'Mr. Grieves already has people who can provide that kind of advice.'

'Who?'

'It's not really any of your business,' replied Jackett.

'I have political connections who can help him.'

'He knows plenty of political people too,' said Jackett irritably now. 'He's connected to Jo Grimond, the former leader of the Liberals. Big enthusiast for normalising relations with the Communist world.'

'I can do better than that.'

Jackett raised his eyebrows. 'Go on then.' The lawyer looked at his watch. 'You've got nine minutes left.'

'First of all, have any of Grieves' companies ever actually dealt with the Eastern bloc? Has he himself ever been to one of those countries?'

'I've only advised him on one deal, with a machine tool manufacturer in Romania for the supply of voltage regulators. But it wasn't straightforward. Lots of paperwork. More facilitation payments to intermediaries than when selling to India or the Middle East. All in all, more risk than Mr. Grieves cared for.'

'More risk means fewer competitors, which ultimately means bigger profits.'

'The stumbling block is enforceability. Making sure the importer formally accepts the goods, so that we get paid by the forfaiting bank. Mr. Grieves also worries about our designs being copied.'

'If you're selling to the right people, people who are personally incentivised in the appropriate manner, then they'll want to buy from you again. And if you can take payment for your products in goods rather than hard currency, they'll have a political motivation to deal with you too.'

'Yes, yes. We know all that. So which of the right people do you know over there?'

'Help me by giving me some idea of Grieves' plans for his business over the next five years.'

Jackett harrumphed. 'That's a somewhat direct question given we hardly know each other.'

The Assassin fixed him with a stare.

'Very well then,' muttered the lawyer. 'Brierly's vouched for you through our mutual acquaintance, otherwise I wouldn't be telling you this.'

'I'm all ears.'

'Grieves' principal investments are in electrical component manufacturing. Items used in both industrial and consumer goods -

bimetallic strips, timers, and the like. But he's considering launching his own line of domestic appliances and selling direct to the retail trade. I even looked into setting up a factory in Ireland for him last year. Labour is cheap and there's grants available from the Irish government.'

'You're late to the household electricals game,' said the Assassin. 'The washing machine revolution happened fifteen years ago.'

'New appliances are coming out all the time,' replied Jackett. 'A couple of years ago, we looked at buying the rights to a "microwave" oven invented by an American firm. Instant cooking could become a big thing.'

'It will be a while before we see any of those on the shelves of GUM in Red Square. But there's bigger opportunities in the East than merely selling luxury goods to the elite. That's what I wanted to talk to Grieves about.'

'What are you proposing?'

The Assassin glanced out of the window at the dome of the cathedral. 'Did you know that East Germany enjoys tariff-free access to the EEC countries?' he asked in a lower voice.

'How come?'

'Because as far as West Germany is concerned, it's part of our national territory. We refuse to treat them as a foreign country.'

'Is their access to the Common Market explicit, or on a nod and a wink?'

'They're the EEC's unofficial seventh member.'

'And your point being?'

'Because if you're serious about entering the appliance market, you'll need to compete against the low-cost Italian manufacturers. Instead of setting up a factory in Ireland, why not contract with an East German state-owned enterprise to manufacture on your behalf? West German quality, Italian cost of production.'

'How would we stop them stealing our designs?'

'That's why you need political cover.'

Jackett mulled this over for a moment. 'It sounds more like a concept, rather than a fully-fledged plan. It also sounds like a lot of effort for an uncertain rate of return.'

The Assassin folded his arms. 'The numbers are what they are.'

'What are your credentials then?' asked Jackett. 'Have you brokered any similar deals in East Germany before?'

'I've worked on the side for an Italian manufacturer of precision instruments. Export of goods to an outfit in East Berlin. Brierly can vouch for me through my boss in Brussels.'

'It still sounds tricky. Were there any export restrictions on the goods?'

'We pulled it off.'

'So who's your contact in East Berlin?'

'I can't say at a first meeting. But it's someone close to the heart of the regime. Ministerial level.'

Jackett tapped the desk with his pen.

'It's the way things work when you're dealing with East Germans,' insisted the Assassin. 'They're naturally secretive. Sorry. No names at this stage.'

Jackett shrugged. 'Well, it's unusual, but it's probably worth fifteen minutes of Mr. Grieves' time.'

Jackett glanced at his watch and the Assassin discreetly checked his too. 'Do you intend to export to West Germany?' he asked.

'Possibly. But they're well entrenched in the areas we currently compete in.'

'You know that once you join the Common Market, you'll be able to employ workers from anywhere inside the EEC? If you want to, that is.'

'Yes. Wilson was complaining about it the other week. But no one's really sure what it will mean in practice.'

'That's because it was only signed into law in 'sixty-eight.'

'What do you mean "signed into law"?'

'Signed into European law.' The Assassin gave Jackett a quizzical look. 'The laws made by the EEC which the member states then adopt.'

'I know what European law is. I'm a lawyer.' But from his tone, the Assassin wasn't sure that he did.

'How about people here who aren't lawyers? Do they understand how the EEC enforces the rules of the Common Market? About the Commission and what it does?'

Jackett blinked a couple of times, not ready for the new direction the conversation was taking.

'The paper today reported that Heath and Pompidou want the individual countries to run the Common Market,' he replied, somewhat flustered. 'Although it seems like a statement of the obvious. Who else would run it?'

The Assassin raised an eyebrow. 'Presumably the people running it now.'

Jackett got to his feet. 'Well, fascinating as this little chat has been, our time is up. Call me tomorrow and I'll let you know when Mr. Grieves can see you. Don't expect anything before next week.'

'Pompidou's summit with Heath will be over by then and the prospect of EEC membership will suddenly feel a lot more real. When it comes to opportunities for acquiring new markets and cheap labour, your competitors won't be sitting on their hands.'

'You'd be surprised at how much he knows about his rivals already,' said Jackett drily. 'Secrets in our industry rarely seem to stay secrets for long.'

Earlier in the week, Selene and the Assassin had arranged their second meeting for that evening at her flat, after she'd finished work. The Assassin would have preferred to have left it longer, given the embarrassment of last time, but she claimed she'd be out of town this coming weekend.

Once he'd left Jackett, he made his way over to Chelsea on foot - down Ludgate Hill, up Fleet Street, and along the Strand past the Savoy. He took a detour around Trafalgar Square and found a tiny pub in Cockspur Street called The Two Chairmen where he sat and ordered a Watneys Red Barrel.

During the past few weeks he'd become practised at killing time in pubs, quietly blending into the background as he made drinks and old newspapers last a whole afternoon or evening. At the very least, the hours spent sitting there and talking with the odd punter gave him a different perspective on Britain from the middle-class world of Reynolds and the world of the Dorchester and the Savoy.

Over his pint he pondered the likelihood that Jackett might have had business dealings with someone who also knew Brierly. Based on Selene's comments in East Anglia about the British Establishment and how they were connected to each other, the Assassin imagined a set of tightly overlapping circles of membership. If nothing else, it drew him a picture to explain why the misdemeanours of people like Driberg and Voaden kept getting covered up.

And that, he supposed, was the crux of the problem. If you covered up for someone like Driberg and his cottaging the first time, then when he did it again, he knew you had no choice but to oblige him once more. Nothing filled a British politician with greater dread than opening the newspaper to read about the latest sex scandal involving one of their party members. When it came to the secret lives of the ruling elite being exposed, they were as paranoid as the Communist parties of the Eastern bloc.

It was still over an hour until the time he'd agreed with Selene, so he kept the first pint company with a couple of Double Diamonds. Sitting there watching the drinkers in jeans and bomber jackets brush past other men in suits on their way to the bar, it struck him again just who the British Establishment and the German Communist Party both feared the most.

Shortly after seven he buzzed Selene's flat from the front entrance to her building. Over the intercom, she told him to come up and that she'd left the door on the latch. When he reached the second-floor landing, he knocked out of politeness anyway, and she called out to him from the bedroom where she was getting ready to go out for the evening.

As he walked through the lounge, he took a swift look around the room. It was dominated by a tufted red sofa, threadbare and over-sized for the space. The rest of the furniture looked like it had come from a house clearance too. She'd attempted a more contemporary feel by putting up modern art pictures on the walls. But there were no photographs, apart from one showing a group of men and women in formal evening wear, posing on the wide steps leading up to a big house. Selene was standing bold as brass in the very centre of the middle row, wearing a blue satin ballgown and a wide smile. The ornate porch behind them reminded the Assassin of Voaden's monastery and he gave an involuntary frown.

He knocked again before entering her bedroom. She was already dressed, apart from her shoes, but hadn't finished doing her makeup. They talked as she sat before a spotted mirror propped up on an ancient dressing table. Various brushes and tins of cosmetics were spread out over its deeply scored surface.

'So, how was your party at Club Clubs?' she asked.

'Smythe got some photographs,' he replied, sitting down on a chair next to the bedroom door.

'What did they show?'

The Assassin looked embarrassed. 'Annersley holding my hand. But it's not what you think,' he added quickly.

'How did you get that far with him? I didn't think he was that way inclined. I was told that touching up young girls was more his thing.'

The Assassin grimaced. 'I was told he wasn't particular either way.'

He walked over to stand behind her. Then he raised his hand up to the mirror and flipped it back and forth a couple of times to show how something had penetrated it and come out the other side.

'People are always interested,' he said.

Selene stretched her mouth to apply a line of lipstick. 'It takes more than that to impress me. What did you do? Try to grab the top of some railings to steady yourself when you were drunk?' She smacked her lips together to ensure the scarlet was even.

'I won't bore you with the story then.' He sat back down again.

She bent down closer to the mirror to apply a thin stroke of turquoise eyeliner, taking her time about it. Her cleavage was visible in the reflection, and he made himself look away.

'What happens next?' she asked, once she was done with the first eye.

'Next is a dirty party in Devon where we're going to get Barker. Smythe says he's been invited too, as a bouncer.'

She didn't reply immediately, instead concentrating on the final touches of the turquoise, the tip of her tongue between her teeth.

Closing the eyeliner tin with a snap, she started on her mascara. 'And what do you think of our policeman friend on better acquaintance?' she asked, scraping the excess from her brush before applying it.

'What? As a person or as a professional?'

'Both.'

'He has his moments. But he's not the sort of individual I'd naturally warm to.'

'I've only met him recently,' she said. 'But he's in too deep to the scene for my liking, even if he is meant to be undercover.'

He watched in silence as she delicately brushed on her mascara. When she was finished, she screwed the bottle shut and turned round to face the Assassin. 'What do you think?'

The Assassin coloured slightly. 'Different to how you looked when I first met you.'

She took a silver-backed brush and started to work on her hair with long, even strokes to alternate sides. 'Have you given any more thought to what I asked you last time? About making your time here count for something?'

'Aren't we doing that already?'

'You know what I mean.' She looked at him expectantly. He recrossed his legs.

'The whole premise of this operation is that Heath is at risk from blackmail,' he said. 'But blackmail over what? You've described his arrogance to me at length, but I've not heard from anyone that he's sexual to any great degree, in whatever form that might take. Maybe the two are linked and arrogance comes from shyness in the other area. I don't know him. You do. Or at least, you know him better than I do.'

Selene frowned. She took a break from brushing and ran her hand slowly through the strands of her hair, twisting their ends around her fingers. 'I suppose you think Heath is some kind of machine who needs to be taken apart to understand how he works. But he's not, he's only human. The underground culture the three Marks operate in is very simple. Brutally direct. The threats against Heath aren't sophisticated because they don't have to be.'

'All well and good,' he replied. 'But I'm the one who's being photographed by Smythe in some potentially highly compromising situations. All because we think Heath's personal secrets might be at risk of exposure, even though no one really knows what they are.'

'So why did you agree to take on the task for Kramer, then?'

'I owe him, I think. The balance sheet gets confusing. We both know things which the other person wants kept secret, things which should never have happened. Maybe it's more a case of Mutually Assured Destruction.' He gave a faint grin, but there was no warmth to it.

'Sounds like you have your own issues back in Brussels.'

'Anyway, I've started this now, so I need to see it through to the end. Definitely before the middle of June.'

'What's happening then?'

'I told you in Devilliers' garden. I have something else I need to take care of.'

She finally finished brushing. 'I never offered you a drink. Do you want something?'

Without waiting for an answer, she strode out of the bedroom to the lounge in stockinged feet, the Assassin following along behind. She went over to a side table on which stood a dusty decanter and tumblers and poured him a brandy, half-filling the glass. He swirled the amber liquid while she poured a smaller measure for herself.

They sat down with their drinks, she on the tufted red sofa, he in an armchair with shot springs. Looking at one other over the rims of their glasses, they each took a sip at the same time. She took a second sip, then spoke.

'If you're suspicious about what Smythe wants you to get up to with the Marks, then why don't you take out some insurance? Some ability to blackmail him and the others for yourself?'

'What are you suggesting?'

'Before I explain, let me ask you something first. I saw you flinch a moment ago when we talked about Annersley. When I said he touched up "young girls", how old did you think I meant?'

'Fourteen, fifteen? Ones with breasts and hips who're starting to look like older girls?'

'Please. Don't be so naïve.' She looked at him with a hard expression. 'Try eleven or twelve. Some are even younger than that.'

'Who told you this?' he asked. 'Smythe?' She shook her head impatiently, her face still grim.

Somehow the Assassin didn't really want to hear her answer. 'Did you know that back in March, Smythe took me to meet a reformed abuser?' he said. 'The idea was to give me some background on the scene. But I don't believe that the man I met has reformed much, if at all. More like he's toned it down and has been hidden away in the country where no one will find out.'

'And?'

'It was pretty unpleasant. Not least because he showed almost no remorse.'

'So what are you going to do about it?' she asked in a more diplomatic voice. 'What would it take to make you act? That's the question I asked you the last time we met.' The Assassin shuffled his feet under the table.

She was in earnest now. 'You can't just be an observer.'

'Isn't that what you are for Brierly? I thought you wanted to get into politics, not spying?'

'And I still do. But when he gives me an assignment to manipulate known child abusers for selfish political reasons, I can't turn a blind eye to who they are underneath.'

'How well did you know Brierly before you started working for him?'

'He's a friend of the family.' She pursed her lips and a look of bitterness flashed across her face for a second.

The Assassin gave her a glance. 'You said at the restaurant that the Establishment figures who are part of the child abuse scene need to be exposed to the light of day. What are you suggesting we do? Within the constraints of the task in hand, obviously?'

'I've no idea what regime-ending secrets out there are being covered up by the Establishment,' she said. 'But their ongoing fascination, or rather horror, over Profumo's downfall tells you all you need to know about their sensitivity to being found out.'

'I realise that. It's why they put Smythe in place to watch for them.'

She bit her lip. 'Frederick, the married man I know in the Whips Office, says he never goes into battle with awkward MPs without having a trump card up his sleeve.'

'Of course.'

'But for the Whips, it means having a real ace. They don't have much time on certain Parliamentary occasions. Their trump card has to work immediately. Other blackmailers can take their time. The Whips need results within hours or minutes.'

'So what trump card do you imagine we're going to discover in the next four weeks to use on these people?'

'I don't think we will. But I've had an idea for one we can make ourselves. First, though, I need to know that I can trust you,' she said in a solemn voice.

'I have my immediate task for Brierly, dealing with the three Marks. And as I already told you, I've less than a month left to do it. Then I'm gone. How much can you really come to trust me in that time? This is only the third occasion we've met.'

'Then I don't have a lot of choice in the matter,' she said, her voice strangely distorted now.

'Don't worry,' he said with a sneer directed more at himself than anyone else. 'The people running the English side of things don't trust me either. Did you know that this is my second time in England on this mission? When I first came in March, I was only on probation.'

Selene looked at him with wide eyes. 'You and I want the same thing,' she insisted. 'Not merely to be Kramer or Brierly's pawns, but to take action. To hit the three Marks hard - and any other abuser we might come across too.'

The Assassin smiled to himself as he listened to her exhortation. 'You're right. Of course I want to see these people finished off for good.'

She bit her lip again, but gently so as not to spoil the carefully applied gloss, he thought.

'Let's get a photograph of you and Heath together in a social setting,' she said quietly.

He stared at her.

'At some point in the future we, or someone else, might be able to use it to suggest that he has unexplained links with the Eastern bloc.'

The Assassin's eyes widened to become saucers. 'You'd be right about them being unexplained - because they wouldn't exist.'

Now he snorted. 'Selene, *putain*. I can tell you think he's arrogant and needs humbling. But how would this help put child abusers in jail?'

Yet even as he said this, a wild look crept into the corner of his eye. If she had been pushed, she would have described it as one of greed more than anything else.

'The problem isn't a lack of witnesses or evidence,' she said. 'Not really. It's inertia, an unwillingness to prosecute on the part of the authorities - the Home Office civil servants and their ministerial masters. Mainly because the members of the Establishment are all so connected to each other, as I've been telling you.'

'Have you been spending time with Smythe? That sounds like his line. He told me all about the MP Tom Driberg, to whom nothing seems to stick.'

She frowned. 'What's your point?'

'How is a photograph of me and Heath sitting together on a sofa going to change a reluctance going all the way up to Cabinet level to even acknowledge child abuse by insiders? Surely the whiff of a sex scandal will make them even more unwilling to bring it to the public's attention?'

'Because I'm not going to give them any choice. The next time I hear a rumour from Frederick in the Whips' Office about an abusive MP whom the Establishment has chosen to turn a blind eye to, I'm going to threaten to start some rumours of my own. And when I say "abusive", I don't mean an MP paying for a fifteen-year-old in stockings and lipstick who looks a lot more experienced. I mean grossly abusive.'

'You would go that far? Use another photograph out of context to start a scandal like the one with the Kray twin and Lord Boothby? I didn't expect...,' he said, breaking off.

'What? You didn't expect me to be this concerned? But surely you can imagine what it's like for someone, boy or a girl, to be all alone with a group of men? Beyond help and out of earshot?'

Now it was Selene's turn to be puzzled. The Assassin's face first flushed, then drained white. She could even have sworn there was a glisten of sweat on his temple.

He took a slug of the brandy. When he spoke again, his voice was cold. 'If you feed your rumours and uncorroborated photograph to the right journalist at the right time, they could spin a story that might bring down the government. Is that what you want? Or what Frederick's faction within the Conservative Party wants? To replace Heath with someone more amenable to the right wing of the party?'

'I'm not that close to Frederick. I only sleep with him to find out information for Brierly and Devilliers. And for my amusement.'

'Do you remember what happened to Ward and Keeler over the Profumo affair, when their entrapment play went wrong? The same people who came after them will come after us too.'

'Come on, Thomas. Be a man. Fire needs to be fought with fire. If the Establishment is never forced to confront child abuse within its ranks, then who knows how far it will eventually spread throughout society?'

The Assassin swirled his brandy some more and took another long slug. He got up and went to stand by the window with his back to her, looking out at the darkening eastern sky.

'What are you saying?' he asked. 'The sins of the Establishment will one day be taken on by an entire future generation?'

She waited on him saying more, but for the time being he carried on standing there, gazing silently out of the window. He turned round to face her full on.

'Do you really think you can set something up where I can compromise Heath?' he asked. 'How would it work? He must meet hundreds of people each month.'

'I have an idea for getting to him privately, away from the public. If I take a calculated risk at the office, I can get access to his appointments a couple of weeks in advance.'

The Assassin raised his eyebrows. 'This is good stuff,' he said, waggling his glass.

'It should be. It's a nineteen twenty Bas Armagnac. My father gave it to me as a house-warming present.'

'But it's not absinthe, and I'm not delusional.'

To his surprise, there was hurt in her face. 'It will be our secret,' she said quietly. 'We'll do it in such a way that the others won't find out.'

He stared at her, his expression cool. 'I still need to think about it,' he replied.

She eyed him up for a moment, then reached round the side of the sofa for her boots, bending down to pull them on and zip up the sides. She leant back into the cushions and crossed her legs. There was the briefest of pauses before she ran her hands slowly down the outside of each thigh over her miniskirt, before bringing them together to clasp under her knees.

He finished off his glass in a vain attempt to distract himself from this performance. She gazed at him with watchful eyes.

Coming to some sort of decision, she took a breath. 'I'm going to get laid tonight after the party. I don't know who with, I'll decide when I get there.'

He gave a half-shrug. 'It's a free world.'

He opened his mouth to say something else, then shut it again.

'I was serious a week and a half ago when I invited you up here after lunch. I still want to make love to you, Thomas. I want to do it now before I go out. I want to know that you're on my side.'

She uncrossed her legs and lay back even further into the sofa, knees slightly apart. Just so that he got the message, she ran her hands back up over her thighs, her fingers brushing the hem of her skirt as they passed, lifting it slightly.

The Assassin made himself take a breath. 'Why are you doing this to yourself?'

'What do you mean?' she asked with an edge to her voice. 'You just said it was a "free world"? We've talked, we've had a drink, and just now I'm in the mood. I like the look of you, and I want you to screw me.'

'The last time you propositioned me, I said you deserved better than a quick fling. I still think you're better than that.'

She sat up straight again. 'What if I don't want to be?' she asked sourly.

He carried his empty glass over to the table. 'I'll think seriously about the idea with Heath. Go ahead and start planning the details of how we might do it.'

She let her arms slump down by her sides.

He walked across to the door. As he reached for the handle, he turned and gave her a solemn look.

'If we do this thing together, I only have one condition. Nothing is to be used to pressurise Heath over abuse by his, or any other political party's MPs, until after accession is complete. Which might not be until the end of next year.'

'I suppose I'll have to live with it,' she said grimly.

'Well, good night then. Enjoy your party.' And with that, he was gone.

Chapter Fourteen

One street over from Piccadilly was a nondescript, narrow-fronted building, sandwiched in the middle of a terrace of other sooty grey offices.

The Assassin hurried up the steps to the front door, past a nameboard listing the businesses located at the address. Once inside, he climbed to the first floor and knocked at the door of a travel agency claiming to specialise in holidays to the Levant.

The floor of the reception was covered with green-grey linoleum, lifting at one corner, and the walls looked like they hadn't been painted since the fifties. But despite the unprepossessing canvas, someone had made a valiant attempt to brighten the room with a pot of purple bougainvillea.

An assistant was sitting at the front desk reading a paperback and looking bored. He handed over his passport, telling her who he'd come to see, at which point she suddenly came alive and snapped to it.

As she made an internal call, he picked up one of the magazines fanned out on the counter. He flicked to an article on the night life of Beirut from spring nineteen sixty-nine. Girls in minidresses squired by moustachioed Omar Sharif types sat at tables in a nightclub watching a belly dance being performed in the middle of the floor. A jazz band played on stage and waiters ferried trays laden with cocktails to the diners. He began to understand the attraction that Lebanon might have had for the notoriously louche Kim Philby, who'd chosen to live there for the last eight years of his life in the West. Moving to the Soviet capital must have come as a shock.

After half a minute, a heavyset figure appeared behind the frosted glass partition to the inner part of the office. The door opened a crack, and the Assassin was beckoned inside with a finger accompanied by a '*Par ici.*'

The security man led the Assassin down a corridor to a room with a plaque on the door which read 'Directeur - Privé.' Inside was a desk flanked by pot plants and on top of the desk, a light-grey phone with an oversized handset. Next to the phone was a calendar whose picture for this month was a colour photograph of an imposing medieval castle towering over an arid valley in the foreground. The Krak des Chevaliers, according to the caption.

The Assassin's escort nodded at the phone. 'You know how to use this model?' Without waiting for a reply he told the Assassin what he needed to do.

'*Décrochez, attendez le feu rouge, appuyez sur le bouton.*'

The manager left him to it. The Assassin glanced at his watch to make sure that the lunch hour, or rather hours, at the Berlaymont could reasonably be said to be over and dialled the special number for Kramer's office.

After a few seconds' delay, Kramer answered himself.

'*Hein?*'

'It's Thomas.'

'*Attendez.*'

A bang came down the line as the door to Kramer's outer office was slammed shut. 'What's happening? You're meant to be keeping a low profile. Brierly said he would keep me updated on your progress.'

'A couple of things have come up.'

'You haven't picked the best time to call. It's the first day of the summit with Heath. I'm standing by this afternoon in case the minister needs to be briefed at short notice.'

'I know exactly where our ally is today. It was in the morning papers here.'

'How are they reporting it?'

'He spoke at the conference of the Conservative Party women's organisation yesterday, just before he left for Paris. He told them he was going to achieve through negotiation what Hitler and Napoleon had failed to achieve through conquest. The clipping agencies won't have it at your end yet.'

Kramer took several seconds to reply. When he did, it was in an icy voice. 'His utter, pompous arrogance will be our downfall. Which can't be allowed to happen.'

'The Conservative women seemed to lap it up though. He got a big cheer, apparently.'

'Well thank God for that,' said Kramer sarcastically. 'Who'd have known they were such enthusiasts for French hegemony.'

'And then they sang a patriotic song. Which wasn't *La Marseillaise*.'

'Eh?'

Realisation dawned on the Assassin too. 'They think Heath's going to conquer Europe where the other two failed.'

It was Annersley who'd claimed in Club Trèfle that the British would one day run Europe. Brierly had scoffed at that idea on the drive up to East Anglia. But to be fair to Annersley though, he might have been high on cocaine when he suggested it.

'Stupid, naïve little fools,' said Kramer. 'They deserve everything coming to them.'

The Assassin frowned. He disliked it when people sneered at the rank and file, regardless of which organisation they belonged to. Hubris came before nemesis.

'So what happens when Heath eventually outlives his usefulness to us?' he asked. 'You'll send me back here to take care of him? Ask me to transfer secret funds to the trade unions so they can fund a national strike or two and bring him down?'

'Save the creativity for the professionals. What's your news, then? Make it quick. And no more use of real names, even on a supposedly secure line.'

'We made a play at compromising the first Mark, but the photos weren't good enough. We're going to try again at another social event which the policeman is taking me to. The second Mark is meant to be coming to that one as well.'

'Whose fault was it that the images didn't come out?'

'The light levels were too low. The policeman took the shots.'

'Do you believe him?'

'I believe him more than not.'

'When's this next attempt to take place?'

'We're waiting to be told the date. The policeman says it'll be a couple of weeks yet.'

'And what did you think of the first customer?'

'As sleazy as I imagined,' said the Assassin. 'But I've no real indication that he's a threat to the top guy, or that any of the Marks are.'

'Why's that?'

'Two reasons. No one can say definitively if our English ally is homosexual, likes children or is some kind of eunuch - mentally that is. He's a mystery in that area. No one can say for certain if he even has anything to hide.'

'And the second reason?'

'Because so far, I haven't come across any real opposition to accession here - at least not amongst the people who make the decisions. There's some malcontents in the Conservative Party, but they're being worked on. At this stage there's no real risk at the party political level, even if the top guy were to have to resign for personal reasons.'

'But that's not the whole story, as you ought to realise by now,' said Kramer.

What do you mean? A new leader might think twice about the opinion polls and the lack of popular support for joining.'

'What figures have you heard over there?'

'The general public are two to one against. And the numbers haven't changed in a year. Got worse, if anything - depending on which poll you believe.'

'You need to have faith in the plan,' said Kramer. 'Let me tell you a story. Do you know how the negotiation back channel between the two leaders came about?'

'The Foreign Office man who I met with your old colleague back in March mentioned it. He was complaining because it cuts their own diplomatic service out of the loop.'

'What does he expect, when the top man is a close personal friend of the President's chief of staff? All because he met Jobert by chance on vacation in Spain ten years ago, sitting at neighbouring tables in the same restaurant. I promise you, we've had this sewn up for years. Their top man doesn't care about those polls, and neither does his party or any of his likely successors.'

'Did he and Jobert really meet by chance, or did someone make sure they ended up sitting together?'

'Decide for yourself.'

At the London end of the line the Assassin opened his mouth as if about to retort. Instead, he lifted one corner of the calendar page for May to see what image was in store for June. The Grand Mosque in Damascus apparently. He came to a resolution.

'I said there were a couple of things that have come up. One of your old colleague's team has come to me privately. She wants me to work with her on a freelance operation on the side.'

'Who's this again?'

'The girl that he has working inside the top man's office. She's also the cut-out between me and him right now.'

'Oh, her. His secret weapon. I didn't realise he was intending to avoid direct contact with you,' said Kramer. 'What does she want you to do?'

'To set the top guy up for a Stasi smear, just like we're doing with the Marks.'

There was a long moment of silence. 'Was this her idea or yours?' asked Kramer incredulously.

'Hers.'

'And her reason?'

'She claims it's a matter of conscience. She's not happy with the idea that at most we'll only be smearing the Marks. She thinks if we can get some kind of hold over the top guy, she can put the entire network of Establishment abusers under pressure.'

Kramer tutted. '*Putain.* I've never heard such idealistic *degueulasse.* You're meant to be getting more experienced at this game, Thomas. Don't you recognise a trap when you see it?'

The Assassin pursed his lips at this. 'I never said I believed her.'

'Wake up. By the time you finish your work for them, who knows which laws they'll have asked you to break over there. But if they catch you doing this on the side, you'll have given them all the excuses they need to cover their tracks. Don't you realise what the words "deniable" and "untraceable" mean? Don't you realise what can happen to people involved in these kinds of operations who go out on a limb?'

'You don't need to spell it out for me.'

'It seems that I do. Or maybe you're getting greedy on someone else's behalf? Maybe you want to make a big splash in the intelligence world with a photograph of you and the top man together? One that all kinds of people would be keen to possess?'

The silence between them stretched out even longer this time.

'Am I going to have to come across the Channel and fetch you back at some point?' asked Kramer. 'If only to protect you from yourself?'

'Think what you could do with that kind of material. It's worth the risk. The top guy hasn't delivered accession yet.'

'He doesn't need any extra incentive just now,' said Kramer. 'He's desperate. He can hardly sell out England to us fast enough.'

Both of them waited for the other to speak. In his mind's eye the Assassin could see the blond wood fittings in Kramer's office and the view over the Parc du Cinquantenaire from the top floor of the Berlaymont. A world away from sex parties in Devon - or so one might imagine.

'Use your judgement,' said Kramer finally. 'You have to live or die by your own decisions. But this time you might not have any friends to rescue you in case of trouble.'

In London, a flash of annoyance sharpening to anger crossed the Assassin's face. 'I have a question for you,' he said.

'Yes?'

'Did you know that when I saw your old colleague last, he asked me how much I trusted you? Have you ever trusted him?'

'He and I were allies of convenience. I was grateful in my own way for the assistance of the English. I didn't become bitter like De Gaulle and resent them for it. I was a realist.'

'Even so, why would you turn down extra material on their top man, even if it is fabricated?'

'What's happened to you these past few weeks?' asked Kramer.

'You haven't heard the things I have about these abusers. The ages of the children involved. You told me yourself last year that someone needed to bring them to justice. And in any case, I'm not well disposed to give any English political leader an easy life.'

'That's because of your ongoing obsession about what they did to Hamburg.'

'It's my home town. The only place my family has a connection to, now that East Prussia is gone.'

'Really? Someone I know in Brussels might be surprised to hear you say that.'

There was another strained silence.

'Anyway. The liaison girl and I are only discussing a smear. She's going to work out how feasible it might be to get him into a private setting. And he is very private.'

'Whatever you're planning, don't drag it out. You're meant to be finished in England within the next four weeks.'

'You don't appear to be protesting this very hard,' said the Assassin tersely.

There was a hiss of static on the line which passed as suddenly as it came.

The Assassin continued. 'Because this whole effort to protect the top guy isn't just about ensuring Britain joins, is it? That's almost in the bag, if our contacts and the Conservative Whip's Office do their job right.'

'What do you think is going on then?'

'I think part of you wants the blackmail material which the Marks claim they have on the top man. Or any other material that's on offer right now. Because you want to make sure that Britain follows the French line after they join, don't you? Above all, you don't want the top man getting too friendly with Brandt.'

'I'm saying nothing. But we're at least a year away from being in the happy position of having that problem to solve. But you forget. All we really care about is getting the British to fund the CAP. If they do that, their man can take centre stage in Brussels as much as he likes. We'll hold as many pointless summits for him to chair as he's got time for.'

'It always comes down to cold hard cash, doesn't it?' replied the Assassin. 'Anyway, that's where we are so far. I'll check back in when I have more details - but only if I think her plan is feasible.'

'Forget what I said about abandoning you if things turn sour. I'm not a heartless bastard.'

'What happens if I get some hot stuff on the top man and have to leave in a hurry? Were you serious about the emergency plan you described in Paris?'

'I can make it happen. Does Jimmy still have your gear?'

'Yes.'

'Then think of a codeword and let me know it.'

Chapter Fifteen

Grieves' companies were spread across the south east of England. In London, he owned an industrial unit in Bermondsey but also kept an office in the City, presumably for the cachet of the address. However, as the Assassin headed north towards Islington and the warren of streets next to Broad Street Station, he realised that the only people it would impress would be those who'd never actually been there.

After walking up and down the road a couple of times, unsure if he was in the right place, he rang the only bell he could see at the number Jackett had given him over the phone. The area was a jumble of offices, warehouses, shops, and terraced houses. Around the corner from Grieves' building was a pub, and on the other side of the street, a print works. The Assassin knew something from personal experience about the secrecy of Swiss holding companies, but this was taking discretion to extremes.

He was buzzed in and climbed the stairs to the first floor where he was met by a much better class of secretary than at Jackett's. She gave him a cool, disdainful look as he was shown into the inner office. If Grieves didn't indulge himself with the latest Danish office furniture as Kramer did, then he at least hadn't stinted himself when it came to choosing his personal assistants.

'Mr. Hofmann,' she announced.

Grieves was younger than Brierly and Fryatt, closer to Smythe in age. His hair was receding but he made no obvious attempt to disguise it. That said, the curls at his temples seemed to be unnaturally dark. He waved his secretary out of the room.

'So you're the person that someone wanted me to meet about doing business behind the Iron Curtain?' he asked, getting straight to the point.

'I saw your lawyer last week. I was told I had to go through him first.'

'Jackett? He's an old woman. Typical lawyer - never prepared to come down on one side or another of an argument unless there's a fee involved.'

'Why do you use him then?' asked the Assassin.

'Because he doesn't think like me.'

'Fair enough, I suppose.'

'So what did he want us to talk about?' asked Grieves.

The Assassin frowned - he thought he'd already discussed this at length on Wednesday. He decided to start again from the beginning.

'It's no secret that the Comecon countries are way behind the West when it comes to meeting demand from their own people for civilian products,' he said. 'A couple of years ago the Soviets even had to go to the Italians to get them to set up a manufacturing plant for small economy-model cars.'

'Did Jackett tell you that we tried selling to Romania a few months ago?'

'He said you'd found it difficult. But when it comes down to it, doing business in the Eastern bloc is no different to anywhere else. You just need to know the right people.'

Grieves snapped his fingers. 'Everyone claims they know the right people and wants to charge me for access to them.'

'East Germany's new leader, Honecker, has only been in power for three weeks. The "right" people change all the time, sometimes unexpectedly so.'

'I heard about Germany. It was no big deal apparently, a very smooth transition.'

'So the papers say,' replied the Assassin drily.

But Grieves' interest in the internal politics of the East German Politburo had already waned. 'You told Jackett there was a way we could manufacture at low cost in East Germany and have tariff-free exports to the EEC?'

The Assassin raised an eyebrow at Grieves' tacit admission that he'd been paying attention to his lawyer after all.

'I was in Luxembourg last year and had a private meeting with the East German Deputy Minister for Foreign Trade. He told me they were always on the lookout for money-making ventures.'

'Did you discuss local manufacturing with him then?'

'No. But he asked me to bring him any opportunities I found through my work.'

'He actually said that to you?' asked Grieves sceptically. 'Jackett told me you'd helped an Italian manufacturer export equipment to East Germany recently. Was that before or after you met this minister?'

The Assassin shrugged. 'His people in Berlin were pleased with what I did for them. I have some credit there now.'

'So why are you in London? Are you scouting for your minister contact?'

'As I told Jackett, I work in Brussels for the EEC. I'm here for a couple of weeks to meet my professional counterparts ahead of Britain agreeing the accession treaty. I'm taking the opportunity to meet friends of friends who might want to extend their networks in Europe.'

'You're a real Good Samaritan, aren't you? How did Jackett come across you again?' he asked.

'Through one of his contacts. He knows someone I'm connected to through people in Brussels. A Mr. Brierly.'

'I've never heard of him,' said Grieves shortly.

The Assassin thought for a second. 'Is there any sensitivity because of the topic we're discussing? What's the attitude of the government to trading with the Communist bloc? I thought Heath was all for it?'

'Heath?' Grieves almost spat with contempt.

The Assassin raised an eyebrow. 'What's your problem with the Prime Minister?'

'He should have been a member of my father's party. Not masquerading as a Tory toff.'

'Which party is that?' he asked, guessing that Grieves was one of those characters who needed humouring through life.

'The Liberals. My father was a town councillor in Northampton.'

'He wasn't a businessman like you?'

'By day he was a postman.' Grieves glanced at a black-framed photograph on his desk, then looked at the Assassin again. 'I've made my own way in life so far. I had to. There was no family money to get my first business off the ground. I worked every hour God gave me during those ten years it took to become established.'

'Why do you say Heath is masquerading as a Conservative?'

'His own father was a builder. Heath might be ashamed of his background, but I never forgot mine.'

'But you're a plutocrat now?'

Grieves snorted derisively. 'What are you then? That sounds like something only a socialist would say.'

The Assassin reddened. 'I don't always use the right words in English.'

'Don't get me wrong. I'm not unsympathetic to the broad aims of the communists - the British ones at least,' said Grieves. 'But governments can't just snap their fingers and create prosperity out of thin air. The Communist Party talks about everyone having the same standard of living, but in their world we'd all end up equally poor. Ultimately, you have to let people make their own way in life.'

'But despite their failings, you don't mind trading with the socialist countries? And enriching their government officials?'

'I don't care how I make my money. Or who buys my products. I'm a liberal in the truest sense of the word. In all areas of human activity.'

The Assassin shifted in his chair.

'So what's the trick to selling to the East Germans?' asked Grieves. 'If I wanted to pursue this idea?'

'They're German. Do everything by the book, treat them fairly, and they'll do the same by you.'

'I've always thought that we were some kind of long-lost cousins. I wish there was a way we could have avoided going to war.'

'If you ever get to meet an East German, don't say that, whatever you do. Their first leaders were old-time communists who fled to Moscow from the Nazis in the thirties.'

'I can lay on the Brother Socialist act if I have to.'

'I wouldn't make fun of them either. They're not stupid. They expect people to see past the slogans to a degree, especially hard-nosed Western businessmen.'

'How about the secret police over there?'

'Why do you ask?'

'What if I went on a business trip to East Berlin, said the wrong thing to someone in a bar, and got arrested?'

'I think you're confusing East Germany with Stalin's Russia. They're not savages. I told you before, everything by the book.'

'Have you ever met them? Their secret police?'

'I suspect that when you hand over your passport to be stamped at the border, you're giving it to a Ministry employee. And when you visit a company, at least some of your hosts will be reporting back on you to the Stasi - not that you should be aware of it.'

'Awkward though. Unsettling.'

'I'm sure the British secret police do the same when the representatives of Communist combines visit London.'

'Possibly,' replied Grieves. 'But as you were hinting at earlier, to avoid confusion on anyone's part, this discussion needs to stay between you and me.'

'Doing business with the Communist bloc isn't illegal, but I understand.'

Grieves rocked back in his chair. He glanced past Assassin, looking at something or someone behind the glass partition dividing his office from the rest of the room. 'So if I wanted to go ahead with this idea of contract manufacturing in East Germany, who in Berlin would I approach?'

'First things first. We're dealing with a true bureaucracy here. It takes time and patience to work your way up through the hierarchies at the relevant ministries.'

'You said you knew the Deputy Trade Minister? Well, do you? Can't you go directly to him?'

The Assassin fished in his wallet and passed over a slightly dog-eared business card with 'Schalck-Golodkowski' printed on it.

'There you go. But as a German, I guarantee that even if I were to call him up this afternoon, his first question would be if I'd already gone through the proper channels. Then he'd politely ask me to start there. Of course, if you had military technology or other industrial secrets to sell it would be different.'

'Well I don't,' said Grieves. 'But having said that, the inclusion of certain items on the export restrictions list makes little sense. For all the Soviet posturing over Czechoslovakia three years ago, I don't believe the Cold War will amount to anything more than that.'

'That's a bold statement, even in an era of détente. It wasn't "posturing" in Czechoslovakia,' said the Assassin, looking at Grieves closely. 'It was a full-blown invasion with tanks and paratroops. People died.'

'I suppose you're a lot closer to them in Germany than we are. I'll at least give you that.'

'Let me ask you a different question then,' said the Assassin. 'Just how relaxed would you be about exporting new technology? Are you planning to develop anything that they might be interested in?'

Grieves rocked back in his chair again and tapped his teeth with his pen. He looked at the Assassin coolly. 'Why do I think there's more to you than meets the eye, man of many scars?' The Assassin clasped his hands together self-consciously.

Grieves savoured his small triumph for a moment. 'So who are you going to take me to see at the East German Foreign Trade Office?' he asked. 'To discuss what I might have to sell, or might want to have made for me in private behind the Iron Curtain?'

The Assassin hadn't expected Grieves to be this keen. 'So you want to give this a go? And work through me?'

'I make decisions quickly. No point in beating around the bush. Deals don't do themselves.'

'Before we discuss names of trade officials, is anyone else getting something out of my approach to you?' he asked.

'What do you mean, "anyone else"? The people who brought us together?' replied Grieves.

'I don't know. People usually expect something.'

'If that's what you're worried about, I'll speak to my lawyer and have him draw up an introducer's letter. We pay good rates for worthwhile opportunities.'

The Assassin gave a slight nod.

'Would we start off by meeting someone here in London or in East Germany?' asked Grieves.

'Berlin? You're prepared to go out there for a first meeting?' asked the Assassin somewhat dubiously.

'Time is money. If you have the contacts you say you do then let's go to East Berlin and check them out.'

Now it was the Assassin's turn to pause and think. 'I would need to make some calls first. It wouldn't be right away. As I said, this is a bureaucracy we're dealing with.'

'Speak to my secretary on the way out to arrange another meeting. I'm a member of the City of London Club, I'll take you there for lunch.'

'Give me a week or two.'

'Don't make me wait too long. I'm an impatient man once I get going.'

Chapter Sixteen

When the Assassin got back from the pub on Friday evening, unusually for a weeknight, Reynolds was still sitting reading in the lounge.

'You didn't stay up on my account?' asked the Assassin as he came through the door.

Reynolds pursed his lips. 'I can never get hold of you otherwise. You go jogging in the morning and come back after I've left for work. Then you're out all evening. I hardly ever see you.'

'Secret of a happy marriage,' grinned the Assassin. 'Or so the lads in The Three Feathers said tonight.'

'"Lads"? You're going native Hofmann. You need to get back to Germany or Belgium, or wherever it is you live these days.'

'So what did you want to ask me?'

'It's a bit embarrassing,' said Reynolds.

'Go on.'

'My… my girlfriend.'

'That's right,' grinned the Assassin again. 'Your girlfriend friend.'

'How much have you had to drink?'

'You sound just like someone I know.'

Reynolds shook his head and gave himself a few seconds. 'You've been invited to lunch on Sunday at her parent's house.'

'Why?'

'Because I think they want to know that you actually exist.'

'Oh. Am I spoiling your plans for her to move in with you?'

'I'm guessing she wants to make sure that my German flatmate isn't another woman. She got suspicious after I had to stand her up last weekend when I was working.'

The Assassin couldn't think of anything clever to say in response so didn't. He waited for the other man to fill the silence, but something else seemed to be troubling his flatmate.

Reynolds pursed his lips, stood up, and went over to the chimney breast. A three-bar electric fire stood in the grate where coal had once been laid. He leant with one elbow on the mantelpiece and looked the Assassin in the eye.

'East Germans living in Britain have to renew their visas every six months. For obvious reasons, at renewal time we pay special attention to any government officials working here.'

The Assassin suddenly sobered up. 'All the East Germans living here work for the government,' he said. 'When you say "we", is it your service which conducts the interviews?'

'I never said how they're vetted.' Reynolds looked narrowly at the Assassin who sobered up some more. 'But in the case of your contact at the East German Foreign Trade Office and certain others at Belgrave Square, there's a special arrangement - a man from the Department of Trade and Industry meets them on an informal working basis every couple of months or so. Any tidbits the DTI man picks up are reported back to us to help inform our views as to their real occupation.'

'What do they discuss at these meetings?'

'It's not a set questionnaire,' said Reynolds guardedly. 'General topics. The reaction in Berlin to visiting delegations of British MPs and trade union officials. Speculation about which countries might also be considering granting diplomatic recognition to East Germany. Gossip about Heath's desire for more trade with the Communist bloc and his encouragement to British firms to find ways around American technology export controls. All topics designed to take the temperature of détente.'

'But that's not what they talked about this time?'

Reynolds raised an eyebrow at the Assassin.

'No. Earlier this week your Herr Uhlmann complained bitterly about you, about how he had been tricked by an MI5 agent provocateur into defaming the regime in Berlin.'

Reynolds waited for a reaction, but Assassin was impassive. 'What happened between you and him?' asked Reynolds. 'I saw something going on at your table when we were at the Savoy.'

Now the Assassin looked at Reynolds with narrowed eyes, despite his supposed inebriation. 'Go on. What else did he say to your contact?'

'An agent provocateur was only his first suggestion.'

'What do you mean by his "first"?'

'Because he also said that he'd checked back with Berlin, and they'd denied all knowledge of you.'

'Why did he do that?' asked the Assassin carefully. 'And why would he share that kind of information with a British official?'

Now Reynolds fixed the Assassin with an icy look. 'Because he was giving us an indirect signal that he didn't believe Berlin's denial of you. In so many words he asked us to either stop provoking him if you were acting for us, or to have you deported as a Stasi operative if you weren't.'

'Really?' replied the Assassin. 'Then he's spent too much time in London learning your arts of equivocation. A real German would just have come straight out and told you what they thought.'

'So why do you think he said what he did? And how should I explain this away inside the Service?'

The Assassin seemed unconcerned. 'Make use of what he said. Write down your interpretation of his story to the DTI man and have it added it to my file. Don't we want people in MI5 thinking that I'm one of them?'

'Yes...but.'

Reynolds tailed off. Then he frowned, pursed his lips, and with a new resolution came to the point.

'I... I have to ask. I know you have a cover story for what you do in Brussels. I understand that. But are you here under any other kind of false pretences for the French... or anyone else?' Reynolds blushed as he said this.

The Assassin slowly shook his head, a mournful look of disappointment on his face. 'No wonder your rivals in MI6 are in such a mess. No one trusts anyone else in this country.'

'Do you blame them? Over the years all kinds of unlikely people later turned out to have divided loyalties. And you're not that unlikely.'

'When your counter-intelligence people investigated the former head of MI5 did you really believe the rumours? Did you really imagine that Roger Hollis was a KGB spy? It's preposterous. Don't get sucked into that world of madness, John.'

'I had to ask,' said Reynolds defensively.

'Surely you must realise the reason for Uhlmann's accusations? The situation inside Belgrave Square is more complicated than you think. We all know things are about to change for East Germany as regards diplomatic recognition by the West. But it's an open secret that when that happens, the Stasi will want to place their own people in Berlin's new embassies.'

'An open secret to whom?' asked Reynolds, puzzled.

'Just listen. For the East German Trade Ministry, it means a loss of some of their precious overseas postings. Maybe one day in the future, even a high-level position like that of the ambassador himself might be filled by an HVA operative, rather than someone who works solely for the Foreign Ministry. So of course the trade officials want to create difficulties for the politicals ahead of time. And it's not only the Stasi who'll be disturbing their cosy existence. The Volksarmee's military intelligence service also runs overseas operations.'

'A turf war. I get it. We test the boundaries with Century House all the time.'

'And on top of that, Ulbricht was replaced by Honecker as East German leader only this month. The entire map of political connections in Berlin is being redrawn as we speak. Who knows which faction our Herr Uhlmann is acting for right now?'

Reynolds drummed his fingers on the top of the mantelpiece for a few seconds and gave a sigh. He turned back to look at the Assassin with another frown. 'I'm never going to know who you really are, am I?'

'I'm coming to put in a good word for you on Sunday with your girlfriend's family. So I can't be all bad.'

Chapter Seventeen

On Sunday the Assassin and Reynolds took the Central Line to Mile End and walked up Grove Road to a leafy terrace of Victorian villas in Bow. The weekend traffic was light, and the tube almost deserted compared to a weekday, or so the Assassin helpfully informed Reynolds.

'How much do you use the Underground, then?' Reynolds asked his companion.

'I get around. Like it says in the song.'

'So what do you do during the day when you're not doing your thing for Brierly? Surely you only go to the pub in the evenings?'

'I'm never going to get a chance to live on my own in London again,' replied the Assassin, side-stepping the question.

'Indeed. Sounds like you're having your last fling of freedom.'

They walked side by side past a row of dilapidated terraced houses marooned in an expanse of cleared wasteland.

'Last remnants of houses bombed during the war,' said Reynolds. 'Left to moulder, along with their current occupants. Probably to be replaced by a concrete tower block one day,' he added distastefully.

'Like in Germany,' replied the Assassin. 'On both sides of the border.'

'Look,' said Reynolds pointing up at a railway bridge which they were about to walk under. 'This spot was the first place in England to be hit by a V1 flying bomb.'

'What was the damage?' the Assassin asked with professional curiosity.

'Six people were killed. The original bridge was destroyed.'

'Lucky hit,' said the Assassin. 'Not for the people of course,' he added quickly.

Reynolds said nothing.

They neared Reynolds' girlfriend's house.

'Her father is a bookkeeper at the docks, you said?' asked the Assassin.

'Yes. Further out east. Somewhere by the Royal Docks. A bookkeeper or an accountant. I'm never sure which is which.'

'Nice family? Any problems with Germans?'

'Her father's the one who told me about the V1 so don't push it,' said Reynolds. 'Why do you ask? Have you had some trouble down the pub lately?'

'No. The solidarity of the international working class is a real thing,' the Assassin replied in a deadpan voice. At least that's that they told him in The Three Feathers, even if he suspected they were making fun of him.

'What reason did Linda give for her parents inviting me today?'

'They thought it would be rude not to. They didn't want to leave you sitting alone in the flat - although knowing you there wasn't much chance of that.'

Reynolds rang the bell, and his girlfriend answered the door with a quick smile for Reynolds and a guarded look at his companion. The Assassin turned to his flatmate and saw in the other's expression what he'd by now come to recognise as a faint embarrassment. He wondered if it was because Linda seemed to be only a couple of years out of school. It would make Reynolds a good five or six years older than her at least.

They walked through the hallway, past the kitchen, and down a set of steps to a basement-level room. French doors opened out into a back garden which lay below the level of the street.

A short man in horn-rimmed spectacles was just finishing laying the table. He looked up as they came in. On his day off, Pryce had dispensed with a tie, but was wearing a jacket in acknowledgment of the family's guest. He came round to greet them.

'You must be John's friend. You're most welcome.' He saw the Assassin glance about the room. 'This is where we eat when we're not being formal.'

Pryce offered the two younger men drinks and his daughter disappeared back upstairs - presumably to help her mother finish preparing. The Assassin watched her as she climbed the narrow staircase, taller than her father but with the same raven hair, in her case falling ruler-straight down her back. The Assassin thought that Selene could learn a thing or two about the power of unavailability.

The conversation over lunch soon turned to the Assassin and what he did in Brussels. When that topic was exhausted, he was quizzed about life in Hamburg. Unlike at a certain Sunday lunch in the suburbs of Dublin last year, no one brought up the Beatles.

The Assassin asked them how many Germans they knew personally. He occasionally put this question to people he met down the pub, once they began to give their opinions on the war. Sometimes he felt as if he was in England on a one-man mission to establish West Germany's democratic credentials, as much as for anything else. When the conversation called for it, he'd even have a go at justifying East Germany's attempts to leave the past behind.

Reynolds slyly dropped in the Assassin's five years spent in the French Foreign Legion, and then wished he hadn't because that finally piqued his girlfriend's interest. But the questions she asked the Assassin weren't the ones he was expecting.

'What did your family think about you leaving to join the French Army?' she said.

He thought quickly. 'They knew what I was like as a person. It wasn't a surprise to them.'

'And your mother? Was she happy to let you do whatever you wanted?'

He recognised a loaded question when he heard it. He gave a glance at Miss Pryce's own mother, who was sitting next to her. 'Of course she had regrets,' he said. 'But I was only nineteen. It was hardly a life sentence for either of us.'

'How old was she when you were born?'

'Twenty.'

Now Linda flicked her eyes to the side, as the back and forth of family politics played out under his nose.

To the Assassin, she reminded him of a cat, happy to sit still and watch as the conversation flowed. But when she wanted to know something, she pounced. He wondered if that was how she conducted her relationship with Reynolds too.

The Assassin also saw a new side to his flatmate's character emerge during the course of the meal. He and his girlfriend sat opposite each other, virtually in silence. But when they did speak, Reynolds' faint air of constant underlying uncertainty seemed to be replaced with a more natural confidence. He wondered what it would take to make him that confident in his professional life.

When the meal was finished, Pryce invited the Assassin to join him in the garden. Reynolds helped his girlfriend and her mother clear away.

Her father took his guest down to the bottom of the path where they sat together on a bench against a warm yellow brick wall, looking back at the rear of the house.

'I didn't want to bring it up earlier,' said Pryce. 'But I'm curious, what did your family in Germany do during the war?'

The Assassin shrugged. 'This and that.'

'How did they get by afterwards?'

'With difficulty. What did you do back then yourself,' asked the Assassin.

'Same as I do today, an office job down at the docks. I was fourteen during the Blitz, just old enough to be a messenger for the ARP. Air Raid Precautions,' he explained. 'What happened in Germany? Did the Hitler Youth do the same?'

'I don't know. No one really talks about their time in it much. I know that they drafted teenagers to be *Flakhelfer*. Loaders for anti-aircraft guns, that kind of thing. My...' Whatever he was going to say, he thought better of it.

'This area of London suffered badly?' he asked instead. 'How about the docks?'

'It was hit all over. Not this street though. You came from Mile End?'

The Assassin nodded.

'Just up from there is where the first V1 hit London. We called them "Doodlebugs."'

'Reynolds pointed it out to me.'

'What do you think of Linda's young man?' asked Pryce.

'I've only been lodging with him for a few days.'

A flicker of a smile passed over Pryce's face. 'That's a careful answer,' he said. 'Do you know what he does for a living?'

'He works in the Agricultural ministry.'

'Hmm. From what my daughter has hinted at, we think he might be something in the Ministry of Defence.'

The Assassin shook his head firmly in denial. 'Maybe his actual job at the Agricultural ministry isn't that important, so he's embellished it a little? You know how men try to impress girls.' Then he realised how this might sound to her father. 'But to be fair to Reynolds, he's been pretty open with me during my stay.'

'Maybe it's because you're an international colleague of his?'

'I'm definitely not that.' The Assassin shook his head and gave a faint laugh. 'What do you do down at the docks?' he asked, turning the focus back on his host.

'I run the numbers for a shipping company. Thankfully, it's a skill that's always in demand in every industry.'

'Why do you say that?'

'Because the writing is on the wall for the East End docks. Saint Katharine's by Tower Bridge closed three years ago, the London Docks in Wapping the year after. The Surrey Docks on the south side of the Thames closed last year. There's talk of those ones being filled in to build an airport. All that's left upstream of Tilbury are the Millwall and the Royal Docks.'

'Why all the closures? Because your colonies are gone?' asked the Assassin.

Pryce shook his head in amusement. 'It's more down to earth than that. Before they started building container ships, do you know how long it took to load and unload cargo at the beginning and end of each voyage?'

The Assassin dutifully shook his head in ignorance.

'A general cargo vessel can take ten days to cross the Atlantic, but it can spend the same amount of time tied up in port. Manual loading of freight means just that: pallet by pallet, barrel by barrel. Cut the port time by half and you make the ship a third more productive. The numbers speak for themselves.'

'How does that affect the docks here?'

'Because once the shipping lines finally complete the switch to using standardised containers, the ships themselves will grow ever larger in pursuit of economies of scale. And most of the East End docks were built for sailing ships.'

The Assassin pondered this for a moment. 'So we're at the point where the cost of shipping is about to fall significantly over the coming years? And the maths work for longer voyages too? From places like Australia?'

'Of course. From everywhere. What do you know about aviation?'

'A little. My grandfather worked in an aircraft factory.'

'At the start of this year, Ted Heath nationalised Rolls Royce, the aero engine manufacturer. They'd underestimated the development cost of their new turbofan and went bust.'

'That's why you need accountants,' said the Assassin drily.

'Heath nearly became one after Oxford. But then he decided that he had more to offer society as a politician. Anyway, he was advised to rescue Rolls-Royce, not least because their new engine design is vastly more fuel efficient than those currently being sold by the American manufacturers.'

'So you're saying the cost of flying is going to come down too?'

'It's a mathematical certainty. The turbofan combined with the jumbo jet will revolutionise the economics of long-haul air travel.'

'Not Concorde then?'

'Not for the masses. BOAC is already asking IATA for permission to offer cut-price fares to ensure they can fill their 747 flights to America.'

'And all this is happening just as you join the EEC,' said the Assassin. 'So you can switch to importing goods from France and West Germany instead.'

'I doubt if many in Parliament are fully aware of the implications. Most of our politicians seem to think that ditching our Commonwealth trade partners is a good thing, even if they claim to regret doing so. We need to move on in the world, apparently.'

'And you, Mr. Pryce? What do you think?'

'It scarcely matters. The Labour MP Tony Benn wants a referendum on joining the Common Market, but the government's ruled it out.'

'I saw it in the newspaper,' said the Assassin. 'How can they avoid taking it directly to the people, though? Each of the other candidate countries are having referendums. Next year at the very latest.'

The article had come out a couple of days after his trip to East Anglia, otherwise he'd have asked the same question to Devilliers and Brierly.

'That's not how the British system works. We don't have a constitution for one thing and even if we did, we delegate those kinds of powers to Parliament.'

'So was the last election a kind of referendum on joining?'

'Wilson wants to join too, as does Jeremy Thorpe. The option to stay out of the Common Market wasn't on offer at the ballot box last year. I suppose the thinking goes that the politicians are better placed than we are to make those kinds of big decisions,' said Pryce.

They both gazed skywards for a moment at a jetliner making its way up from the south, flying high, streaming a long contrail behind it. Long haul, headed to northern Europe, probably from somewhere sunnier than London.

'Going back to what you think about the EEC. Do you personally want Britain to join?'

Pryce polished his spectacles, taking his time over it. When he was done, he held them up to the light to check the lenses were clean. 'What's the West German public's opinion about Britain joining the Common Market?' he asked instead.

'We're in a completely different situation. You live in an old country.'

'What do you mean, "old"?' he asked, puzzled.

'Germany only became a nation a hundred years ago. Our centenary was in January this year. That's why our first anthem was "Deutschland Über Alles" - Germany first and foremost. An exhortation of loyalty to Germany over Bavaria, Prussia or the other constituent states.'

'What's your point?'

'You trust your politicians because your system of government has survived for so long. It's an asset which no other country in Europe possesses.'

'I don't know about trust,' murmured Pryce. 'It seems that they don't trust us.'

'I think it's worthy of you to want to join France and West Germany in political association,' said the Assassin. 'But as I said, your country has survived quite happily for centuries. I can't see that the EEC will make much difference to you over the long run.'

'Now I'm confused,' said Pryce. 'Are you saying we should or shouldn't join? You work in Brussels, surely you support what Heath is doing?'

'I'm trying to say that our perspective and yours are entirely different. And Heath's is different again. He actually said the other day that he wants to complete the work of Napoleon and unite the continent. I even kept the cutting from the paper. I'm going to have it framed for the office.'

Something made the Assassin glance up just then to the windows at the back of the house. 'No one's invaded you for nine hundred years,' he continued. 'My country was razed to the ground twenty-five years ago and isn't even whole anymore. Divided and chopped up. The amputated parts given away to Poland and the USSR.'

'You make it sound like Germany was the victim. You've forgotten which part of London we're sitting in.'

'The Luftwaffe isn't coming back to the East End. Not under any circumstances.'

'I suppose you're right.'

'Hamburg lies only thirty kilometres from the border to the east. The reckoning is that the Soviets will reach the outskirts within the first thirty-six hours and will take a week to fight their way through the city, based on how long it took your troops last time. Assuming they only use conventional weapons, of course. We both have bigger problems right now than the vanishingly small chance that France and West Germany will ever go to war with each other again.'

'In one sense we've hardly moved on from nineteen forty-five. We simply replaced an old threat with a new one. It doesn't feel like peace, not real peace. I remember the fortnight of the Cuban Missile Crisis only too well. It wasn't even a decade ago.'

'Our best defence is to persuade the people running the regimes over there that we're happy for them to continue doing so as long as they don't interfere with us in turn,' said the Assassin.

'But that's selfish of the West. What hope does that attitude give to the people oppressed by Communism?'

'Some of them think that it's we in the West who are being oppressed - by the American capitalists. Most of them don't have an opinion either way, they just want to get on with their lives. They have families too.'

'They don't have much choice about it, I suppose. Are you trying to defend the Kremlin somehow?'

'No, not at all. But although I don't agree with their system, East Germany is still part of Germany. As West Germans we have an obligation to help our countrymen however we can. But I'm also realistic. No one is coming from the West to free them from Moscow's rule. All we can do is not make their situation worse.'

They watched as someone appeared at the french door into the basement room.

'Look, there's John.'

Reynolds and the Assassin retraced their steps to Mile End. Reynolds' girlfriend saw them to the door of the house and gave her boyfriend a half wave as they left, but that was as far as any demonstration of affection between them went.

'What did you think?' Reynolds asked the Assassin, once they'd walked a little way down the street.

'Nice family. Nice to meet some normal people for a change.'

'How about your chums down at the pub?'

'They're okay. They have their own sense of humour, though.' For a moment Reynolds wondered if the Assassin was lonely in London.

'Did I put your girlfriend's mind at rest about your living arrangements?' asked the Assassin.

'She's happy enough for the time being,' replied Reynolds. 'I did what she asked by bringing you along today.'

'You have to give people the impression from time to time that they're in control,' said the Assassin impassively.

'What did you speak with her father about?' asked Reynolds.

'He asked me if you were at the Ministry of Defence. I said you weren't. They'll eventually work it out for themselves, you know.'

'I'll cross that bridge when I come to it.'

They walked on for a few yards while the Assassin considered his reply. 'You need to find a way to tell her the truth without her realising what you've told her.'

'Is that how you salve your conscience with all of your girlfriends?' asked Reynolds.

The Assassin cocked his head to one side, but said nothing.

Just before they went inside the tube station Reynolds dropped a screwed-up packet of something from his closed fist into the litter bin by the entrance.

The Assassin saw how he tried to hide it and suppressed a grin. They bought their tickets and went down to the platform to wait for the next train.

'You dirty dog,' said the Assassin to his flatmate. 'Where was her bedroom? Top floor at the back of the house?'

'How do you know?'

'I thought I heard a noise when I was sitting in the garden with her father.'

'It's not like we have much opportunity with you in the flat.'

'I can't believe you left me alone with Pryce while you were upstairs banging his daughter.'

Reynolds reddened.

'I could stay away from the flat one night if you want me to,' said the Assassin. 'Just say when.'

'You'll be gone soon enough.'

The Assassin smirked at Reynolds' discomfort. 'What did her mother say when the knives and forks were finally put away and you sneaked upstairs hand-in-hand?'

'We're in the East End. She's probably been encouraging Linda all this time.'

'You know that once you've had sex with a woman, you're meant to be partners with her for life?' asked the Assassin in a flat voice, his change of tone catching Reynolds by surprise.

'Where does that notion come from?' replied Reynolds irritably. 'Some weird Eastern religion?'

Now the Assassin looked knowingly at Reynolds. 'You could say. Not a church-going man, are you?'

'Why? Are you?' said Reynolds darkly.

'When I need to be. Mainly to keep my mother happy, to be honest. Although that's not a real reason I suppose.'

'Devout believer, then?'

'We can't always be what we want to be,' said the Assassin.

'Someone's in a mellow mood today. Are you often this flippant?'

The minutes stretched out, but the train indicator still didn't change. They stood together in silence, listening for the approach of the train.

The Assassin felt the need for rapprochement. 'It's only half-past two. Let's go and visit the docks before they're all gone,' he suggested. 'We'll find a sailors' pub that neither of us has been to yet.'

Reynolds didn't react to this proposal.

'It wouldn't take us long to get there,' added the Assassin by way of extra incentive. 'Did you know there's a branch of the Metropolitan Line which goes south of the river? You can take it all the way to the old Surrey Docks.'

'Be my guest,' said his flatmate. 'I can only cope with so much fun in one day.'

Chapter Eighteen

For the briefing on Devon, the Assassin had come back to Smythe's house. Once again, the policeman took him down into the basement den.

As before, the red velvet curtains and the artificial half-light from the orange shades gave the room a sickly, unwholesome appearance. Given the choice, the Assassin would rather have met anywhere else, not least because of the faint, acid smell of Smythe's body odour.

While Smythe poured himself the inevitable drink, the Assassin looked around the room again. There was a second door on view this time. On his last visit it had been behind a wall hanging which was now pulled back to one side.

'Don't stand there like a scalded cat,' said Smythe, sitting down in the left-hand recliner chair. The Assassin took the other, deliberately angling it away from the blank wall and towards Smythe, making his mark in the other man's den.

'Avoiding the office again today, are we?' he said.

Smythe gave him a sardonic look. 'They've promised me a desk at Paddington Green when it's fully up and running, if it'll stop you asking all the time.'

'You see? Progress. Why don't you tell me which department you're meant to be working for?' The Assassin was happy to put off the discussion about the coming weekend for as long as possible.

Smythe shook his head. 'I'm on the books of "A" Department, even though I'm not uniformed. "Administration,"' he explained.

'So you're undercover within the police too?'

'People assume I'm some kind of troubleshooter.'

'Which problems are you meant to be fixing?' asked the Assassin.

'Bent copper problems. Sometimes the Met pays them off, retires them quietly.'

'Retires them quietly? Like what happened to Voaden?'

Smythe coughed. 'Right. Except that he wasn't with the police. Look, here's a diagram of the house in Devon.'

He opened his notebook and leant over the table between the recliners to swiftly sketch out a floorplan in the shape of a long rectangle.

'The main party with the usual supplies of stimulants will be downstairs in the main drawing room.' He pointed to the top half of the outline he'd drawn. 'It will be wild, people swapping partners, adult prostitutes, the lot.' There was a twinge of regret in his voice.

'The main staircase is here,' he tapped on the middle of the rectangle with his pencil. 'Up that way is where the children will be taken to be abused. There's a set of bedrooms on the first floor.'

'You make it sound so matter-of-fact. You call it the "first floor", we call it the second in Germany. But whatever it's called, I won't be going anywhere near there,' said the Assassin in a hard voice.

Smythe sat back in his seat and shook his head. 'You may not have a choice, Fritz. Not if you want to help nail these guys.'

'What do you mean? Where are you planning to take the photographs from?'

Smythe pursed his lips. 'It's not easy to get people in front of concealed cameras in these old houses. They're just too big - too many places where people can wander off to for privacy.'

'Where have you put the cameras then? The first-floor bedrooms?'

'The last two on the corridor. They're connected directly to each other. The wall between them is a couple of feet thick. There's a connecting door on each side which makes a space in the middle big enough to hide in. I'll drill a spyhole in the door beforehand, or maybe take out a screw holding a coat hook and drill all the way through that hole.'

The Assassin looked dubious but didn't say anything.

'I'll carry a miniature too,' said Smythe. 'In case the opportunity presents itself downstairs.'

'I can't see anyone being very happy if you're taking souvenir snaps in the drawing room.'

'You never know. Later on, when people are drunk the chance might arise.'

'You're just saying that to persuade me to turn up. But I'm telling you for the last time. I don't know what I'll do, but I won't take any part in that kind of perversion.' His eyes were adamantine.

Smythe eyed him speculatively. 'Anything goes these days. But no one's saying you have to join in. Lots of things can happen in those bedrooms. Annersley or Barker might only want you to watch. Some men get off from having an audience to cheer them on.'

The Assassin shook his head. 'I'm not even doing that.'

'So what will you do, once they get started?'

The Assassin shrugged. Smythe gave a sigh of frustration. 'Look. You're not going to save any children on Saturday. They're there for a reason and we can't stop it happening. Not in Devon. If something's going to change with the powers that be in London, it's going to require something special. I've said it to you a couple of times now, this whole story of East German spies might just be the thing to shake people into action.'

'But the photographs you take aren't going to be used for that.'

'If we're patient, the opportunity might come along,' replied Smythe.

'What if it doesn't? What if the circumstances change in some way?'

Smythe's face darkened. 'What do you mean? If society changes? The paedophiles get their own civil rights group and persuade wishy-washy middle-of-the-road types like Heath to lower the age of consent? So that all my work will have been for nothing?'

'I hadn't thought that far ahead,' said the Assassin, frowning. 'But there's no way I'm going to let myself be photographed inside one of those rooms with children in the background.'

'We'll think of something together. If it puts your mind at rest, I can always trim the negatives to crop out any real nastiness.'

The Assassin pursed his lips.

'Anyway,' continued Smythe casually. 'Maybe they'll want to get you upstairs on your own account, with no children present. I saw the way that Annersley was looking at you in the club.'

The Assassin rubbed his temples. 'Do you have a darkroom here in the house?' he asked by way of distraction, no easy answers presenting themselves to his dilemma. The one he'd known long before he left Brussels that he'd have to face at some point.

'Just through there.' Smythe pointed to the new door in the corner. 'In the other part of the basement.'

'Where do you store the negatives?'

Smythe gave a quick frown. 'Some here, some in a safe at my office.'

'So you have a personal collection of the choicest ones somewhere?'

Smythe said nothing. He gave the Assassin a disapproving look and went over to the drinks cabinet for a top up.

'Why can't we sit upstairs?' asked the Assassin. 'Is your wife at home?'

'No. But she might turn up at any moment.'

'What does she think of you being out at all hours of the night? And all the hours you spend down here?'

Smythe came back with the entire bottle of Bell's. 'She's a policeman's wife. She's come to expect it.' He refilled the Assassin's glass, perhaps in the hope of fortifying his resolve.

The Assassin changed the topic again. 'Who's the owner of this house in Devon? Will he be at the party?'

'He's a decaying aristocrat who's constantly short of cash. He lives virtually on his own these days, although there might be a couple of part-time servants. The house was requisitioned during the war by the Americans who left it in a bad state of disrepair, and the estate's never generated enough income to fix it up properly since. We're basically taking over the only usable parts of the building.'

The Assassin grunted. 'Not all aristocrats did badly out of the war.'

Smythe looked at him contemptuously. 'Whether they did badly or cashed in, none of them are anyone to be in awe of. I've seen enough of them naked.'

'How secluded is the house?' asked the Assassin.

'It's at the end of a steep valley leading down to the sea. The only access is by a narrow lane and the nearest property is at least a quarter of a mile away.'

'Sounds like it was carefully chosen.'

'In its heyday it must have been quite something. Times have changed. Nowadays, the Victorian morality only lasts as long as it takes to rip the corsets off the tarts.'

The Assassin topped up his own glass this time. 'You sound like you resent missing out.'

'I know the dangers of getting sucked in,' replied the policeman.

'What precisely do you do at these aristocratic parties, beyond running security?'

'I told you before. I try not to get sucked in. Or at least, not get sucked in too deeply. It isn't always easy, knowing when to stop. There's a lot of temptation.'

The Assassin took a sip of the whiskey. 'Do people ever ask you to take photographs of them in the bedrooms? I suppose some men want a record of their exploits to look at later?'

'Not at a party like this. There'll be too many guests for them to be comfortable with someone making home movies.'

'How many will be there?'

'Fifteen or so actual players, like we had at Jimmy's.'

'Why can't we do the same again? He's expecting us to host another party at Club Trèfle.'

'Aside from the fact that a concealed camera didn't work there last time, this is a chance to get some spicier shots. The more compromising they are, the better for you and your mission.'

'You're really not giving me much choice, are you?' said the Assassin. 'How do we play it on the night, then?' he asked, unwillingly coming back to the main topic of the meeting.

'Get Annersley to introduce you to Barker. Then go upstairs with them, together if you can.'

'Why together? Even though I said I wouldn't.'

'Harder for them to later deny what was going on.'

'But trickier to manage with two of them in the room.'

'You would need to play it by ear. The party will go on all night. But if you only take one upstairs, I can't guarantee the other won't drift off somewhere else. Perhaps into a different bedroom followed by an early exit.'

'And once inside the bedroom?'

'Say at first that you just want to watch. And then make sure you can't participate when it's your turn.'

The Assassin frowned.

'I'm not going to spell it out for you.'

Now the Assassin shook his head in disgust. 'Fucking hell. This is the worst job I've ever done. How close would I have to be to get into the photograph?'

'Stand on the far side of the bed from the connecting door. I'll take care of the rest.'

'And if they insist that I take part somehow?' asked the Assassin.

Smythe looked at him contemptuously. 'Then do it, if you really have to. Or if you want to. As I said, these children are corrupted already.'

The Assassin shook his head some more, his face darkening.

'What's the worst that can happen if I refuse? In the first couple of minutes before they get started properly, surely you'll get at least some photographs from your hiding place?'

'Yes, but if you don't even try to play along, your cover story will be blown. And we've still got to get to Grieves. Anyway, all of this is on you.'

'How do you mean?'

'Whatever it was you said to Annersley last time, he came away with the impression that you were happy to take your turn with a nice clean boy. Maybe you shouldn't have led him on.'

'So now it's my fault, somehow?' The Assassin shook his head. 'Some people must have second thoughts when it actually comes to doing it.'

Smythe shook his head. 'I'll say it again. You'll have to make at least some kind of effort in that bedroom. Trapping newcomers in an unspoken web of mutual blackmail is how these people operate.'

'Are you speaking for yourself there? Enmeshed in a web of blackmail?' asked the Assassin.

'That's what the punters think,' replied Smythe without missing a beat. 'They wouldn't come to these parties with me otherwise. In their minds, I'm just another corrupt policeman a hairbreadth away from exposure.'

'If I don't play along, might they think that I work for the police too?'

Smythe looked shrewdly at the Assassin, weighing something up.

'If they think that, then they'll get suspicious of me for letting you come. They'll want answers as to why I didn't warn them that someone else in the police was running an informer at their party. And then what happens to my access to their world? Let alone anything else they might do to me? Ronnie Kray held homosexual parties at his place in Clapton. But no one talked about them much outside of Cedra Court. Or at least, not to his face and not for long.'

'Why?'

'Because he was a fucking psychopath, that's why. He would go from reasonable to murderous in a flash. They even sent him to the looney bin for a time. I try to give the underworld types who occasionally make an appearance at these parties as few reasons as possible to cause trouble.'

The Assassin glanced away into the corner of the room. Smythe shook out a cigarette from his packet and lit up while he waited for the Assassin's next question.

'If the Marks are as casual about mutual blackmail as you say they are, how is a suggestion that they're linked to a known East German agent going to have an effect on them anyway?'

'Because as we've touched on before, with a communist spy in the picture, everything changes. It's no longer a matter of paying off someone in the Vice Squad, it becomes a question of national security.'

'Brierly told me in March that the procurer in the Profumo Affair had supposedly committed suicide.'

'Almost ten years later there's enough ongoing speculation about Stephen Ward to make people wary of crossing the intelligence services.'

'What if the Marks get suspicious of me at the party and go public with some of the information they have on Heath? Just to give us a warning?'

Smythe rattled the ice in his glass impatiently. 'You're worrying about things you can't control.' He sucked in a half-melted cube and crushed it with his teeth. 'You'll just have to work something out on the night and make sure that they don't suspect you.'

The Assassin got to his feet and walked over to the grimy window, drawing back one of the curtains for a moment. 'It's not you whose name will be contaminated forever,' he said.

He turned back to look at the internal door to the other part of the basement before staring at Smythe again. 'Would they respond to threats of physical violence? You mentioned how people were scared of the Krays.'

Smythe cocked his head to one side. 'You'd need to be very convincing. And you're neither Reggie nor Ronnie.'

The Assassin shrugged. 'What if I brought a gun to Devon? To threaten them with.'

Smythe caught his breath and frowned. 'Yes, but what if you ended up using it?'

'What would happen, theoretically speaking?'

Smythe gazed at the opposite wall. The unadorned white one, against which the Assassin was prepared to bet Smythe projected the movies and slides he'd rather no one else saw, going by the way he kept talking about 'spicy' shots.

'What are you getting at? It would end the threat from Annersley and Barker for sure. And word would leak out into the wider network.' Smythe shrugged slowly. 'It would kill off any other embryonic blackmail attempts against Heath as well.'

'You do realise that I'm asking theoretically? And that I explicitly told Kramer I wasn't going to do an assassination?'

Smythe nodded. 'Yes. But pull out a loaded gun and you need to be prepared for what happens if it goes off.'

'What would happen, practically, if it went off by accident?'

'You'd have one witness, the child. But anything they say can be dismissed as fantasy. Especially as they'll probably be sedated to some extent.'

The Assassin looked quizzically at Smythe.

'You know? Dilation.'

The Assassin grimaced. 'Jesus. You're making the floor shows in the clubs for specialist tastes just behind the Reeperbahn sound like wholesome family fun. Go on.'

Smythe looked at the ceiling for inspiration for a second. 'It would have to be portrayed as a mystery disappearance into thin air,' he said. 'Annersley lives alone in a swanky block of flats off the Grosvenor Road with a load of other hoi-polloi. He has a reputation for enthusiastic debauchery. No one would be surprised if a rumour was set running that a homosexual lover had gone too far during one of their kinky games and disposed of his body.'

'That's one of them.'

'Barker is unhappily married, often away on trade union business. Very partial to trips to the Eastern bloc countries and we all know what gets laid on for favoured foreign delegates there.'

'How would you explain both Marks disappearing on the same night?' asked the Assassin.

'No one at the party will be volunteering the information that they saw them together. And every day that passes will make remembering the faces of the people present more difficult.'

'How long would it be until they're missed?'

Smythe shrugged. 'How can I answer that question? At a guess, they'd most likely be reported missing on different days, though.'

'Wouldn't Barker's wife raise the alarm?'

'If he's gone away for the weekend to Devon, he'll have made some excuse to her. I imagine they have an unspoken agreement that she doesn't ask too many questions about his trips. In any event, she won't want the police to dig too deeply at first, in case they expose any serious wrongdoing on his part. He brings in his trade union salary after all.'

'And when she finds out that he's really gone?'

'It might be a relief to her. People in these situations put up with a lot. Often more than they should.'

'This is a very dangerous conversation. Just talking about these things can make them real,' said the Assassin.

'The questions are all coming from your side,' replied Smythe.

'Would you do it?' asked the Assassin. 'Kill them, if there was no other way to avoid being forced into taking part in abuse?'

'If it came to a choice of committing murder, I'd rather just stick my dick in the kid's backside and be done with it.'

The Assassin's brow furrowed. 'If there were bodies, how would you make them disappear?'

Smythe put his head on one side. 'That would be for me to know. I would need some insurance against you developing a conscience later on.'

'I suppose so.' The Assassin rubbed his hand over his face. 'Do things ever get seriously out of hand at these events? People get too rough with the entertainers? Or someone overdoses like at Voaden's farewell performance?'

Now Smythe gave a quick frown. 'It's not a vicarage tea party. I've had to disarm some of the tougher customers before letting them in. The gangster types I told you about earlier, who come hoping for a night of mischief and mayhem.'

'Do you have a gun?' the Assassin asked.

'Why? Fuck me Thomas, for someone who keeps saying how much they don't want to do anything illegal, you're making a lot of detailed enquiries about how to pull it off.' Smythe raised his eyebrows. 'Are you serious? Do you want me to arrange a gun for Devon?'

The Assassin was silent for a moment.

'What if all the action is downstairs in the drawing room?' he asked instead.

'How do you mean? Before they bring on the kids, the canapés and wine turn into an orgy because someone takes their clothes off and the rest want the same high from losing their inhibitions?'

'You tell me. You've been to these things. I haven't,' replied the Assassin.

'Whatever happens, to be sure of success you need to go with them upstairs. Take a tart with you as well, not just a kid. Then no one will ask you to take part in the worst of it.'

'People will be upstairs for the kids.'

'Stop being so German about it. There's no rules at these parties. One more thing, before you go up there, I'll need some kind of warning to get into position. When we're downstairs, I'll be watching you as much as I can, but I don't have eyes everywhere.'

'You and the dregs of British society.'

'We need to work together, Thomas. It's going to be tricky enough on the night without us fighting beforehand. Some of the tarts scrub up well. Screwing them isn't a hardship.'

The Assassin gave a shrug.

'Last thing,' said Smythe. 'Hire a reliable car. There's no point in us going to all this effort and then you don't show up because of a broken fan belt.'

'You mean hire a German car?'

'Don't be cheeky. Something quality, but not flashy - like a Rover 2000.'

'You're the expert.'

'And don't forget it on the night. No clever ideas or going off by yourself. Stick with me and I'll make sure you get through it with your conscience more or less intact.'

Chapter Nineteen

On the way down to Devon in the car he'd borrowed from Jimmy, the Assassin was deeply troubled. Smoking a spliff in Club Trèfle and riffing along to Annersley's innuendo at midnight was one thing, but Devon was quite a different matter. He knew it wasn't an exaggeration when he'd told Smythe that his name might be contaminated forever. He hadn't told Smythe in whose eyes though.

After leaving Smythe he'd thought long and hard about what he might be forced to do this weekend. No good answers came to him, even at two in the morning as he stood staring out of his bedroom window at the blank wall of the house opposite. His least-worst option was to walk away if things got really out of hand - to get out of England and deal with the consequences from Kramer and Brierly later.

The hours passed slowly on the single carriageway roads. As if to torment him further, in contrast to the pollution he expected to find at his destination after crossing into Devon the countryside only became more picturesque.

After South Molton he turned off the A-road and headed north for the coast. The villages became smaller and the roads ever narrower. The place he was heading for wasn't easy to find. He had to pull over a couple of times to consult his road atlas, before finally turning into the lane which led to the house, zig-zagging down the side of a tree-covered valley. Before he'd driven very far, the lane became a single track, and the wing mirrors of the Rover were brushing past hedgerows bejewelled with tiny pink and white flowers.

The house was set in a wide grassy clearing, almost at the end of the valley before it tumbled away down to the sea. It wasn't merely secluded as Smythe had described, it was an oasis of utter calm and tranquillity. In the warm evening sun, the golden stone of the main building glowed softly against the emerald of the sheep-cropped turf, and the cooing of doves provided a background chorus to delight all of the senses.

How fortunate was the person who owned this place thought the Assassin. No wonder he didn't want to give it up. How unfortunate were the children whose activities helped pay to keep him there.

The Assassin drove through the gate and round the back to park out of sight in the stable yard, just as he'd been told to by Smythe. Not that there'd be many casual passers-by at this time of day in this lonely, forgotten spot at the margins of the land and the sea.

Returning to the front of the house, he met Smythe just inside the open doorway. They acknowledged each other only perfunctorily. Smythe made a show of checking the Assassin's name off a list, then he took an envelope from him, discreetly riffling the tenners and one of the new twenty-pound notes that were tucked inside.

Through the open doors into the main drawing room the party was just getting started. People were serving their own drinks from well-stocked tables set out along one side of the high-ceilinged room, but otherwise everything seemed prim and proper so far. Even the prostitutes were dressed like the women at the Piccadilly club, as if they were simply out for a formal evening.

'After everyone's arrived and been fed and watered, the host will announce the start of fun,' said Smythe. 'You'll need to change into your toga at that point.'

'What do you mean, "toga"?'

'Like an ancient Roman - if they'd worn bedsheets. Get changed in one of the last two bedrooms so that your clothes will be there when you go back up with the Marks. Then you'll have the option of getting dressed and slipping away without being seen downstairs again.'

'I'd better go through,' said the Assassin without much enthusiasm.

The Assassin hadn't been in the drawing room long before he was spotted by Annersley from across the room. He came over to greet the Assassin with more bonhomie than he was comfortable with.

'So,' said Annersley slyly, a flute of champagne in his hand and an arm around a bottle blonde in a red sheath dress that was a size too small for her. 'You came after all? Ready for fun and some new experiences?'

'What do you mean "new experiences"?'

'Don't act all coy with me. Didn't Smythe tell you what to expect?'

'I'm sure I'll find out at length over the next few hours. How about you? I thought men were more your thing?' asked the Assassin with a half-nod at the prostitute's straining bustline.

'I've come here to forget my troubles and I'm open minded as to who with. Anyway, why should people limit themselves to half the menu, or even to a quarter of it?'

'Who else do you know here?'

'Not as many as I once did.'

He set down his champagne glass to take a cigar from the breast pocket of his jacket, his arm still held tightly around the woman's waist. The Assassin took out his own lighter and offered it to the Englishman, who bent his head to the flame.

'At least one of those things in your hands is no good for you,' said the Assassin. The tart gave him a sly look, as if daring him to find out which.

Annersley took a long drag on the cigar. He exhaled, wreathing them in aromatic smoke. 'I told you in Soho, seize life while you can.'

With an empty smile, the Assassin left Annersley to his current companion and drifted off to find Smythe. The policeman was still outside in the hall, watching the door with a grim expression.

'Has Barker arrived yet? asked the Assassin.

'Don't talk to me you bloody fool. No, he's not here yet and there's no guarantee he'll come. Get back in there, pansy.'

In the drawing room, the curtains had been drawn and someone had put on some light classical music. The Assassin thought it was a shame about the curtains - there was still plenty of light outside. He made his way through the growing numbers to the table of drinks. Annersley was no longer to be seen.

More tarts were arriving and filtering through the guests, more than one for each man he thought. A couple of them marked the informal start of proceedings by starting to dance together, but it was tame stuff, even less believable than in a kitsch cabaret bar in West Berlin.

In an attempt to raise the temperature, the tarts' dancing became more provocative, and they started kissing to ironic cheers from the men and some of the other women. Before long, a handful of the onlookers joined them in the middle of the floor and started moving too. The Assassin had seen enough. He tried the handle of the French doors and stepped outside onto the terrace.

The sun was just dipping below the western treeline and to the east, the surface of the sea was darkening as twilight approached. Below the terrace was an overgrown lawn which had been allowed to go to seed and right over by a low boundary wall, an ancient rusted grass roller. Annersley was sitting on its drum, leaning back against the upright handle, still smoking his cigar. The Assassin stepped down off the terrace and followed the track Annersley had made through the long grass to the wall.

As he approached, Annersley looked up at him. 'You're not a very convincing homosexual, are you Thomas?'

The Assassin opened and closed his mouth.

Annersley raised an eyebrow. 'Don't beat yourself up about it. You tried your best.'

'What are you saying?'

Annersley shook his head ironically. Amusement danced across his face. 'We can tell, you see. A lifetime lived in secret teaches you these things - how to pick up on the signals, how to dissimulate. How to detect the real thing.' He shook his head once more. 'Who sent you then?'

'Jimmy Malta. He thought you might be somebody.'

'I haven't done anything to upset Jimmy. I bet it was your sneaky, slimy friend who put you up to it, though.'

'I don't know what you're talking about. Which friend?'

Annersley sighed. 'Sit down over there where I can see you.' He pointed to the wall.

The Assassin did as he was told, but chose to sit facing out to sea, his back to Annersley. 'It's beautiful here. I never knew England could be so *bezaubernd*.'

'I'm not going to see it for much longer. The doctors have given me six months.'

The Assassin turned around. 'Is that what you were hinting at inside a few minutes ago? About seizing life?' There was a glimmer of compassion behind the mask the Assassin was wearing tonight.

'I'm sorry to hear that. But you shouldn't have threatened Heath,' he said, judging there was little to lose now.

Annersley gave a half-shrug. 'I'm sorry for that too. I said before, I think that deep down, at heart he may be one of us.'

'The rumour you started was that he likes children.'

Annersley slowly shook his head. 'I don't think he knows what he is. I don't know if it's ever truly been presented to him.'

'What do you mean?'

'If he'd gone to a school like Harrow, he might have found out.'

'I'm a foreigner. I don't understand what you're trying to say.'

'Redecorated Number Ten with white and silver patterned wallpaper and gold *moiré* curtains. Artistic after a fashion with his music. Enjoys the manly rough and tumble of life under sail and his mother is the only woman he ever loved. It all adds up to me.'

'But not to him. Is that what you're saying?'

Annersley didn't reply. He pulled on his cigar and gazed out across the Bristol Channel towards the Welsh shore, thirty kilometres away.

'If you think you know him so well,' said the Assassin, 'then tell me this. Has he been trying to prove something to himself his whole life?'

'What? That he's a real man?'

'Do you think he even knows enough about himself to care in that way? Doesn't he just want to believe that his life has significance? In his case, being known to history as the Prime Minister who took Britain into the EEC.'

'You keep coming back to that topic. Is that what this is really all about?' Annersley shook his head again. 'International politics and big business?'

'The budget of the Common Agricultural Policy is the same size as the American space programme. Even with your investments in Africa, you and I are just the little people. And right now you're in some bigger people's way.'

'You want to know Heath's real motivation? I gave you a clue that night at Jimmy's club as to how he became the darling of Conservative Party. Britain needs a role in the world commensurate with its importance.'

'Says who?'

'Says virtually the entire Conservative Party. It was Macmillan's grand idea, but when his time had passed, Heath took up the baton. A grammar school boy faithfully following the path set out by the Old Etonian, the type of grandee so beloved by the shires.'

'Heath has been a supporter of the EEC in his own right since at least nineteen fifty. He's not doing this, just because he resents his lowly background and wants to become one of the snobs. If he ever does anything, it's because he's chosen to. He's developed extreme stubbornness over the years, or so I've been told.'

'"His lowly background"? I'm not sure he sees it that way. He went to Oxford and sloughed off his old skin like a snake.'

'And afterwards, what was left of his true self? In later life it seems that his obsession with Europe has consumed his entire personality.'

'Why are you so concerned anyway? Surely Belgium wants the UK to join the EEC and provide a counterbalance to France and West Germany? Don't you?'

'After my service in the Legion, I'm now a French citizen. And France has its own reasons to support the UK's accession.'

'Obviously. Otherwise you wouldn't be here. To take care of the hares we set running.'

'Are you going back inside the house?' asked the Assassin.

'No, not tonight. I've changed my mind, if it's all the same to you. I'll finish my cigar shortly and push off.'

The Assassin pursed his lips.

'Whatever it is you wanted from me, you won't get it tonight,' said Annersley.

'What would it take to make you drop your threats against Heath?' the Assassin asked him back.

The sun was gone from the sky now, but in its red afterglow the Assassin could see that the skin on Annersley's face was loose and sagging.

'I'm not acting alone. All of us are free from harassment or none of us are.'

The Assassin gave a quick frown. 'Is that what the threats were? A form of insurance?'

'We did what we needed to do.'

'You realise that if you're not open to reason, then the next people who come along won't bother with a soft approach?'

Annersley curled his lip contemptuously. 'If you don't go back inside soon, you'll miss first go with the bunnies. I heard a rumour that there's candy floss tonight too.'

The Assassin glowered. Getting up off the wall, he walked over to the ancient grass roller, casting Annersley into deeper shadow. The Englishman looked up at him, faint amusement on his face again.

'You don't know what to do anymore, do you?' he said. 'Some tough guy you are, with your conscience. Well, I'm not going to make it easy for you. I can die tonight or in six months' time.'

The Assassin balled his fists in frustration. 'I could leave you with a loaded pistol.'

Annersley's expression turned into an outright sneer. The Assassin hesitated and went to sit back down on the wall again. 'Did you have any ulterior motive for attacking Heath?' he asked. 'You say you support the idea of Britain regaining its place in world politics, but maybe you're lying?'

'We wanted our threats to be taken seriously. But we didn't think we'd attract attention from Brussels, or wherever it is you're from.'

'Does the Conservative Party truly understand the nature of the EEC? It seems like they haven't been honest with the public about the end of your thousand years of independence.'

Annersley sighed. 'Who cares what the public think? And why do the plebs even need to understand these things anyway? As long as there's a Conservative government in power, we're joining the EEC whether Heath is in charge or not.'

'Why aren't the public more suspicious then? Where's that fierce British love of independence, of standing alone and feeling you're superior to everyone else? You bastards bombed my country to hell without a second thought.'

'I thought you said your country was either Belgium or France? Or do you come from further east? But I suppose the play-acting is almost over now.'

'I need to understand how we got here tonight. Before what happens next.'

'And you think I have the answer? Sometimes there's no great conspiracy. Maybe for Britain, it all started with Vicky's Albert and his desire that every European nation should embrace liberal values. Maybe it just grew from there, the sense that as Europe gradually became enlightened, we were destined to come together one day. Or maybe it really was triggered by the First World War.'

'It's the nineteen seventies. It's an age of global nuclear superpowers. You seem to be saying that Heath's still trying to solve the domestic issues of nineteen fourteen Europe.'

'It's one way to look at it.'

The Assassin took a deep breath. 'I spend every evening in a different London pub. From time to time I ask these same questions, trying to puzzle it all out. The vision you speak of might have been that of aristocratic Europe, but it's not that of the people I've met drinking.'

'Then I don't have your answer as to why Britain's leaders have almost pulled it off.'

The Assassin looked across the wilderness of the former lawn. The curtains in the French doors were drawn tight and no one was to be seen, either inside or out. He reached into his jacket pocket and pulled out the Makarov automatic he'd retrieved from Jimmy's safe, the same day he'd picked up the car.

'Over the wall.'

Annersley slowly got up. 'Fuck. I made it all the way through the war without a scratch.'

He sighed again as he stepped over the low stonework into the field beyond. The Assassin directed him towards a clump of gorse bushes which blocked the view from the house. The butterscotch scent of their bright yellow blossom was heavy on the air.

'*À genoux.* On your knees.'

Annersley shook his head as he sank down onto the grass. 'I'd have willingly knelt in front of you that night in Soho, without you needing to use a gun,' he said, half to the Assassin, half to himself.

The Assassin shifted the gun in his hand and hit Annersley on the side of the head with its butt. '*Ta gueule, connard.*'

Annersley touched a hand to his cheek where the blood had run down from his scalp. He held his hand in front of him, seemingly transfixed for the moment by the red smear on his fingers.

'Did you ever fuck children?' demanded the Assassin.

'No. Not me,' said Annersley, looking straight ahead of him. 'That was Voaden's thing. I just talked the talk. But then they pushed him to one side. Me?' he half-turned towards the Assassin, '*J'adore les hommes. Et les femmes.*'

The Assassin hit him again with the butt of the gun. 'Who were "they"? Smythe and Jimmy?'

Annersley bit back a cry and put up his hand back up to touch his head. 'No. It was Fryatt's idea to take over Voaden's contact book,' he said more urgently now.

The Assassin's eyes widened. Far overhead a swift piped out its call.

'Fryatt? Are you sure?'

'Yes, that was the slimy bastard who spoiled Voaden's fun.'

The Assassin was even more confused. He bored his eyes into a spot on the ground just above Annersley's crown, desperately hoping that the next course of action would somehow present itself.

He came to a resolution, moving to one side and raising the gun to Annersley's temple. 'You don't have any evidence that Heath fucks children, do you?' he asked Annersley in a final question.

'No one does. But he might well have done so in the past.'

'You were foolish to make up that story. But now it no longer matters.'

The Assassin ground the muzzle of the gun into Annersley's temple, forcing his head back round to face the front.

Annersley closed his eyes. The Assassin stood there for the longest second of his life, pressing the gun against the side of the other man's head.

The Englishman opened his eyes again and looked up. The Assassin was returning the pistol to his jacket.

'Go.'

The drawing room was warm with the fug of sweaty people when the Assassin returned. He shivered as he saw the crowd of revellers. It had been far too easy, holding the gun to Annersley's head. Balanced between death or life, the old sensations had started coursing through his veins again.

But there was no time to quiz Smythe on the things Annersley had said. As soon as they spotted one another, Smythe headed straight across the room, closely followed by a short man with a toothbrush moustache and broken red veins in his nose.

'Thomas, this is Barker,' he announced. 'Barker, this is the boy with the fetish that Annersley talked about.'

Barker gave the Assassin a keen look. 'Annersley said you liked feeling pain? Being stabbed, was it? Me, I like to inflict it.'

The Assassin suppressed his distaste with difficulty.

'Where is Annersley, by the way?' asked Smythe, looking suspiciously at the Assassin.

'He's not feeling well. He's gone home early.'

Smythe's eyes widened for a brief second, but the Assassin's expression was blank. The Assassin turned to Barker. 'What's your pleasure then? Whipping?'

Smythe raised an eyebrow. 'God. I definitely need to spend more time with the two of you.'

The Assassin eyed him coldly.

'Don't forget that we're here to have fun tonight, ladies,' said Barker. 'Ah, here we go.'

The two women who had been dancing together when the Assassin left for the terrace earlier now came back into the drawing room, hand in hand and stark naked. They lay down on the carpet in the middle of the floor and began to writhe against each other. People craned their heads to watch and encourage them to greater efforts.

'They're just to whet your appetite for upstairs,' said Barker. 'Our host has organised some real sweeties for later.'

The Assassin closed his eyes and gave himself a moment. 'Where does he find them?' he asked Barker.

'I believe he got these ones from a supplier in London. Which makes a pleasant change for once.'

'Who runs the trade? Englishmen? Or foreigners?' asked the Assassin.

'No one cares,' said Smythe. 'Don't be inquisitive. People will think you're a snitch.'

A tall man, thin almost to the point of emaciation, walked up to the drinks table. He tapped a glass with a metal swizzle stick and cried out in a reedy voice. 'Clothes off and togas on. Togas being optional, of course.'

People began to leave the room and return dressed as Romans, even as the floor show continued. The two women had been taking their time about things so far, but now they started to work themselves up into a frenzy that almost seemed real.

'Well?' said Barker, moistening his lips as the women eventually came to a conclusion. 'I'm going to slip into something more comfortable.' He left the room, but the Assassin couldn't see where he'd gone.

Smythe gave him a malicious grin. 'Go on Thomas, your turn now. Don't show too much leg.'

Unwillingly, the Assassin left and slowly climbed the main staircase. The corridor of bedrooms lay just off it, and at least one of the rooms was already in use going by the sounds coming from behind the closed door. He made his way to the end of the passage and found the last bedroom. It was empty and from the lack of discarded clothes, no one else seemed to have discovered it yet.

He pulled a sheet off the bed, trying to remember how the early changers had dressed. He thought back to pictures he'd seen of Romans in togas, racking his brains to work out how it should fold. But try as he might, either the sheet kept bunching up or wouldn't stay on at all.

There was a knock at the door and Smythe came in wearing an immaculately folded toga, one end draped over the left arm in the approved manner.

'What's keeping you? This is a farce. The entertainment is being paraded downstairs right now and you're nowhere to be seen.'

He quickly rearranged the folds of the Assassin's garment, then slapped his behind.

'What's this?' he asked incredulously. 'You're wearing underwear? For fuck's sake Thomas, if you're not going to go through with this then leave now.'

He looked coldly at the Assassin for a fleeting moment, then left him to make his own decision.

The Assassin caught up with Smythe before he reached the stairs. Together, they hurried back down and into the drawing room. The last of a group of similarly be-togaed children was joining a line up, having finished walking up and down the middle of the floor a couple of times for the delectation of the guests. It might have been a game to the adults, but the faces of almost all the children were blank. The Assassin guessed the false smiles on the others were because they'd been to these parties before.

'Go over to Barker and do your stuff.'

Barker was engrossed by the show, his hand continually straying to scratch his crotch. The Assassin stood next to him, watching him for a while. He mouthed a silent obscenity and gave Barker a nudge. 'Which one do you like?' he asked flatly.

'I'd happily take 'em all. All at once.'

The Assassin gave a sickly grimace. 'It's your fantasy. How about that one over there by the end?' He nodded to the smallest child, a boy of about eleven or twelve, he thought. The Assassin had the vague idea that if he and Barker took the boy instead of someone else, then he'd be able to limit the worst of the abuse.

'That other one has been giving me the eye.'

Barker licked his lips at the teenaged boy who had just walked past them with a cheeky toss of the end of his toga and a hitch of its hem to show a buttock.

The Assassin bit his lip and hardened his resolve. 'No, let's take the smallest one together. I've got a stash of blow upstairs.'

The Assassin glanced over at Smythe who gave him the very slightest nod in return.

By now some of the children were being led off by various men. A couple of the remaining guests went over to the sofa where the naked tarts from earlier were still lounging and started to perform with them. One or two of the other women looked like they were getting ready to join in too.

The Assassin strode over and took the smallest child by the hand, just before an older man with an aquiline nose reached him. The other man had obviously been to a Roman orgy before, because he was wearing a fancy-dress toga - one with a purple edge. Perhaps a theatre prop, thought the Assassin inconsequentially.

'He's under my protection,' he hissed at the thespian type.

Barker arrived and took the boy's other hand. The Assassin let go.

'I normally like watching for a bit first, to let the anticipation build,' said Barker. 'But we might as well take one while it's fresh and clean.'

As soon as they were out of the drawing room, Barker let go of the boy's hand and took him by the ear instead. He dragged him across the hallway and up the stairs accompanied by faint yelps from the child. He scolded the boy as they went.

'Naughty boy. Little bitch. Filthy thing. You've got something coming to you all right.'

The boy himself showed little reaction. Maybe he was used to the talk, or else he was drugged, just as Smythe had suggested. But regardless of any opiates there might be in the boy's system, the

Assassin himself felt like someone observing the scene from afar - an entirely different person, one who wasn't actually there. At the top of the stairs, he looked back and saw Smythe disappearing down the ground-floor corridor directly below them, heading for a second set of stairs somewhere, he hoped.

'I'm in the end room,' the Assassin said to Barker.

'Wait a moment. I need to fetch something.' Barker opened the door of the room they were just passing.

A boy was there with two men. He was wearing lipstick and a stoned look on his face. Barker reached under a chair by the door and pulled out a small, battered travelling case. The Assassin looked away from the scene in the room, feeling guilty for not stepping in there and then to punch the men between the eyes.

They walked further down the corridor. Two rooms along, the door was open and all three of them looked in to see a girl lying on the bed, clearly not wanting to be there. A naked man stood facing them, bald all over, with a tattooed snake bunched in a coil on his glistening chest.

The Assassin saw the look on the boy's face and his own expression became even grimmer. As they approached the end of the passageway, he struggled to catch his breath as the anger mounted inside him. He bit the inside of his lip again, and this time he tasted blood.

They reached the end room. From grabbing the boy's hand in the drawing room it had only taken two or three minutes to get here. No time to make a real decision on how to play things next.

Barker dragged the boy roughly into the bedroom and shoved him face-down on the bed. He hissed something at the child under his breath which the Assassin couldn't catch, but the boy wriggled up to the headboard and looked like he was trying to burrow his way underneath it.

'No you don't, you filthy thing,' said Barker. He placed the case on the bed, flipped it open, and took out two pairs of handcuffs and a length of steel chain.

He fastened one set of handcuffs on each of the boy's wrists, then threaded the chain through the cuffs and around the bedstead with one expert hand while he pressed the other into the small of the boy's back to keep him flat on his belly.

The Assassin's mind wandered from the waking nightmare unfolding in front of him. The thought came that the cuffs were adult-sized restraints and he wondered why the boy didn't simply slip them off and be free. Maybe he was already locked up inside his head, incapable of even imagining escape. Maybe it was the same for himself.

The sound of a slap on the boy's behind as the Mark finished his work snapped him back to the present. Barker grasped both of the child's ankles and dragged him down to the end of the bed, pulling the chain taut. His short toga rode up to expose a pair of thin buttocks and Barker gave them another, sharper slap. The bile rose in the Assassin's throat.

'Come here you little bitch. I'll fix you.' Barker rummaged inside his case. 'Let's see what we've got in my box of tricks.' He took out a wire contraption. 'This will open you up.'

Realisation dawned on the Assassin. He wasn't going to watch any more of this. He stared hard for a moment at Barker, then protested to him in an almost normal voice. 'That's too much.'

The other man wavered but held tightly on to the metal device. 'I know what I'm doing.'

'How many times have you done this then?' demanded the Assassin. 'Made them yell as you use that thing?' He forced himself to smile as he said it.

Barker's moustache twitched. 'Too many times to count,' he replied, smirking. 'I like to hear them squeal. It gets me going.'

Something broke inside the Assassin, something he didn't even know was there to break. His eyes glazed over and he seemed to depart briefly to another place. But all too soon, he came back to the bedroom with its stained mattress, and his false smile widened to a broad grin.

'Wait. I've got a toy he won't have seen before. I hope he doesn't shit himself when he sees it.'

'You hear that, Thing? We've got a new toy which we're going to play you with.' Barker slapped the boy's behind again, then stood back.

'Be quick, for fuck's sake.' He looked inquisitively at the Assassin, then shrugged off his toga to stand pale and naked on the carpet.

The Assassin gave a half-glance at Barker and put a conspiratorial finger to his lips for silence. He went over to where his clothes were hanging behind the door to the corridor and made sure it was shut tight.

From the inside of his jacket, he took out the stubby automatic he'd used earlier on Annersley, and from the side pocket, a silencer which he proceeded to screw onto its muzzle.

He raised the elongated barrel to his lips, just as he'd done with his finger a few seconds back and winked slowly. Then he placed the end of the silencer inside his mouth, closed his lips over it, and gave it a suggestive suck. He took it out and offered it to Barker to suck too.

'You utter pervert,' said Barker, trembling with excitement. He grasped the silencer hard with one hand, slipped it inside his own mouth and closed his eyes.

The Assassin's face froze, and a bitter coldness came into his eyes. With a sweep of his foot he chopped Barker's legs from under him and the small man collapsed slowly onto the discarded toga. For a moment or two he kept his grip on the silencer, pulling the Assassin with him, all the way down to the floor. In the next instant, the Assassin had placed a knee on Barker's chest and forced the silencer back inside the other man's mouth. There was a suppressed cough from the gun and the toga sheet stained red.

'Don't look. Stay face down,' said the Assassin to the boy, his heart racing.

There was a rattle from the connecting door to the adjoining room and Smythe burst out of his hiding place. He stared at the limp figure on the ground and then the Assassin.

'You actually did it, you crazy bastard,' he said hoarsely. But he sounded more excited than displeased.

The Assassin unscrewed the silencer and returned it to his jacket along with the Makarov. He looked at Smythe with a hostile expression.

The policeman prodded the boy lying on the bed in his back. 'Where did you come from today?'

'London, mister,' he said into the sheets, his voice muffled.

'Okay.' Smythe gripped the Assassin's forearm hard with one hand and pointed at the boy with the other. 'I'll get him dressed and you can take him back to London. He can tell you where to go once you're on the road.'

He poked the boy again. 'Where's your clothes? Do you remember which room?'

'I think so,' he replied.

'Right,' said Smythe, turning again to the Assassin. 'I'll go with our young friend and then we'll meet you back here. Make our grown-up friend comfortable through there.' He pointed to the connecting door.

'Right, little lad. Look at me and only at me. Our friend has been taken ill. Mr. Smith is going to take him into the next room and fetch a doctor.' With a wave of his hand he motioned the Assassin to hurry up.

The Assassin quickly wrapped Barker's body in the blood-stained toga. He shrugged off his own sheet and used that too, before dragging the body into the space between the rooms. He had to bend Barker's legs to get him to fit. When he was done, he looked up and saw a fancy SLR camera hanging by its strap from a nail in the panelling.

Once the Assassin had closed the connecting door, Smythe unlocked the boy's cuffs, pulled him up off the bed, and straightened his toga. 'Move you little bugger. And don't stare. You've seen plenty of men's todgers before.'

As soon as Smythe and the boy had left, the Assassin ducked back into the connecting passage. He quickly opened the back of the camera and took out the film. He shut the door on Barker's corpse and sat for a moment on the bed, pressing his hands on his knees to try to stop the trembling.

Shaking his head to clear it, he dressed, putting the roll of film inside his jacket next to the gun. What was done was done, but there was no need for anyone to have a record of it.

Chapter Twenty

There was a soft knock on the corridor door. The Assassin opened up to see the kid in a grubby T-shirt and jeans, his worn gym shoes laced up tight.

'Off you go now,' said Smythe. To the boy he said, 'Behave yourself, and do as Mr. Smith says.'

Behind a flush door in the end wall of the corridor there was a narrow staircase with uncarpeted treads, the one that the Assassin guessed Smythe had come up by. Presumably it had once been used by the small army of domestic servants the house must have had before the Great War.

The winding stairs led down to the ground floor, where they found themselves in another corridor with several doors leading off it. The Assassin chose one of these at random, taking the boy into a darkened room cluttered with furniture covered in dust sheets. Striding over to the full-length window, he struck the warped wooden frame with several blows of his fist, forcing it open. The unlikely pair stepped out onto grass wet with dew. In the distance, the crash of breakers could be heard on a lonely beach.

By the light of the moon and the fainter glow of the stars, the Assassin cautiously led the way around the side of the house to the stable yard. Since his arrival earlier that evening, the yard had filled up with the cars of other guests. He found Jimmy's Rover between a Ford Zephyr and a Range Rover - a style of vehicle he hadn't seen before. Clearly only the well-off could afford the entertainment laid on tonight.

Quietly unlocking the doors of his own car, he made the boy get into the front passenger seat, while he went to the boot and returned the Makarov to the black flight bag he'd concealed it in for the journey down to Devon.

Coming back round he got in next to the boy. 'It will look less suspicious if we sit together,' he told him.

'I know what to say to any policemen if we're stopped. I've been in cars with men before.'

They drove out of the entrance to the grounds and up the lane to its end. A few hundred metres down the public road, the Assassin stopped by a shut-up chapel he'd noticed on the way there and consulted his road atlas by the interior light.

When he was done, he glanced over at the boy. His face was pale and drawn - from the drugs as much as the tiredness, thought the Assassin. It was getting on for eleven o'clock.

He released the handbrake and got going again, driving slowly so as not to miss the turns. In the deep darkness of the countryside, perspective changed by night. He saw the boy shivering and switched on the cabin heater.

'How old are you?' he asked, in an attempt to stop the boy thinking about what had gone on in the bedroom.

'Eleven.'

'Where do you go to school?'

'In Streatham. When I get to go. Some days I have to miss class because it hurts too much.'

'Do you live in Streatham too?'

'Yes. With foster parents. Right now it's just me and my little sister. We have to call the man "uncle."'

'Did he send you here tonight?'

'He said I had to go or he'd send my sister instead. But then he always says that. Normally I go to the flats of men we meet at the arcade.'

'Which arcade?' asked the Assassin, his horror mounting again.

'The amusements at Piccadilly Circus. He gives me money to play the machines.'

'I think I know where that is.' The Assassin had criss-crossed London many times in the past weeks but had tended to avoid Soho. From back in March he vaguely remembered a devil's tail logo above a well-lit entrance when he'd gone by way of Piccadilly Circus to the toy shop on Regent Street.

'He sends you off on your own with other men?'

'No. He comes with me. Sometimes there's more than two of them.'

The Assassin shook his head and paused for a moment. 'Where is he tonight?'

'Dunno. I came with two other boys. Someone different drove us down in their car.'

'What was the story to the police if you'd been stopped?'

'We were from a children's home and were going on a camping trip to Devon - like the Famous Five.'

'Okay,' said the Assassin uncertainly. The name meant nothing to him.

'You're different,' said the boy. 'You're not one of them, are you?' The Assassin glanced at him.

'Do I really have to go back to Streatham?' asked the boy. 'Why can't I go to a proper children's home for a while? He makes me drink to forget.'

This was proving more complicated than the Assassin had first thought. In the heat of the moment he'd only intended to take the boy away from the party and dump him at one of the big London terminus stations to find his own way back to wherever he was staying.

'I don't know what you can do. Which street do you live on?'

'Ellison Road.'

The Assassin's trusty London A-Z was in the glove box, he never went out without it.

'Have you ever tried to run away?' he asked.

'I couldn't leave my little sister behind. She needs me.'

The boy was silent after this. The seconds stretched out and when the Assassin looked over next, he'd dropped off to sleep. At rest, the child appeared younger than his eleven years. His cheeks were plumper and his forehead smooth and unworried, almost baby-like. He wondered how old the boy's sister was.

The hours rolled on and the kilometres rolled by. He passed the ghostly form of Stonehenge on the left, half an hour before the brand-new motorway which Smythe had told him about back in March, opened only that Friday.

Maybe it was the interruption to his concentration which triggered it, but just then a wave of nausea washed over him. He pulled off the road onto the verge and got out of the car. The fresh air revived him for a second or two, but then came a renewed urgency and he reached out to grip the nearest fence post, leaning over the wire to be sick.

When the feeling had passed, he was left hollow inside. Once more he'd crossed that forbidden line, the one drawn in scarlet. But unlike that afternoon back in 'sixty-nine, these days he had even less excuse for not knowing right from wrong. The silent stones didn't care. They looked on impassively as they'd done for the past six thousand years, but the shadows behind them cast by the first quarter moon spoke to something even older.

After another thirty minutes they reached the motorway and arrived in London along with the grey dawn light. It wasn't until the car had slowed right down as they reached the outskirts that the boy woke up again.

He moaned about being hungry, but the Assassin was unwilling to be seen in his company, even at one of the anonymous early morning cafes he saw as they passed through Wimbledon. Eventually though, he couldn't ignore the child's distress any longer, especially when he complained about wanting to use the toilet.

Another cafe came up on the left and he stopped around the corner from it. Stuffing a handful of pound notes into the boy's hand, he told him to buy whatever he wanted for breakfast.

'You won't drive off and leave me, mister?' the child asked plaintively. 'I don't know the way home from here.'

The Assassin had been considering doing just that, reckoning that if the police were called to pick up a child, the boy and his sister might have a chance of being rescued from their foster parents. But whose story would the police believe? That of the adults, or the accusations of a child who'd apparently run away from home?

While the boy went to the cafe, the Assassin consulted the A-Z and realised he was only ten minutes or so from Streatham. For the second time in less than twelve hours a decision couldn't be put off for much longer.

The boy must have been hungry, because when he returned to the car, he had grease around his mouth. He handed the Assassin a paper bag containing a second bacon sandwich and all of the change, even the brown half-pence coins.

'You could have kept some of the money for yourself,' said the Assassin, wondering for a moment how well the boy got fed at home.

'I have to give my uncle all the tips I get from the men. Otherwise I get beaten.'

'Do you want me to take you back there?' Even as he asked the question, the Assassin felt ashamed for making the child decide.

'I've nowhere else to go,' he whispered. 'And if we got split up, who would look after my sister?'

The Assassin said nothing to this, but began to drive more slowly as he neared their destination. One thing was clear to him, with pressing certainty - right now, he was a fugitive from the law - even if the law didn't know it yet. Time wasn't on his side. Not only could he not go to the police with the boy and explain how he'd found him, if he wasn't to flee the country immediately, he'd have to find somewhere to hide for a few days until any hue and cry had died down.

Before he knew it, they were there, driving along a road several hundred metres long. The boy didn't give him a house number, but instead told the Assassin to park on the corner with Kempshott Road. He sat with his hands resting on the steering wheel, looking straight out in front of him.

Turning to the boy, he opened his mouth as if he was about to say something, but then closed it again.

The boy looked back at him.

'Don't worry about me mister. Or yourself. You're one of the better sorts, really. Thanks for my breakfast.'

'Stay a minute. Does your "uncle" do anything to your sister?'

'No. He's saving her for when she's older. She'll be worth a lot to the first man. I was told that by one of the men who does things to me.'

Before the Assassin could reply, the boy jumped out and started trotting up the road. The seconds passed and the distance between them increased.

The Assassin felt sick again. He put the car into gear and cruised along the road, keeping a few metres behind the boy. Coming to a resolution, he leant across the seats to roll down the window of the passenger side, intending to call out. But suddenly the boy darted down a side path between two houses and in a flash was lost to sight.

-

The Assassin drove to Soho and parked a couple of streets away from Club Trèfle. He went hunting for Jimmy Malta.

The club owner was sitting up at the bar, looking over a cash book when the Assassin walked up to him.

'Back already? You look like shit. Like you want to murder someone.'

The Assassin's face was thunderous.

'What's Smythe said to you?' he asked tightly.

'Nothing. How was your trip to the country?'

The Assassin closed his eyes for an instant. 'I need somewhere to lie low for a week or so.'

'Really?' The Corsican looked at him askance. 'It went that well?'

'Just tell me a place where I can go,' said the Assassin grimly.

From where he sat, Jimmy reached over behind the bar for a red telephone and placed it down on the counter in front of him. Taking a slim address book from inside his jacket, he consulted it briefly before dialling a number. The person at the other end took a while to answer. When they did, only Jimmy's side of the conversation was audible.

'It's Jimmy… Do you still have that room upstairs?… He'll pay you when he gets there… Yes, keep it on the QT… Okay, I'll tell him.'

Jimmy hung up and replaced the phone behind the bar. He scribbled a note and turned to the Assassin.

'There's a room you can have above a pub in Limehouse. Here, I've written down the address. If you don't need the Rover any longer, you can take the train from Fenchurch Street.'

'Whose place is it?'

'Some friends of mine. People I trust. Are you going to take the rest of your gear from my safe?'

'No, I need to leave it here. I've parked the car in Wardour Street.'

'Any new distinguishing dents or scratches I should know about?'

'No. When can I go to Limehouse?'

'It's not a hotel, they're not laundering the sheets and getting in fresh flowers from Covent Garden.'

The Assassin nodded to the row of bottles behind the bar. 'Can I have a couple?'

Jimmy looked at him coldly. 'Make sure you stay out of trouble. Or is it too late for that?'

'I'm going to be holed up for a few days - or at least until I know what's happening next. I need to pass the time somehow.'

Jimmy sighed, slipped off his stool and went round behind the bar. 'What do you want?'

'A bottle of scotch and one of vodka.'

'Pace yourself and don't draw attention.'

'I know how to look after myself.'

'No mistakes. For Kramer's sake as much as your own.'

Chapter Twenty-One

Limehouse, London - Sunday-Monday, 30th-31st May 1971

When the Assassin got to the pub he was shown to a room on the top floor with faded red flock wallpaper, a single light bulb connected to the switch by exposed wires, and old damp stains in the corner. There were two other bedrooms and a communal bathroom and kitchen. Family accommodation for when the pub had a live-in landlord, he supposed.

As soon as the current landlord had tramped back downstairs again, the Assassin poured half of each bottle of spirits down the kitchen sink. For the rest of the day he stayed out of sight in his room, catching up on his sleep from the night before. His facial scar was softening over time, but it was still too distinctive for comfort.

He only emerged once, late in the evening after dark. He left the pub by the back way, heading for the phone box on the corner, hoping to catch Kramer at his apartment in Brussels.

But the Assassin's luck was out and so was his boss, doubtless off enjoying dinner at one of the smart restaurants near the Royal Quarter, he thought sourly. Cursing, he gently closed the door of the kiosk, eyeing up the chip shop across the street but not willing to risk it.

He re-entered the pub by the way he'd come, past the saloon and its raucous patrons by the bar. The door was ajar, and through the crack he caught a glimpse of the revellers. A group of older women out for an evening without their husbands, talking at the tops of their voices. They were in a cheery mood tonight. Some of them even broke into a ditty as he walked past. But not him. He wouldn't be singing for a long time.

In lieu of food that evening he turned to tobacco. He lay on the narrow bed, staring up at the cracks in the ceiling, chain-smoking in bursts of three or four cigarettes at a time.

He thought about the things he'd done over the past two years, both in England and elsewhere. And about the things he hadn't done but should have. He thought about the road back to a semblance of normality, to a time and a place in the future where he could leave death and killing behind him. At four in the morning, trying to stay awake to put off the inevitable nightmares, he envied the rest of humanity. Almost all of it.

As he dozed, he kept replaying the final scene in the bedroom - from the moment he and Barker walked through the door, to the first bloom of crimson on the crumpled toga. The crimson stain which wouldn't stop spreading. But just as often, he replayed the image of the boy running down the path between the houses and swerving out of sight.

On top of his troubled conscience, he had professional woes to keep him from sleep too. The thing he'd been turning over in his mind all the way up from the West Country - Annersley's last minute disclosure that Fryatt had wanted to take over Voaden's network.

Someone had decided it was time for Voaden to retire after the party where the girl had died. But when the Assassin and Smythe had discussed it, the impression he'd got was that it was unnamed Establishment figures on the abuse scene who'd arranged it.

What if Fryatt wasn't merely Smythe's liaison at the Foreign Office? What if he'd taken part in Voaden's entertainments at some point? In that case, it would be perfectly understandable if he'd been one of those seeking Voaden's retirement because things had gone too far. But actually taking over his operation was quite a different matter. There had been no opportunity to quiz Smythe about it in Devon, as they'd soon had bigger problems to deal with.

Who was Fryatt, really? Words like "liaison" could imply any number of different meanings. Having worked for Kramer for two years, he found it all too easy to believe that Fryatt might also be linked to the British foreign intelligence service - perhaps in the informal way that his own boss was to France's SDECE.

Maybe one day someone senior at MI6 had come across a previously unknown surveillance operation in London. A deniable, semi-official one, whose operators were open to persuasion to switch allegiance from their current sponsors. Maybe MI6 had simply encouraged Fryatt to try his luck at recruiting them, knowing that their own involvement could be kept safely at arms-length.

How likely was it that MI6 would want to run their own entrapment operation inside the UK? Smythe had talked once before about foreign persons of interest visiting Britain these days, taking advantage of all that Swinging London had to offer by way of culture and entertainment. Even more happening than Philby's bohemian life in Beirut, before he exchanged it for the dubious charms of socialist Moscow.

But regardless of any possible official objectives for such an exercise, why couldn't MI6 have had some unofficial ones too? According to Smythe, their Secret Service rivals already funded 'Eve's' - the nightclub off Soho where the Bishop of Southwell had come to grief. What if that patronage also gave MI5 a hold over politicians who approved intelligence budgets?

Thirty years ago, Kramer had told Jimmy that the various agencies had been at war. Not only with the Axis powers, but with each other too, fighting for personnel and secret funds. The Assassin doubted that their battles had stopped in nineteen forty-five.

He started a fresh chain of cigarettes to a sudden burst of singing from the pavement below his window, almost instantly drowned out by a late-night train rattling across the bridge over the road nearby.

If Voaden had been pushed to one side by Fryatt, then where did Smythe fit into the picture? What did it even mean to take over someone's address book in the abuse underworld? Despite all the insults which Voaden and Smythe had traded at the monastery in Hampshire that day, they'd seemed to get on with each other well enough. If Fryatt really had taken over Voaden's network, surely it must have been done with Smythe's knowledge, or more likely, with his connivance.

But despite what Annersley had said about it being Fryatt initiating a takeover, maybe it had been the other way around? Maybe Smythe was frustrated in his role as an observer, watching other policemen pull in bribes from the very people he was spying on. Greedy for a bigger share of the profits, had he brought in Fryatt to help him get rid of the future Brother Clement?

But both possibilities begged a further important question - if Voaden had been forced to retire to Hampshire because a girl had died from a drugs overdose at a party, had the overdose been accidental or intentional?

And what was the real relationship of the three Marks to Fryatt and Smythe, and to each other? Why had they put themselves on Brierly's radar with their dangerous accusations against Heath in the first place? What was it that Annersley had said yesterday evening, sitting on the grass roller as he looked out to sea, bathed in the red glow of the evening sun? 'All of us are free from harassment or none of us are.'

Was it anything more complicated than that? They'd banded together for mutual protection because they'd worked out for themselves what had happened to Voaden? They'd seen how someone had caused a girl to die in order to get what they wanted.

But Barker wouldn't be telling any more tales and the Assassin had no easy way of getting hold of Annersley again either. That only left his upcoming meeting with Grieves, if that was even still on the cards after Devon.

Maybe there too lay yet another twist to their story. When Annersley said 'all of us', the Assassin had assumed the phrase included Grieves, but he only had Brierly and Smythe's word for it. He began to wonder why they'd specifically suggested a different approach for getting close to the businessman, in contrast to the casual social encounters with the first two Marks.

Was Annersley connected to a third person then? Someone who wasn't Grieves? But if that was the case, why had Grieves made it onto the list of targets for a smear? Perhaps Fryatt and Smythe were trying to deal with several problem characters all at the same time, whether they were connected with the Heath threats or not. Selene had wanted to reuse the Stasi smear idea for her own ends, why mightn't others want to do the same?

And lastly, what of Brierly and Selene? Thirty years ago Brierly had been in the wartime SOE. How close were his links to the British security services today? And if there was a link between Brierly and MI6 or MI5, why couldn't Selene be working alongside them too, right at the very heart of the Number Ten operation?

*

He came down into the empty saloon on Monday morning and read the papers before opening time, while the barmaid wiped and dusted around him. The radio news was on in the background, but there was no mention of any murders in the West Country. He supposed it would be a while before Barker's body was found, if Smythe had taken care of things properly.

The landlord knew better than to take an interest in the Assassin, only speaking to him once all morning to suggest that he go up to his room before opening time.

When he climbed back up the narrow, creaking stairs, he discovered a new occupant on the top floor, a young woman whom he met in the shared kitchen. She offered to make him tea and put the kettle on to boil.

'How long have you been here?' he asked, as she set out two chipped mugs and a sugar bowl on the draining board next to the rust-stained sink.

'Since this morning. I had to leave my last place in a hurry. When did you get here?'

'Yesterday.'

'People come and go from this pub all the time,' she said. 'I had a room up here once before, back at the start of last year. I mainly work nights.'

The Assassin opened the cupboard and found the teabags.

'Where are you from?' she asked.

The Assassin told himself this was why he should have stayed in his room until the evening. She got to work breaking up the hardened sugar in the bowl with a spoon, just as the kettle began whistling on the hob.

'Belgium.'

'I went to Bruges on a coach trip once.'

'I live in Brussels.'

'Heath wants to take us into Europe,' she informed him.

The Assassin reflected for a moment. 'I don't follow the English news much. I'm only over here for a couple of weeks.'

She poured the water into the mugs, using a spoon to carefully squeeze the single teabag, before she transferred it from one mug to the other.

'What do you do?' she asked.

The Assassin hesitated again. 'I came to see if I could get a job as a barman in the West End.'

'What? Like an Australian?'

'I guess.'

'And how's that going, chuck?' She passed him a mug and the sugar bowl. After a careful sniff, he added milk from a bottle he'd found in the fridge.

'I've served at a couple of parties. As a waiter,' he said.

'So the big city lights of London attracted you too?'

'Something like that,' he replied, keen to bring the conversation to a close. 'Thanks for the tea.'

The woman watched the Assassin from behind as he returned to his room and shut the door.

That evening the Assassin went out to eat in the anonymity of an American burger bar on Commercial Road.

When he left the restaurant, instead of going back to the pub, he turned left and kept walking, further and further away from Limehouse. Eventually in Shadwell he found what he was looking for - a badly lit side street with a phone box. The kiosk stood hard by a corrugated iron fence surrounding an old bomb site, going by the peeling wallpaper on the gable end of the last house.

It had been almost forty-eight hours since the shooting in Devon. As the Assassin stood in the booth, instead of laying out his change along the shelf holding the phone directories, he would happily have been taking the next available flight to Brussels and leaving the whole mess in England behind him. He dialled the international number for Kramer's apartment, unsure if it would work first time, or if he'd have to go through the operator instead.

After a long series of clicks, followed by several rings, Kramer picked up and the Assassin pressed the button at his end to connect the line.

'It's Thomas.'

'Well?' said Kramer snappily.

'I went with the policeman to the social event I told you about, in order to get photographed with the first and second Marks. It didn't go as planned.'

'Why does that sentence fill me with foreboding?'

The Assassin ignored Kramer's question. 'Before we get onto that,' he said, 'there's something else I need to tell you.'

'What?'

'I'm beginning to suspect that the threat to our ally from the Marks may have really been meant as a warning to the Foreign Office man and possibly the policeman. I think the Marks were buying themselves some insurance.'

'Insurance against what?'

'Being shunted off to a monastery because they'd outlived their usefulness.'

'What's prompted this revelation?' asked Kramer, trying to disentangle the strands of the Assassin's story.

'Because I've just come back from a party in Devon where the first Mark told me outright that the Foreign Office man wanted to take over the contact book of the ex-abuser I met in March - the monk from Hampshire. That same evening, he also hinted strongly that "all" of them, whatever that means, were working together for mutual protection.' The Assassin decided not to complicate things with his other theory about how the overdose of the girl at Voaden's last party might have been murder.

'Why do you say "all" in that way? All three of the Marks, surely?'

'He didn't give me any names or how many people. At the time I assumed he meant the three Marks, but now I can't be sure.'

'And are you certain that the first Mark was pointing his finger at the Foreign Office man? That's not an allegation to be made or even repeated lightly,' said Kramer solemnly.

'I'm trying to come up with an explanation that fits the facts.'

'Why did he tell you all this in the first place?'

The Assassin took a breath. 'Because I put a gun to his head. He thought it was his final confession.'

'How in the Devil's name did you end up in that situation?'

'I had no choice. I was desperate. He said he was leaving the party early before the policeman had the chance to photograph us together.'

'Threatening him with a gun was an overreaction, to say the least. You could have just met him another time.'

'I've been hanging around for weeks waiting for this opportunity. The policeman doesn't move quickly.'

'Was he there too, when you questioned the Mark?'

'No. None of the others were. The policeman knows nothing of what went on between us,' said the Assassin.

There was an awkward pause.

'But this isn't the end of the story, is it?' asked Kramer grimly. 'What did you do next? Don't tell me you pulled the trigger?'

'No. But later that evening the second Mark died.'

The Assassin heard an exclamation of deep disgust at the Brussels end.

'You can't help yourself, can you?' said Kramer coldly. 'You're addicted to killing.'

'You're the bloodthirsty one. You're the one who said to me last September that you might need me to go to England to kill some people.' The Assassin could sense Kramer's shrug from two hundred kilometres away.

'What can I do with you?' retorted his boss. 'Without self-control you're no use to anybody.'

Back in the grimy phone booth, the Assassin pursed his lips. 'You weren't there. You don't know what the second Mark was about to do in that bedroom.'

'Was the policeman present for that particular performance?'

'He saw everything that took place. But if anything, he seemed pleased about it. Surprised, but not unhappy. Which was strange, considering that he says he still wants to recover the blackmail material on the top man at some point.'

There was a long silence at the other end.

'Okay,' sighed Kramer. '*Dites-moi*. I need to know exactly what happened. Maybe, just maybe, there's a way out of this.'

'I was with the second Mark in a private room. The policeman was watching, concealed so that he could take pictures. But then the situation developed. The second Mark was going to take things too far with one of the children.'

Kramer exhaled. The sound came down the line as a harsh hiss.

'I told you last year. These people need to die. Someone has to give them what they deserve. But you said "no." So I went through a rigmarole for months with my wartime colleague, persuading him you were right. Eventually, we did manage to agree on an alternative plan. One which you've now completely compromised.'

'It is what it is.'

'Where are you speaking from?'

'I'm back in London, staying in a place that only Jimmy knows about. I'm going to call the policeman either tomorrow or Wednesday to see what happened after I left.'

'You left him there in Devon to take care of things?'

'That's what we agreed to do if the situation arose.'

Another hiss came down the line. '*Putain*. You actually discussed it beforehand? He's as crazy as you are.'

The Assassin was silent.

'And you're sure that the policeman doesn't know what the first Mark told you about the Foreign Office man?' asked Kramer.

'No. And I don't think he suspects either. I told you, he didn't seem that bothered about what happened to the second Mark. That's why I've been wondering if he and the Foreign Office man really were being pressured by the three Marks all along. It wouldn't surprise me. This is a filthy, deeply morally corrupt game.'

'I know all that.'

'I have to carry on for the time being as if the first Mark said nothing to me. What I've just told you is based on a couple of sentences spoken two days ago and the time I've spent since then thinking about them.'

'Give me a minute to think for myself.'

'When you're ready, call me back on this number,' said the Assassin. He gave Kramer the details and rang off.

After a minute, the phone rang shrilly. The Assassin picked up. '*Oui?*'

'Assuming that what you said is true, I need to probe my old colleague to see what he knows or suspects about those two jokers he has working with him.'

'Don't you agree there's a chance that he's in on this too? The Foreign Office man and his accomplice have a problem and they call up your old colleague to fix it for them? Is he implicated somehow along the way?'

'There's nothing untoward going on with him, unless I've badly misunderstood him over the years. Fixing things is precisely my ex-colleague's job,' said Kramer. 'To evaluate any threats to the top man which he gets to hear about and neutralise them. Maybe the Foreign Office man played on that.'

'However the threats against the top man came about,' said the Assassin, wanting to salvage at least something from the wreckage of his mission, 'the people behind them still need dealing with and the material recovered. I need to finish the job on the third Mark, if only to avoid raising the other pair's suspicions. We also need to find out where the third Mark himself fits into the picture.'

'Why? The smear plan is ruined. We can never use any of the photographs of you with the Marks now, even if someone managed to get one.'

'Don't you want to know what your old colleague and the Foreign Office man might really have been getting up to? What if they've been colluding against you?'

'Does it really matter at this point? It's almost time to lower the curtain on your English performance.'

'But don't you at least want to have something to hang over the British after they join? You may have outmanoeuvred them in the run up to accession but it's dangerous to assume they'll always remain on the back foot.'

Kramer said nothing for a few seconds. 'You really hate them, don't you, *mon gar*?'

'Who?'

'The English.'

The Assassin thought back to a night last year in a quayside pub on the River Liffey, where he'd explained at great length what had happened to Hamburg during the war. 'Operation Gomorrah' they'd called it.

'The ones at the party I've just been to, for sure,' said the Assassin. 'But it's hard to hate people collectively, once you start living amongst them.'

There was another pause at the Brussels end. 'Okay, then,' said Kramer. 'Offer to carry on for now. I'll probe my old colleague to see if he believes your story about the monk being pushed to one side.'

'Make sure he doesn't make the other pair suspicious about our willingness to finish the job.'

'Why? I've just told you to carry on. What are you planning now?'

'Let's not forget about the possibility of obtaining that additional material on the top guy which the girl talked about.'

'Thomas, *putain*. Don't get greedy. Know when it's time to quit.'

He broke his journey back to Limehouse with a visit to a different pub, where he sat with a Courage in the corner and a copy of the Evening News propped up in front of him to discourage the inquisitive.

But even here he couldn't escape Devon. He discovered that the Mary Whitehouse who Smythe had mentioned a couple of weeks ago was someone who ran a public pressure group, and that they were unhappy with the BBC for broadcasting excerpts from a new sex education movie to schools. They accused Guy Burgess' old employer of having a 'calculated amoral approach' to children and had complained about it to Margaret Thatcher, the education minister. But whatever the attitude of the BBC broadcasting executives, it couldn't be worse than the boy's experience at the hands of his foster parents.

He wondered what Kramer would say if he really did manage to get himself photographed in Heath's company. He wondered too, what use Selene would be able to make of it, if the whole story about an East German operative in Britain was now dead. Not that she knew it yet. When all was said and done, the Assassin had more confidence in her determination to make a success of her scheme, than in Kramer's willingness to actually do something with the magpie treasure he was offering to bring him.

When he got back to his own place, he could hear unmistakable sounds coming from the woman's room next to his. After a couple of minutes there was silence, a murmur of voices and the slam of her door. An hour later the noises started up again, and then again even later still, around two in the morning.

There was a final bang of her door and shortly afterwards the sound of the kettle coming on to boil in the kitchen. Maybe her work was done for the night.

Chapter Twenty-Two

The following day was Tuesday. The third day after Devon, the Assassin knew he was still in denial about the disaster that had taken place there, justified as it had seemed in the heat of the moment.

At this point in time, he still had no idea whether Smythe had managed to cover up what had happened in the room. For all the Assassin's talk about carrying on, about continuing to investigate Grieves, even about waiting to see what plan Selene came up with to compromise Heath, he knew it was only displacement activity to stop himself thinking about the party and its aftermath.

But the blue devils couldn't be kept at bay forever. He also knew he had to give himself something to do as a distraction, no matter how trivial it seemed. For want of any better idea, he decided to make the visit to the docks he'd suggested to Reynolds after Sunday lunch at the Pryce's, wondering just how much of the city was still a working port. He might as well take a look. After all, it felt like he'd been virtually everywhere else in London already.

Pryce had said that only the Millwall and Royal Docks were still in operation. Setting off, he first went south, hitting the Thames by the Limehouse Basin, where the Regent's Canal joined the river. The basin was surrounded by brick warehouses in various states of dilapidation with shuttered doors and rusting hoists. Walking east along Narrow Street, he crossed the canal lock over a lifting bridge. Next, after more industrial premises, came a cleared bombsite and then a series of modern low-rise council flats.

The whole place gave off an air of quiet decay. There had clearly been attempts to rebuild after the war, but it had neither been restored to what it was before, nor completely torn down for a fresh start. A ship's horn sounded from the river, and he caught sight of disembodied yellow masts and derricks gliding across the top of the roofs of the buildings by the Thames.

He pushed on east. From what he could see, the Millwall Docks were surrounded by a high brick wall, blocking any view of what was going on behind it. To get to the other working docks, the Royal Docks, he'd have to head inland again to East India Dock Road to get past Bow Creek. It hardly seemed worth it anymore. He reversed direction, retracing his steps all the way back down Narrow Street and then west to the docks which had already closed a couple of years ago - the London Docks and Saint Katherine's.

In order to keep on his general heading, he had to take long detours along silent quays and over lock gates which would never open for a ship again. At one point, he tried to take a short cut and got thoroughly lost in the jumble of derelict buildings between Wapping and Hermitage Basins. He paused for a smoke, sitting on an old bollard under the overhanging roof of an abandoned warehouse, his feet on a length of mouldering hemp rope which trailed down into the scummy water of the dock below.

He'd already taken a quick look at Saint Katherine's dock after a visit to the Tower back at the start of May and decided to give it a miss today. Eventually, he found his way north, up past the Highway and Cable Street towards Commercial Road and the land of the living, where the council house developers had been at work again. But the East End wasn't giving up without a fight and there were signs of resistance to the changes in the area. Peeling posters from last July were still to be seen on walls, exhorting the dockworkers to shun strike breakers. Fading echoes of the national dock strike which Selene had told him about in East Anglia, when Heath had been forced to have a state of emergency declared. And as he walked along, he came across signs of a different kind of social conscience too.

Outside a post-war church built in red brick, there was an advertisement for a talk to be given that evening by an Englishman who smuggled Bibles behind the Iron Curtain. The Assassin's socialist lecturer friend from the Free University in Brussels wouldn't have approved. The Soviet Union had spent over fifty years trying to eradicate the opium of the masses.

The *Pfarrhaus* stood next to the church. As he read the poster for a second time, a man came out with a bunch of keys in his hand. He gave the Assassin a searching look as he stood there by the railings.

Something about the man's expression pricked the Assassin's conscience, newly fragile since Devon. Embarrassed, he turned and retreated slowly down the street. The man closed the front gate behind him and went off in the other direction.

The Assassin pursed his lips, angry at himself for his nervousness. He retraced his steps and gave the advertisement a final glance. He'd vaguely heard stories about Bible smuggling into the Communist bloc before, but if he'd thought much about them at all, it was only to wonder what sort of person took those risks.

The notion began to form in his head of actually trying to find his way back there that evening to listen to what these people had to say. He'd have to appear properly in public at some point and he couldn't see the harm of going to an anonymous meeting. If nothing else, he'd learn what the churches in Britain thought of life in the socialist countries. And he knew he'd hear stories of people behind the Iron Curtain who were worse off than himself. *Schadenfreude*. It would certainly be one way to avoid the temptation of staying in his room and claiming depression to justify seeking comfort from the prostitute next door.

He had dinner at six, then made his way over to the church, slipping in unnoticed at the back, past the remnants of a sandwich supper laid out on trestle tables by the door. He'd had some experience of these kinds of events from before and arrived deliberately late to avoid any well-meaning members of the congregation who might accost a stranger with a welcome.

As he looked around, he saw an oddball collection of characters who'd come this evening, people of all shapes and sizes. Some wore smart clothes, perhaps their Sunday best. Some had come straight from work: the factory, the office, the shop.

He wondered what they in turn would think of him, dressed in his battered black leather jacket, worn over an open-necked formal shirt, and with stubble on his chin. As out of place as any of them he supposed. But he wasn't the only stranger there. An anarchist type with spiky hair and a CND peace logo printed on her canvas shoulder bag was sitting at the end of one of the rows of rickety chairs, looking from time to time like she was desperate to break into the flow of the speaker's talk.

The smuggler, or maybe only a representative of the missionary society, because the Assassin had missed the introductions, was telling his audience about the state of the church in Russia. He listed some of the restrictions faced by Christians who shared their faith: loss of employment, their place at college, and prison for persistent offenders. For Communist Party members who converted, the even bigger sacrifices they made by publicly opposing the Party's teaching - including the risk of their children being taken away and put into orphanages.

The anarchist called out 'Not true' at this, to disapproving looks from some of the audience. Whether she was disputing the idea of religious persecution under socialism or that a communist could become a Christian wasn't clear.

The speaker talked about the hunger for Bibles and how they were passed from person to person like precious relics, despite the risk people ran if caught reading one. He didn't say what would happen if a Westerner was discovered smuggling them into the USSR.

As the talk unfolded, the Assassin was transported by the stories of faith in the gulags, where some of the unluckier victims of Soviet justice had ended up. In his mind's eye he left east London and soared over labour camps dotted across the windswept tundra of Siberia - a better prison fence than anything men could devise. Rather them than him.

The speaker exhorted the audience by telling them how privileged they were. Privileged to live in a country which allowed free speech, where any of them could walk out into the street and share the Gospel without fear of arrest. As people living in freedom, they were under an obligation to help the underground church behind the Iron Curtain to share the Christian message of love. He told them with utter conviction that giving the Bible to Russia would shake the foundations of communism more surely than an atom bomb. This left the anarchist silently opening and closing her mouth, in conflict between the speaker's reactionary attack on dialectic materialism on the one hand, and his implied advocacy of nuclear disarmament on the other.

The man whom the Assassin had seen earlier that day, tonight's host, but surely also the minister of the church, came up to the front to close the proceedings. He reminded his audience of the warning he'd given at the start of the talk which the Assassin had missed - that although names had been changed for the protection of the secret believers, their stories shouldn't be repeated too widely.

'Although it's unlikely that anything will get back to the KGB from Limehouse tonight,' he said with a reassuring smile. 'As far as I know, there's no Soviet spies sitting here amongst us this evening.' The audience tittered, despite the gravity of the topic.

Life sounded a lot more repressive in Russia than the Assassin had understood to be the case. Even East Germany tolerated the Lutheran church to an extent. At their instigation, Berlin had gone as far as allowing conscientious objectors to carry out their compulsory military service in unarmed construction battalions. They were the only Warsaw Pact country to have done so.

After an appeal for funds, a final hymn and a prayer, the meeting was at a close. Assassin weighed up whether to slip away or to approach the speaker and satisfy his natural curiosity as to what sort of a person tweaked the Bear's tail. East Germany might begrudgingly tolerate their own Christians, but every German knew they weren't averse to jailing West German tourists on the flimsiest of excuses. There was even a going rate on the payments which East Germany extorted from the rival government in Bonn for the release of their citizens.

The decision was made on his behalf when the host buttonholed him, just as he was sidling away in the general direction of the exit. In another corner of the room, the gamine anarchist girl was arguing passionately with the speaker.

'I saw you earlier today outside the church,' said the man to the Assassin. 'What brought you back here tonight?'

What indeed, thought the Assassin. 'I had a free evening. I didn't know what Bible smugglers really got up to and the Soviet dissidents have always intrigued me.'

'Where's your accent from?' asked the man.

The Assassin's time spent in the pubs of London over the past month speaking with the locals had obviously done enough to disguise his origins on initial acquaintance.

'Where do you think I'm from?' he asked, momentarily pleased with himself for the first time in a few days.

'I'm not sure. Holland?'

'Close. I live in Belgium.' The Assassin gave the man the same story about seeking work in England that he'd given to the prostitute in the pub. 'And you?'

'I'm the minister here.'

'I guessed so.'

'Did you want to meet the speaker properly and hear some more stories?' asked the minister. 'I'm inviting him next door for a late supper.'

Without waiting for a reply, he led the Assassin over to the smuggler and the anarchist girl.

'This is Thomas, from Brussels in Belgium.'

The Assassin was rewarded with an enquiring look from the anarchist and a neutral one from the smuggler.

'Are you ready to go?' the minister asked the speaker. 'Would you both like to come round for a bite to eat?' he asked the two strangers.

The Assassin and the girl glanced at one another.

'Sure, why not?' said the Assassin, knowing he really shouldn't.

The minister led them out through the vestibule, acknowledging a deacon on the way past. The guy who was going to spend the next half hour sweeping up and stacking the chairs, guessed the Assassin.

They were taken next door to the *Pfarrhaus*, and sat down in the front room, the Assassin and the girl on the same sofa. He tried to angle himself so that he couldn't see her black woollen-clad legs, crossed in such a way that her short denim skirt rode up her thighs.

Now that the anarchist was face to face with the organisers of the talk, she seemed momentarily lost for words. Maybe she'd already put all her questions to them back in the church.

'How long have you been going behind the Iron Curtain,' the Assassin asked the speaker.

'I've done a couple of trips. We have to think carefully about who we send and how often they go, so that they don't get recognised by the authorities.'

The Assassin nodded silently in agreement. He could sense the girl next to him holding fire, perhaps trying to decide how she should come across in conversation. But he had no desire to flirt. He spoke to women and passed them over almost every night in the pub.

'Have you ever been to the East, Thomas?' the speaker asked the Assassin.

258

'I've never been to the USSR. Maybe one day.' He pursed his lips. 'How much money did you collect tonight? Enough for another trip?'

'We're not a wealthy congregation,' said the minister. 'But when we hear of our brothers and sisters in need, how can we refuse to help?'

'God honoured the widow's mite,' said the speaker. 'A gift that was insignificant by the world's standards,' he added, when he saw the blank looks coming from the sofa. 'But significant to the widow in the Gospel story. It was all she had.'

The Assassin thought about this for a moment and about the photograph with which Selene planned to take on the Establishment.

'Are you happy with sandwiches for supper?' asked the minister. 'Something for everyone that way.'

'*Merci.*'

The anarchist girl nodded as well.

'How did you end up here tonight?' the Assassin asked her, as the minister left the room to fetch the food.

The speaker looked shrewdly at the pair.

'I'm... I'm not sure. Someone at Queen Mary asked me to come along but they didn't turn up. I'm a politics student there.'

'You must have an opinion on the Soviet Union, then?' asked the speaker. It was all the invitation she needed to restart their earlier argument from before in the church.

The Assassin let them get on with it. While the pair of them duelled over philosophical points of principle, burning in the back of his mind was the thought that at a house somewhere in Streatham right now, a boy ought to be going to bed and getting his eight hours before school in the morning. But that he might not be.

The minister returned, his wife following along behind, pushing a trolley laden with plates of sandwiches and small cakes. It looked like they were the leftovers from the tables that had been set out at the back of the church when he arrived.

'Norman will pour,' she announced. 'I have to put our children to bed.'

'How old are your kids?' the Assassin asked the minister after she'd left.

'Six and nine.'

'Are they easy to manage? Children in general, that is?' From the corner of his eye he sensed the anarchist girl turn towards him.

The minister raised an eyebrow. 'They're a blessing, not a burden. How about you, Thomas?' he asked. 'Any family?'

'No.' The Assassin gave a faint mocking laugh. 'Maybe one day. How big is your congregation?' he asked, changing topic.

'Around fifty adults.'

The minister handed the Assassin a plate of sandwiches. 'Pass them round, Joyce has made plenty.'

The Assassin turned to the anarchist girl and felt the warm touch of her fingers under the plate as he handed it over.

'Do you have a church background, Thomas?' the speaker asked.

'My mother goes, and my aunt.'

The minister gave him another look as he handed out cups and saucers for tea.

'So not your thing then?' he asked.

'I never really got into the habit.' This was enough for the anarchist girl though. She launched into another speech about how she didn't see the point of the church either, which gradually became more and more hectoring in tone, as the speaker and occasionally the minister debated with her.

The Assassin sat out this one too, half-listening while the minister deftly defused the worst of her accusations as she perched on the edge of the sofa with a saucer balanced on one knee, taking the occasional bite from a ham sandwich.

Eventually, the conversation petered out. The Assassin glanced at the clock on the mantelpiece and made his excuses.

'If you'd like to come back again, you'd be most welcome Thomas,' said the minister. 'You too Diane,' he added, not forgetting the girl. 'Our normal midweek meeting is a Bible study on a Wednesday.'

The Assassin nodded along, admiring the minister's optimism when it came to trying to recruit the anarchist girl to his talks. With a final word of thanks, he stretched and got to his feet. She was quick to join him.

'Thank you for coming tonight,' said the speaker, but saying it mainly to the girl. 'I hoped you learned something about the persecuted church.'

The Assassin wasn't so sure. Come the revolution, his guess was that she'd be the first with the denunciations of Christians to the secret police.

'Which way are you going now?' he asked her, as they stood on the pavement outside the minister's house. 'Back to your college campus?'

'I'll catch the 277 bus from Burdett Road.'

They started walking together. 'What's your plans for tonight?' she asked.

'I'm heading home. What did you think?' he asked with a nod behind him towards the church building.

She shrugged. 'They're deluded. It's the nineteen seventies. No one believes in that nonsense anymore.'

'Some people in Russia do. They believe in it enough to go to prison.'

'Do you want to come back with me to Queen Mary?' she asked casually, but with an underlying edge of intent. 'We can go for a drink in the college bar. Beer is ten pence per pint.'

The moment passed.

'No, but thanks for the offer.'

They arrived at the bus shelter. 'I'm going this way.' He pointed back down the street they'd just come along. 'I'll wait with you until your bus comes.'

'I don't need your protection. Or your male condescension.'

The Assassin supposed that if being out on her own after dark in the East End was so dangerous, she wouldn't have stayed for supper. But he'd let the boy run back home from Ellison Road, and he wasn't going to have something else on his conscience.

'It's okay,' he said. 'I wanted a cigarette anyway.'

He offered her his pack, but she shook her head with a fierce gleam in her eye.

He sat and smoked a Silk Cut. He started another one, getting half-way through before her bus arrived. With a final, regretful look, she got on.

He continued sitting there under the lamplight, the blue smoke slowly curling upward. At that time of night there was only the occasional pedestrian. They glanced at him and hurried on by.

The Assassin made his way back to the lonely room at the top of the pub. The temperature in London had been hitting the twenties for the past few days, but his room still felt as damp and cold as it did at every other time.

He lay in the gloom for a long while, tracing the cracks across the ceiling, as he'd done every evening since arriving. Tonight, he relived the speaker's stories of the Russian Christians, which at least were more wholesome than what he'd been thinking about the night before.

Mechanically, he slowly worked his way through his last pack of cigarettes, as car headlights shining in through the thin curtains chased each other across the wall. After a while, the noises from next door started up again.

He stubbed out his final cigarette and rubbed the three-day growth on his chin. It was time to buy a change of clothes and a razor. Part of him wondered if looking rough was why he'd been invited to supper.

One Bible verse had stayed with him over the years, one about showing kindness and heaping fiery coals on an enemy's head. The apparent contradiction had always puzzled him.

The Assassin hadn't gone to the church tonight looking for hospitality, but the minister had gone out of his way to show it to the two strangers in their midst. As had Reynolds' girlfriend's family that Sunday, despite Reynolds' cynicism about her motives.

Here he was, running around England on Kramer's behalf, working to ensure the British political class got its way over joining the EEC, against the wishes of their voters. Denying the people the referendum which Pryce had talked about as they sat together that sunny Sunday afternoon in his garden in Bow. And here he was, back again in the East End, receiving kindness from ordinary folk to whom unkind things were being done.

Chapter Twenty-Three

Mid-morning the next day, after a diversion to Whitechapel to buy a pair of jeans, fresh shirts, and wash things, the Assassin presented himself at the *Pfarrhaus*. The minister's wife took him through to the study where her husband was already preparing his sermon for Sunday.

The Assassin wanted to know if there was someone in the congregation whom he could lodge with.

'Why do you ask?' said the minister with a hint of scepticism. 'You hardly know us.'

'I need to move for personal reasons.' Some of these included making sure Smythe couldn't trace him to where he was staying, but he couldn't very well explain that in present company. 'After last night, I had the idea of staying with a Christian person.'

The minister gave him the same searching look as the previous afternoon, when he'd caught the Assassin looking at the poster for the talk outside the church.

'Why's that important to you?'

'I need to be around different people to the ones I've been with in England so far,' said the Assassin clumsily.

'I confess that I didn't really expect to see you again after last night.'

'I have money. I can pay up front.'

'Let me think about it for a minute.' The minister twirled his pencil as he sat. He looked up through the open door where his wife was just passing with a basket full of laundry.

'There's a Caribbean lady who lives on her own, but who's had lodgers before. A Mrs. MacDonald. Would you like me to ask her?'

'Sure. Tell her I'll keep out of her way. I won't be any trouble.'

263

'I'll go and see her now,' said the minister, glancing at the clock on the wall. 'She'll be cleaning the church. We have a rota,' he added hurriedly, placing a bookmark in the page of his concordance.

After five minutes he returned.

'You can move in any day. This evening, if you want to. It will be six pounds per week, payment in advance. She can provide an evening meal as well, two pounds extra.'

It was half the price of staying with Reynolds, not that Kramer had ever cared about expenses when it came to the Assassin's assignments.

He went there just after six. The minister accompanied him and made the introductions, making sure that the Assassin handed over the first week's rent in advance.

It was hard for him to tell, but he thought his new landlady was somewhere in late middle age. She had a tiny spare room at the back of the first floor overlooking a narrow backyard with a washing line and an outhouse. Even the room at the pub was bigger, but he didn't have any baggage apart from the clothes he'd worn to Devon and his spare shirts, now bundled into his black flight bag on top of the Makarov.

Mrs. MacDonald went off to make tea for the three of them. They sat in a chilly front room with a crude painting of a tropical island hanging over the fireplace while the minister attempted to make small talk. He struggled, for his landlady didn't seem naturally loquacious, at least not in front of the Assassin. The arrangement would suit him just fine.

There was a further awkward five minutes of desultory remarks, during which the minister again invited him to the midweek meeting. Eventually, the Assassin judged enough time had passed for politeness' sake and asked for directions to the nearest working phone box.

As he opened the front door, he heard the conversation in the room behind him start to flow freely at last - minister and congregant, from opposite sides of the Atlantic. United in spirit too, with political prisoners in Russia whom they had never seen nor ever likely would. And all the while, Brierly was labouring to build his own perfect system of government on earth.

-

Before he called Smythe, he decided to check if Selene had heard anything since he'd got back from Devon. She answered after a couple of rings.

'Where have you got to? You didn't return to Reynolds' flat after your trip to the West Country. I needed to speak with you urgently.'

'I've found somewhere else to stay.'

'What happened at the party?' she asked.

'What do you mean "what happened"? What have you heard?'

'Smythe called me up to see if I knew where you'd been, and then I called Reynolds.'

'What did Smythe say to you?'

'Nothing. Nothing much. He didn't seem overly worried that you hadn't made it back to Earl's Court. He thought that you might be out of contact for a couple of days. He told me to call him if I heard from you.'

'I'll call him myself after we hang up.'

'How far away are you from central London? If you need to, you can always stay at my flat. There's no one else here at the moment.'

There was a pause. 'I have a spare bedroom even if there was.'

'My current landlady looks like she needs the money. I'll have to pick up my stuff from Reynolds' place at some point, though.'

'I needed to get hold of you, so we could talk about our other plan. The top man is going yachting this weekend. This is our chance.'

'Is "going yachting" a euphemism for a dirty weekend with a kid or two on board?'

There was silence at the other end for a couple of seconds.

'You've really been getting into the scene, haven't you? No, as far as I know, he's actually going yachting. How else would you describe the team selection races for the America's Cup in August? We need to get down there on Friday night to see if we can bump into him socially, either that evening or the following one.'

'Sorry.'

'You have a car?' she asked.

'Let me think it through one last time. Give me a moment.'

'Why, for God's sake? This may be our only chance. You said you wanted to help me stop these people. Are you seriously saying you're now having second thoughts?'

The Assassin closed his eyes, trying to come to a final decision. If nothing else, he had to do something to make up for leaving the boy in Streatham. 'Okay. Let's do it. How can it make things worse?' he said half to himself.

'Good. Don't let me down. How about a car?'

'I don't have one anymore. I can't easily get one either.'

'Really? I normally don't bother driving when I go down to the South Coast for a weekend.'

'Do you go sailing too, then? You never said.'

'Since I was a teenager. Meet me at Waterloo on Friday evening at ten to seven, under the main departure board. There's a Southampton train at five past which I usually take when I go day-running from the Hamble.'

'Okay.'

'Are you certain that you want to do this? Once you're committed, we have to go through with it.'

'More certain than you can know,' he said, his doubts banished for now. For even if Selene's plan to threaten the Tory grandees never came off, the Assassin was determined to make Heath pay some other way for what he'd been forced to do in Devon. Someone, somewhere had to.

-

The Assassin's next call was to Smythe, but this time his luck was out. He waited, then tried another couple of times before admitting defeat. But there was no way he was going over to Stockwell in person. Not before he'd seen the lie of the land from a safe distance first.

The Assassin returned to Mrs. MacDonald's house and knocked for admittance.

'Can I get a key?' he asked, as she opened the door with a cautious look up and down the street.

'Next door has one, if I'm not in.'

The minister must only have recently left, for she went into the front room to clear up the tea things.

'What are you doing in England?' she asked, giving all her attention to the dirty cups and saucers. From the door into the hallway, he watched her stacking them on the tray one by one.

'I told Reverend Thompson, I'm looking for work,' he said.

'You needed to get away from Belgium? You had some trouble at home?'

He stared back at her for a moment. He suspected she would prove to be more perceptive about his affairs than he cared for.

'Life always brings trouble of one kind or another,' he said.

'No temptation we suffer is beyond what we can bear. That's the promise of the Lord.'

He shook his head. 'I don't remember ever hearing that.'

'It's in Corinthians. How well do you know your Scriptures?'

'Not well,' he answered with a half-shrug. 'What does it say?'

'Look.' She picked up a well-thumbed Bible lying open on the sideboard to show him. As she flicked through the gossamer-thin pages he could see where sections had been painstakingly underlined in pencil.

She brought it over and he read the whole of the verse she pointed to. The second part of the text, about how God would *'with the temptation make a way to escape, that ye may be able to bear it,'* made as bold a claim as the first about not being tested to destruction.

'I've never seen an English Bible,' he said in reply. He wasn't ready for a deeper conversation which might reveal what he himself was escaping from right now.

'It's the version we used back home. The proper version.'

'Where was that?'

'Saint Kitts.'

'And when did you come here?'

'Fifteen years ago.'

'Will you ever go back?'

'My family is the church now.'

Chapter Twenty-Four

First thing on Thursday morning the Assassin tried Smythe from the phone box again, hoping to catch him before he left for the day to go wherever it was he went to meet his informers, or perhaps his clients.

'It's Thomas,' he announced, once the line connected.

'Well, you've taken your time to resurface. Playing hard to get for some reason, are you?' asked Smythe sarcastically.

At least he was in a half-joking mood this morning. 'Did you sort out the problem in Devon as you said you would?' asked the Assassin asked icily, declining to play along for now.

'It's been taken care of.'

'How?'

'I said I wasn't going to tell you. Where are you now?'

The Assassin had the sense that to give any answer at all would somehow be to commit himself to staying in England. Which in turn meant he'd be going after Heath with Selene, wherever that path might take him. He only had to replace the receiver and a lot of possibilities might never come to pass.

'I'm staying with a friend of a friend,' he said.

'Turned into a shrinking violet, have we? Afraid to show your face in public? As you damn well should be.'

'You didn't seem that conscience-stricken when I left you on Saturday night. What happened? You couldn't sort out the problem in the end?' asked the Assassin.

'Don't be cheeky. You're in no position to mock right now.'

'Okay. Should I be heading for the airport then?'

'Fuck you, Thomas. I said I wouldn't tell you. But if you must know, it was a stone clasped to his chest, the whole lot wrapped in chicken wire, and a boat trip out to the mouth of the bay at four in the morning.'

'You managed it on your own, did you? How did you get him down the stairs?'

'The owner of the house gave me a hand the following day.'

'So he was up there for almost twenty-four hours before his boat trip?'

'I know what I'm doing.'

It was an interesting admission given the circumstances, thought the Assassin to himself. 'How long do we have before his wife goes to the police?' he asked.

'People usually leave it a couple of days.'

The Assassin grunted. 'We're well past that point now.'

Outside the booth a milk float went by, the whine of its electric motor another thing about England that he was still getting used to.

'We need to meet,' said Smythe. 'I need to look you in the eye and know you're still onside for going after Grieves.'

'You still want to smear him?'

'Do you think he's agreed to stop with the blackmail threats against Heath?'

'You said there were no threats yet.'

'Devon changes things. We need to speed things up,' said Smythe.

'Why?'

'Because when Barker's disappearance eventually hits the press, if you're somehow linked to it, then the smear attempt will be ruined forever, and bang goes our chances of getting you and Grieves together.'

'But if it hits the press, at that point it's all over for our play with Grieves anyway.'

'Not if we can link you to him before that happens. If we can do that, then he'll also be linked to Barker's disappearance. And for him that would be even worse than the idea that he might have a Communist business partner.'

So far there had been no mention of the missing film from Smythe's camera.

'You wouldn't be making any of those links on behalf of the police at some point?' asked the Assassin in a cold voice, trying for a reaction. 'Perhaps after the three Marks are safely neutralised and you've recovered their blackmail material?'

'Do you think I want to be connected to Devon any more than you do?'

'I don't know how the British police work.'

'That much is obvious.'

'So, how are we going to speed things up?' asked the Assassin, moving on.

Smythe waited a second before replying. 'Stage an arrest of you and him. Make him think he's been caught with a spy.'

'That sounds like a convenient way to get me into custody, if you wanted to frame me for Devon.'

'What do you mean by "frame"? You're losing touch with reality. I've been working like a dog to cover things up for you since Sunday night, you ungrateful bastard.'

'Okay,' said the Assassin, unable to refute Smythe's logic. He paused for a second. 'Just how would we stage an arrest? I've already agreed to meet with him early next week at the City of London Club. But doesn't he need to be caught doing something illegal to make an arrest look convincing?'

'What do you suggest then, Mister top secret spy?'

'I'm just pretending at being that.'

'I suppose I'll have to think of something then,' said the policeman. 'Anyway, right from the start I've never liked this whole soft, indirect approach.'

'It's an impression you keep on giving me.'

'Let's finish this thing now then,' said Smythe. 'Go out with a bang. Don't you want to see the expression on Grieves' face when we slip on the gyves?'

'It would have to be the very last thing I do here. Then it's straight out of the country for me the same day.'

There was a pause again at the other end of the line, as if Smythe was weighing something up.

'You said that you spoke with Annersley before he left the party. What did he say to you?'

The Assassin thought quickly. 'He told me he suddenly didn't feel like it anymore that evening. Like he was weary of the whole thing. You and I saw him inside the drawing room, he appeared to be getting ready for a night's entertainment. But then I went outside for some air and there he was at the bottom of the garden, having a smoke and a think.'

'Did you say anything to frighten him off?' asked Smythe suspiciously.

'No. When he said he was leaving I was surprised as you were when I told you. You think he's getting sick of it all? Sick in the head, like Voaden?'

Smythe grunted. 'Voaden got himself into all kinds of trouble with powerful people. And even worse trouble than that. Dark, occult stuff. Things not meant for this world. By the end I think he was only too glad of the excuse to give it all up.'

'Voaden didn't know his limits.'

'You're one to speak,' said Smythe. 'You saw only a small taste of what these guys get up to and then you immediately flipped to become judge, jury and executioner. You're the unstable one who needs help.'

The Assassin didn't have an answer to that.

'Don't meet Grieves yet,' said Smythe. 'Come to my place this weekend instead and we'll discuss our next steps.'

'I can't. I have something on.'

'What's more important than this?'

'I have a social engagement away from London. I'm leaving on Friday. If I cancel it will look suspicious.'

'A "social engagement"? Pull the other one. You're taking a girl out of town for a dirty weekend, aren't you? Don't try to deny it.'

The Assassin gave a sharp tut.

'Is this what my life has come to?' asked Smythe. 'Putting everything on hold, just so you can get your leg over?'

'You're the one who told me to make the most of the summer in London.'

'Jesus. You Germans just love following orders, don't you? If you'd done less of that thirty years ago the world wouldn't be in the state it is today.'

The Assassin decided not to reply to this either.

'But I suppose getting your end away with a woman is better than the games Barker wanted you to play with the kiddies. Call me first thing Monday then. No later.'

-

The Assassin looked over his shoulder to make sure no one else was waiting to use the kiosk. In Brussels just about now, Kramer's secretary would be bringing him his morning coffee on the top floor of the Berlaymont. He fished for a fifty-pence piece and made his call to report.

'I spoke with the policeman. He claims he's taken care of everything in Devon.'

'Do you trust him?' replied Kramer.

'On this occasion, yes. He doesn't want to be implicated any more than I do. But I'm still not certain I didn't inadvertently do him and the Foreign Office man a favour by solving whatever problem they had with the second Mark.'

'What's his plans for you now?'

'He wants to hurry things up and stage a fake arrest of the third Mark. Catch him red-handed in my company doing something that would suggest treason.'

'I have a bad feeling about this,' said Kramer. 'What if he's got more than an arrest planned for the Mark. I don't trust any of them anymore.'

'What's changed since we last spoke three days ago? Have you come round to the suggestion by the first Mark that the Foreign Office man engineered the monk's retirement?'

'I don't know what to think. Not until I've spoken with my old colleague.'

'Well, that's where we are for now. Let's see exactly what the policeman proposes for the third Mark.'

'Anything else?'

'I spoke with the liaison girl about getting some new material on the top guy. We're going to give it a go this weekend.'

'*Putain*, Thomas. One thing at a time. And this really isn't the time just now.'

'There may not be another chance.'

'I don't need that kind of hold over the top man, and I never asked you to get it.'

'You didn't tell me not to do it when I first mentioned it.'

'We've been over this at length already. It's not a question of me giving you permission. It's a question of you using your common sense.'

'I take it you're not going to forbid me now, then?'

'This is your self-destructive streak coming out again. You think you've escaped any consequences from Devon, so now you have a new compulsion to put your head in the guillotine.'

'You think you know me that well?'

'I'm trying to help you recognise yourself for who you are. I can't be there every hour of the day making your decisions for you.'

'You've no idea what decisions I've had to make on my own in the past.'

'And how have they turned out for you so far?'

The Assassin was silent. Kramer spoke again in a calmer voice. 'Before we sent out new agents during the war, my colleague and I made sure they understood their own weaknesses. The ones that would end up getting them killed or worse. That's all I'm doing here.'

'I'm not an agent. I'm not really anything, to anyone, anywhere.'

'You've been useful to me at least, over the past couple of years,' said Kramer. 'I don't know what people in other places think about you.'

The Assassin shook his head at the London end of the line. 'I'll wait until I hear her plan for the attempt on the top man. Then I'll decide nearer the time.'

'You know I can't stop you from trying. But if you want to keep working for me, I need to know you'll do as I say when I decide on a course of action.'

'And what are you saying about this venture?'

'Think of your priorities. For God's sake don't get caught, not before the middle of June.'

'I know that only too well.'

'Maybe secretly you want to get caught?'

'No one wants that. Don't overthink it, Kramer.'

Chapter Twenty-Five

Waterloo Station, London - Friday-Sunday, 4-6th June 1971

As agreed, the Assassin met Selene at Waterloo on Friday evening at ten to seven under the departure board.

'What happened to your hand?' she asked over the clacking sound of the train indicators as they changed above their heads. The knuckles on both the Assassin hands were skinned and bruised.

He wondered how little he could get away with saying. 'Last night some guys were hanging around outside the place where I'm lodging. They were insulting my landlady, so I dealt with them.'

'You're a real German gorilla, aren't you?'

'I've been telling people recently that I'm Belgian. It seems to stick.'

She gave him a look, wondering how seriously he was taking it all.

'I've booked us into the hotel where he might stay if he decides to spend the night in Southampton. His club, the Royal Southern, is out of town on the River Hamble.'

'What's the plan? Surprise him at dinner?'

'Pretty much. If he's not at the hotel, I'll go down to the club and ask in the bar to find out what he's doing tomorrow evening. I'm hoping he'll skip down the coast to spend Saturday night away from Southampton. He might do that. He likes his privacy.'

'And what will we do?'

'We're going to follow him. I've borrowed a yacht belonging to a friend for the weekend. He keeps it in Port Hamble, the marina next door to Heath's club.'

The train was hot and crowded, packed with commuters homeward bound for the weekend. Selene and the Assassin found a spot in the vestibule where they were forced to stand close to one another. The Assassin couldn't tell if the warmth he felt was the ambient temperature of the carriage or the heat coming off her body. He reached across her shoulder to slide down the window behind them.

'How was your party the other night?' he asked.

'Different to the ones the other girls in Number Ten go to. I don't think any of them are into the spade scene.'

'What's that?'

'The suit in cards. Spades.'

He shook his head, still puzzled. She rolled her eyes.

'What colour are they?'

'Oh.' He rubbed his knuckles again.

'I don't care though. I'll go with anybody. I believe in the equal right of anyone to fuck anyone else. If they're adults and are willing, of course.'

A woman standing beside them deliberately turned away, showing them her back.

'You're obsessed with it,' he said to her quietly.

She bit her lip for a moment. She opened her mouth to say something then closed it again.

'And you're not?' she asked finally.

The Assassin looked out the window as Clapham Junction slid past.

After Woking they got a seat.

'Have you been down to sail out of Southampton often?' he asked.

'Yes, a few times. But strictly speaking, no one sails out of Southampton anymore. The Hamble is the closest place for yachts. My own club is on the Isle of Wight.'

'Where did you learn?'

'In the Girls Venture Corps.'

The Assassin frowned.

'It's like a youth club for the Army and the Air Force. Mainly for the latter,' she explained.

'Your father was in the military? I thought you said he was a farmer?'

'No. No-one in my close family was. It's a club run by volunteers to teach girls about aviation. To encourage them to choose the Air Force as a career later in life.'

'Because you don't have conscription?' The Assassin was confused and not a little dubious.

'Anyway. That's where I learned.'

Their train arrived at Southampton Central, and they walked the short distance to the Polygon Hotel. The Assassin idly wondered if the hotel had been named for the building's angular Art Deco frontage or if it had been the other way around.

'Why here?' he asked.

'Smartest hotel in Southampton. Heath only stays at the best places. Big ballroom, if you're into dancing.'

'I can't imagine we'll see him doing the foxtrot tonight,' snorted the Assassin.

They stood outside on the pavement, the evening sun still bright an hour before sunset. Selene looked up at the red-streaked clouds passing high in the sky above. 'Tomorrow is going to be a good day,' she said. 'Plenty of wind forecast.'

'You're the expert.'

'It's still a long shot that Ted will be here. After I check in, I'm heading off for a drink at the Royal Southern.' There was a glint in her eye as she said this.

'You want me to come along with you?'

She looked at him coolly.

'Oh. I see. You're hoping to meet someone there? What time do you want to have breakfast?'

'Let's say half six.'

'Do you normally get up that early?' he asked.

'You had your chance to find out.'

As Selene had expected, Heath wasn't staying at the Polygon. After she left in her taxi for the club, the Assassin waited in the hotel's bar until it closed at midnight on the off chance that he might show up.

But by the time it came to finish off his last whiskey and make his way up to the room, she still hadn't shown up either.

*

In the dining room the following morning, Selene was uncharacteristically quiet. When she returned to their table from the buffet with a plate of scrambled eggs and kipper, he avoided the topic of what she'd got up to the night before.

'What's our movements for today?' he asked instead.

'We're going to pick up my friend's yacht, then we'll shadow *Morning Cloud* as best we can - all day if necessary. From what I managed to overhear in the club yesterday evening, I think he really is going to spend tonight somewhere down the coast. We'll need to keep a close watch once he's out on the water. But not too close.'

They took a taxi from the front of the hotel to the village of Hamble-le-Rice where the Royal Southern had its clubhouse and where her friend kept his yacht at the marina just upstream.

As they neared the end of their journey, Selene broke the silence between them.

'Devilliers spent several months near here during the First World War,' she announced out of the blue.

'Training?'

'There used to be a big military hospital that way,' she said, with a nod of her head to the right. 'It's since been demolished. Devilliers took almost as long to recuperate from his wounds as Macmillan did.'

After another few minutes, the taxi pulled up at the marina. From the shore, it didn't look to be much more than a large car park with a boat repair shed at one end. The Assassin searched his pocket for the fare while the driver dumped their bags on the tarmac.

'The Royal Southern is just there,' she said pointing downstream. A couple of hundred metres away, the clubhouse where she'd been last night looked to be no more than a row of cottages.

Selene led the Assassin across the car park to the quayside, acknowledging the other early starters with a nod. She informed him that they were looking for a thirty-two-foot glass-fibre yacht called *Tatterdemalion*.

'A what?'

'A plastic-hulled boat about ten metres long.'

'They all look the same to me. How about that one?' He pointed to a vessel almost at the very end of the northern pontoon.

'Come on.'

They crossed the sloping bridge from the shore down onto the deck of the pontoon and made their way along it.

'You were right. Here we go.' She jumped aboard and motioned him to follow her.

'From now on I'm entirely in your hands,' he said with a faint grin.

'Have you ever been sailing?' she asked, as she unlocked the cabin door.

'I've only been to sea two times. And one of those was only a half-hour excursion from Kiel down to the mouth of the fjord and back.'

'They have a big yachting festival there,' she said.

'I know. Have you ever been?'

'Friends have. I might go myself one year. And your second time at sea?'

'A trip on a fishing boat to an island off the coast of Donegal.'

'What were you doing out there?' she asked.

'If I told you, you wouldn't believe me.' Not that the Assassin had any intention of telling her, or anyone else in England.

'Don't be so bloody mysterious.'

She went below with her bags and stuffed them into a locker. He followed her and did likewise. He looked around at the hand-finished wooden interior fittings and the clever space-saving table and bunk units.

'What does all of this cost Heath?' he asked. 'To run a yacht and crew and go to international races?'

'I doubt he sees much change from twenty thousand pounds a year, which is the figure that's been rumoured.'

The Assassin's lips moved silently as he worked this out.

'That's completely crazy. That's like buying three new Ferraris each year. No wonder Brierly was complaining when we met at Devilliers' house. And no wonder he was so evasive about who's really paying the bills.'

But it was only a fifth of what the Syndicate cleared each week in Soho, according to Jimmy Malta. British Prime Ministers were cheaply bought by comparison.

Selene shrugged.

'Does Heath know how much his hobby is costing his backers?' he asked.

'He doesn't care. His view is that they wouldn't pay for it unless they wanted to.'

'Does he ever stop to think about what they want from him in exchange? Or is he so selfish or arrogant that the idea of returning a favour would never cross his mind?'

'It's the way manipulation works,' she replied. 'The person being manipulated doesn't realise it's happening to them.'

She took him around the yacht, pointing out the ropes she wanted him to pull if she yelled 'Lee-Ho' or 'Gybe Ho'.

'Don't forget that on a boat, left is "port" and right is "starboard."'

'On a German boat, right is *"Steuerbord"* - "steering board" I guess.'

'Rudder. It must have been from a time when they shipped a steering oar out to starboard. Most people are right-handed.'

Close to the end of the pontoon, their yacht was unencumbered by other boats, and at that time of day the river traffic was still sparse. She decided to not bother with the engine and used the foresail alone to get underway and out into open water.

They headed across to the far side of the Hamble and then downstream, past the Royal Southern to where the river widened out, so she could put him through the basic manoeuvres.

'Watch for the swing of the boom and whatever happens, don't fall in.'

'"Boom" - *"Baum"*,' he said happily. '*"Baum"* is "tree" in German. *"Boom"* is also the Dutch word for tree.'

'We're here today to sail, not to play word games.'

He got the hang of it quickly enough and after a couple of experimental tacks she spilled her wind to stem the current a couple hundred metres from the Royal Southern's jetty.

They waited. It felt strange to the Assassin that he was actually going to see Heath in the flesh, after all these weeks and months of preparation. He wondered if the top man, as Kramer called him, would ever know just how much trouble people had gone to on his behalf.

The past couple of days the Assassin had gradually stopped thinking about Devon, but just now a coldness came over him again, a resentment at the position he'd been put in, all for the sake of protecting the Prime Minister's reputation.

He went below again and found some binoculars in the cabin. Propped up with his elbows on the coaming, he watched the comings and goings at the club for a while. The first crews of the day appeared, and he followed the figures of a group of yachtsmen clad in a variety of jerseys and windcheaters down the jetty. He looked more closely for a second, and then suddenly, without any warning, there was Heath himself emerging from behind them.

The Assassin lowered the glasses to see the Prime Minister with his own eyes as he walked along the pontoon to *Morning Cloud* followed by a couple of crew members. The heavy figure and grey side-parted hair unmistakable from a thousand photographs.

At a distance, Selene and the Assassin heard the barking of orders as Heath's crew went aboard and were told to jump to it. But it was only after a while, after what seemed like a lot longer than it had taken Selene to get going, that *Morning Cloud* finally slipped from the jetty.

Selene immediately let the head of *Tatterdemalion* swing round to point downstream and got underway first. Heath's boat followed them as they crossed the track of the Warsash ferry and approached the pier of the navigation school near the river's mouth. She wore a hat pulled down close over her ears and a windproof jacket with its collar turned up - not that the Assassin imagined Heath would take much notice of the downstairs staff at Number Ten.

Just as they left the river and joined Southampton Water, Selene gave a quick look back to see the set of *Morning Cloud's* sails and then up at her own masthead pennant to see the wind's direction. She steered a wide line as she turned to the south, only one of many yachts now heading to the Solent for the day. Heath started to follow her round, then trimmed his sails and cut the corner to overhaul them without so much as a curt acknowledgement that she'd given way.

They watched as he put distance between them, speeding down the Water towards the Solent. She nodded to herself as he turned west at Calshot Point and cruised up to a yellow spherical buoy with what looked to the Assassin like a 'X' symbol on top.

'He's taking part in the Poole Bar race today,' she informed the Assassin. 'And there's a couple of timed courses being run off Cowes tomorrow. I want to watch where he goes tonight, so we'll cruise between Gurnard Ledge and Lymington up by the Needles until they come back from Poole.'

He was clueless as to where they were going, but she seemed to know what she was talking about. Already in the short time they'd been out on the water, there was a steelier edge to her voice, even to her stance at the wheel. An energy infused her that he'd never seen before, all the more striking because she herself seemed unaware of it.

'I didn't tell you before,' she said, as they watched *Morning Cloud* swing round the first buoy. 'Along with Heath's arrogance and need for control, he's also developed a paranoia of the media over the years.'

'In what way?'

'It's a vicious circle. He reads a negative article about himself in the press and instead of going on the front foot to woo and charm the journalists he treats them with ever greater disdain. The feeling is reciprocated.'

'He just won an election last year, what does he care?'

'We have an expression - "plain sailing" - for when things are going well. But those times never last. At some point you need people in Fleet Street you can call in favours from.'

'You said "paranoia" just now. That's a lot stronger than professional dislike.'

She took a breath. 'He thinks the press take an active pleasure in misquoting and distorting what he says, or trying to entrap him in other ways. His suspicions came to a head last September when he decided to take personal control of the negotiations over the release of Leila Khaled, the Palestinian terrorist who had a go at hijacking an El Al flight and was arrested at Heathrow for her troubles.'

'When did his mistrust of others first start? During childhood?'

'I don't know, however it's my belief that the Khaled affair marked his final break with Fleet Street. The right-wing press didn't hold back from criticising how he'd caved into terrorism by exchanging her for British hostages being held in Jordan. And on his side, he didn't hold back either - he started cancelling press lunches and cutting off disfavoured journalists and editors.'

The Assassin pursed his lips. 'Then we'd better be careful about how we approach him tonight, if we get the chance.'

'We'd better. Also, I don't know who's with him in the boat, whether or not it's just his regular crew. The IRA threatened to kidnap his father last year and anarchists bombed the home of a cabinet minister this January just past. We should assume he's taking precautions.'

Selene shadowed Heath until the racers left the Solent, heading for the entrance to Poole harbour. After they had disappeared into the haze beyond the Needles, she cast to the north of the western Solent and then to the south, killing time as she tried to teach the Assassin the finer points of sailing. She even let him steer occasionally too, but only when they were running steadily before the wind and at a distance from other traffic.

When he was at the wheel, she kept one eye on the masthead pennant at all times, wary of the wind suddenly veering and causing them to gybe unintentionally. She helpfully informed him that a gybe was the opposite of a tack, leaving him not much clearer as to the meaning of either.

He didn't begrudge her his limited time on the wheel for he saw how happy she was skippering. He was quite content to be her crew and allow himself one day when someone else could make the decisions. When not needed to pull on ropes, he sat in the cockpit, his back against the cabin bulkhead turning over in his head the events since he'd landed at Northolt in March.

'Why did Smythe take me to see Voaden?' he suddenly asked, as he gazed at the fort at the end of Hurst Point. 'It doesn't make much sense.'

'Who's Voaden?'

'I told you about him the evening I came to your flat, but I didn't mention his name. Voaden was the real-life abuser that Smythe took me to meet at an Anglican monastery in Hampshire in March. It was preparation for meeting the Marks. They wanted me to learn how these people think and speak. I was told he was someone who used to be on the scene but was strongly encouraged to give it up and retreat from public life.'

'Why are you asking me about him now?'

'Do you know of him?'

'Not by that name,' she said.

'His time in society came to an end after a girl died of an overdose at one of his parties. She died in a corner and no one realised it for hours. They managed to keep it quiet from the gossip columnists, though.'

'That must have been the same party that Brierly told me about when he and Devilliers first briefed me. But he didn't say that the person who'd organised it was connected to our assignment.'

'Really? Brierly didn't give you a name?'

She shrugged. 'Even before he told me, I'd already heard about that party from one of the girls who works in our office. That's how widely the rumours had spread.'

'And he didn't mention at any point that he was planning for me to actually meet this person?'

She shook her head.

'I suppose he did say that this operation was compartmentalised,' said the Assassin.

'But I know something about that party which you might not. According to Brierly there was someone else there that night who's involved in our case.'

'Who?'

'Barker. That's when Brierly told me we had a good chance of success at warning these people off Heath - because they'd already started crossing the line in different ways.'

The Assassin gave her a quick frown as many possibilities ran through his head. He looked away to the Dorset shore, just visible on the western horizon.

'What sort of party was it?' he asked, turning back to her. 'I was told that the girl who died was the daughter of a judge but not how old she was.'

'It wasn't that kind of party.'

'Do you know anything else about Barker that Brierly might not have told me?' he asked.

She shrugged again. 'From what Brierly said, he was a supplier of children.'

'Did he say where they came from?'

'I believe Barker's a trustee of a council-run orphanage or perhaps it's a children's home. Somewhere up North. Brierly said that Smythe knew the exact details.'

The Assassin nodded to himself. Back in the drawing room in Devon, Barker had said that having a new procurer of children for the party made a pleasant change for once. Presumably a pleasant change for him not to have any additional responsibilities as a supplier that night. The last night of his life.

'Barker must know as many, if not more of the secrets of the participants on the abuse scene than anyone else. No wonder...' He had to consciously make himself use the present tense.

'No wonder what?'

'Nothing,' said the Assassin quickly. It was hardly a surprise that Smythe hadn't been overcome by grief at Barker's demise. Especially if

Smythe was connected in some way to the overdose at the fatal party which Barker had attended.

He stared out at a passing frigate a couple of hundred metres away, as it churned the water on its way to the naval base at Portsmouth. Faint streaks of orange rust ran down from its hawsehole and a large figure '8' was painted on the ship's grey funnel. The echoing rasp of an announcement came over the Tannoy as it passed. A ship crewed by men who fitted into a system, who knew where they were going and what they were doing when they got there. Unlike the Assassin.

'Do you think there's a more plausible reason for the three Marks' threats to Heath than the non-explanation I was given back in March?' he asked.

'What non-explanation was that?'

'Brierly said they might be tempted into blackmail at some undefined point in the future. Smythe suggested a couple of general reasons that could apply to any and everyone. But that was it.'

'And what are you thinking now?'

'Firstly, that the overdose might not have been an accident. Someone might have wanted to cause a scandal to force Voaden into retirement and take over the running of the business, as I suppose you might call it. But if Barker was at the fatal party, he might have seen who that person was. Maybe one of the other Marks was there that night too and they formed a pact for mutual protection?'

'You're sounding cagey about the potential names. Why? There's not that many in the frame.'

'Hear me out. I'm testing a theory.' He wondered again how close she was to Brierly professionally. Not as close as Kramer's former colleague might imagine, given the trick that they were planning to pull off on Heath this weekend.

'Okay. But what protection would the three Marks need? Even if, for the sake of argument, they saw someone slip the girl the drugs, the perpetrator wouldn't expect anyone at the party to go to police about it.'

'Not unless there was a personal connection. Maybe one of the Marks knew the girl's family?' suggested the Assassin.

'Is it a strong enough reason to threaten Heath?'

'Were Smythe or Fryatt at that party?' asked the Assassin instead.

'Not as far as I know,' she replied. 'Anyway, why would Fryatt have been there? He's the person who originally put Brierly and

Smythe together, but he's not a participant - at least not that I've been told.'

The Assassin grunted and turned to stare at the Needles for the tenth time, just in view past the end of Hurst Point.

The hours slid by, but the Assassin didn't notice. Out on the water time passed differently. As they sailed up and down West Solent, the waypoints became more familiar to him with each leg: Yarmouth, Newtown Creek, the Beaulieu River on the northern side. Eventually, the racers reappeared mid-afternoon, and Selene tracked them all the way to the finish line just outside Cowes. After a further short while, the yachts began to disperse, their racing done for today. Heath set a course to take him back up Southampton Water and they followed him at a discreet distance, all the way to the mouth of the Hamble and then on into the river.

'What's he doing?' asked the Assassin, as *Morning Cloud* headed for the jetty of the Royal Southern. 'Is he done for the day?'

'That's not what I heard last night. Maybe he's dropping off some of his crew.'

Selene looked on with pursed lips as she and the Assassin beat slowly up and down the river between Port Hamble and the lifeboat station, keeping *Morning Cloud* in view from a distance as Heath brought her alongside the club's pontoon.

Using the binoculars again, the Assassin watched as three of Heath's crewmen got off. One stayed onboard with Heath. The pair of them went around *Morning Cloud* checking the ropes, then hauled down the jib to change it for a smaller sail. At last they cast off, and Selene could finally breathe a sigh of relief. Unlike this morning, she let Heath get underway first before tracking him down the river and out into Southampton Water. Once *Morning Cloud* reached Calshot Point, this time the helmsman steered a course for the eastern Solent and Portsmouth. Heath's boat lent over into the wind and the chase was on.

Whatever passing friction there had been between Selene and the Assassin so far that weekend was now long forgotten. Her entire focus was on the performance of the yacht as she constantly flicked her eyes up to the sail to check its set. He watched her there, standing at the wheel with legs braced, caressing its spokes as she made tiny adjustments for wind and current, utterly at one with the boat. Like a pirate queen he thought. The wind caught her hair and it streamed straight out from under her woollen hat. A tattered flag of bronze.

'You were born to this,' he shouted back at her. 'You're a natural.'

She grinned.

'All thanks to the Venture Corps,' he said.

She was silent for a while, gazing beyond any horizon that the Assassin could see. A sadness slowly came into her eyes. 'Growing up, my parents never showed me much real affection,' she said in a voice scarcely audible above the sea breeze. 'Looking back, going to the Thursday drill nights and adventurous training with the other girls was the only time I was unconditionally happy.'

The Assassin wasn't sure what to say to this, so said nothing. Now a sourness came over her face, a bitter anger he hadn't thought it possible before for her to express.

'And then one day, even that was taken away from me,' she said in a harder voice. Her eyes glittered in the sunlight.

She glanced up at the sail again. 'Take out the bottom row of reefs.'

The Assassin turned to his task.

They were both quiet for a long time after that. He gave her an occasional glance when he thought she wasn't looking. Eventually the sourness seemed to fade, but only gradually.

They beat against the wind across the choppy brown waters of the Spit Sand in the approaches to Portsmouth harbour. Heath had taken the lighthouse rising above Southsea Castle as his headmark and Selene did the same, another fort on an artificial island lying off to starboard as they approached the point. Once they reached the old castle, they turned the corner and paralleled a long shingle beach for four or five kilometres until they met the channel which marked the western edge of Hayling Island.

The two boats tacked eastwards against the wind for another forty-five minutes. *Morning Cloud* with her deeper keel lost less leeway and drew steadily ahead. Just as a darker frown started playing on Selene's face, the Assassin saw the start of the opening of a second channel marking the far side of Hayling. Heath tacked around a buoy and she gave a yell of triumph.

'I knew it. He's heading for Chichester. He's probably going to the marina. Maybe Itchenor. Let's see.'

They followed Heath in and watched him thread his way north, before taking the right-hand fork in the channel to leave first Hayling, then Thorney Island and its airfield to port. A bright yellow helicopter with a red-white-and-blue roundel on the side of its fuselage took off as they passed.

'What kind of aircraft is that?' he asked her.

'RAF Search and Rescue.'

Another muddy channel with banks of grey ooze opened up to port, and *Morning Cloud* swung left to enter it. Selene gave a frown.

'Bosham?' she asked herself out loud.

She dropped back as Heath set a course for Bosham Quay.

'I hope he's not going to stay at a house owned by one of his chums.'

'Maybe there's a pub in the village with rooms?' suggested the Assassin.

She tried to keep the disappointment from her face. 'Then cross your fingers there's somewhere like that or else we've lost him for this weekend.'

As they sailed north, the other river traffic suddenly dropped away.

'Boats of our size can't go alongside at Bosham. Even Bosham Channel is pushing it.'

'What does that mean?'

'We're rowing ashore. I think there's an inflatable dinghy in the forward locker. But we'll hardly be inconspicuous.'

Heath didn't steer up the channel for long. After another five minutes they saw *Morning Cloud* stemming a buoy and Heath's companion hooking on. The Assassin started to look around for a free buoy for themselves, but Selene shook her head.

'It's a long pull to the village from here. We'll carry on for a while. We can moor closer in than he can.'

They watched as a boat put off from Bosham, heading in their direction.

'Let's get the sails down. We'll follow them in using the engine,' she said, glancing at the chart before counting something off on her fingers. Tide heights and times, he supposed.

The boat from Bosham reached *Morning Cloud* and her crew clambered in. With a sudden roar from the ferryman's outboard, he headed back to the quay.

'Let's go,' she said.

She steered the other boat's wake until she judged she'd gone as far as they could. They found a free buoy surrounded by cabin cruisers and sailing dinghies, all smaller than them.

'When are we going after Heath?' asked the Assassin, as the ferryman's boat neared the far shore.

'Patience,' she replied. 'We can't catch him on the water, even if we could do it without drawing attention to ourselves. Get out the binoculars again and let's see where he goes.'

They waited until Heath finally reached the shore, then watched as he and his companion walked along the quay to a large pub and disappeared inside.

'So far, so good,' she said.

The Assassin found the inflatable and a foot pump where she said they would be. Unrolling the deflated hull in the cockpit, he started pumping while Selene assembled the oars.

'We'll need to travel light,' she said, going below to repack her bags.

Just as he finished fitting the dinghy's seats, she returned with a canvas grip.

'Over the side with it and take a turn of the painter around that cleat. Tie it up,' she said, when she saw his puzzled expression.

He did as instructed. She threw in the oars, then stepped over the side into the little boat.

'Okay, untie the rope, keep it turned round the cleat, then throw the free end down to me.'

He followed these instructions too, then stepped gingerly into the dinghy himself.

'Can you row?' she asked. 'Never mind, I'll do it.'

'No. I will,' he reached over and grabbed the shafts of the oars, taking them from her.

She pouted at him. 'Don't catch any crabs.'

He shook his head and started dipping the oars in silence.

The pub had four small guest rooms and served food too. Only a twin bedroom with an ensuite was still available. They registered under the names of 'Mr. and Mrs. T. Smith' and the Assassin paid from a roll of ten-pound notes.

'What time is supper?' Selene asked the landlady.

'Six-thirty,' she replied. 'We've already started serving. Are you dining here tonight?'

'Is there anywhere else nearby?'

'Nowhere closer than a fifteen-minute walk.'

The Assassin nodded. 'It'll do.'

Once in their room, the Assassin asked Selene when she thought they should make their next move.

'Let's leave it fifteen minutes before going down to the bar. From what I saw on the way past, you can see the dining room from there.'

'This place seems a little downmarket for Heath. I would have expected the woman at reception to gossip about him staying here this evening.'

'Maybe he's been before and they know not to.'

She went to use the shower over the tub in the ensuite, emerging from the bathroom in a linen button-through dress she'd brought from the boat. The Assassin made do with running a comb through his hair.

Arm in arm they descended the stairs together. As they reached the turn, they saw that Heath was already downstairs in a room off to one side of the main bar, his back to the public area. The Assassin wondered if it was what the Irishmen he'd been with last year would have called a 'snug.'

'Here we go,' she said, linking her arm tighter into his.

'Wait,' he said, pausing for a moment on a step. 'When you introduce me, I'm an Italian. Thomas Di Luca.'

She turned to look at him, first in puzzlement, then with scepticism. 'Which part of Italy are you meant to be from?'

'Tell them Alto Adige. South Tyrol. And call me Tommaso, Tommaso Di Luca. Got it?'

'That's a different surname to what you wrote in the register.'

'It can't be helped now.'

They walked up to the bar and he ordered drinks. She turned to look around and gave a nod of acknowledgment to Heath through the open door of the anteroom where he was sitting at a table. He frowned back at her, a grim set to his jowls. Undaunted, she approached him. Heath's companion stopped talking and turned to look, one hand grasping the table's edge.

'Mr. Heath?' she said.

'Who are you? Oh, the girl from downstairs.'

'Miss Warrington-Williams, I work for Jane Parsons.'

'What are you doing here?'

'My boyfriend Tommaso and I were sailing in the Solent today.' She turned round to wave the Assassin over, but he'd already come up behind her. 'Tommaso, Mr. Heath.'

The Assassin dipped his head. 'Tommaso di Luca.'

Heath gave him a peremptory nod in return. 'What do you do?' he asked in a strained accent which managed to sound both fruity and gravelly at the same time.

'*Lavoro per...* I work for the Commission in Brussels.'

'Indeed. Which area?' asked Heath, almost despite himself it seemed to the Assassin.

'Agricultural policy. Calculating subsidy allocations.'

'Important work, I'm sure,' said Heath loftily. He nodded at Selene to speak.

'We met through mutual friends,' she explained.

'Indeed. You're not thinking of leaving us for Brussels, are you?' he asked, his piercing blue-grey eyes narrowing slightly.

She gave a nervous laugh. 'Tommaso is a great admirer of yours.'

'*Per favore, Signor Heath*, a photo?'

The Assassin took a compact camera from his side pocket and handed it to Selene. He stepped around the table, unsure whether to hunker down to Heath's level where he sat. The decision was made for him when Heath and his companion both got to their feet at the same time.

There was a look of distaste on Heath's face. The Assassin had to force himself to go up to stand next to the Conservative Party leader. He flicked a wary glance at Heath's companion whose knuckles were whitening as he gripped the back of his chair.

'If you don't mind, sir,' said Selene.

'I do mind,' he snapped. Then he relented. 'Make it quick.'

An open smile spread across the Assassin's face. '*Mille grazie, Presidente Heath.*'

Selene pressed the shutter button and quickly wound on the film. She raised it a second time. The impatient look on Heath's face hardened.

The Assassin smiled, seemingly oblivious. 'Thank-you, *Presidente.* Europe salutes your endeavour of peace.' He turned and gave Heath a kiss on his leathery cheek, roughened by a day on the water. At the same time, Selene released the shutter and an instant later Heath jerked away, horrified.

The Assassin clasped his hand to his chest in thanks and gave a half bow. Heath's companion bristled.

'*Ancora, mille grazie,*' said the Assassin, his face all happy innocence.

'*Grazie Signorina Warrington-Williams,*' he said, dipping his head to Selene now.

'That's enough,' said Heath's companion suspiciously. 'Ted's had a long day.'

'I'm so sorry,' she said. 'Tommaso got a little overwhelmed by the occasion. He's Italian,' she added by way of explanation.

Heath waved his hand in dismissal and sat back down again to his drink. His companion did the same and suddenly it was as if Selene and the Assassin had never been there.

They immediately went back upstairs to their room. By silent, mutual consent neither of them wanted to try the restaurant and risk being buttonholed by Heath's suspicious companion. The thought even occurred to the Assassin of rowing back to the boat there and then to spend the night afloat. As she climbed the stairs, Selene kept a tight hold on the camera, determined not to let go of her prize.

'We won't know if we even got anything until it's been developed,' she said, placing the camera on the table between the two beds. There was a note of exhaustion in her voice.

'We've had a stroke of luck,' said the Assassin encouragingly.

'More than a stroke. It's a bloody miracle,' she said more fiercely now. At whom her defiance was directed at, the Assassin wasn't sure. She sank down to sit on the edge of the bed, knees pressed tightly together.

The Assassin stood by the door, watching her warily.

Now she leaned forward, elbows on her knees and gave a great sigh.

'I still can't believe we managed to get it. When did you come up with the idea of being an Italian? On the way downstairs?'

He nodded.

'I hope to fuck it was worth it,' she said. 'I hope to fuck we can actually use it and make a difference. Fuck. What have we taken on?'

The Assassin frowned. 'You really needed this, didn't you?'

Her face took on the same bitter, twisted look she'd had earlier on the yacht when she talked about her childhood.

'You want to tell me?' he asked gently. 'What happened when you were in the Venture Corps?'

'Can't you work it out for yourself?' she snapped angrily. 'Haven't I given you enough hints already?' She glared at him.

Her anger seemed to pass. She swung her legs up onto the bed and curled into a ball, facing away from him. He watched her for half a minute as she lay there, hair tumbled on the covers.

Still facing the wall, she began to speak in a low, dull voice.

'After it happened, nothing else mattered for a long time. My parents were no help. I tried to summon up the courage to tell them, but it was no good. They would just have blamed me for it,' she said, her voice rising up to a quavering high pitch.

A sob came, and then another.

'Afterwards I didn't care who I did it with,' she managed to say through the tears. 'I lost all my self-respect.'

The tears were coming in floods now, and the bed shook with her trembling.

The Assassin watched Selene in her anguish and his heart was pierced. He stayed by the door for a few seconds longer, then went over to the bed and sat down next to where she lay, placing a hand softly on her shoulder. She let it rest there while the sobs eventually played themselves out, slowly subsiding into sad sniffles.

She turned over on the bed to face him, eyes still red, tear streaks down her cheeks.

'They stole my teenage years from me,' she growled. 'And now no one wants me. Not for who I am.'

She wiped her eyes for a final time and looked up at him as he sat on the edge of the bed watching her.

'What about you?' she asked, her voice a little calmer now. 'Has anyone ever hurt you?'

The Assassin looked away and gazed out of the window at the darkening sky in the direction of Portsmouth.

'Not in that way.'

Silence filled the room, overpowering silence. It grew and grew until he felt compelled to speak.

'My mother was raped by Russian soldiers at the end of the war, and I was born,' he said, still staring out of the window. He turned to her. 'But she kept it secret from me. I only found out a couple of years ago.'

'Jesus. I wasn't expecting that.' She sat up again, tucking her legs in underneath her and leant back against the headboard, her right knee pressing gently against the outside of his thigh.

'Is that why you're always so grim, apart from today on the water?' she asked with a faint smile. He thought he heard a sense of relief there too. She wasn't the only woman with a story.

She reached out a hand to touch his cheek, but he caught it first, holding it lightly in his own. He looked into her eyes for a second, then lifted her hand to his mouth and gave it a quick kiss. Getting up from the bed, he walked over to the door and stood looking back at her, their moment of intimacy over.

'A lot has happened in the past two years.' He was silent for a second. 'My wife is pregnant.' There was a strange inflection in his voice which made her hold back from what she'd been about to say.

Silence fell again. 'Are you hungry?' he asked her. 'Do you want to eat something?'

'No. I'm tired. I'm ready to turn in.'

He went over to his own bed and dragged the mattress across the floor, laying it down in front of the door.

'I'll sleep here tonight.'

'Are you that cautious?'

'I don't trust Heath's bodyguard or whoever he is. Or myself,' he added in a quieter voice.

She watched him as he rearranged the blankets that had fallen off the mattress as he'd dragged it over.

'Is it your child?'

He didn't answer her immediately. He sat down to unlace his shoes, before lying back on top of the covers.

'Life can be hard,' he said, staring up at the ceiling.

*

In the small hours of the morning the Assassin suddenly woke for no reason that he was conscious of. He lay still, listening hard. Selene was silent under her blanket. Just outside the door he could hear heavy breathing, as if someone was short of breath. The person stood there for one, two minutes before he heard the sound of footsteps disappearing down the corridor.

He gave it another five minutes, then went over to Selene's bed and shook her gently.

'Let's go.'

'Now?' she asked sleepily. 'Why, Thomas?'

'I can't explain. I just have a sixth sense.'

She came back to full wakefulness.

'Okay,' she said quietly and without fuss.

In the pre-dawn light they crept downstairs to the deserted lobby. The Assassin placed their keys softly into the night box by reception and unlatched the front door. They emerged into a cold, grey world in which they were the only inhabitants. But even as they made their way down to the quay to untie their dinghy and start rowing back to the yacht, the glimmer in the sky to the east was already strengthening.

The Assassin worked the oars again, the exercise warming him and soon they were clambering aboard *Tatterdemalion*.

'No wind,' she said. 'We'll have to use the engine.'

They unmoored under Selene's direction and headed for the open sea. As they exited Bosham Channel, the very tip of the mast glinted rose red from the upflung rays of the strengthening sun, still just below the horizon at ten to five.

'How long will it take to get back to Port Hamble?' he asked.

'Three or four hours.'

'If we turned left, how long would it take to reach France?'

'I told you yesterday. On an English boat it's called "port". At this speed, it would take the best part of a day to get to Cherbourg, assuming the wind and tide were in our favour.'

The Assassin looked out to port, staring as if he was trying to see the far shore.

He sighed in frustration and turned to look at Selene.

'You realise that Heath will probably send someone after you?' he said.

'Yes. It will start politely: "Do you mind giving us the film? We don't like the places where Ted goes for relaxation being identified." They'll use the security excuse.'

'But then you'll say you don't have it, because you took the photograph using your Italian boyfriend's camera.'

'And then I chucked him out that very weekend. I found he'd been cheating on me with another woman. He broke my heart and I wanted nothing more to do with him.'

'We need to agree on a story.'

Selene looked up at the masthead for a moment. The wind was freshening and they would need to take in sail at some point, but she decided to make the most of it while they still could.

'We left London to spend a weekend together away from the city. We deliberately chose Bosham as it's off the beaten track and we came across Heath by sheer chance. Our disguise when booking the hotel was that you were Italian. But you never kissed him on the cheek. We admit everything up to that point.'

The Assassin gave a low laugh. '"Our disguise"? We're not an unmarried couple from last century. Still, I think we'll get away with it. After the first rebuff they'll give up and tell themselves it's not worth the effort.'

'It wouldn't surprise me. The Establishment's instincts are always to let sleeping dogs lie. By the time they realise that the photograph might be construed as Heath giving a signal about his sexuality to a supposed East German agent no less, it will be too late.'

'Their only way out would be for Brierly to come clean about what he did. How he set the Marks up for a fall by creating a fake spy to implicate a Soviet satellite in a fake entrapment operation. And as I've been warning people since I arrived, he can't afford to be discovered doing something of that nature. If the Soviets ever were to find out and inform the international press, heads will roll. Who knows? The government itself might fall.'

'The Party would need to decide which of losing Heath or losing power was the lesser of two evils,' she said. 'It wouldn't take them long to choose. Our photograph is a Sword of Damocles hanging over the entire Establishment.'

'Only while Heath is Prime Minister,' he replied.

They arrived back at Port Hamble marina just after half-past eight. Selene snapped her orders at the Assassin as they flemished ropes and got her friend's yacht back to the same state as they'd picked it up in. There was no sign of *Morning Cloud*. The time trials in the Solent would take all day, but presumably she needed to return to the Royal Southern to pick up her crew first.

The nearest phone box was in the High Street. They walked there and called for a taxi to the railway station in Southampton. When it arrived, they asked the driver to hurry. Thirty minutes later, they were waiting impatiently on the platform at Southampton Central for the next train, a slow stopping service. The Assassin hung the camera around his neck, buttoning up his jacket to hide it.

It was a Sunday morning and when it finally pulled in, the train was almost empty. They found a compartment to themselves and sat facing one another in silence until they heard the slam of the doors and the train started moving again.

Now that the distraction of physical activity was finally over, they had nothing much more to say to each other, the day after the night before. They had a brief discussion as to where they could get copies made of the negatives with no questions asked, and after some resistance, the Assassin persuaded her he'd get a contact in Soho to take care of it. He promised to bring her a copy as soon as it was done, no later than midweek.

The train picked up speed past Eastleigh and the miles soon started to roll by. The Assassin stared out the window, lost in his thoughts. After half an hour he got up to study the route map displayed in the vestibule. Selene watched him through the corridor window as he muttered softly to himself.

After Basingstoke, the conductor went past their compartment again. The Assassin looked up, then stood to follow him into the next carriage. After a couple of minutes he returned and made an announcement to Selene.

'I'm getting off at Woking. I'm going to take a taxi and see Voaden while I'm down this way.'

'Why?'

'I want him to fill in the gaps in the story of how his retirement came about, and more importantly, why.'

'Which gaps? Because you think the girl was overdosed deliberately?'

'I'm not going to speculate any further. Not until after I've spoken with him.'

She looked at him solemnly.

'Am I invited too? Aren't we joined in this thing together now?'

'My instinct is that you should stay away. You're in this deep enough already and I don't want Voaden identifying you later, if someone asks who visited him today.'

'I don't need your protection,' she replied evenly. Then she relented. 'Will he be more likely to open up if you go on your own?'

'I don't know. Going along there with a woman might seem less intimidating. On the other hand, if you were to come, it would be two of us against one of him.'

She bit her lip.

'Go on your own then. Tell me what you find out when you bring me the negatives. But before you go, you need to tell me where you're staying,' she said.

He thought for a moment as they slowed down for the stop at Farnborough.

'I'm lodging with a Flora MacDonald,' he said. He gave her the address of the neighbour next door who held the spare key.

'Scottish lady?' she asked, writing down the details.

The Assassin shrugged. 'She's careful with money for sure.'

'There's worse vices,' said Selene.

'I can guarantee it.'

Chapter Twenty-Six

Drops of rain from a summer shower spattered the windscreen of the Assassin's taxi as they turned off the road into the driveway up to the monastery. After the good weather of recent days, it felt like the temperature was on its way back down.

On the journey from the station he'd been having second thoughts about whether he was acting rashly. He didn't have an excuse for coming here today, and if Voaden clammed up he'd be worse off than if he hadn't called. Either way, he was almost certain that Smythe would find out about his visit at some point. This afternoon he was counting on there still being vanity inside Voaden, and a secret sense of loss for the life he'd known. And a desire to talk about it.

But even the thought of speaking with Voaden troubled the Assassin. It wasn't so much the new stories of abuse that he might hear, as fresh examples of Voaden's moral ambiguity. That was what truly frightened the Assassin. Given what he'd done in Devon - and not done in Streatham - he increasingly had secret, gnawing worries of his own on that score. Certain sins were unforgivable, or so he'd heard at some point.

His landlady had tried to give him some words of encouragement about not being tempted beyond what he could bear. But somehow, when he'd thought about it afterwards, he felt worse than before. For whether he'd completely understood the words or not, he now knew he had even fewer excuses for his actions in England so far.

He walked up the steps of the monastery and into the hall, shaking the water from his jacket, and made his way to Voaden's room. Knocking, he entered.

Voaden looked up, initially in surprise and then with a knowing expression.

'Well darling? You look like a man who wants answers to something.'

'Do you want to guess?' asked the Assassin, deciding that bluff was as good an opening gambit as any.

'My final fling? My greatest triumph and my downfall?'

'How did you know?' The Assassin frowned.

'Annersley said you might come. He said you were on a mission. An avenging angel come to dispense a justice of your own making.' Voaden moistened his lips.

'Is that all he said?' replied the Assassin as nonchalantly as he could muster. 'Quite a fairy tale he told you there.'

'No, he said more than that.'

Voaden waited for the Assassin to ask, but he didn't take the bait.

'When did you speak to him?' asked the Assassin instead.

'A couple of days ago. He said that he'd seen you in Devon at one of Smythe's parties. Apart from anything else, he was disappointed that you didn't seem to appreciate the treats that had been laid on.'

The Assassin shook his head slowly. 'It wasn't Smythe's party,' he said. 'Someone else organised it. Smythe was only there to help run it.'

'Please. I had higher expectations of you after what Annersley said.'

The silence opened up as the Assassin digested the first indirect confirmation, albeit an unreliable one, that Smythe was more than a supporting player in this affair.

'Is he a friend of yours?' asked the Assassin

Voaden looked at him contemptuously. 'Who? Smythe or Annersley?'

'How about both of them? Was Smythe also an example of you leaving no corner of the Establishment uncorrupted, as you said the last time I was here? And was Annersley more than a friend perhaps?'

'I can't be responsible for other men's consciences.'

The Assassin's eyes narrowed for an instant. 'Smythe seems an unlikely nut for you to have been able to crack.'

'He fell all by himself. And he knew what he was getting into when he started helping me run the parties.'

The Assassin frowned again. All kinds of possibilities now began to unfold. There was regret too, for Smythe's sake, at the idea he hadn't been able to stop himself being sucked in after all.

'How did the two of you get together in the first place?' asked the Assassin. He suddenly had an urgent need to know what Smythe's path had been, if only so he could avoid it himself.

'You're not a policeman and I don't have to answer your questions,' said Voaden

'But Smythe is, or perhaps was one,' said the Assassin. 'How did it start? To be convincing as a corrupt cop he had to do things he shouldn't have?'

'I'm saying nothing.'

'And to get really close to the scene, he eventually asked to be your assistant? Or was it cruder than that? Did he offer to pay the running costs of your debaucheries from secret police funds?'

'I don't know how you do things in Belgium. But that's not how things work in this country.'

'Then enlighten me. I'm a naïve foreigner in awe of your sophisticated British ways.'

'Do you want some tea? The pot's still warm.' Voaden placed the back of his hand on the china.

'I thought I was so clever at the start. But then it became a bigger thing than I could handle. I was too good at ensnaring people and eventually I ensnared too many of the wrong sort.'

'The wrong sort?' asked the Assassin incredulously. 'Is there a right sort at these parties?'

'I hinted at it before. Dabble in the occult and don't be surprised if bad things happen.'

'What kind of things?'

'Schizophrenia. Uncontrollable rage. Extreme violence.'

'On whose part?' asked the Assassin, trying to suppress the guilty tone in his voice.

'That's when I realised my pastime would end up killing me.'

The Assassin shook his head again in disbelief at Voaden's description of his activities with the children. 'But someone did die,' he said. 'A girl comes to one of your parties to get high, lose her inhibitions, and then regret it all the next morning. Except that she doesn't, does she? The next morning never came for her.'

'It was no one's fault, darling. Not particularly. People understand that these things happen. It's not as if the pills come in a bottle with a manufacturer's label on the side, telling you how many to take.'

'If they're barbiturates and amphetamines from a pharmacy they do,' replied the Assassin coldly.

Voaden looked at him defiantly. 'Anyway. You can't pin that one on me.'

'I never said I was going to. But someone did. Someone who wanted you out of the way. Was it Smythe? Were you eventually bested by your apprentice?'

Voaden's face went dark. 'He'd never have had the nerve. No, it was someone connected to the diplomatic service who came to me the day after.'

'Who? Someone with black and white streaked hair? Puts you in mind of a badger?' asked the Assassin.

Voaden nodded slowly.

'And that's all you have to say? You're not angry or even bitter at how you got sent here into a form of retirement, and how someone else stole your network?'

Voaden shrugged. 'I've made my peace. With myself and with the people who pushed me out. After all, I'm meant to forgive, aren't I? That's what gets me off, doesn't it?'

Once more, the monk's religious hypocrisy unsettled the Assassin. The monk talked about forgiveness for sins, and then he met choirboys in his room after music practice.

'Tell me this, then. Why did Fryatt and Smythe want your address book in the first place? I know who Annersley was and I also know about the man called Barker. He was at your final party. A supplier of children from the north of England, isn't he?'

'Who told you all those details?'

'I've been speaking to more people than just Smythe. People keen to make sure that their version of the truth becomes the accepted one. So what was Annersley's speciality? What did he do for your network that you couldn't do for yourself?'

'He recruited a certain type of guest. He has his own networks within the more reactionary wing of the Establishment.'

'Was it lucrative? Did you resent losing the income from your parties when you came here?' asked the Assassin.

'Who said that I stopped making money? I still get paid a retainer for my silence. People with access to enough funds and influence to shut down any investigation by the authorities, no matter how high up the instructions come from. Did Smythe ever tell you the story of how the Boothby exposé was brought to a halt?'

The Assassin ignored the question. 'Were Annersley and Barker working together with Fryatt and Smythe to exclude you, then? How did it all start and end?'

Something just then made the Assassin refrain from mentioning Grieves.

'Why didn't you ask Annersley all this when you met him?' asked Voaden. 'Or Barker? Annersley told me the other day that Barker hasn't been heard of since that weekend in Devon.'

'I don't know what happened to him after the party.'

'I've been sitting listening to your questions for a while now,' said Voaden. 'But I'm confused. I thought Smythe brought you here last time because you were helping him?'

'How would I have been doing that?'

'Aren't you an international police colleague of his? Someone they'd brought in to put pressure on people who were being awkward?'

So much for Brierly's highly compartmentalised operation, thought the Assassin. The scene was so incestuous that real secrets were few and far between, at least, not ones that could be kept from the long-time players.

'I came to England to research the British trade. That was all. Smythe was going to take me to some parties undercover. Let me see things for myself.'

'What finally prompted you to come here today, then? You've grown uncertain over the past few weeks as to which side of the moral boundary Smythe is standing on?'

'What do you mean, "which side"?' asked the Assassin. 'From what you've been hinting at, I think Smythe's long given up trying to do any real good.'

'Then what are you going to do about it? Purify them of their sins. One by one?'

The Assassin frowned, his face troubled.

'You're no different to them, you know,' said Voaden. 'If you choose to involve yourself with Fryatt and Smythe, even at arm's length, then you're tacitly approving of what they do. Your coming here today is proof of that, otherwise you'd be at the nearest police station trying to find an honest copper.'

'What exactly are you accusing me of?' asked the Assassin. 'Are you saying I need to take them down to save myself?'

'I'm saying you need to get on the next plane to wherever it is you came from. You're sailing in some treacherous waters, darling. If they can get rid of me in a manner of speaking, then they can do the same to you when your usefulness is finished. Or even faster than that. I only have to pick up the phone to Smythe and after you went behind his back to come here today, it'll be all over for you.'

'Is that what you really want? Or wouldn't you prefer if the tables were turned and some heat was put on Smythe for once?'

The Assassin went over to the window and stared out at the car park. A squall of rain swept over the tarmac, lashing the disused fountain with sudden a violence which passed as quickly as it came. Voaden got up to rinse out the teapot and cups at the enamel sink in the alcove by the door.

'Are you done with the guesswork?' he asked the silent Assassin. 'I have Divine Office in a few minutes.'

The Assassin turned round, his face sombre. 'I'll ask you one last time. Why did Fryatt want your address book? And why did he even arrive on the scene in the first place? Was he working for himself or for an organisation?'

'Why do those two reasons have to be exclusive? He's a cruel man, cold. Driven by selfishness. I think his employer values those qualities.'

'Do you know who his real employer is?'

'I know everyone, darling. Who works for whom. And I love collecting their secrets, even yours.'

'Can I guess at Fryatt's? Was he doing it for the money, using his employer as a convenient excuse to muscle in on you?'

'That one doesn't need the income I earned from laying on private entertainment to gentlemen of discriminating tastes. His family is wealthy. The money we made wouldn't have made any difference to him.'

No wonder Fryatt knew what a marrow spoon was at the *Herrenklub*. The Assassin nodded. 'Then he was doing it for the power. I bet Smythe was doing it for money though. Perhaps each of them thought they could get more out of the network than you'd done up to that point. Is that why they got rid of you?'

'I really must go. I've indulged you long enough.'

The Assassin shook his head and slowly placed a hand in each side pocket of his jacket.

'Tell me, what happens after choir practice?'

'Father Chevalier picks out a couple of the more compliant and then they get extra lessons here in my room. I don't do anything with them that they won't be getting up to once they go to boarding school. In fact, I'm doing them a favour.'

The Assassin's brow furrowed. Voaden wagged a finger at him. 'I'm helping them learn how to deal with the older boys they're going to meet later on. Sometimes a real tenderness develops between us. Affection, you could call it. Love of a kind.'

It was all the Assassin could do to stop himself from visibly gagging.

'Once your sort starts, you can't stop, can you?' he said after a few seconds. 'No matter how hard you try. But if you had come here after a true change of heart, you'd have wanted to put it behind you. When you pray with the other monks, instead of going through the motions, why don't you open your mind and actually communicate with the person who's listening.' The Assassin pointed upwards with his finger.

'Are you speaking for yourself or for me? I know in my heart what you did to Barker.'

'Barker was what he was. But the girl at the party, she was someone's daughter for sure.'

Without further ceremony, he turned sharply on his heel and left, slamming the door on his way out.

–

On the way back to London he turned over in his head the things he'd learned this past week.

If he were to take everything he'd heard at face value, then Fryatt and Smythe had worked together to push Voaden to one side, and some combination of the three Marks had seen them do it. He could think of several reasons of his own why the pair might have wanted to take over Voaden's address book. But whatever they were, two, probably three, of the Marks had been worried enough to threaten Heath as a form of insurance.

And when they'd done that, they'd put themselves in either Fryatt's or Smythe's crosshairs, so to speak. Neither of the new bosses of the network wanted the risk of the Marks making good on their threats and someone tracing a connection back to the Foreign Office or the police. From that point on, some kind of pre-emptive action had been almost inevitable.

But all of this assumed that Annersley and Voaden were reliable witnesses. It also assumed that Selene was telling the truth about Barker being at the party. But he didn't believe she'd lied about anything she'd said so far. She certainly hadn't faked her tears yesterday evening in Bosham.

He urgently needed to see her again and test his latest theory. He wondered how she would take it. She'd wanted to make a stand against abuse within the Establishment, but now he strongly suspected that he and she - and Brierly and Kramer - had been unwittingly working for Fryatt and Smythe all along. Enabling the filth to carry on.

Angry didn't begin to describe how he felt. He could scarcely imagine how Selene would feel towards the others when she realised for herself.

As the train rattled through Queenstown Road, past terraces of houses similar to those in Streatham, he stared unseeing at his reflection in the window. But instead of a hard-faced German, he saw the back of the boy as he ran down the path between the houses. Running home to his sister, if 'home' you could call it.

At Waterloo he scanned the faces of the people going to and fro on the concourse, looking for Selene, even though he knew he was being irrational. She'd be long back in Chelsea by now, only a fifteen-minute taxi ride away. He reached into his jacket and touched his wallet with the photograph inside. One temptation in England he would continue to resist.

Having missed every meal since breakfast the previous day he was ravenous. No wonder Selene kept her figure. Across the road from the station, its upper storeys divided by a railway bridge to nowhere, was a pub called The Wellington. The Assassin gave a wry smile at the name. They were still serving roast beef and he spent a couple of hours making up for lost drinking time too.

Feeling human again, he dived back into the dusty tube and made his way back to Limehouse via Fenchurch Street, arriving at Mrs. MacDonald's at half-seven.

She opened to his knock, still wearing her Sunday best. He could see a hat with plastic fruit on the brim and a mock veil sitting on the table in the front room.

'You've just come from church?' he asked her.

'The evening service.' She took a look at his still-drawn face. 'Would you like some supper?'

He wasn't hungry anymore, but didn't want to offend. 'Sure. Why not?'

She made them buttered toast and a pot of tea which they took together in the front room. The Assassin had long given up caring about any social awkwardness. The days of effort he'd spent trying to stay out of Reynolds' hair and maintain the peace in Earl's Court seemed pointless now, given what he'd had confirmed over the weekend.

Reynolds was another one he had to check off his list. But whatever deceptions Fryatt and Smythe had been practising on those around them, the Assassin was certain that his earnest former flatmate was innocent of any more sinister involvement in their game. At least not consciously.

'Would you like to go to the midweek meeting this coming Wednesday?' she asked, taking him by surprise. 'Have you ever been to a church service before? Either in England or in Belgium?'

He paused before replying, like a miser, doling out the words one by one.

'I've been to church in my home town. My mother goes. I join her when I'm there.'

'Do you believe?'

It was the one question which the Assassin had been hoping she wouldn't ask. He looked at her with vacant eyes. 'I can't unknow what I know.'

And that was his real problem. He knew right from wrong, he'd even told Smythe so when they met two months and a lifetime ago, out at the hotel by Heathrow. But in Devon he'd given into the rage that consumed him when he'd seen what Barker was about to do to the boy.

If he'd merely laid out Barker with his fists, he could have gone along the corridor and done the same to the abusers in every bedroom. He even had a gun he could have threatened them with, chased them all back downstairs. And then instead of skulking in the car at the corner of Ellison Road and letting the boy run to his foster parents, he would have been able to take him to a police station. Or gone to the boy's house with the gun and rescued his sister as well.

His landlady broke into his thoughts and brought him back to the present.

'Have you confessed your sins to God and repented of them?'

She lived in a tiny house, only a couple of rooms on each floor, with cracked walls from the blast effect of Luftwaffe bombs and a dingy outside toilet. In the eyes of the world she had no power, but just at that moment she dominated the room.

'I have,' he replied. 'I did. But then afterwards I let myself go,' In the aftermath of Italy he'd given up any thoughts of even trying to go to church in Brussels. He hadn't been cut off from the community of believers, because he'd never made any real attempt to be part of it. And look where he'd ended up now.

'So what happened?' she asked. 'Why do I catch a look from you from time to time like you're haunted by the Devil?'

If only she knew.

'I'm angry. And I'm tired. I'm tired of being made to do things I don't want to. I have obligations to so many people. Ones I'll never be free from.' He passed a hand over his face. 'I'm angry at everyone, almost all of the time. At the people closest to me. At myself.'

She took a sip of tea while she digested this outpouring. 'The verses for tonight's sermon were from Romans.' She closed her eyes for a moment to bring them back from memory.

'"*Dearly beloved, avenge not yourselves, but rather give place unto wrath: for it is written, Vengeance is mine; I will repay, saith the Lord.*"'

'And the next one is: "*Therefore if thine enemy hunger, feed him; if he thirst, give him drink: for in so doing thou shalt heap coals of fire on his head.*":

His eyes widened momentarily. Of all the verses she could have quoted, it was the one that had stayed with him from his teenage years. The coals were even described the same way as in the Luther Bible: '*feurige Kohlen.*'

'I don't understand all of the words. What does "give place unto wrath" mean?'

'Leave room for God's wrath. His, not yours. Don't push God from his rightful place as a just judge.'

Better to be given the message later rather than never, he supposed. He didn't believe in coincidences. And he didn't need any more warnings of the consequences of not listening. Barker's bloodied body was the evidence of that.

'A lifetime wouldn't be long enough to finish punishing all the evil I've come across in England,' he said.

'If you believe, you have to live your life as if the words in the verse are true. All that's being asked of us is to step aside and let God exercise his right of judgement. For mercy-giving and for punishment.'

'Easier said than done,' he countered.

'I had to, once.'

Her pupils went large and dark and far away. She glanced up to the painting of the island above the fireplace. The Assassin looked at her again, a woman far from the land of her birth, speaking out her words of faith from under the shadow of her own troubles.

'God took the hatred out of my heart once. He didn't tempt me beyond what I could bear.'

The Assassin finished his toast and tea.

He looked at her solemnly. 'I'll come with you to your church meeting on Wednesday evening, no matter what else I'm doing earlier that day.'

She nodded. 'There's nothing God cannot forgive, other than not wanting to be forgiven.'

'I need it to be true.'

'You're no different to the rest of us. No better and no worse in God's eyes.'

Chapter Twenty-Seven

The following day the Assassin arrived at Club Trèfle just after ten. Once again, he was shown upstairs to Jimmy's office and the seats by the low table. Once again, the nightclub owner played host and poured them both drinks. Cognac this time.

'I've come to check on my gear,' announced the Assassin. 'And I have two new requests.'

'More?' asked Jimmy. 'I heard that the room I found for you wasn't good enough? You moved out?'

'It was fine. It's just that I don't like staying too long in one place.'

'What do you want now?'

'I need a film copying. No questions asked and no one to look at what it shows. And I need it done right away, immediately after I leave here.'

'And the second thing?'

'Someone to pick locks and crack a domestic safe. Housebreaking.'

Jimmy shrugged his shoulders. 'If whatever you're planning goes wrong, it's Kramer you'll answer to.'

'I know that.'

'Do you?' Jimmy gave a half-smile to himself. Thirty years ago I'd have had a go myself. Housebreaking was how I started out. When are you planning this for?'

'I don't know yet. Sometime this week. Not before Wednesday night.'

'Two days is short notice.'

'I'll take anyone who's competent.'

'There's a man who does the occasional job for us. Reliable guy. He ought to be available if I ask.'

'Okay,' said the Assassin. 'I'll call you late tomorrow to confirm. Get your guy to clear his schedule. Agree whatever payment you think is necessary.'

'I presume this is almost the end?' asked Jimmy. 'Did you get done whatever it was Kramer wanted?'

'You have a soft spot for him, don't you?' said the Assassin. 'For some strange reason he has that effect on people.'

'And how about you?' asked Jimmy again. 'Do you work for him out of loyalty or necessity?'

The Assassin hesitated, unwilling to give an answer. 'Both. But that's irrelevant. The operation concludes this week. One way or another.'

Jimmy looked into the bottom of his glass.

'Kramer's never asked much of me since the war. One of his people was hidden by my family for several months at our farm in the maquis above Corte. He's shown his gratitude to me in different ways ever since.'

'Good to know he cares.'

But Jimmy was still in the mood to reminisce. 'It was the winter of 'forty-one when my cousin Ghjorghju built that false room under the log store. Towards the end of the war, we used it as a cell to hold communist partisan leaders from France who Kramer asked us to interrogate.'

'Nothing like a civil war to bring out the best in people, is there?' said the Assassin glibly.

'He felt under an obligation to us for that particular service. But he didn't need to. We'd have gladly done it for free.'

Jimmy looked up again and stared hard at the Assassin. He leaned across the table and jabbed a finger into the scar in the middle of the Assassin's right hand. The Corsican's eyes were pools of the deepest black.

The Assassin stared back, measure for measure. 'Maybe he knew that one day you'd help him again.'

Jimmy grunted. 'Are you planning something that needs muscle? I have some guys keen to prove themselves. Nephews of a kind.'

'Possibly. What can they do?'

'What do you want them to do?'

'Are they French citizens? Have they done their *service militaire*?'

'One of them was in the Chasseurs Parachutistes.'

'Useful man to know,' said the Assassin with a slight nod.

'You must have done conscription too?' asked Jimmy. 'Which part of the German army did you serve in?'

'It wasn't any regiment you'd have heard of,' said the Assassin. Something in his voice told Jimmy not to ask any more questions.

'Tell me more about your nephew,' asked the Assassin.

'First things first.' Jimmy got up and went back to his desk. He picked up the phone and made a call, speaking for a minute in a low voice.

He looked up at the Assassin. 'There's a man near here who can copy your film. He does development work for people who make their own very private home movies.'

'Spare me the details. When's he free?'

'I'll take you over there myself. He said to give him half an hour.'

Jimmy fetched the bottle of pastis from under his desk and the glasses.

'Let's have a drink while we wait.'

For whatever reason, the nightclub owner was in a good mood this morning. The Assassin struck while the iron was hot.

'Let me check my gear while we talk. Also, one more thing. I'll need to borrow a car again before the weekend.'

Jimmy's man worked out of a bookshop in Walker's Court, between a topless bar and a clip joint. After the Assassin was done with the contents of the green holdall, Jimmy took him over there.

Walking straight past the greasy long-haired hippy type behind the counter, they pushed through the beaded curtains dividing the shop front from the private room to the rear. A short man wearing thick glasses was sitting there, perched on a high stool as he hunched over a workbench.

'Bert will do whatever you need. He's very discreet,' said Jimmy with a wink.

'Don't worry,' said the technician. 'I've seen a thing or two on celluloid during my time.'

'Okay. I'll tell you what to do in a minute.' The Assassin looked at Jimmy for a second, who gave him a shrug. 'I'll see you around,' he said. He shook hands with the Assassin and left.

The Assassin set the camera on the table.

'How many sets of negatives?' asked Bert, bending over his work again.

The Assassin stared at the bald patch on the top of Bert's head. 'Three. But you only ever made two. Got it?'

Bert looked up. 'Keep your hair on.'

'Apart from the cameraman, you'll be the only person to know what the picture shows. I promise you, if you tell even one other person, I'll find you and kill you.'

The other man glanced at the scars on the Assassin's hands and face. 'Come back this afternoon after three,' he said, his expression carefully blank.

–

As soon as the Assassin was happy that Bert had got the message, he made his way at speed to the specialist travel agency off Piccadilly. He was shown without ceremony to the same office as before and called Kramer on the secure line. The Frenchman himself picked up.

'Well, what's the news from England?' he asked. 'Did you get something on the top guy at the weekend?'

'I got a lot more than "something."'

'What did you and the girl manage to do?'

'She got a photograph of me kissing Heath. Full on the cheek. Head to one side like a lover.'

Kramer gave a low whistle down the line. Then he laughed softly. 'My God. Where's the film now?'

'I'm having a copy made for her and a copy for us too. That was the agreement we came to.'

'Have you given it to her already?'

'No.'

'Then find an excuse not to. It's only of use to us if we have full control over its release. Did you take the photograph on her camera or yours?'

'She took it, on mine.'

'There you go then. It's the property of France,' said Kramer brusquely.

'That's not all that happened this weekend.'

'*Putain*, don't use that tone of voice. It makes me dread what you're going to say next.'

'No. It's not that,' said the Assassin. 'Something else. Problems of a different kind.' He looked at the calendar on the desk. It still showed May's picture of the Crusader castle from his last visit. He flipped over to June's Grand Mosque.

'Well?' asked Kramer.

'After what I've learnt this weekend, I'd suggest that the entire rationale for this assignment is now in doubt.'

'What do you mean?' said Kramer coldly.

The Assassin decided to dispense with the indirect references to people and just name them. The scrambling device attached to the line either worked or it didn't.

'One of Fryatt or Smythe might have arranged a drug overdose for a girl who attended one of Voaden's parties, in order to force him into retirement. Voaden is the one who's the pervert monk.'

'How do you know all this?'

'I went to see Voaden yesterday in Hampshire. Privately, without Smythe's knowledge. He confirmed what Annersley told me, that Fryatt was the one who came to him after the party to tell him to quit the scene. He indicated that Smythe has taken over his old network and is now actively running it, not merely spying on its members.'

'Sounds circumstantial. How trustworthy is Voaden?'

'None of them are. But Voaden also said that he'd been called up by Annersley sometime last week, after the party in Devon. Annersley warned him about me. Said that Barker hadn't been heard of for some days.'

'So much for getting away with it.'

'I also learned from the liaison girl this weekend that Barker was at the same party where the overdose happened. Now we have a reason for why they initiated the threats against Heath.'

'Which is?'

'I suspect the Marks saw something. They definitely saw how Voaden was pushed to one side afterwards. Both are reasons for Annersley to say they'd banded together for mutual protection. I'm almost certain of it.'

'Almost certain isn't certain. And you can hardly quiz Barker anymore.'

'Do you have a better idea for how the pieces of the puzzle might fit together?'

'Why do you say Smythe's role as a party organiser is a new one?' asked Kramer. 'The impression I got from Brierly when we were first planning this back in late summer last year was that Smythe had always run the parties. Brierly never mentioned anyone called Voaden. Nor did Fryatt when he was brought into the discussion.'

'Then at a minimum, Fryatt was lying by omission. Voaden and Smythe worked together, possibly long before Fryatt was even on the scene. Smythe was conducting a long-term, deep cover police surveillance operation - according to himself, that is. He says it was set up to provide early warning to senior police officers of entrapment operations being run by rival agencies. They didn't want to be caught unawares by MI5 again, like they were eight years ago over the Profumo Affair.'

'So are you suggesting that Fryatt's now collaborating with Smythe? He somehow won the allegiance of Smythe away from Voaden and helped him take over Voaden's network?' asked Kramer.

'I've never seen them in each other's company. I don't know whether Fryatt or Smythe is the leader. But surely the bigger question is whether Fryatt is doing this on his own account, or on behalf of an employer connected to the Foreign Office, somewhere within the British intelligence apparatus?' said the Assassin.

'Why couldn't Smythe be doing that?' asked Kramer

The Assassin shook his head in London, although no one was there to see it. 'He doesn't strike me as the class of person who they would have working for them. Social class, I mean. It would have to be Fryatt.'

'Social class? You've spent too long over there,' said Kramer with a grunt. 'Okay, then. Were the three Marks acting in concert? And why those three in particular? What kind of partnership did they have going on?'

'I don't know. But Barker may well have been more than a passive observer at the fatal party.'

'Why do you say that?'

'Because the liaison girl also told me he was a supplier of children to abusers. Perhaps only an occasional one, but I don't know for sure. He had access to a children's home in the north of England.'

Kramer was silent for a few seconds. 'Then maybe you've stumbled across a business association that's gone sour? An illegal enterprise that connects everyone: the three Marks, Fryatt, Smythe and

Voaden. Maybe the threats that the Marks made about Heath may just have been normal precautions between criminals. Or maybe they were threats in general terms about what they would do if they were ever threatened with exposure? As opposed to threats directed personally against Fryatt or Smythe?'

'They blackmail each other all the time in their world, or at least, Smythe insinuated that they do. Nothing would surprise me,' said the Assassin.

There was another moment's silence as both ends of the line digested this possibility.

'I wonder what talents Annersley and Grieves could have brought to the table?' asked the Assassin out loud.

'Forget that for now,' replied Kramer. 'If the three Marks were close to Fryatt and Smythe, that could explain why the English took their time about giving me the green light to send you to England. Perhaps Fryatt was happy for Brierly and me to fall out for a few months.'

'And did you? Fall out?' asked the Assassin.

'The three of us took forever to agree an approach on neutralising the danger to Heath. But don't you see? Maybe if the three Marks did make a general threat to release their Heath material, it suited Fryatt and Smythe to wait a while and lull them into a false sense of security.'

'Do you still trust Brierly after all that's gone on?' asked the Assassin.

'Give me another moment to think,' said Kramer.

The line went quiet for half a minute. The Assassin wondered if Kramer was scribbling with the same silver propelling pencil he'd seen the Frenchman use at a hundred meetings in Brussels. Drawing the same map of connections as he was doing right now in his own head.

'If Brierly has been set up or misled by Fryatt, my first concern is to get him disentangled from any resulting complications,' said Kramer finally. 'Right now I can't risk losing one of my key inside sources in England.'

'Then you'd better make friends quickly with him again. Just in case he gets to hear about the photograph of me and Heath.'

'What story did you agree with the girl?'

'Admit to almost everything. Claim it was a joke, a prank. But deny the kiss.'

'It might work, but only if you both stick to your story under pressure. Dangerous though.'

'You still can't believe we did it, can you?'

'One to laugh about when this is all over,' said Kramer. 'In the light of what you've just told me about Fryatt and Smythe, we need to decide once again whether it's the end of your sojourn in England.'

'No.'

'What do you mean, "No"?'

'We need to take down both of them. Permanently if possible.'

There was a long silence. The seconds stretched out.

'Is this another joke?' asked Kramer coldly.

In the office in London the Assassin shook his head again at his own reflection.

'What are you planning to do?' asked Kramer again.

'I don't know yet. I'm going to speak with the liaison girl this evening. We'll think of something.'

'Am I going to have to fly over there and talk to Brierly about you? Get you taken off the streets by force?'

'Trust me. Wait and see if the girl and I can come up with a plan. I promise I'll discuss it with you first before we actually do anything.'

'Don't you dare go rogue on me. Who are you actually working for right now?' asked Kramer.

'The good guys. Always the good guys.'

–

The Assassin left the travel agency and walked down Dover Street until he found a phone box. He called Smythe. It was late morning, but the policeman was still at home.

'Well?' said Smythe with a sarcastic edge to his voice. 'Did you get your leg over at the weekend?'

'I got what I wanted.'

'I bet you did. I bet you gave her some German discipline.'

'You're a sleazy shit,' said the Assassin.

'Don't knock it. Some girls like dirt.'

'What are we going to do about Grieves?' asked the Assassin. 'When are we staging an arrest, and who's going to carry it out for us?'

'I'll find someone not known to anyone on the scene.'

'Why not Reynolds?'

'Brierly doesn't want to involve him and his boss any more than we have to.'

'What's the danger?'

'They might be getting to the limit of how far they're prepared to go in deceiving their superiors.'

'Why? Because this is a very unauthorised operation?'

'Put it this way, Brierly doesn't have an official status in any government organisation.'

'So what is the plan then?'

'It's got to be something dramatic,' said Smythe. 'Something that's going to hit Grieves hard. I think you should persuade him to leave the country with you, and then we'll arrest you both, just as you're about to get on the plane with a briefcase of secrets.'

'That's not dramatic, it's completely mad. Which TV programme did you get that idea from??'

'Well you think of something, then.'

The Assassin tapped the top of the phone cabinet with a ten pence coin masquerading as a florin. 'We could trick him into attending a fake business meeting with an East German trade official at the hotel by Heathrow where you and I met in April. He doesn't actually need to be standing on the runway to be accused of trying to skip the country.'

'Not the Skyway. It needs to be somewhere private. Somewhere he can't kick up a fuss and call for help.'

'Where then?' asked the Assassin.

'Maybe we don't need to play it that way after all,' said Smythe quickly. 'You just said, an actual plane trip doesn't need to be part of it. We could do the arrest at an abandoned wartime airfield. Get him there under false pretences.'

'What kind of false pretences?'

'Claim you want to take him to inspect warehouse space as part of your cover story. Say it's for a new import-export venture you want him to invest into. A lot of the buildings at those old places have been converted to industrial units since the war.'

'It sounds overcomplicated. He's an impatient man. He's not going to waste his own time checking on the size of the shelving.'

'As I said, you think of a better idea then.'

'Where would we find an abandoned airfield?' asked the Assassin.

'East Anglia?'

'Could do. Some lonely place near the north Norfolk coast.'

'Why all the way up there? And how would we get him to go there voluntarily in the first place? It's hardly convenient for London.'

'Tell you what,' said Smythe. 'Where are you now?'

'In town. Dover Street.'

'Meet me halfway. There's a pub next to Vauxhall Bridge called the Morpeth Arms. Go there for one o'clock. I'll give it some thought between now and then. You do the same. We can have lunch and talk, or if it's busy, we can go to the gardens behind the Tate for privacy.'

'Why don't I call Grieves' office this morning?' said the Assassin. 'Just to keep him warm? We'd already arranged last month that we'd meet this week to discuss opportunities in East Germany. At the very least I could confirm the appointment.'

'Do you have enough to say to him to keep the conversation going?'

'About East Germany? Plenty.'

-

It had been almost three weeks since the Assassin had last spoken with the businessman. When he called the modest building next to Broad Street Station, it was Grieves' secretary who answered - the supercilious one whom the Assassin reckoned might have other duties around the office.

In a cool voice which gave the impression she didn't much care which answer he gave, she asked if he could come to Grieves' office there and then. He glanced at his watch, reckoning he could just about squeeze it in before he was due to meet Smythe.

Retracing his steps from May, the Assassin made his way to the northern edge of the City. Today, the flight of stairs up to the first floor seemed less dingy than before, maybe because he'd unconsciously adjusted his expectations since his first visit. The secretary showed him through to the inner office behind the glass partition.

'You wanted to see me right away?' he asked warily.

Grieves was sitting at his grey-painted steel desk, scribbling some notes. He made the Assassin wait until he'd finished before looking up.

'I heard a rumour that Robert Maxwell was in Vienna last month.'

'Who's that?' asked the Assassin, still standing.

'The former Labour MP. Czech Jew who fled the Nazis, changed his name and served in the British Army during the war.'

'What was he doing that close to his home country?' asked the Assassin, immediately suspicious of Frolík's old employers, the ŠtB, and their success at penetrating Westminster.

'He's traded in Europe for years. His big break in life was thanks to your lot, just after the war. West German publishing house who gave him the worldwide distribution rights to their scientific journals. He only became an MP to indulge his own sense of self-importance.'

'What's his connection to you?'

'None. I heard about his visit through another consultant. But I've decided I want to give this idea of manufacturing in East Germany a go. I don't want shysters like Maxwell suddenly tapping into their Central European connections to get a head start on free trade with East Berlin once we join the EEC.'

'It's a reason, I suppose.'

'But I'll need more senior advice than what you can give.'

'How do you mean "more senior"?' asked the Assassin sharply.

'I want someone who knows the internal politics of the regime. Who's in favour, which minister is on the way out. East Germany isn't a normal country. I need to pick the right business partners.'

The Assassin considered this for a moment. 'You're suggesting that you need the kind of insight only available to governments.'

'Or to people who do business there all the time. I appreciate your initial prompting, but there's a group of politicians at Westminster whom I know. MPs who are supportive of trade with East Germany. The ex-leader of the Liberals, for one. A whole string of Labour MPs too. There's even a Tory, Lord Boothby. They ought to be able to give me introductions in Berlin.'

The Assassin frowned momentarily at the mention of Boothby. Given the level of his competition, he reckoned he had nothing to lose. 'I could take you along to the East German Foreign Trade Office in Belgravia Square today,' he said in a matter-of-fact voice. 'But if you want to meet the top people you would have to come with me to Berlin, as you suggested the last time we met.'

'Which top people? The trade minister whose name you mentioned?'

He drummed his fingers on the desk. 'Okay. Talk to your contacts in Berlin and give me some evidence you know what you're talking about. I want to know who's on their way up and who to avoid.'

'There's no immediate answer to that. I told you last time, Erich Honecker has only just taken over as leader.'

'Yes,' said Grieves. 'But that means that right now is the time for his underlings to make their moves, while the political situation is still fluid. In business, disruption spells opportunity.'

'I'm only in England for another week or so. My assignment got extended. But I can place a couple of calls to Berlin before I leave, just to get the ball rolling. Then we should meet again before I leave London to decide on a plan.'

'Okay. But very discreetly. My name's not to come into it.'

'Naturally. But before I can start speaking with the ministry people, I need to know a few things from you first.'

'Go on.'

'Firstly, how serious are you about this idea, really? How soon could you go out there, if the right opportunity came up?'

'I could afford a couple of days at short notice.'

'How do you feel about doing business with the socialists that you seem to dislike so much?'

'The ones over there are communists, not socialists. And they're a completely different breed from Labour. Not the halfway house type that we have over here, neither hot nor cold.'

'The East Germans would probably agree with that assessment,' admitted the Assassin.

'In any case, I'm liberal about how I make my money.'

'If the people at the trade office were to ask me, how would you run a business division over there, practically speaking?'

'I might set up a trading subsidiary in a neutral country like Switzerland or Austria. But local manufacturing is an even bigger step than import-export. I suppose I could bring in a West German partner for local management, maybe as a co-investor. Someone who knows the lie of the land.'

The Assassin glanced away for a second and a disapproving look came over his face. 'I know some people who might be up for it. A West German holding company. The principals might listen to me, if I catch them on a good day.'

'How soon will you have something to report back from the trade office?' asked Grieves, without waiting on an answer 'I've had a lunch cancellation for tomorrow. Talk to my secretary on the way out and ask her to keep the slot clear for you. I said before that I'd take you to my club, but if you haven't already been to the Mirabelle on Curzon Street, ask her to get us a booking there.'

'How much time would you really be prepared to invest into this?' replied the Assassin. 'You might need to spend a couple of months in East Germany over the course of a year to build up trust. Especially if you want access to their most lucrative markets.'

'When I make a decision, I do whatever it takes to follow through.'

-

On his way to the Morpeth Arms, the Assassin reflected on coincidences. Only this morning Smythe had suggested that the Assassin trick Grieves into a simulated escape from Britain. It wasn't even lunchtime and now Grieves was offering himself up to go on a trip to Berlin. Even if it hadn't already been planned that way, Smythe would jump on it immediately.

But for all Smythe's cunning, when all was said and done, the Assassin still didn't see why an arrest couldn't be staged at Heathrow. Either Smythe or even Reynolds must have contacts at the Customs service, who would be happy to help on an informal basis. A tap on the shoulder and a firm grip on the arm as Grieves was escorted to an interview room at the airport. But going by Smythe's hints so far, he supposed that whatever was being planned for Grieves, it wasn't a chat over tea and biscuits while the businessman assisted the police with their enquiries.

When the Assassin entered the pub, Smythe greeted him with a half-wave. The policeman had already ordered food and was munching his way through a plate of fried whitebait. Two pint glasses stood on the table in front of him, one half-drunk, the other still full to the brim. The Assassin sat and they stared at each other in silence for a few seconds.

'I've met some hard cases in my time,' said Smythe. 'But you really take the biscuit.' He shook his head in wonderment.

'What else could I have done in that bedroom?'

'We went over it a hundred times beforehand. Stick it in or watch.'

The Assassin shook his head now. 'I don't know why I even thought I could be in the same room as him.'

'Well, there's no point in going back over it now. What's done is done.'

'Any word about the man in question? Any reports to the police?'

'Not yet. Give it until the end of the week.'

'Then let's get a move on. Let's finish this before the weekend,' said the Assassin.

'Did you speak with Grieves' secretary? Is he still on for a meeting?'

The Assassin pointed at the full pint glass. 'Is this for me?'

'I thought you should try some real beer.'

'I've been in London for almost six weeks. Where do you think I've been each evening?' The Assassin took a sip. 'Back to Grieves. Better than a meeting, when I phoned this morning, I was asked to come over to his office in the City there and then. He's got a bee in his bonnet about his competitors getting a head start in trading with the EEC.'

'Typical,' said Smythe. 'Greed is always the downfall of these guys.'

'Who are you talking about? Obscene Publications?'

'Them and half the Met. So what did he say?'

The Assassin rubbed his hand over his face. He saw Smythe's eyes following the scar between the third and fourth metacarpal bones.

'He's really bought into my cover story about having access to importers in the East. He wants me to set him up with contacts in Berlin.'

'Lucky for you that you're being arrested before you have to deliver on that promise.'

'And where's that going to take place exactly?'

Smythe tapped his plate with his fork for a moment. 'Why can't we combine both ideas? Tell him you can organise a flight to Europe from a remote airfield.'

The Assassin attempted nonchalance. He'd only told Smythe that Grieves wanted contacts in Berlin, not that he was prepared to travel there. 'Why would he suddenly feel the need to take a clandestine flight to the Eastern bloc?' he asked the policeman.

'Rudolf Hess in reverse,' said Smythe half to himself.

'I don't understand. What's on Grieves' conscience that would make him do that?' asked the Assassin.

'Please.'

'Yes, but he's not been worried about being found out before. Why suddenly now?'

'We could make him worried,' replied Smythe.

'He thinks he's protected by his threats against Heath,' said the Assassin.

'There you go. Someone drops him the hint that he's gone too far with the threats and that it's time to leave the country fast.'

'And who does that?' asked the Assassin 'You? Brierly? Fryatt?'

'Fryatt's got no connection to the juve scene. I'm the one who gets their hands dirty on other people's behalf. You seem to be getting confused about something.'

The Assassin supposed that Smythe had no choice but to maintain his lie. 'So what do you suggest?' he asked out loud. 'Because if you put too much pressure on Grieves, he might release his smear material on Heath after all.'

'I don't know. Maybe it's too much of a stretch. Maybe we just knock him on the head.'

'What? And arrest him when he wakes up? Put an Interflug ticket to Berlin via Battersea Heliport in his jacket pocket?'

'No. Let me think about it some more. I'll come up with something better by tomorrow.'

'Are you done eating?' asked the Assassin. 'What are the little fish like?'

'Try some.' Smythe pushed his plate across to the middle of the table. The Assassin took one with his fingers and ate it in two bites.

'Not bad,' he said. He looked around the pub and the decorations on the walls. Old oars hung from the ceiling, the names of long-forgotten rowers picked out in faded gold on the blades. 'Nice spot. You like coming here?'

'It makes a change from the places I usually have to go to.'

'Where do you go in the evenings to relax?'

'What do you mean "relax"?'

'Whatever you want it to mean.'

'None of your fucking business. I didn't pry into who you were with at the weekend.'

'I didn't mean it that way,' said the Assassin.

'So what did you mean?'

'I'm just making conversation,' said the Assassin, coolly.

'I really don't see what Annersley saw in you,' said Smythe,

The Assassin looked pointedly at him. 'By the way, what happens with him now?'

'I've no idea. Something else to worry about.'

Smythe leant forward, his elbows on the table, and lit a cigarette. 'Did Annersley say anything else to you in Devon? Anything at all?'

'He mentioned something about doctors giving people bad news.'

'What? He was talking about his own health?'

'I think so. I don't always understand the phrases that people use here.'

'Really? You seem to understand well enough most of the time.'

'If you smile, people assume you're following along.'

'Then they must think you're as thick as two short planks because you're as dour as a Scots Presbyterian.'

There was a pause for a second or two as the Assassin tried and failed to puzzle this one out. 'If Annersley really is sick with some fatal illness, I suppose the problem eventually takes care of itself?'

'Eventually, yes.'

Smythe finished his drink.

'Let's speak again tomorrow. Call me in the evening and we'll discuss a plan. In any case, something new might have come up by then. It often does.'

-

At three o'clock, the Assassin returned to Bert's shop in Soho to pick up the negatives. On the train up from Portsmouth yesterday afternoon he'd agreed with Selene to get a copy over to her by midweek. But based on today's meetings with Grieves and Smythe, he suspected that events were about to speed up. And in any case, he wanted to tell her what he'd learned from Voaden and hear what she thought about it.

He assumed he'd have a good chance of catching her at home on a Monday evening, so killed time by walking to Chelsea via The Two Chairmen in Cockspur Street, followed by a detour through Belgravia. When he buzzed her flat from the street at half-six, he was in luck, and after a few brief words over the intercom, she let him into the building.

Once again, he climbed the wide stairs with the coir runners, up past the two first floor flats to the second-floor landing. Her neighbour's door was slightly ajar, and he heard jazz music as he waited for Selene to come to the door. She answered his knock in a dressing gown, her hair wrapped in a towel.

'Who's the Ray Charles fan?' he asked her.

She stepped over the threshold to peer round at next door.

'Oh. That's Helen. Come in. I've just had a shower. I'm going out again later.'

She gave him an expectant look, but he didn't ask for the details. She closed the door behind them and told him anyway.

'With the same boy I picked up in the club bar at the Royal Southern.'

The Assassin shrugged. They sat down facing one another across the low table in her lounge. She lit a cigarette and drew on it heavily.

'You didn't expect me to give you yet another chance, did you?'

The Assassin shook his head. There was such a thing in life as trying too hard. It didn't become her, but he wasn't going to blame her for it either. Some events from your past you never fully left behind. He set a pale blue envelope down on the table. 'First of all, here's your copy of the negatives, as we agreed.'

'Did the image come out?'

'Crystal clear. There's a print inside the envelope too.'

She took out the photo and studied it.

'It's more suggestive than I remembered. You really put in some effort there Thomas. Puckering and everything. You ought to get some kind of acting prize.'

Little did she know just how many characters he was playing right now. 'Okay. Don't wave it around, keep it for when you really need it,' he replied. 'Listen, I need to tell you what Voaden told me about Fryatt and Smythe. How much time do you have?'

'An hour.'

'Before I start, I wanted to say that you should consider lying low for a bit.'

'Why?'

'Things are moving in ways I didn't expect. And I'm having second thoughts about how seriously they'll view last Saturday night and what we did to Heath.'

'It's finally dawning on you, is it? But how can I lie low? I have work to go to. And anyway, why should I?'

'It's only Monday. But give it a couple more days and if Heath's said something to someone, then they might start to take action by the middle of the week.'

She shrugged. 'I don't care. I won't take orders from any man ever again.'

'I wasn't trying to insult you.'

She looked at him neutrally. 'I didn't mean you when I said, "any man."'

'So what are we going to do about Fryatt and Smythe?' he asked.

'What do you mean "do about" them? What did Voaden say to you?'

'The short version is that they took over his network to run it for themselves. What will Brierly say when you tell him?'

'I still don't understand. You're saying that Fryatt and Smythe are running a vice ring together? They came to Brierly with talk of blackmail against Heath.'

He gave her a second to let it all sink in.

'Smythe might have started off observing the party scene, but not any longer. He and Fryatt are now running these sex parties for some other reason or reasons of their own. Money and influence I'm guessing.'

'So the threats against Heath might not even be real? Or they might be connected somehow to a turf war in the vice underworld?' she asked, scepticism tinged with hope in her voice.

'I can't say that the threats aren't genuine. And I can't say that the Marks don't have compromising material on Heath. Right now, my working assumption is that they made some half-credible accusations, but they did it for their own protection because they suspected that someone - Fryatt or Smythe we have to assume - arranged the death of the judge's daughter at Voaden's final party.'

'You can't be serious? You're actually suggesting they might have committed murder? Or at best, manslaughter?'

If only she knew how easy both of those things were.

'As sure as I'll ever be,' he said.

She frowned deeply. 'That's a big leap of faith you're making. It doesn't sound like the kind of risk someone in the Establishment would need to take. What if it was a genuine accidental overdose and Fryatt and Smythe just hinted that it wasn't?'

'You were the one who told me that the abuse scene was a brutally direct one. Why couldn't someone have done it?' He stopped himself from asking her what she imagined actually went on at those parties. Maybe she already knew.

'Is that why you're saying we need to be on our guard over Bosham?' she asked. 'What real evidence do you have for your theory about the girl who died?'

'It was you who told me the second Mark was at that party. Then Annersley told me that they took out some insurance afterwards. We don't need evidence to be on our guard.'

'And Annersley said all that? How long have you known?'

'He told me at the party in Devon.'

'Have you met Smythe since we got back from Southampton?' she asked.

'I met him today at lunch. Mostly we discussed Grieves. I obviously didn't mention my visit to Voaden at the monastery yesterday.'

'Who else have you shared your theories about the girl at Voaden's party with, apart from me?'

'Only Kramer. I told him I'd discuss with you what we're going to do next.'

'What do you mean, "do next"?'

'How we're going to take down Fryatt and Smythe.'

Her furrows on her brow creased even more deeply. 'Your French boss agreed to that? I didn't.'

'I said I was going to go after them. But I need your help. You're British. You know the levers to pull. You knew how you were going to use this for maximum effect.' He tapped the envelope containing the negative and the print.

She hesitated. 'I had some ideas on how and when to use a one-time nuclear option. But trying to gradually undermine a shadowy operation being run jointly by the Foreign Office and the police is a very different matter. Where's their pressure points? Who's the right person to target and make it all unravel? With the Heath photo, when the right time comes, I can just go to Frederick at the Whips' Office -

throw the print on his desk, promise him another weekend in Brighton, and then hide behind him while he does all the dirty work on my behalf. With this…'

'So you don't want to help? You're the one who persuaded me to join this crusade in the first place,' he said in a colder voice.

'I didn't say I wouldn't help deal with Fryatt and Smythe. I only said that I don't know how to.' Her voice was frosty now too.

The Assassin wondered what more he could say to encourage her.

'What if Fryatt has a political motivation that clashes with Heath and the Conservative Party? Won't Brierly be concerned that someone with the kind of power that comes from compromising members of the Establishment at Smythe's parties might be a loose cannon?'

'What do you imagine his motivation in life is then?'

The Assassin thought back to the spat between the pair at the club in Piccadilly.

'I've only met Fryatt once, for dinner with Brierly back in March. Apart from general complaints at Britain's economic weakness, the only specific political opinion he shared was when the topic of the European Parliament came up. He said, "the whole point of joining the EEC is to keep the plebs well away from power."'

'Then maybe that's Fryatt's thing? Maybe he just despises the little people? It's hardly an unknown trait amongst the English upper classes. What's your point?' she asked.

'But don't you see?' he said more confidently now. 'Whatever material Smythe has been collecting over the years equals power. Power to manipulate powerful people from behind the scenes. Fryatt spends years overseas in the Arab world, negotiating Britain's exit from the Gulf amongst other things. Maybe while he was out there, he got a taste for intrigue and secret deals? Like how Britain's running a war in Oman, supporting the sultan who deposed his own father?'

'I think you're making some very heroic assumptions there.'

'I'm drawing a quick sketch, not painting a Rembrandt. Voaden said that Fryatt's family were rich, so I presume he's doing it for the hidden influence it gives him. Smythe's almost certainly doing it for the money. I put those suggestions to Voaden by the way, albeit indirectly. He didn't say no.'

'You said a lot of things to Voaden. That was dangerous. I imagine gossip is what he's always lived for. If he gave you a secret or two, then you paid for it by passing on some of your own, whether you realised it or not.'

'I was careful. I didn't mention you.'

'Even so. I'm still not certain I can do anything much against Fryatt directly. Not against someone who's got general ambitions but no obvious plan.'

'What would Brierly and Devilliers think about being misled by Fryatt and Smythe? They seem honest enough in their own way. At least as measured by their dedication to the cause of EEC accession.'

'I suppose so. Devilliers' certainly kept alive the flames of his passion for a European state over the decades. But I wouldn't be surprised if when it came to it, he'd view that whatever steps Fryatt might have taken to protect Heath were a necessary evil, for the greater good of the country.'

'That's crazy,' said the Assassin. 'Fryatt and Smythe most likely triggered the threats in the first place.'

They looked at one another for a while.

'How can you be certain?' she asked. 'Maybe taking over the network was necessary to protect Heath from a completely different set of people to the Marks, ones whom we know nothing about. Maybe he does have other secrets? Maybe something as simple and boring as bribery? He is somewhat of a miser, after all.'

He slowly shook his head. 'We may never know. It just proves that you shouldn't underestimate men's ability to do the wrong thing for the right reasons.'

Selene unwound the towel from her head and began to slowly rub her hair. 'I need to start getting ready in a few minutes. You said that Smythe photographed you with Annersley and presumably also with Barker in Devon. But is he still intending to smear Grieves?'

The Assassin composed his face at the mention of the second Mark. 'He wants to do more than that. He's preparing a finale. One last scene to make it very explicit to Grieves that he's under suspicion of working for the other side.'

'What's his plan for doing that?'

'Stage a fake arrest of Grieves and myself as we flee the country. Smythe wants me to get Grieves to a remote location somewhere. An old airfield perhaps.'

'Sounds melodramatic.'

'That's exactly what it would be. We'd be putting on a show for Grieves to scare him permanently into silence.'

'Really? Why would Grieves agree to put himself in that position? What if after your visit at the weekend, Voaden's already warned Grieves that you're sniffing around? You're hardly nondescript with your scars.'

'I don't know if Voaden and Grieves know each other. I don't even know if Grieves knows the other two Marks.'

'Don't you have to assume that they do?'

'I met Grieves yesterday, you know. He tells me he's considering a business trip to Berlin.'

'That sounds convenient for Smythe's arrest idea.'

The Assassin drummed his fingers on the table.

'You see what I mean?' she insisted. 'Or what if Smythe has already done a deal with Grieves to get, not him, but you to a remote location? Maybe Grieves has already handed over his blackmail material on Heath and is off the hook? What if Smythe and the others have prioritised you because what we did to Heath is more of an immediate threat?'

'What? And all of that's happened in the past forty-eight hours? By the way, if I'm in danger, then so are you,' he said.

'Yes, but I'm not in the photo, you are,' she replied.

'At the end of the day, it's only a photo.'

'But what a photo. A picture of Heath being embraced by an unknown German? That's all the press will talk about for weeks'

'Just like the Boothby photograph with the Kray twin?' he suggested.

'Like Profumo and Boothby rolled into one. All the rumours about Heath and the mythical Czech organist finally coming true after a fashion. He won't survive.' She shook her head at the audacity of it. 'When I go to Frederick, I'll tell him there's more photos where that one came from. Allowing the police to finally prosecute some junior minister after being caught for the fifth time with a boy from Piccadilly Circus will easily seem the lesser of two evils.'

'It's not the sort of dusty, dry document which could have been knocked up in a KGB forgery lab, I suppose.'

The Assassin took the photo out of the envelope again. It showed only himself and Heath, with nobody else in the background. He knew the picture had been taken in a pub, but there were no obvious features or other decorations on the wall behind them to identify it as such. It could have been a private function room at any venue.

'Smythe hasn't come up with a firm suggestion yet for how we could get Grieves to leave London. I was the one who talked to him about taking a trip to Berlin. If there is a plan to silence Grieves and myself, I'm not sure it's not one that had been devised at eleven o'clock this morning.'

Selene drew on her cigarette and looked at him with narrowed eyes.

'Where is this fake arrest meant to be taking place?' she asked.

'Smythe talked about finding an old airfield in East Anglia.'

She cocked her head and raised an eyebrow.

He ploughed on. 'What state are the runways behind Devilliers' house in? Could they still take a light aircraft?'

'Because you're actually thinking of leaving the country that way?' she asked in an amazed voice. 'You're not just staging something for Grieves and Smythe? What then? Are you planning to take Grieves with you? Take him out of the picture entirely?'

The Assassin was impassive. 'Maybe.'

'I've no idea about the place near Somersham,' she continued. 'But there's tens of other disused bomber airfields in East Anglia.'

'Are there any old airfields near the coast that you know of?'

'I stayed in a house in Acle a couple of years ago. Sailing holiday with friends on the Broads. I've got an Ordnance Survey map for the area somewhere.'

The Assassin waited while she went to look on the shelves of an antique mahogany bookcase with glass doors.

'Here,' she said, returning to unfold the sheet on the table, smoothing it out with her long, lightly tanned fingers. He wondered if she'd be wearing her silver rings again tonight.

'There's one place that might do. From what I can remember, it didn't look too broken down a couple of years ago when we drove past.'

As she bent over the table, the front of her dressing gown gaped slightly. She sat up and retied it tighter around herself. The Assassin made a show of keeping his eyes fixed on the map.

'Which one is it?' he asked. There were two or three triangles of former runways marked on the section she'd spread out.

'There - that one.' She circled it with a pencil. 'You can have this map if you like, but it's a few years out of date. Take a note of the sheet number and you can buy the most recent edition at Stanfords in Covent Garden.'

The Assassin traced the outline of the coast on a page of his notebook, carefully copying the perimeter track of the airfield she'd circled.

When he was done, she folded the map up again. Setting it to one side, she placed the blue envelope on top.

'What do you think is going to happen to the first two Marks now?' she asked.

'I'm not sure. The smear attempt with me was only one method of blackmail. I suppose Smythe has other material he can dip into if he has to. He told me he's been collecting evidence for years.'

'There's Westminster rumours of a kind of black book, just like the one the Whips maintain on the MPs. But this one supposedly contains the secrets of the entire Establishment, all the way from the top to the bottom.'

'What if Smythe's dossier is it?'

She shook her head. 'It's probably just a rumour intended to scare people.'

'Maybe that's why Brierly was open to helping Fryatt and Smythe?' he asked. 'Just in case it wasn't? Maybe Brierly helps them silence the three Marks and in exchange Heath's real secrets stay hidden - if he has any.'

'Everyone has secrets. Stop thinking the best of people. But Brierly doesn't give me the impression that he's under any kind of pressure from Fryatt,' she replied. 'He's somewhat dismissive of him, if anything - even though they're both working for accession to the EEC.'

The Assassin gazed at the opposite wall, deep in thought. The seconds of silence stretched out.

'What does the man that you met in the bar of the Royal Southern do?' he asked.

She gave him a puzzled look. 'He's something in the City.'

Then she frowned. 'I would have slept with you in Bosham, you know. You only had to make a move. It would have been our secret. No one need ever have known.'

'I told you, I'm married. At some point the destruction of lives has to stop.'

'Every time I start going out with someone new, there's always a chance that it will be the real thing.'

'I wish I could make love happen for you.' He got to his feet.

'Is this goodbye?' she asked looking up. 'Do I get a kiss?'

He remained where he stood. 'I really do think you're in danger. Call in sick to work. Go and stay with your parents until next weekend.'

'Men have been trying to tell me what to do all my life,' she said. 'Staying in London is my choice. They can come and get me. I'm not running.'

'You have a life ahead of you. Don't risk it by stubbornness.'

'You have a cheek saying that. You're the one who wants to take on the world. The three Marks, Heath and now Fryatt and Smythe - all at the same time.'

'What are you saying? I'm acting like a man? I want to have it all?'

'Don't forget that you have a life as well. A wife waiting for you at home, or so you say.'

'I won't forget. I signed my life away for her.'

Selene frowned. '"To her" or "for her."'

'For her. For all women.'

-

After leaving Selene, the Assassin called Reynolds' flat from a phone box around the corner from her apartment.

'Are you going to be in for the rest of the evening?' he asked when Reynolds answered.

'Yes.'

'We need to talk,' said the Assassin.

'And you need to clear your things out of my spare room.'

'I'll be over in an hour. I'll take you out to dinner, if you like. We never had that meal at the restaurant on the Old Brompton Road that you talked about.'

'Come to mine first. You can let yourself in with your key,' said Reynolds drily.

Half an hour later, Assassin presented himself at the flat in Earl's Court.

'Where have you been this past week?' asked Reynolds, as the Assassin entered the lounge. 'I thought you'd vanished off the face of the earth.'

'And good evening to you too. Did you want to have dinner or not?'

'I've eaten already.'

'Suit yourself. And in answer to your question, I haven't been anywhere, I've been working with Smythe on my assignment.'

'I hope to hell you people know what you're doing. You're in the book by the way. Classified as an East German sleeper agent operating in the West, because we couldn't think of how else to describe you.'

'Does it have a secret mark to show that I'm not? It wouldn't do for there to be confusion at some later point in time.'

'I'm sure you'll be cross-indexed elsewhere on another file. Don't ask us how we do our job.'

'Did my being out of touch this past week cause you any problems?'

Reynolds shrugged noncommittally. 'Now that a decision has been made about you, work expects me to kick you out soon. But not in a way that would make a supposed Stasi agent suspicious.'

'So I'm not to be kept under observation?'

'You're not rated important enough for that. We have to prioritise our objectives.'

The Assassin gave him a wry look. 'I'm not going to take offence at an imaginary status,' he said with a half-smile.

'Can you pack up quickly please?' asked Reynolds. 'I'm meeting Linda in Leicester Square shortly.'

'Cinema?'

Reynolds pursed his lips. 'Yes. Her choice.'

The Assassin's expression was neutral. 'Come through to the bedroom while I pack,' he said. 'I need to ask you something before I leave.'

Curious despite himself, Reynolds dutifully followed the Assassin into the box room.

The Assassin dragged his bags from under the bed and started to empty drawers. Suddenly, he stopped what he was doing, and looked

Reynolds in the eye. 'How far would Masterson go to further his career?'

'What are you cooking up now?'

'I want to understand how he might have benefited professionally from my being here.'

'How would I know that?' replied Reynolds. 'You haven't even told me what you're doing in London in the first place.'

'But you guessed, right? You must know why MI5 would want a supposed East German agent on their books? One they can bring out to embarrass people with at the drop of a hat?'

'Yes. We'd already worked it out. Some kind of smear. But we don't know who it's directed against or why.'

'And your boss really doesn't know?'

Reynolds gave another shrug.

'If Masterson's already gone this far for Brierly and Fryatt, how much further would he go again?' asked the Assassin a second time. 'What would he be prepared to do for the chance, say, of a transfer to MI6?'

'It's none of your business. And anyway, I can't speak for him.'

'Is it a possibility? Think. This could be important. Anglo-French relations might be at stake. I'm not exaggerating.'

Reynolds was unconvinced. 'All that Masterson cares about is advancing his career,' he grumbled. 'He's just at the point where the next step up in grade puts him on the inside track to reach the very top. If he gets that promotion, he's got it made.'

'Maybe by getting me into your books he's already sitting pretty? Even if MI5 doesn't come through, maybe he's already secretly earned the transfer to Century House he's always craved? The chance for a fresh start in a new organisation?'

'You make it sound all so cynical and corporate. We're here to defend the nation's interests, not jockey for a bigger desk.'

'Yes. But Masterson has to explain to his wife why that's more important than a pony for their daughter,' said the Assassin.

'You don't know anything about him or his family. Stop making things up.'

'Stop avoiding the point. What if his loyalties are divided right now?'

'Like yours,' muttered Reynolds. 'Where are all these questions leading to, anyway?'

'Patience,' said the Assassin. He finished packing his bags and followed Reynolds back to the lounge. To the other man's disappointment, instead of leaving the flat, the Assassin dropped his bags and sat down on the sofa.

'My mission in England is almost over,' he announced.

'So when's your last day?' asked Reynolds, suppressing his annoyance.

'This coming weekend, I think.'

'You think?' This time the edge of sarcasm in his voice couldn't be disguised.

The Assassin crossed one leg over his knee and waited a second before replying. 'You asked me the reasons for my questions about Masterson. Here's why. All of us right now, we have *un grand problème*. The kind of problem that you feared this informal arrangement might lead to.'

Now Reynolds sat down, his face serious. 'Go on.'

'I'm not going to spell out every last detail for you. Trust me, when I say that for your sake, you don't want to know. But in short, the SDECE's arrangement with MI6 has gone sour.'

'With MI6?' repeated Reynolds uncertainly. 'Are you sure about that?'

The Assassin raised his eyebrows at the other man. 'Hence my questions to you about Masterson.'

'Is he in trouble somehow for agreeing to work with you?'

'If Masterson's in trouble then so are you. But in truth, we're all in trouble right now. There's been a falling out over the correct operational approach towards the people that we were jointly targeting.'

'What happened?'

'It turned out that our MI6 contacts didn't just want the SDECE to smear our troublesome customers, they tried to trick us into killing them. They tried to use us for their own dirty work. On your service's home territory.'

'Are you joking? I can't tell with you sometimes.'

'You decide. My French boss in Brussels is furious. Angrier than you can even imagine. I was sent here in good faith because he thought that he and MI6 had an understanding. There was a joint plan that we'd carefully worked out together.'

Reynold rested his head in his hands. He gave himself a moment or two. 'What's going to happen next? Are Masterson and I implicated?' he asked.

'I have a proposition I want to make to your boss. A chance for us to get even with MI6. If Masterson helps make things right with France, my own boss will ensure you both get the credit within your organisation for rescuing the situation. You'll be the heroes of the hour.'

'Those are big claims you're making.'

'No, not claims. Opportunities, for you and your boss.' He nodded encouragingly at Reynolds. 'Can you reach Masterson tonight? I need to speak with him in private, no later than tomorrow evening.'

Reynolds grumbled.

'I just told you it will be worth your while,' insisted the Assassin.

'If you say there's trouble brewing, I have to let him know in any case. I'll tell you what he decides.'

'I can wait downstairs in the hall with my bags if you like. Give you some privacy.'

After ten minutes, Reynolds appeared at the top of the hallway stairs. He slowly descended to meet the Assassin at the bottom.

'Masterson's agreed to meet you tomorrow afternoon at four,' he said to his now ex-flatmate. 'Here, I've written down the address. It's in Seven Dials. Knock loudly when you arrive.'

He reached out with a slip of paper. 'And don't waste our time chasing wild geese.'

'Trust me.'

Reynolds held on to the note a moment longer. 'You keep asking us to do that. But trust is finite, and at some point in the not too-distant future, it will all be used up. Just make sure you've still got enough to see you onto that plane at Heathrow.'

Chapter Twenty-Eight

Next morning the Assassin went to the travel agency to speak on the secure line to Kramer.

But before he could report, Kramer had news of his own.

'Well, I didn't have to call Brierly in the end,' announced the Frenchman. 'He called me, and now you're in all kinds of trouble.'

'How about the girl? Is she in trouble too?'

'I imagine he's taking care of her in his own way.'

'What's he said? What's he going to do to her?'

'You're showing a dangerous level of interest in her welfare for someone in your domestic situation. Forgiveness isn't in the nature of your wife's family.'

'I can't help that.'

'Well, Brierly wants your head on a platter for sure.'

'What can he do? He works for a think-tank, not the Mafia.'

'He's threatened to disrupt the accession talks and make sure I get blamed for it.'

The Assassin really needed to see Kramer's face just then, he could only pick up so much from the tone of his voice.

'That's a preposterous reaction. And "disruption"? We both know that's only code for stage-managed delay. If Heath and Pompidou have come to a final agreement on terms, then the Conservative Party can't afford to back out now, they've invested too much politically into this.'

'You're sounding very confident for someone who's got no friends left over there.'

'What? Not even my police buddy Smythe?' So what else does Brierly want, apart from my head?'

'He's demanded the return of the film and your immediate departure from England. I must say, that's one way to get out of a job you never really wanted to do.'

'Are you coming over to England to straighten things out with him?'

'No. For now, I'm denying all knowledge of you and your hare-brained scheme on the side. You'll have to give him back his film. I'm sorry. It seemed too good to be true, and it was.'

'I need to stop calling you from this line then. Brierly can't find me, and he can't make me give up the negatives. Anyway, why should we? Knowingly or not, he's spent all of his political capital with you to protect MI6's new network of child abusers, even if he didn't realise it.'

'Until Heath's signature is on the accession treaty, Brierly can never overdraw his account with us.'

'When did he call you?'

'Late last night.'

'Okay. I'm ringing off now. I need to warn the girl.'

'She's your problem now.'

The Assassin replaced the handset then dialled Selene on the regular unscrambled line. There was no reply, which was hardly surprising as she ought to have been at work by that time.

He took some stationery from a tray on the desk and scribbled a note, sealing it inside an envelope printed with the Air France hippocampus. Leaving the agency, he jumped in a taxi on Piccadilly and headed for her flat.

The street door was ajar. Pushing his way inside, he took the stairs up to her landing two at a time and knocked. No one answered, so he slid the envelope under the door and tried her next-door neighbour's flat. There was no answer there either.

On his way down the stairs, he met a young woman coming up with a cardboard box in her hands. He'd seen her earlier by the side of the road, unloading other boxes from the back of a Hillman estate car.

'Excuse me. Do you know Selene?' he asked.

'I live next door. Who are you?'

'A friend. Have you seen her today?'

'No. I imagine she's at work. You ought to know that if you're a pal. But even if you are, you shouldn't be hanging around here. It's not polite.'

'Look, I know she's popular. But I really am a friend of hers, it's just that I haven't heard from her for a few days. I'm getting worried.'

'It's none of my business, but for your information she has lots of male friends. You're only one of many. For all I know, she's simply becoming tired of you. Leave her alone, for your sake as much as hers.'

'Don't worry, I'm going. Keep an eye out for her these next few days, will you? If she doesn't turn up, call the police.'

The woman looked at him disbelievingly. 'Really? You're that worried?'

'I might call back tomorrow. What's your name?'

The woman frowned. 'Whereabouts are you from with that accent? I report creeps too, you know.' Then she relented. 'I'm Helen.'

'I'm Thomas.'

'I'll tell Selene you were asking after her when I see her next.'

—

The Assassin walked the short distance to Hyde Park and sat on a bench near the Corner, smoking for a while. Coming to a resolution, he ground out his cigarette on the path and made his way up Park Lane to the Dorchester where he paid for a room until Sunday. Collecting the key, he went up to the fourth floor.

His new room was bigger than the one which Reynolds had booked him into, but the Assassin wasn't paying for this one either. Checking his watch, he sat down at the desk and looked in his notebook for the number of Grieves' office.

'This is Mr. Hofmann,' he announced to Grieves' secretary when she answered. 'I'm calling to confirm the lunch booking for next week with Mr. Grieves.'

'One moment. He asked me to put you through to him straight away if you called again.' She sounded different today, as if he wasn't a piece of dirt under her shoe

A click came down the line as she put the call on hold. Grieves picked up. 'Hofmann?' he asked.

'Yes?'

'Where are you calling from?'

There was a moment's hesitation on the Assassin's part. 'I'm staying at the Dorchester. If you have any messages for me, you can leave them here.'

'I need to meet with you. Today, if possible.'

'What's going on? You have some new information about who Maxwell saw in Vienna?'

'No. I can't talk about it over the phone. Let's meet somewhere off the beaten track.'

The Assassin thought quickly. 'There's a pub called the Scots Arms by Saint Katharine's Docks. I've been there before. It's not busy, not now that the docks have closed.'

'What's the address?' asked Grieves.

'Wait a minute.' The Assassin consulted his A-Z. 'Almost at the western end of Wapping High Street, at the junction with Redmead Lane. Meet me there in an hour's time.'

Grieves was already inside the pub when the Assassin arrived. The last time he'd been here, the landlord had explained at length how the original building had been destroyed in the Blitz, as the Assassin was learning to call it. That evening the Assassin had successfully side-stepped any questions about where he was from, otherwise he might have been tempted to tell them what happened to cities when the real experts at carpet bombing got to work.

Grieves was sitting on his own with a gin and tonic and gave him a cautious nod. The Assassin couldn't swear to it, but he thought by the glint on his brow that the other man was sweating. He went up to him and rapped on the table.

'I don't want to speak in here,' said Grieves. 'Let's talk outside.'

'Okay.'

Grieves gulped down his drink and they left, walking the short distance to the derelict south-east corner of Saint Katharine's Dock. The warehouses which formerly stood there had been demolished and the site cleared in preparation for the arrival of the developers, much to the delight of the pub landlord.

The Assassin pushed through a gap in the hoarding and led the businessman past lumps of fallen bricks and over lengths of rusted steel wire to the middle of the quayside. Almost directly opposite on the far side was a wooden-framed building. They were out of earshot of any living soul.

Grieves sat down on an old bollard, its layers of paint flaking to the touch. The Assassin stood on the very edge of the dock and peered down into dark water, waiting for Grieves to begin

'I have a confession to make,' he said at last. 'Three or four years ago I accepted an invitation to several parties that in hindsight I wish I'd never gone to. Now I'm being threatened over one of them.'

'What kind of parties were they?' asked the Assassin, turning around to face him.

'I'm not being blackmailed over my own behaviour, if that's what you're thinking,' replied Grieves more defiantly now.

He lowered his voice again. 'But I've been told that someone I knew has recently disappeared, someone who went to the same events. The rumour going around is that he was murdered by the secret services. I was warned that they're coming to get all of us in my circle of contacts.'

The Assassin's heart missed a beat. Only two other people apart from himself - three including the boy - knew what had happened in Devon. The source of the rumours heard by both Grieves and Voaden surely had to be Smythe.

'Again, what kind of parties could possibly have justified those consequences?' he asked.

'I'd prefer not to say. Just take my word for it.'

'Have you heard some general gossip, or has someone threatened you directly?'

'Can't say. My situation is what it is. But I won't be held prisoner by the past,' said Grieves fiercely.

'Why are you telling me this? You're looking for my help in some way?'

'You can give me a legitimate reason to leave the country for a while.'

'Why do you need a legitimate one? I'm not getting involved in anything criminal, such as helping you run from the police.'

'I want a change of scenery. I'll run my businesses from overseas for a couple of months until the rumours are confirmed one way or another.'

The Assassin turned away to look across the dock again.

The businessman continued. 'I can kill two birds with one stone. I can spend time overseas making a start on my plan of opening up shop in the Communist bloc. And it couldn't hurt to find a country where I'd be beyond the reach of the law in Britain, if it ever came to that.'

The Assassin turned round to face Grieves once more. 'For the third time of asking - what on earth happened at those parties?' he said in apparent amazement.

Yet again Grieves refused the question. 'How likely it is that one of the communist countries would host a Western businessman?' he asked.

'What do you mean "host"? Grant a form of asylum?'

'Not necessarily right away. Maybe at some point after I've made the initial move to the Continent.'

The Assassin whistled through his teeth. 'Sounds expensive. Especially if you're seeking some kind of political sponsorship from a Communist regime. What do you have to offer them in return?'

'I have money salted away from the taxman in various locations.'

'That's not what I meant.' The Assassin wondered whether to take the plunge and ask Grieves if the idea of leaving England had come to him all on his own. The Englishman interpreted the Assassin's silence differently.

'Don't waste your time thinking of ways to gouge me,' he suddenly snapped. 'I can walk into the East German Foreign Trade Office myself, if it comes to that. I know the way to Belgrave Square.'

'Yes, but I know how to make them take you seriously, if you do.'

The Assassin kicked a loose stone from the dock's cracked concrete surface into the water.

'You say that someone you know died, or was killed? When did this happen?'

'A week or two ago.'

'Have you seen anything in the newspapers to confirm the rumour?'

'No. But I'm frightened and I'm not faking it. I've cancelled all my outside appointments for the time being. It will be straight to work and straight back home for a while.'

'You need to vary your travel routine, if you're worried about your security,' said the Assassin. 'Who told you about this person who died?' he asked, probing for confirmation it was Smythe.

'Never you mind. Someone I trust who moves in that world.'

'I can't help you unless you tell me what was so sinister about these parties. I already said that I'm not getting involved in anything criminal. And definitely not while I'm in a foreign country. Was it a specific party that made you a target, or just a certain type of party in general?'

Grieves gazed past the Assassin's shoulder out over the dock, weighing up what to say next.

'There was one party I went to a couple of years ago. Something untoward happened there. The person I was with that evening saw things he shouldn't have. And then we watched in the days and weeks that followed as some prominent players were threatened and their lives destroyed.'

'Really?'

'We decided that it wasn't going to happen to us,' said Grieves more confidently now. 'So we made sure word got out that we also knew some personal secrets. Secrets about certain people in government - very high up in government. Dark ones that they wouldn't want to come to light.'

The Assassin slowly shook his head as if in despair.

'That was bloody stupid. Do you have any records or proof of these secrets? Photographs? Handwritten letters? Otherwise it's your word against theirs.'

'I just know. I can draw you a diagram of my contacts. Who's connected to whom but would rather not have it known. There's just too many coincidences for this person not to be involved.'

The Assassin thought for a few moments, his forehead knotted.

'Forget East Germany for now. That idea could take months to bring to fruition. But if you can produce enough hard evidence, I know people in French politics who would do more than sponsor your residence permit. They could take direct action on your behalf right away. Get you out of the UK, almost immediately. Quietly too, outside the usual channels. And then keep you hidden in France or its overseas territories afterwards. There's worse ways to spend six months until the dust settles than sitting on a beach somewhere in the French Caribbean drinking rum.'

'How can I trust you? Where's this French idea suddenly come from?'

'You forget where I work. In Brussels I have access to influential people from all six EEC countries. People who in turn have influence in several capitals at once.'

'You didn't tell me that before, about being connected to France. I thought it was people in East Germany who were your prize contacts? The Deputy Trade Minister, wasn't it?'

'Introducers are allowed to know people in more than one country. I'm not slavishly loyal to one place over another.'

'Just get to the point,' said Grieves. 'What are you expecting by way of compensation?'

'Tell me something first. Who are these people in the British government whom you know things about? Or is it a person?'

Grieves gave the Assassin a sly, sideways glance.

'The man in question is one of the very top people in the Cabinet.' He pointed his finger up into the air and gave a grin.

'"One of" you say? It wouldn't be your bachelor Prime Minister by any chance? Or are we talking about a second Profumo here?'

'For argument's sake, let's say you were right the first time,' replied Grieves.

'Then all I can say is no wonder you're in trouble,' said the Assassin gravely.

Grieves looked at him with an air of anxiety. 'Well?' What would it be worth to Paris?'

'The people I know would definitely be interested in having something to hold over Heath. Just to avoid confusion, that's definitely who we're talking about, right?'

Grieves nodded dumbly, his riddling finished for now.

'Why so despondent?' asked the Assassin. 'From what I've heard since coming to England, you may have more friends than you think. I've been told his arrogance grates on many within his political party. That and his pompous sense of destiny.'

'What's your credentials with these French political figures you say you know?'

'Give me a day to speak to someone at the right level. If it will convince you, I'll set up a meeting at the French embassy.'

'What other proof do you have?'

'If it helps, I hold French citizenship after my service with the Foreign Legion.'

'You never mentioned that before,' said Grieves, suddenly suspicious now.

'Look.' The Assassin reached into his jacket and handed over a French passport. Grieves flicked through it.

'Thomas Hofmann. Born in Wismar in nineteen forty-five? Where's that? Alsace-Lorraine?'

'No. It's in what's now known as East Germany. Part of my family escaped to Hamburg just after the war. I still have cousins in the East, so I have an excuse to go there as often as I need to.'

'How did you end up in the French Foreign Legion?'

'I got into trouble with the police as a teenager.'

'Get me to France quickly and with no fuss and I'll pay you well.'

'Give me something to show my main French contact in Brussels. Some hard evidence, or one of your diagrams of contacts. Then we can talk.'

Grieves' shoulders slumped. 'I told you already. I don't have anything to hand. But once I'm in Paris, I'll happily tell everything I know to anyone you like.'

The Assassin sighed. 'I'll talk to my guy, but I can't promise you anything. You understand the risks they'd be taking if the British secret services really are after you? People connected to the French government can't afford to be caught interfering in British internal affairs.'

'It needs to be soon. You're not the one looking over your shoulder at every shadow.'

'Then just leave right now. Take a taxi straight to Heathrow and go.'

'I can't. I still have business arrangements to make. Powers of attorney to sign. I need to brief Jackett.'

'That's the problem with wealth. It slows you down.'

'How do you know?' asked Grieves sceptically.

'I don't. But I know people who do. I'll phone you at your office tomorrow at midday. Make sure you're free to take my call.'

-

The Assassin walked with Grieves as far as the tube station at Tower Hill, past the modern office block on the north side of the dock and the first of the yachts to be moored in the new marina.

As he rode the District Line to the Embankment and his meeting with Reynolds and Masterson in Seven Dials, he thought long and hard about Smythe's next move, if indeed it was Smythe who'd called up Grieves and not a panicking Annersley. Whatever Smythe was planning, everything was coming together too neatly for the policeman, and for the Assassin's liking.

Just like Grieves, the Assassin could leave this evening himself if he wanted to. He'd paid Mrs. MacDonald upfront, and Jimmy could return his gear to the French embassy. It would certainly avoid a confrontation with Brierly over the photograph with Heath. But he needed to know that Selene was safe from harassment, even if she was only in trouble in the short term. And he had something else on his conscience too, over and beyond the caged body at the bottom of the Bristol Channel being nibbled at by the crabs.

As he walked past the pubs and theatres of Saint Martin's Lane, he thought one last time about the incentives he was planning to offer Masterson to switch his support from Brierly, and perhaps Fryatt, to Kramer and the SDECE.

He had several cards in his hand, selections from the treasure trove of secrets he'd been provided with at his last operational briefing in Brussels. If he played them right, he ought to get most of what he wanted from the MI5 men. And in any case, a secret never spent had no value at all.

Whatever the outcome of the next meeting, he was determined that he wasn't going to East Anglia alone, for that was where all roads seemed to be headed right now. If Masterson wouldn't give him the extra insurance he sought by drawing MI5 into the endgame, he still had plenty of credit with Jimmy. The block of high-grade heroin he'd handed over to the nightclub owner in March would have covered a month's employment of the old Kray gang - and he didn't imagine Jimmy's nephews were as expensive as that.

-

The meeting place with Reynolds and Masterson was a room above a shuttered shop. It sat just back from the Seven Dials junction itself, but the only antiques it offered these days were the collection of dead flies in the shop window. The upper room was bare, apart from two bentwood chairs, a rickety card table in one corner, and a well-worn sofa bed which had been left folded out by the room's previous users.

Masterson took one of the chairs, turning it so that he faced the door. He motioned to the Assassin to take the other one, but he declined and remained standing against the outside wall, a grimy sash window on either side of him. Reynolds also chose not to sit, instead stationing himself by the door, opposite Masterson. The sofa bed appeared to have been nibbled by rodents and there was a suspicion of fleas.

'So,' said Masterson, looking up from where he sat, legs wide apart. 'I understand you have a proposition for us? Some cock and bull story about you and Kramer falling out with the other lot?'

'You're not taking this seriously. See it from our point of view. We're invited by MI6 to help them solve a mutual problem in an intelligent, legal way. You're brought into it as well, to support the operation from the MI5 end, by people you trust too.'

'And?'

'And then MI6 turn the tables on the SDECE, try to get us to do things which are very illegal. All so that they can keep their own hands clean. As far as France is concerned, it's a hostile act. Just as Britain needs all its friends in Europe.'

'Why are you coming crying to me?'

'Because you're going to fix this.'

'Or else?'

The Assassin looked deliberately between Masterson and Reynolds and then back again. 'Or else Brierly will say you've been hosting a real Stasi agent - one to whom you've just given a clean bill of health.'

'He would drop you in it like that?' asked Masterson.

'I'd survive. Reinvent myself again.'

'So you'd be prepared to smear us with exactly the same smear as Brierly was organising for your targets? All because you're pissed off at Century House?'

'It's not a fair world. And there would be no "us" about it,' said the Assassin coldly. 'It would be you in the hot seat.'

Masterson looked disgustedly at Reynolds, as if this was all his doing. 'Unlike the ponces and nonces that Brierly's trying to scare off, I'm a much tougher proposition,' he said.

'Is that what this was all about?' asked Reynolds. 'You were smearing a bunch of dirty old men? I assumed it was preparation for a first strike against suspected KGB illegals.'

'If only,' said the Assassin.

'So what did these people do to merit the attention of the intelligence services?' asked Reynolds.

The Assassin looked at Masterson and raised his eyebrows. Masterson coughed. 'It was never said so explicitly. But it was obvious whose reputation we were working to protect.'

'Are you going to tell him?' asked the Assassin.

Masterson gave a couple of slow nods. 'Edward Heath.'

Reynolds shook his head in wonderment, but he wasn't as surprised as the Assassin had expected him to be. Maybe everyone had sneaking suspicions about the Prime Minister.

'Protect his reputation how?' asked Reynolds.

'The people we targeted claimed they knew things about him. Private things of a personal nature,' replied the Assassin.

'And now you know too,' said Reynolds' boss.

'So tell me this then,' said the Assassin. 'Now that we're all clear about what's at stake, why wouldn't you jump at the chance to stab MI6 in the back over this shambles with the SDECE? No one from Century House will be sweeping in now to pluck you out of obscurity and give you a fresh start south of the River. If I've learned anything from working for governments, it's that no one likes to be associated with failure.'

Masterson shook his head in mock disbelief. 'What's this? German diplomacy?' But he sounded amused rather than angry.

Reynolds' tone was sharper. 'That's enough Hofmann. I told you last night not to be presumptuous.'

Now Masterson gave the Assassin a speculative look. 'What's in it for us if we help you?'

The Assassin took a moment. He peered round the edge of the window, looking down at the shoppers in Tower Street before turning back to face Masterson.

'One juicy secret, and one offer to collect some even juicier secrets together,' he said.

'Go on.'

'There's a reason why MI6 were keen to protect Heath. Or rather, there's one person in particular who's keen. Someone whom the

SDECE has known about for a very long time. Someone with a secret which they've managed to keep hidden from a succession of your interior and foreign ministers. Whoever it was within MI6 that Fryatt or Brierly may have introduced you to, he won't be higher up than this man. Or have more to lose.'

The Assassin paused. Masterson frowned. 'You're really laying it on thick, aren't you?' he said, trying to keep the curiosity out of his voice.

'I don't like where this is going,' said Reynolds. 'Who's Fryatt, by the way?'

'Shut up. Let's hear what Hofmann has to say. Go on,' said Masterson warily.

'Allow Reynolds to help me fix this, and I'll give you a name. For now I'll call this person "Treasure."'

'Who is he?'

'Someone who reports to the head of MI6. A homosexual who's lied about it for decades to the security vetters in the Secret Intelligence Service. Someone who's in the running to be the next Director. Someone who, if this gets out, can't be trusted by his political masters not to lie again.'

'Everyone who reports to the Director is in the running for that post. Just how do you know all this?'

'Because the SDECE operates in the same places around the world, and on the same incestuous embassy social circuits as Treasure did when he was posted overseas. Fryatt and Smythe aren't the only ones with an unhealthy interest in niche sexual practices.'

'It's not illegal in England anymore,' said Reynolds.

'That's not the point. Treasure is protecting one of his own. Someone like him.'

'Where's your proof of this?' said Masterson.

'There's no proof about Heath that I know of.'

'I should bloody well hope not,' interjected Reynolds.

'But I do know where we can search for evidence that Fryatt was trying to smear all sorts of people - not only the ones who made the claims about Heath.'

'Who's this man Fryatt?' asked Reynolds again.

'Someone in the Foreign Office who was Smythe's liaison contact,' said the Assassin. 'The man whose house in Stockwell you drove me to the day I arrived in England.'

'But if this Fryatt is connected to MI6, then protecting the Prime Minister and the state's interests is his job,' said Reynolds. 'Just as it is for us. So what's he done wrong?'

'Because it's not MI6's job to be running entrapment operations in this country involving British citizens, even if it is in support of the government. They're pissing on your lamp post.'

Masterson glanced at Reynolds who frowned back at him.

'Entrapment operations?' asked the Assassin's former flatmate. 'You mean something other than the smear plot involving you?'

The Assassin shook his head. 'Fryatt's been running one with Smythe for some months now. They may well have started out with Treasure's blessing, but it's taken on a life of its own and gone much, much further than the immediate objective of protecting Heath.'

'Really?' said Masterson, now frowning himself.

'I believe that Fryatt in particular has been making plans to acquire undue political influence over certain public figures, independent of any direction from Treasure or his own bosses in the Foreign Office.'

'What kind of undue influence?' asked Masterson.

'He's taken over an existing vice ring. One which his accomplice Smythe had been watching for years in order to protect prominent people. My guess is that they're keeping black files on the entire Establishment. Probably without your Service's knowledge.'

'Vice ring?' repeated Reynolds faintly.

'A circle of acquaintances on the underage sex scene who went to parties put on by the ringleader of the network. One into which they drew more and more people.'

'So where are these black files?' asked Masterson.

'I can't say for sure. But there's a place where I want to take a look before the week is out.'

'You mean the house we drove to in Stockwell?' asked Reynolds.

'Maybe. We'd have to break in, though.'

'I need more than conjecture about these people's intentions before I give my blessing to that kind of potential Career-ending caper.' said Masterson. 'You told Reynolds last night that MI6 wanted the SDECE to kill someone. What gave you that idea?'

'Because one of the people we're trying to smear is in fear of his life. He claims MI6 are out to get him.'

'But it doesn't follow that MI6 wants the SDECE to do it. Or that this threat is even real. Sounds more like something a fantasist would say. You, perhaps?'

'The guy wants to flee the country. And he doesn't scare lightly. I think MI6 are getting impatient and are preparing the ground to blame us if something does happen to him. I need to get him out before they do anything.'

'Who is this person?'

'A British businessman whom I've spoken with a couple of times this week. He's talking about leaving England permanently and going behind the Iron Curtain to help the Comecon countries develop their electronics industry there.'

'That sounds like an embellishment. What do you think, Reynolds?' asked Masterson.

Reynolds had been in turmoil ever since the Assassin first mentioned Heath. He thought the odds of his old flatmate's story being true about the Prime Minister, a Deputy Director, and other unspecified people being persecuted by MI6 were fifty-fifty at best.

'I believe Hofmann,' he said simply, reasoning that the only way to find out was to play along for the time being. It didn't help that his earlier suspicions about an unexplained relationship between his former flatmate and East Germany were still nagging him too.

'There's a couple of rooms in the basement of Smythe's house,' said the Assassin. 'How can it hurt for us to go and take a look together? We might find gold.'

Masterson rubbed his hands over his face. 'Can you do it and not get caught?' he asked the Assassin.

'Yes. I have people right here in London that we can use.'

'Is that your price for telling me the name of "Treasure"?'

'No. That comes later. If we find hard evidence at Smythe's house that he and Fryatt have strayed beyond collecting information on behalf of someone at MI6, I want their network shut down and the pair of them taken out of the picture.'

'You know I can't bargain with you over that? The tentacles of vice extend deep into society, and if you ask me, into some places too difficult and dangerous even for the Secret Service to reach. I won't make promises I can't keep,' said Masterson.

'You have to choose your priorities, Hofmann,' said Reynolds.

'But how could it upset your bosses if you found evidence that MI6 were crossing the line in that particular way?' asked the Assassin. 'It would be terminal for me if it showed any direct involvement by someone I report to,' said Masterson.

'How can you lose? Either you'll be able to blackmail your superiors, or if they're clean, they can use the material themselves to undermine MI6. If you start letting your foreign intelligence service rivals operate within England, then where does that eventually leave you?'

'The Service could use it to raise a stink and keep them out of Ireland,' suggested Reynolds.

'I can't make Reynolds break into someone's house,' said his boss.

The Assassin shrugged unconcernedly. 'Okay. Anything I find I'll keep for the SDECE.'

Masterson shook his head. 'You're not leaving us with much choice, are you? When do you propose doing this?'

'I don't know yet. I'll need to get back to you. I suspect that as part of the show being staged by Smythe, I'll be taking the person who's in fear of his life up to East Anglia towards the end of the week. Probably at the weekend.'

'You want Reynolds to go to Smythe's house while you're up there?'

'No. We'll go together to Stockwell.' The Assassin glanced at Reynolds.

'I'll do it,' said Reynolds. 'But how will we know if Smythe's away when we go to his house?'

'He doesn't have any set routines as far as I can tell.' The Assassin turned to Masterson. 'Why don't you approach Fryatt and suggest that you go for drinks with Smythe this Saturday evening? Somewhere like Brierly's club in Piccadilly. But do it casually. Either we'll find out where he's going to be that night, or he'll be out with you and the house will be empty.'

Masterson tilted back in his chair and gave the Assassin an appraising look. 'I never said that I knew Fryatt.'

'Did you need to?'

Masterson cocked his head to one side. 'You're a little sneak, aren't you? As well as a bully. You'd have done well at Stowe. Bring me something on Saturday night that I can believe in, and I'll start taking you seriously.'

The Assassin was the first to leave the safe house. He made his way to Leicester Square, intending to lose anyone who might be following him in the early evening crowds.

Soldier Blue was showing at the Odeon, but he'd seen enough of sex and violence in England already. He hoped for Reynolds' sake he hadn't taken his girlfriend to see it yesterday on their date. Those kinds of indirect suggestions could sometimes backfire.

He himself didn't believe that Heath and "Treasure", as he'd called Maurice Oldfield, were members of a secret British homosexual mafia. But planting the seeds of doubt in people's minds was just that. Given the right conditions, they grew into trees all on their own. Especially in Masterson's case, if he already wanted to believe the worst of MI6.

Chapter Twenty-Nine

The next morning the Assassin made his way west from Mrs. MacDonald's house to the Dorchester and let himself into his room. He left it until nine before calling Stockwell, wondering if the policeman had waited in for his call.

Smythe picked up, but only after six or seven rings. 'Well? You took your time. You were meant to call me last night.'

'Word about Devon has leaked out,' said the Assassin.

'How do you mean?'

'I spoke with Grieves again yesterday. He said he'd been told by an old acquaintance of a rumour going around that someone they both knew had been murdered by the Secret Service.'

There was a half-second pause.

'Shit.'

'What do we do now?' asked the Assassin.

'Did he say anything else?'

At the other end of the line, the Assassin smiled grimly to himself at Smythe's nonchalance. 'He's now desperate to leave the country. By any way he can.'

'Really?'

'Aren't you pleased? You know what this means for us?'

'If he's getting nervous, then let's not delay any longer. Let's do it. Trick him into going with you to an airfield in Norfolk by claiming we'll fly him out and let's give him the fright of his life when we arrest him. When are you seeing him next?'

'I said I'd call him. But there's an alternative to arresting him that I wanted to run past you.'

'Go on.'

'Let's not pretend we're flying him out. Let's get Kramer to actually do it. We could take him to Paris and interrogate him there.'

He'll give up what he knows soon enough, once the SDECE gets him hooked up to a car battery. Kramer can make him disappear into the system afterwards.'

Smythe gave a low whistle that came a fraction of a second too quickly. 'Does Kramer really mean it?' he asked more solemnly now.

'Why not? It's just a variation on your arrest theme.'

'And you're certain Kramer could arrange all that?'

'You'd be surprised at the things he can get people to do,' replied the Assassin drily.

'Well, if you're serious, I'll need to speak with the others.'

'Which others? Brierly?'

'And Fryatt. There's a Foreign Office angle to consider.'

No kidding, thought the Assassin. 'Do you have a proposed location for Norfolk yet?' he asked. 'If we really are to take him to France, we need somewhere that a plane could still take off from.'

'I've asked someone that Fryatt knows. He's suggested an old airfield a few miles outside Norwich. It still has runways which haven't been ploughed back into farmland yet.'

'How far away from London is it?'

'About a four-hour drive.'

'You'll have to give me the precise coordinates so I can have Kramer check it out with his people.'

'It's near a place called Reepham. Ten or so miles north-west of Norwich, I believe. But we haven't agreed to this idea yet. And as I said, I have to consult the others first.'

'It can't hurt to prepare some options,' said the Assassin. 'We don't necessarily need to use them. And in any case, we still have to get Grieves to agree to go to Norfolk, whether we end up arresting him there or not.'

'Okay. You work on Grieves and call whoever you need to in Brussels. I'll do the same at my end.'

'When shall we do it? The weekend?'

'Yes. I'll make sure no one's around at the East Anglian end.'

'What? At an abandoned airfield?'

'At the place we're thinking of, some of the old buildings are used by a farmer. Try to get Grieves up there for Sunday night. Tell him he's flying out Monday morning. Even if we decide later on that he isn't.'

The Assassin hesitated a moment before replying. Smythe's plan sounded very detailed for something first mooted only two days ago. 'Okay. I'll try it. If we do decide to go down the road of a staged arrest, who's going to carry it out?'

There was another pause, from Smythe's end this time. 'I'll find someone.'

'Why can't it be Reynolds? He's the most obvious candidate. He's young and pliable.'

'We already discussed him on Monday. I'll get someone from Obscene Publications to do it, someone whose discretion can be bought for a fee. How desperate did Grieves sound about wanting to leave the country?'

'I can't imagine he'll be happy to hang around for long. Let's see what he says to the idea of a trip to France first thing on Monday. He told me he'd have some business arrangements to make before he leaves Britain.'

'Maybe I need to shake him up a bit,' said Smythe.

'How would you do that?'

'Get some people to follow him. Act suspiciously near his house.'

'Too obvious. Threats work best when they're subtle. Let the other person use their imagination and they'll frighten themselves into submission. Don't do anything until I've spoken with him first.'

'Be quick about it then.'

The Assassin took a taxi from the hotel to the specialist shop in Covent Garden which Selene had told him about and bought the Ordnance Survey sheet for the Norfolk Broads. For good measure, he bought all of the other sheets which covered the rest of Norfolk too. When he was done, he hailed a cab on Long Acre and made his way straight back to the Dorchester and the privacy of his room.

He unfolded his new map on the bed and used the tracing he'd taken from Selene's older edition to find the airfield she'd circled. As far as he could remember, there didn't seem to have been that many changes over the years. On his copy, some additional grey rectangles had appeared, presumably where the owner had built new structures - perhaps sheds for animals, if that airfield was now also a farm.

He scanned a few grid squares in each compass direction, fascinated by the strange names of the villages. A few kilometres along, at the next nearest airfield to the one she'd marked, the triangle of runways had disappeared completely leaving only the perimeter track in a wide, roughly hexagonal circuit.

He searched too, for the airfield which Smythe had mentioned, using a piece of scrap paper as a ruler to mark off the distance from Norwich. Eventually, he found a triangle of runways north-east of the city. But it wasn't ten miles away as Smythe had said, and it wasn't that close to Reepham either. In fact, there were two other airfields in the same vicinity, and he wondered at Smythe for deliberately holding back the exact location. All three possibilities were in the middle of farmland. Remote places, as Smythe had intended. Places where anything could happen, and no one would ever find out. Just like the house in Devon.

-

Checking his watch, he left the map open on the bed and went over to the desk to dial Kramer at the Berlaymont. After a short delay, the Frenchman's secretary put him through.

'So,' said Kramer. 'Today's Wednesday. It's been two days since you told me about the photo of Heath, and one day since my former colleague asked for it back. Have you thought any more about the position you've put me in, or are you planning some new mischief?'

'The real question is what mischief have the policeman and the Foreign Office man been planning and how long for? And how deeply are they prepared to drag your old colleague into it?'

'What's your news?'

'Yesterday I met the third Mark privately in an out-of-the-way corner of the old docks. He's now saying that he's in fear of his life. That he had a call from someone, I presume he meant me to believe the first Mark, to say that one of their acquaintances was rumoured to have been killed by the secret services. He claims it's because of what they saw at that fatal party from two years ago, but it has to be the policeman playing games.'

'So the third Mark is in on a deception plan of some kind?'

'The liaison girl thought he might be playing a role. I don't know for sure.'

'How convincing did he sound when you spoke with him?'

'He's talking about getting out of England and staying out until he knows if the threats he's heard are serious. He even asked me how he could get asylum overseas. Then he said he'd turn the situation to his advantage and use the time away to investigate setting up business partnerships in the Communist bloc.'

'In East Germany?'

'It was mentioned.'

'I can't think where he got that idea from,' said Kramer sarcastically. 'How serious is he about Berlin?'

'I told him not to bother. I said that as a first step, he should relocate to France. I said I knew people who might be able to make it happen if he could provide evidence of any wrongdoing by the top man.'

'So he admitted that he did make those threats after all? Did he admit to having any blackmail material?'

'No. Only indirect proof of the top man's proclivities. He said that he would give us what he has, if we can protect him.'

'Have you spoken with the policeman since meeting the third Mark?'

'Yes. I told him everything that was said. If the policeman is feeding the third Mark his lines, I can't let him think I suspect it.

'And what do you suspect?'

'I think it's a set up. The third Mark's story about wanting to leave the country fits too neatly with the policeman's arrest plan.'

'There's a fine line between paranoia and caution.'

'I set the policeman a test. I suggested to him that you and I take the third Mark out of the country to interrogate him in France. Force him to give up any information or material he has on the top man.'

'What did he say to that?'

'He said he'd think about it, but that he'd have to ask the Foreign Office man and your old colleague too.'

'What do you imagine the policeman is getting ready to do?'

'I don't know. He and I have a shared interest because of what happened to the second Mark. Maybe he really does just want to frighten the third Mark. Or maybe he wants to manoeuvre me into silencing him permanently. Perhaps in exchange for my freedom from a police investigation into the second Mark.'

'Maybe he's switched over to working for my old colleague for the time being?' said Kramer. 'Maybe he's been asked to recover your film of the top man?'

'The thought had crossed my mind. But the encounter with the top man only happened on Saturday night. If the policeman was coaching the third Mark, they must have been preparing his story for a few days.'

'Is the policeman capable of an assassination?' asked Kramer.

'Possibly.'

'Has he mentioned your escapade with the top man at all?'

'No, but then he wouldn't, would he?'

'Could the policeman be planning to deal with two problems at once? His problem with the third Mark and my old colleague's problem with you?'

'That's possible too. At this stage, anything is,' replied the Assassin. 'Tell me, can we fly the third Mark out of Norfolk on Sunday night or Monday morning? The policeman has come forward with a suggestion for an airfield he claims we could do it from.'

'I suppose it could be one way to avoid further unpleasantness all round. Take you and the third Mark entirely out of the picture.'

'What would we do with the third Mark once we had him?'

'Probably nothing much. A debriefing interview with someone in the SDECE for form's sake, then we'd give him twelve month's residency and let him go. He can make his own way back to England when he's ready.'

'I said to the policeman we'd go heavy on the third Mark. Force him to divulge what he knows.'

'I already said, we don't need any material on the top man to get him to do what we want. His desperation for accession makes him entirely predictable,' said Kramer.

'How's it been going over there?'

There was a pause. 'I'm not going to discuss it on this line.'

Just at that moment, the Assassin felt very cut off from the rest of his colleagues in Brussels, even though he never had much to do with them as they each went about watching different delegations from the accession countries.

'Have you had any calls from London about my photo with the top man?' he asked, coming back to the task in hand.

'No. My old colleague's gone quiet. Do you know if he's approached the girl?'

'He hadn't when I saw her on Monday. I went to her flat again yesterday to check on her, but she was out.'

'Do you think he might take out his frustration and punish her for what you both did?' asked Kramer.

'I warned her about that possibility on Monday night. When you say "punish", what do you mean?'

'He was always a desk man. If he does anything, it will probably be something subtle and indirect. What was her reason for working for him in the first place?'

'She talked about wanting a career in politics.'

'There you go. She can forget about that, if she refuses to give up the film.'

The Assassin thought about this for a moment. He glanced around the room. On the wall next to the bathroom was a print of an old Imperial Airways poster - a fleet of four-engined seaplanes advertising routes to India and Australia.

'So, can you fly the Mark and me out of Norfolk?' he asked.

'We'll use our contingency plan. Then if the policeman tries to double-cross you, you can call on the cavalry.'

'Do you know how those kinds of operations work in practice?'

Kramer grunted. 'Don't be impertinent. I've forgotten less about that sort of thing than you'll ever know. What do you think I was doing after the war up until I was sent to Brussels?'

'No one knows, Kramer. You're a closed book.'

The Assassin imagined the smug look of satisfaction on the top floor of the Berlaymont just then. 'Give me the coordinates for this place where the policeman wants you to take the third Mark,' said his boss.

'So far, he's only told me that it's an old wartime aerodrome near a town twenty kilometres north-east of Norwich. I've found at least three candidates on the map.'

'Let me take a look at my atlas. When's this to take place?'

'I still need a few more days in England. I'm going to suggest first light next Monday, the fourteenth of June. Any time after four o'clock.'

'Where can I reach you once I've been advised whether aircraft can still land at the places you've found?'

'I have a room at the Dorchester. I'm the only person staying there under my current name.'

'Give me a couple of days and check your mail at the hotel.'

-

The Assassin spent the next twenty minutes writing and rewriting a script for his call with Grieves. He even rehearsed some of the arguments he was going to use out loud in front of the mirror.

It was one thing for the businessman to talk about leaving the country, but another to actually do it. He suspected he was about to find out if Grieves really had been coached, and if so, how well.

At half-eleven he dialled the office number in EC2. After a couple of rings, Grieves answered himself.

'It's Hofmann,' announced the Assassin.

'At last. You have news for me from the French?'

'You're in luck. I reached the person I was hoping to get hold of, and I've already made some provisional arrangements. Certain people who'd like to meet you in Paris.'

'Who?'

'Don't thank me all at once. Someone who works for Michel Jobert, chief of staff to the President. Jobert's been running the secret back-channel between Heath and Pompidou during the negotiations. Big Heath supporter, but a man of the world. If anyone is going to take your stories seriously it's him. No one likes to be caught out by people they've put their trust in.'

'How the hell did you get his attention?'

'I told you last time we spoke. In Brussels we have access to all kinds of powerful people. And there's nothing more important to the French right now than Britain's accession to the EEC.'

'Okay.'

'You're sure that you still want to go ahead with this?' asked the Assassin.

'Do you have a plan for me to leave the country?'

There was a moment's silence in the room at the Dorchester. To the Assassin's way of thinking, things given for free in life were rarely appreciated. 'We're going to take a plane from a private airfield. The people I'm hiring want payment in cash upfront. High denomination notes.'

'How much is this going to cost me?' replied Grieves, apparently unfazed by the Assassin's suggestion.

'Flight time, fuel, landing fees in Le Touquet or Paris, depending on what the pilot decides. Maybe an insurance premium for landing at an unofficial strip on this side. It all adds up.'

'Stop dragging it out. Just tell me how much.'

The thought flashed through the Assassin's head of increasing the price he'd worked out earlier that morning. 'Five hundred pounds. But think of the level of access you're getting in Paris.'

'I suppose I don't have a choice, do I?'

'You need to show me the money when I pick you up.'

'You're really selling this, aren't you?' said Grieves sardonically.

'It's one of those take it or leave it offers.'

'No one likes to be robbed.'

'The other day you were jumping at shadows. Now it sounds like you're having second thoughts.'

'That's for me to decide,' said Grieves.

'Don't worry. If you give them what they want, the French will make it well worth your while. If you win the trust of Jobert's man, maybe they'll even sponsor your venture behind the Iron Curtain, as part of their own penetration efforts there. Robert Maxwell wasn't in Vienna the other day to sample the cream cakes. It was worth his time too.'

'Okay. Spending time in Paris is scarcely a hardship. Even if it is in strange circumstances.'

'Then pack your toothbrush and clothes for a week and be ready to go on Sunday evening. Where shall I collect you?'

'You've been to my office in the City a couple of times. We might as well meet outside Broad Street Station.'

'Be there at eight o'clock. Unless there's a change of plan, I won't call you again before Sunday.'

'What car will you be driving?' asked Grieves.

'I don't know yet. My people arrange a different one each time.'

'Cloak and dagger, eh?'

'It never hurts to be cautious.'

The Assassin replaced the receiver, still not quite believing what Grieves had just agreed to. But now the wheels had been set in motion and there was no turning back. Not for anyone, including himself. For no matter how his time in England ended, he knew couldn't put off going home forever.

He dialled Smythe's house in Stockwell next.

'I've been waiting for your call,' said the policeman when he picked up.

'Good, because I don't have any way to reach you,' said the Assassin. 'You never told me the number for your desk at Paddington Green.'

'I don't have it yet. I'm between offices,' replied Smythe. 'Anyway, stop complaining. I don't have any number for you at all.'

'I've taken a room at the Dorchester.'

'Living it up, are we? Nothing too good for our new European friends in Brussels?'

The Assassin ignored this. 'Listen, I spoke with Grieves just now. He says he still wants to leave the country clandestinely and stay away for a week or so until the heat is off his back.'

'Really?' asked Smythe. But the policeman didn't seem that surprised.

The Assassin rowed back slightly. 'Yes. But I got the sense that he's already cooling on the idea, even since yesterday. I think it's still touch and go whether it comes off. You said it was a four-hour drive up to Norfolk. He could change his mind at any time on the way there.'

'What did Kramer say to the idea of taking him out of the country?'

'What did Brierly and Fryatt say?'

There was a pause from Smythe that went on half a second too long. 'Fryatt doesn't care either way what we do with Grieves. At the end of the day, it was Brierly who was worried about Heath. He was the one who took the initiative to call Kramer for help.'

'Have you spoken with Brierly yet? If Kramer agrees to taking Grieves out of the country, will Brierly agree as well?'

'I don't know. There's been some difficulty between him and Kramer recently, as I understand.'

'Well if he wants a say, he'd better hurry up about it,' said the Assassin, carefully modulating his tone.

There was another pause from Smythe. He cleared his throat before speaking again. 'By the way, Brierly's asked me to set up a meeting with you.'

'Any reason?' asked the Assassin without breaking stride. 'Tell him he can leave a message for me at the Dorchester. The room is in my name.'

'Okay.' There was another half-second of silence. 'You and I need to meet again before the weekend,' continued Smythe. 'We need to make some final decisions on how we're going to play things up there. I've been to the place I suggested once before, but we need to go over the plan so that you know exactly where to take Grieves when you arrive.'

'Tomorrow will be too soon to hear back from Kramer. How about Saturday night?'

'Too late, and anyway, I'm out all that evening.'

'So we're meeting on Friday then? Did you find someone to stage the arrest?' asked the Assassin.

'I have a person in mind. We'll rehearse on Friday what you're to say when my fake MI5 man turns up. For a change, why don't I come to the Dorchester. Eight o'clock?'

'I'll buy you a cocktail.'

–

After the call with Smythe was done, the Assassin called Jimmy.

'I need to see you this afternoon. And I need to meet your nephew at the same time.'

'Let me make a call.'

'I'm going on a trip to the country at the weekend. Norfolk. I'll need him to come with me. It's important.'

'What business do you have there?'

'I'll explain more when I see you. It's Kramer's business, to do with Smythe. He wants me to take someone to Norwich.'

When the Assassin arrived at Club Trèfle, he was shown upstairs to Jimmy's office, by now as familiar to him as the travel agency off Piccadilly.

The Corsican was sitting at the low table with another man who had a vague family resemblance. Jimmy stood and shook hands with the Assassin.

'Bert made the copy of the film for you?' he asked.

'Yes.'

They sat down.

'This is Matteu. A nephew of mine, you could say.'

The other man gave the Assassin a curt nod.

'You found me a safe breaker?' the Assassin asked Jimmy.

'He's waiting for your call. Here's the number.'

Jimmy took a card from inside his jacket and quickly scribbled on the back before sliding it across. The Assassin tucked it into his wallet.

'So where are you going to in Norfolk with Smythe?' asked the nightclub owner.

The Assassin unfolded the map he'd bought in Stanfords. The three of them bent their heads over the table as he showed them the locations he'd identified.

Matteu frowned. He looked gravely at Jimmy and said something in Corsican. Jimmy nodded in agreement. Then the younger man turned to the Assassin, and to avoid confusion, spoke to him in French.

'You're certain this is the area he wants you to go?'

The Assassin paused, wondering what came next. 'I'm meeting him again on Friday. He says he'll show me exactly where on the old airfield I'm to take the man I'm escorting. Maybe he didn't realise there were several airfields close together.'

'I already know which one he means. And I already know where you're going when you get there.' Mattheu tapped on the triangle of runways closest to Norwich, the links of his gold bracelet rattling as he did so. 'I've been there to do a job once before.'

The Assassin looked across at Jimmy who nodded slowly back at him. The Assassin raised his eyebrows. 'Like that, is it?' he said. 'Are you absolutely certain it's the same place?'

Matteu pointed to a large building just off the perimeter track, not far from the end of one of the old runways. 'That's where he'll tell you to go. Next to the killing floor.'

The Assassin shook his head in disappointment. 'In some ways I'm not surprised. Which direction will Smythe come from when he arrives?'

'Most likely through the farm. Past the main house. He'll have organised this with the farmer.'

'Can you find a layby somewhere outside the perimeter to watch for him?'

'Might be difficult. The roads are narrow and there's not much cover.'

'Jimmy,' asked the Assassin. 'Can you have my gear fetched?'

'*Un mumentu.*' Jimmy picked up the phone on the table and spoke a few words down the line.

'How many people live on the farm?' asked the Assassin while they waited.

'Just the farmer and his wife. Their farmhands come in from the village.'

'Dogs?'

'Of course. It's a lonely place.'

There was a knock on the door and the bouncer who'd greeted the Assassin at the street door in March appeared carrying his green holdall.

He took it and waited until the other man had left, shutting the door behind him. Placing the bag on the floor behind the sofa, the Assassin crouched down to undo the miniature padlock before unzipping it and rummaging inside. Standing up again, he placed two objects on the table in front of Jimmy and his nephew.

'Starlight scope, US Army issue. Passive night sight, good for a range of at least two hundred metres by starlight or moonlight,' he said. Jimmy looked suitably impressed.

Matteu pointed to the other object. 'I used that model of radio during *service militaire.*'

'Okay. Then you know what to do. Drive your car off the road into a field, hide behind a hedge, then report when you see them coming.'

'You want us to follow them in?'

'No. Stay out of sight unless I call you forward. Hopefully you'll not need to get involved.'

'I think we will.'

'I hope you won't. I'll need you in place well before sunrise. Let's say two in the morning. Sunday is four days after the full moon. You probably won't even need the scope, but just in case.'

'What call signs do we use?' asked Matteu.

The Assassin thought for a moment. 'I'll be *Pfeiffer*. You can be *Ratte*.'

Jimmy mouthed the names silently to himself. 'Makes sense.'

'Is that it?' asked Matteu

'Those are all the plans we can make for now. Just make sure you and your guys are up there in good time. Can all of them drive?'

Matteu nodded. 'How many men do you want me to bring?'

'Two should be enough.' The Assassin pursed his lips. 'Are you free on Friday during the day?' he asked.

Matteu looked at Jimmy who nodded back.

'Yes, I can be.'

'That evening, I have to be back in London to meet Smythe at eight. Let's drive up to Norfolk early on Friday morning so we can find somewhere for you to lie up and watch on Sunday night, and so that I can get the general lie of the land. I want to find a way onto the airfield without going past the farmhouse.'

'Okay. If Jimmy says I need to.'

Jimmy nodded again. But there was a new look in the Corsican's eye.

'You want to come too on Sunday night, Jimmy?' asked the Assassin.

He shrugged. 'Maybe. For old time's sake.'

Matteu glanced sideways at his boss, a neutral expression on his face.

'It would be easier just to look Kramer up in Brussels one day,' said the Assassin with a wry look.

Jimmy put his head to one side. 'Maybe I will. You'll take the rest of your gear when you pick up the car on Friday? I assume you want a car again?'

'Get Mattheu to pick me up at the Dorchester on Friday morning. I'll keep the car once we're done in Norfolk that day and fetch my gear from here on Sunday.' He gave the green holdall a kick.

'Let's have a drink now, in case I miss you on Sunday.'

Without waiting for an answer, Jimmy got up to fetch the bottle of pastis from under his desk and the glasses. He placed them on the table with a jug of water from the fridge.

'*Bonne chance*,' he said.

'Kramer thinks that making a toast before an operation is bad luck,' replied the Assassin.

Jimmy was impassive. 'At some point in life you have to make your own.'

-

Just after six that evening, the Assassin tried to call Selene but without success.

He went straight over to her flat. This time however, the street door was closed and there was no answer to his ring. He buzzed at what he guessed was her neighbour's flat.

'Who is it?'

He thought he recognised the voice of the woman he'd met on the stairs yesterday morning.

'Helen?' he asked uncertainly.

'Who's asking?'

'It's Tom. Selene's friend. We met the other day.'

'What is it? I told you to stay away from here.'

'Is Selene in? I'm worried about her.'

'She went away late last night. There was some kind of argument.'

'What do you mean, a "kind of argument"?'

'Raised voices, bangs, doors being slammed.'

'Has this ever happened before?'

'What? Arguments in her flat?' The woman sounded sarcastic, as if someone who claimed to be a friend ought to have known this already. 'From time to time. Her breakups are usually dramatic.'

'Could she have gone home to her parents for the night?' he asked.

'I wouldn't have thought it likely. She tells me they usually spend June on the Riviera.'

'Do you have any other number for her?'

'Why don't you go to the police if you're a friend.'

'This argument. What did you hear?'

'Just voices. Hers and a man. Maybe two men. But she has all sorts of people over, at all times of the night.'

'Okay, thanks.'

The Assassin stepped back down onto the pavement, his antennae twitching. He wasn't sure what he could do there and then. He could hardly go to Brierly and ask him if he'd sent someone after Selene. His only other option was to try to contact her through Ten Downing Street. But he suspected that whenever he and Brierly eventually did meet up, Selene and her yacht trip along the south coast would be their only topic of conversation.

He looked at his watch and made tracks to catch the Number 15 on Trafalgar Square. He'd promised his landlady he would come to her church meeting that evening, no matter what happened today. No matter what tomorrow might bring.

Chapter Thirty

The following morning, the Assassin headed for British Home Stores on Oxford Street where he bought himself a brown suit, a yellow shirt, and a wide paisley-patterned tie. He carried his purchases to the Dorchester where he changed in his room.

Dressed as he imagined an English social worker might look, he walked to Victoria and took the train to Streatham, buying a clipboard at a stationers on Buckingham Palace Road in a last minute burst of inspiration.

He made his way along Ellison Road to the path between the houses that he'd seen the boy disappear down two Sunday mornings ago. He knocked on the five doors on the right-hand side of the path and then at the five doors on the left. He crossed to the other side of the street and knocked on the ten houses opposite too. The orphaned stretches of post-war housing in the middle of Victorian villas and nineteen thirties semis told their own story about what had happened here thirty years ago.

At most of the houses, someone came to the door in answer to his knock. He asked about an eleven-year-old boy and a younger sister around eight or nine, living with foster parents.

No one had heard of such a family. There were individual children in the area who matched the general description he gave, but not living together as a pair. And there was no foster family nearby of any description, at least none which the people he spoke with had heard of.

The Assassin hadn't really expected any immediate success, but at least he'd got his story well rehearsed by the time he made his own way down the path to see where it led to. After a few metres, he found himself in a turning bay for cars, lined by a row of garages accessed from the next street along, parallel to Ellison Road. Annoyed once more with himself for not having chased the boy when he'd had the chance, he went there and started knocking on doors all over again.

But wherever the boy lived, it wasn't on those two streets. Or maybe it was. At a couple of the houses the replies were shifty, and once there were toys on the floor at a place where the person answering said no child lived.

The Assassin made his way back to Streatham Common station where he sat on a bench at the end of the platform, his face grim. His heart sank as he finally admitted to himself that whatever he should have done a week and a half ago, letting the boy get out of the car wasn't it. It had been a course of action, or rather inaction, that he now had no way of putting right.

What had been the point of going to all that effort last weekend to get the photograph of Heath for Selene? He hadn't helped an actual child in trouble when the boy was sitting right there next to him, telling him what was eventually going to happen to his little sister.

What was being done to the boy tonight? Maybe his foster father only took him out at weekends to minimise the risk of them getting caught. But in the Assassin's heart, he knew he was only telling himself this. If five pounds bought a dirty magazine, then he doubted the money to be made from pimping the boy out on demand would be turned down lightly. Especially as the boy wasn't getting any younger, and at some point his price would likely start to decrease.

The train took a long time to come. When it did, he brushed his hands across his face and wiped them on his trousers before getting on.

On the journey back to Victoria, the Assassin thought long and hard about whether to go that evening to the amusement arcade off Piccadilly Circus which the boy had mentioned. If you could call it luck, he might find him touting for business there.

But the more he thought about it, the more he knew it wasn't rational. What could he do on his own? At best he could drop some hints about a pair of children in foster care in Streatham who were under his protection. But what if the threats backfired and the abuse got worse? Or the children were silenced forever? And if he did walk in there, why would any child prostitute be more deserving than another of rescue?

He retraced his steps to the Dorchester and changed back into his normal clothes. The days of going to the pub to alleviate his boredom were long past. Tonight he didn't feel like doing anything.

After his final failure today to help even a single child directly, he supposed it was back to Selene's long shot after all, in his self-appointed war on the abuse scene - threatening someone in the ruling party into taking action at some indeterminate point in the future, but not before accession next year.

He wasn't sorry for what he and Selene had done in Bosham. He cared little for Heath, for he'd heard enough over the past few weeks to have got the measure of the politician by now.

He'd come to realise that it wasn't Heath's weasel words over the nature of EEC federation which grated on him so much. No, it was far simpler than that. Heath and the Conservative Party simply didn't care what the voters thought in the first place. For no matter how opposed the ordinary people were to the idea of joining, the government was going to sign an accession treaty over their heads anyway, regardless of the terms dictated by France. So much for British democracy. Denmark, Ireland and Norway's referendums put them to shame.

But if Selene's scheme never came off, there was always the equally long shot of Stockwell. He desperately wanted to find something at Smythe's house to prove his story to Masterson about the policeman and his partner from the Foreign Office. He wanted to take Masterson's latent anger at never having made it into MI6 and turn its focus on destroying the members of the network.

He briefly wondered if they found some really incriminating material, whether he should hand it over to the regular police as well as to Masterson - but quickly dismissed the idea as being naïve. Based on what Smythe had said about political interference in the Met, let alone the influence of the Syndicate on the Vice Squad, any evidence would get mislaid long before it reached an investigating judge, if they even had those in England.

Chapter Thirty-One

Mayfair, London - Friday, 11th June 1971

The next day, the Assassin and Matteu set off early in the morning on their reconnaissance trip to Norfolk.

The Assassin asked Matteu to pick him up at the Dorchester where he'd gone even earlier that morning to check for messages. At reception, he'd been handed a brown manila envelope with a London postmark and a sheaf of aerial photographs inside covering all three airfields. No note had been included, but he didn't need one to recognise Kramer's handiwork.

The drive took the full four hours predicted by Smythe, and the Assassin began to have doubts about making it back to London in time to meet the policemen at eight.

Neither he nor Matteu made much conversation. The nephew was even more guarded than the uncle. But from their time together in the car, the Assassin's confidence in him began to grow. A no-nonsense person, someone who could be trusted to think for himself in a tight spot. Jimmy's nephew didn't offer any details about his previous trip to the farm, but then he hardly needed to.

Once past Norwich, the Assassin and Matteu parked up a couple of miles away from the airfield and pored over the black-and-white images.

They drove around the outside of the airfield's boundary, along the roads between the villages, until they found what they were looking for - an old emergency access road, visible on the aerial shots. The entrance was barred by a padlocked steel gate, but this wouldn't present an insurmountable problem. Going by the height of the weeds growing through the cracks in the road's frost-damaged concrete surface, no one had been this way for a long time. Once through the gate, they would be almost immediately onto the airfield's perimeter track, which according to the aerial photo still ran continuously around the old base - a good six kilometres by the Assassin's reckoning.

They arrived back in London late in the afternoon. The Assassin dropped off Matteu in Camden Town and left the Cortina at the underground car park on Park Lane before going back to the Dorchester to change for dinner. Before he'd left Club Trèfle on Wednesday, Jimmy had offered him a Ford Capri, but he prized anonymity above speed.

He made his way to the hotel bar in good time for eight o'clock and sat waiting for Smythe with a scotch for company. Even if he'd been staying here another week, he still wouldn't have had time to get through all the whiskies displayed on the shelves behind the barman's head.

At ten minutes past, the policeman turned up wearing a herringbone suit paired with a grey silk tie and carrying a black briefcase. He looked like a businessman who was finished with his meetings for the day. The Assassin watched as Smythe ordered a Bass at the bar and brought it over to where he was sitting.

'Can we talk freely here, or would you prefer to go up to my room?' asked the Assassin, as Smythe sat down in a padded armchair and lit up.

'The walls of this bar have heard bigger secrets in their time. You want a cigarette?' asked Smythe, waving his pack of John Players at him.

'I have my own.' The Assassin took out a pack of cigarillos with a sailing ship emblem on the front and lit up himself. They each took a drag, eyeing one another warily. Smythe spoke first.

'I've brought a sketch map to show you how to get there and where to go when you arrive. It's a big place.'

'Show me.'

Smythe set his cigarette on the ashtray and took a road atlas from the pigskin briefcase. Laying it on the table between them, he opened it at a page marked by a sheet of squared paper torn from a notebook. The Assassin watched him with interest, not used to seeing the policeman with anything other in his hand than a drink or a cigarette.

'Here,' said Smythe pointing on the atlas. 'That's Reepham. Two miles along this road you take a right, then after another mile you'll come across the entrance to a farm. Turn in there.'

It was the same place the Assassin had just been to earlier that day. Now Smythe switched to the sketch map.

'Go past the farmhouse.' He tapped an oblong drawn in pencil. 'Then continue down this track until you get to the old hangar. You can't miss it, it's the biggest building still standing. Park at the end furthest from the farmhouse. There's a small door in the middle of that side.' He paused to annotate the diagram. 'Go through it, and you'll find an old workshop or office of some kind that was built inside the hangar. You can wait there.'

'And what happens then?'

'You tell me.' Smythe placed the sketch map inside the atlas and closed it before handing it to the Assassin.

'Kramer will lay on a flight if Brierly wants him to. After first light on Monday morning, but no earlier than five o'clock. It's too risky otherwise, given that the place has been abandoned for so long. At the end of the war, I'm guessing?'

'I believe so,' said Smythe. 'Or shortly thereafter.'

'Did Brierly agree to have him flown out?'

Smythe moistened his lips. 'I only spoke with him briefly. If Kramer is happy to take on the responsibility for Grieves, that will be good enough for Brierly. All this time he's wanted minimal involvement in the actual dirty work.'

'And what did Fryatt say?'

'He gave it his blessing.'

The Assassin shrugged. 'So we're in business? The end of this *danse macabre* is almost in sight?'

Smythe looked at the Assassin appraisingly. 'You could say.' He took a long drag at his cigarette and gave it a single, sharp tap into the ashtray. 'There is another way, of course. A path you've already gone down once these past couple of weeks.'

The Assassin swirled his scotch, looking into the depths of the amber liquid. 'If the arrest isn't happening, then I guess you don't need to call on your contact in the Dirty Squad?' he asked.

'It will be just you, me and him up there,' replied Smythe. 'The farmer and his wife know to stay away from that part of the airfield until after midday.'

'Don't they have animals to see to?'

'They can go a few hours unattended.'

The Assassin took a slug of the whiskey. 'If, say, Grieves suffered a heart attack at the prospect of crossing the Channel in a Cessna, what would happen to his body?'

Smythe looked swiftly to each side and shook his head. 'You wouldn't need to worry. It would be taken care of. You could just get on the plane and go.'

'Solving that kind of problem is a specialist skill of yours, isn't it?'

'Why do you ask?' said Smythe. 'Is it likely I'll need it again?'

The Assassin swallowed the last of his whiskey in one.

'Let's go for a walk.,' he said to Smythe. 'And a talk.'

They crossed the road to Hyde Park and went in by the Curzon Gate. Heading south, they kept walking, looking for a spot out of earshot of any passers-by.

After a hundred metres or so they reached the squat plinth of a statue. A classical character stood there in bronze, round shield raised above his head in one hand, stabbing sword in the other. They made their way around the plinth to its far side, away from the path.

'Why shouldn't we take Grieves out of the country?' asked the Assassin. 'What reason would you have for bringing an end to his threats here in England, rather than France?'

'Well for one thing, we'd know for ourselves that they were at an end. He wouldn't be arriving back at Heathrow one day to TV cameras and interviews about how the French secret services had wired him up to a car battery, as you threatened they would. Or worse for Fryatt, he wouldn't travel east in the other direction to tell the comrades behind the Iron Curtain what he knew about Heath.'

'If Kramer says he'll get a thing done, it will get done.'

Smythe pursed his lips. 'But detention and questioning is all that Kramer's offering to do? His talk of assassinations last year was just that?'

'I don't know what was discussed at the start of this venture. But if it's any comfort to you, I can tell you that Kramer's lucky. Even when his operations deviate from plan, they still somehow seem to come off.

'Lucky? What? Like Napoleon's favourite generals? Sees himself as some kind of modern day Bonaparte, does he?'

The Assassin shrugged. 'If anyone thinks he's Bonaparte, it's Heath. He's the one who told the Conservative Party women's conference that he was going to meet Pompidou in Paris and help complete the dictator's work.'

'You know who that's meant to be a representation of?' asked Smythe, pointing up at the statue. The Assassin shrugged as he lit himself another cigarillo.

'Wellington, that's who. He cooked your goose.'

'Prussia was on his side at Waterloo.'

'And whose side are you on, really?' asked Smythe. 'You've been a confusing person to us almost since you first got here. But maybe you're the one who's confused?'

'I'm on France's side. But I'm also on Germany's. The two don't have to be mutually exclusive.'

'Which one would you choose if you had to?'

'Which one has Heath chosen?' asked the Assassin back at him.

Smythe stepped over the low chain encircling the plinth and sat on its lowest step. He lit a new cigarette and took a drag, peering up at the Assassin.

'He's decided that it's all over for Britain. We'll only survive and thrive if we're inside the Common Market. Maybe he's right.'

'So much for helping you guys win at Waterloo.'

'We didn't stay friends afterwards, so it didn't do Prussia or Germany much good,' said Smythe.

'In the long run, it didn't do England any good either. Here you are, standing cap in hand before Pompidou, begging to be let into the EEC.'

'Not very diplomatic words from someone who's meant to be helping us join the Common Market.'

'Oh, I want you to join all right. You have a special role to play.'

'What's that?'

The Assassin bit his tongue. 'Forget it. It was just some nonsense.'

They both stood there a while longer, the tips of their smokes glowing brighter as sunset approached.

'Have you met Brierly in person since we last spoke?' asked the Assassin. 'You said he wanted to speak to me about something.'

Smythe looked away and shook his head. 'I don't know what he wants from you.'

'Was Brierly involved with the party network in any way? He told me once how Heath used to keep a black book of secrets when he was a Whip. Maybe Brierly wants a black book of his own.'

'Brierly?' asked Smythe with an incredulity that sounded real. 'What use would Brierly have for a blackmail dossier?'

'How about to make sure Parliament votes for the accession treaty when it eventually comes before them.'

'That's the Whips' job, not Brierly's.' Smythe pulled on his cigarette and looked at the Assassin with narrowed eyes. 'He's not a man to cross, you know, our Mr. Brierly.'

'Kramer told me that he was only a desk man during the war.'

'You'd be surprised at the things he got people to do for him back then. And still does.'

'Is that a warning of some kind?' asked the Assassin.

'Just make sure that if you and Kramer take on the task of hiding Grieves away in a secret prison, it actually happens. As soon as he lands in France, he's yours and you'll be taking full responsibility for everything that's happened with the Marks on this side of the Channel too.'

'Brierly doesn't scare me. I've faced far worse than him. He can't touch me in Brussels. No one can.'

Smythe was silent. He took another pull on his cigarette.

'And if Brierly threatens me or anyone connected to me,' said the Assassin, 'I'll be straight back to London to take care of him.'

'Big talk. You should tell him to his face.'

The Assassin finished his cigarillo and ground the stub under his feet. 'I guess this is goodbye then, unless there's a problem with the plane in Norfolk?'

Smythe gave a sigh and got to his feet. 'Just in case there is, I'll be up there by five on Monday morning, waiting somewhere nearby out of sight.'

'You, me and him, eh?' said the Assassin.

'Goodbye, Thomas.'

Smythe walked off into the gathering twilight without a backwards look.

Chapter Thirty-Two

Limehouse, London - Saturday, 12th June 1971

It was the Assassin's last day lodging with Mrs. MacDonald but he hadn't told her yet. He was planning to stay at the Dorchester tonight. Until now he hadn't trusted Smythe enough to risk it. But from what the policeman had said last night, he didn't think they'd try anything on in London. Norfolk was where the final act was planned.

'Are you going somewhere?' Mrs. MacDonald asked him at breakfast, having seen that he'd come downstairs with his black bag.

'I'm flying back to Belgium very early tomorrow morning.'

She looked disapprovingly at him. 'It's the Sabbath. You shouldn't be travelling on the Lord's Day.'

'I don't have a choice. It's all been arranged.'

'You always have a choice. Do the right thing and God will honour you for it.'

The Assassin glanced at his feet for a moment as the corollary flashed through his head. 'Thank you for your hospitality,' he said.

'You were a paying guest.'

'And thank you for the Bible verses. And for taking me to the evening meeting on Wednesday night.'

'What time are you going?'

'I've packed. I'm leaving right now. I won't finish work until late, so I've found somewhere else to stay tonight.'

'Then I need to give you back the money for the days you've already paid me.' She got up and went to the hall to fetch her purse.

'No. Please keep it,' he called through the open door.

But she'd already counted out three pound notes and fifty pence made up largely of coppers, and he sensed it would hurt her more if he didn't take the cash.

'Will you promise me something?' she asked.

'What is it?'

'When you get home to Belgium, start going to church. If you really are a believer, you can't keep yourself away from others of the faith. God intended us to live in fellowship with one another.'

The Assassin looked at her gravely. 'I can't make you that promise.'

She pursed her lips, but he didn't want to part on bad terms. 'I was hoping to see Reverend Thompson to thank him before I go up west,' he told her. 'I'll talk to him about it.'

When he knocked at the *Pfarrhaus*, the minister was already in conference with someone in his study. His wife asked the Assassin to wait in the lounge. Through the door across the hallway he could hear murmured voices but couldn't make out the words being said. It sounded like the minister's visitor was in distress.

After ten minutes, the study door opened and the other person left, their head bowed. The minister came into the lounge.

'What can I do for you,' he asked solemnly.

The Assassin shrugged. 'I just wanted to thank you for finding me somewhere to stay. And for your hospitality to a stranger.'

'Are you leaving us?'

'I have things I need to get on with.'

The minister waited in case the Assassin felt like offering further details, but none were forthcoming. 'Is there anything you want to say before you go?' he prompted. 'By the way, Mrs. MacDonald was grateful to you for chasing away those louts who were bothering her the other day.'

'I didn't realise she knew.' He hoped that neither she nor the minister had seen what he'd done to the youths after he'd chased them around the corner. Making sure they didn't come back had been another reason to stay at her house this week past.

'You enjoyed the midweek meeting on Wednesday?' asked the minister, still trying to make conversation.

The Assassin considered the question for a moment. 'It wasn't like anything I've been to before.'

'Are you going to try to find a congregation in Brussels?'

'Mrs. MacDonald just asked me the same question. It's not straightforward at home.'

The minister looked at the Assassin, allowing the silence to open up once more.

'I have a wife. She doesn't believe.'

'I see. Is that the only reason why you don't go to church?'

'How do you mean?'

'Are you here in England because you've got some kind of domestic trouble back home?' he asked more gently.

Only a minister could put those questions and get away with it, thought the Assassin.

'I'm here on a job. My being in London has nothing to do with my wife. It's just that I never got into the habit of going to church. And she wouldn't understand if I started now.'

The minister looked up at the ceiling for a second. 'It's not easy explaining these things to family - I know.'

'I only started down this path last year, but I need help to keep going. I keep falling.'

'In what way?'

The Assassin shook his head, at a loss to explain the thing that Kramer had called his addiction.

'We'll pray for you,' said the minister. 'And for your wife too.'

The Assassin nodded silently. He wasn't going to turn down any offer of help.

'And how have you liked living in London?' said the minister more breezily.

The Assassin raised an eyebrow. 'I didn't know what to expect. I had a certain impression of English people before I came here.'

'And what did you find when you arrived?'

The Assassin shook his head in wonderment. 'So many things. I've been touched by people's openness to someone from a former enemy country. Surprised by small acts of hospitality. But I was also surprised at the corruption you find here. Corruption on so many levels.'

'What do you mean by "corruption"?' asked the minister sharply. 'England isn't Italy.'

The Assassin raised his hands and dropped them again. 'I'm not sure how to explain. I've come across some wicked people in Britain. People who ought to know better.'

'Wicked in what way?' asked the minister, frowning.

'People like the Moor Murderers,' the Assassin replied, suddenly remembering the story that Smythe had told him on the way back from their visit to Voaden in March. 'And there's people in the Church who abuse children too.'

'Which church?' asked the minister coldly.

'I met an Anglican monk who boasted about it.'

Now it was the minister who shook his head. 'Then you should have gone straight to the police. We don't tolerate that kind of perversion in this country.'

'But you do. I've heard stories of certain MPs who are specially protected by the police. People who keep getting away with it because they've been given tacit permission to carry on.'

The minister pursed his lips. 'Where's your evidence of that? "Innocent until proven guilty" is how things work here. There's a reason why our justice system has been copied across the world.'

The Assassin's voice raised a notch. 'I've heard these things with my own ears.' He stopped himself from saying that he'd seen them too. 'There's evil in this society. Evil which runs deep. That's not the sign of a healthy nation.'

'Look,' said the minister more sharply now. 'I'm not saying anyone's perfect. I'm not saying Britain as a country is perfect, but we've had the blessing of Christianity for many centuries.'

'That's what Germans would have said before the First World War,' muttered the Assassin under his breath.

'The churches aren't blind to the moral decay of recent years,' said the minister. 'But God can turn things around.'

'And what is God doing for this country? Heath and the Conservatives are putting their faith in the EEC to restore England's sense of self-worth, although I think they're doing it more for their own sense of pride. We put our faith in the wrong places too, all those years ago.'

'And I'm not saying that it's right to make a god out of the Common Market either,' said the minister with a dark expression. 'You should know that without me telling you.'

The seconds of silence stretched out and the awkwardness increased.

The Assassin rubbed his temples. 'I never told you this before, but back in Brussels, I know people who work at the EEC. They tell me some of the things that are going on right now in European politics.'

'What do they say?'

'You know that Heath is being stitched up over his dream of a united Europe? Or perhaps he already knows it in his heart. Paris has spent the past ten years making sure that when you do join, it will be on terms almost entirely to their advantage.'

'Really?'

'The whole theatre last decade around rejecting Britain's EEC applications, the theatre which drove your politicians to distraction - it was all about loading the dice of the Common Agricultural Policy against you.'

'It was down to de Gaulle's intransigence, everyone knows that.'

'But his departure from the scene isn't the reason why you're talking again. You never withdrew your application. Why is that, by the way? Because it's not what the voters want.'

'Joining the EEC is the policy of both the parties. We had a General Election last year.'

'So they had no choice? Like an election to the East German Volkskammer? Hardly democratic.'

'That's overegging it somewhat. I simply can't imagine that our leaders, of every political party, are anything other than decent men trying to make the best decisions they can in a troubled world.'

The Assassin clenched his fists in frustration. But now that he'd started, he had to finish.

'It's insidious. On the surface their sentiments appear noble, but the people spouting the propaganda know what they're really saying. Promises by Heath that we'll all sing "merry songs of peace" to one another? Doesn't it sound too good to be true?'

'But isn't that what the EEC is about?' asked the minister. 'A fresh start for Europe? Working together for peace and prosperity? Not that prosperity is the answer to a nation's problems,' he added hurriedly. 'And of course, only Jesus can bring real peace.'

'I originally came to your church to hear how people are bringing the truth of the Bible to countries under Communist rule. Those regimes might have had long practice at deceiving uncritical Westerners, but you as a Christian know better. If you can perceive the deception being practiced by the Communist parties behind the Iron Curtain, why can't you see it in your own British political parties?'

The minister pushed his chair back and folded his arms.

'Other people can,' said the Assassin. Those people who protested at Ten Downing Street the other week? The Safeguards Campaigners? They sent a telegram to Pompidou saying that the British electorate are three to one against. What were they hoping for, by the way? To appeal to his better nature? How naïve they were.'

'Everything you say makes it sound like France is an enemy.'

'It's how they see you.'

'Why? What have we done to deserve that?'

'Because your country beat France in a war hardly thirty years ago. It's only human to want revenge,' said the Assassin.

'We weren't fighting France thirty years ago. They were on our side.'

'You wouldn't know it from de Gaulle's attitude. He hated the fact that you remained free and they didn't. Anyway, de Gaulle was only leader of one side in the civil war. I've interviewed officials from the so-called "Vichy" regime too. Except that it wasn't a thing called "Vichy" they worked for, it was the French State, legal successor to the third Republic. Voted into existence by France's own senators and deputies, recognised diplomatically by the US.'

There was a defiant pause. 'We don't even recognise East Germany diplomatically today,' said the Assassin, 'even though they built a wall to mark their border.'

'So you say. Maybe there's some residual bad blood between us and the French for various historical reasons. Maybe Heath is naïve. But that's only a failing, not a sin. You need a spiritual perspective on life.' The minister looked stern now. 'Do you know what's truly important on the eternal scale? Nations come and go as God decides, so why are you getting exercised by this?'

'Heath knows exactly what he's doing. Dishonesty at any level of politics is wrong. And you of all people must know why. *"Er ist ein Lügner und ein Vater derselben."* Or whatever it says in English.'

'I wish your fellow countrymen had been so determined to fight for the truth a few years ago.'

The Assassin stood up. He paced over to the door and then back again. 'I can't help you. I really can't. You British that is. Thanks to a combination of Heath's arrogance and the Establishment's wilful blindness to the opinion polls, he's getting away with changing the very nature of your country. And if the Establishment can get away with that, then what else will they manage to do in the future?'

'We have to put all of these things into God's hands and trust him for the right outcome. He's the one who ultimately directs the affairs of nations.'

The Assassin had walked into the room, grateful for the minister's help and for the sense of fellowship he'd found at the church. Now there was frustration and anger.

'The first evening I came here, I witnessed your concern and your generosity towards the Russian Christians - even though I know that this congregation isn't wealthy. I respect you for that. I just want you to understand what's coming next for your own country.'

The minister stood up and offered his hand. The Assassin looked down, hesitated for a second, then took it. The minister clasped his other hand over the Assassin's.

'When you leave England, go in peace.'

The Assassin seriously doubted it. He nodded but said nothing in reply.

-

After he'd reached his room at the Dorchester, he had nothing else to do until the evening. He tried again to reach Selene, phoning her flat once, twice, and then three times. Still no one picked up.

Once more, he made his way over to Chelsea and the mansion block behind the King's Road, fighting the throngs of Saturday shoppers outside Safeway and the clothes shops opposite the Army barracks. He loitered outside her building until he saw a man and a woman leaving. Averting his eyes, he hurried up the steps and darted inside just as the street door closed behind the couple.

There was no answer to his knock at her door and none at Helen's either. He went back to Selene's door and crouched down on the floor to look underneath. His envelope from Tuesday - four days ago now - was still lying there on the mat.

Shaking his head, he left, frustrated at his helplessness. If he hadn't been going to Stockwell tonight, he would have risked a direct approach to Brierly there and then. For now, he reluctantly concluded there was nothing more he could do.

But maybe it really was as Helen had said. Maybe with a new male distraction on the horizon, Selene had simply got tired of the whole affair and of him too. She was only human after all, just like him.

-

The Assassin met Jimmy's burglar outside Marble Arch tube station at nine. He was a youngish man, compactly built, with close cropped hair going grey at the temples and a practical look about him.

They walked down Park Lane to pick up the Cortina from the underground car park and the Assassin drove them to Stockwell where they waited at a cafe by the station for Reynolds to arrive.

The Assassin bought two teas at the counter and carried them back to the formica-topped table where they'd installed themselves.

'Which part of Germany are you from?' asked the burglar, cupping his hands round his chipped white china mug.

'Hamburg.'

'I was stationed there during my National Service. 'Forty-seven to 'forty-eight.'

'What did you think of the locals?' The Assassin took a sip of the dark brown tea.

'Mixed bag. A few of us had German girlfriends, even though it was frowned on. Pretty girls some of them. Immediately after the war they were starving. Freezing in winter too - they'd do anything for a pack of cigarettes.'

'That might have been my mother you're talking about.'

'Well, there's no airs and graces about you, are there?'

The Assassin put his head to one side. 'She never talks about those first couple of years. I get the impression they were hard.'

'Where was your father?'

'Gone.'

The burglar nodded to himself.

A familiar face appeared at the door. The Assassin raised a hand in greeting to Reynolds as he came over to join them at the table.

'We're not staying,' said the Assassin. 'Let's go.'

The burglar sat in the back of the car as they drove a short distance up Lansdowne Way and parked ready for a quick getaway, should it come to that.

They approached Smythe's end-of-terrace house from the rear, bunking up over the side wall to the garden. The house was in darkness and the curtains hadn't been drawn.

All three of them slipped on gloves. Reynolds and the Assassin waited in the shadows of the bushes while the burglar quickly picked the lock of the garden door at the back of the house, opening it with care. No burglar alarm went off, no dog barked, and no cat made a break for freedom.

They trooped inside. The kitchen didn't look like it had seen much use recently. A couple of dirty plates stood in the sink and a row of empty wine and beer bottles were lined up against the wall behind it.

'This guy lives on his own,' said the Assassin. 'If there's a Frau Smythe she's an ex- one.'

'Where are we going?' asked the burglar.

'Through here, I guess, then downstairs.' The Assassin led the way to the basement den.

'Nice pad. Like a tiny nightclub,' said the burglar.

'What are we looking for and how long do we have?' asked Reynolds, glancing at his watch.

'Knowing something of Smythe, I doubt he'll be back here early on a Saturday night. We can allow ourselves an hour, I think. Let's start here.' The Assassin pulled back the drape hanging against the wall on its rail to reveal the door into the other part of the basement. He tried the handle.

'Let me,' said the burglar. He worked with his picks for a few seconds and opened the door.

'Careful,' said the Assassin. 'It's a darkroom of some kind,'

'You should have said,' remonstrated the burglar. 'Turn off the main light,' he told Reynolds.

The burglar shielded the torch with his hand, and let the faint glow briefly play around the interior of the darkroom before going inside to flick on the light switch.

Standing against one wall was a developing tank and on a table in the middle, a portable Ilford-Elmo 8mm sound projector. Lengths of string were stretched across the ceiling and empty pegs showed where prints had been hung to drip dry.

Reynolds and Assassin started to go through the drawers of the metal cabinets under the work top. Inside, they found folder after folder of negatives. They took out the strips at random and held them up to the light. The images mainly showed group shots that had been taken at parties - adult men and women. Nothing unusual or incriminating that the Assassin could see. He didn't know any of the people in the shots. Maybe one of Smythe's covers was as a party photographer.

'There's got to be something else,' said the Assassin. 'A safe. Or a diary. Let's look upstairs.'

'How about this?' The burglar pointed with his foot to the drinks cabinet. 'False front, I'd bet.'

He slowly felt along the bottom of the cabinet. With a click, the front section with its shelves of bottles swung to one side to show a grey-painted steel safe behind it.

'What do you think?' asked the Assassin.

The burglar glanced at his watch. 'I'll give it a go. It's a pre-war Chubb. Nothing too fancy.'

He unrolled a canvas tool carrier on the floor and took out a long pick. The other two watched as he got to work, but the old safe was a tougher proposition than the burglar had at first thought.

The Assassin became impatient. 'You,' he said to Reynolds. 'Go back upstairs and watch for anyone returning. I'm going up to the first floor to check the bedrooms.'

The upper storey of the house had three bedrooms and a bathroom. The Assassin found Smythe's room and drew the curtains before turning on the main light. He started with the drawers in the bedside table, methodically going through their contents. Almost immediately, he found a leather-bound diary.

Opening the volume, he turned to the month of June. The notes he saw there were terse and cryptic. Flicking back to the day of the party in Devon, the entry was simply marked 'Mk1, Mk2, TH' - the initials of the name by which Smythe knew the Assassin. Despite the sparseness of the entries, he took out a miniature camera and snapped the pages for the dates he'd been in England. Replacing the diary where he'd found it, he started examining the chest of drawers and wardrobe. But after the first rush of success at finding the diary, he now felt it draining away from him again.

Increasingly frustrated, he turned off the light and reopened the curtains. One by one he tried the other bedrooms, taking the same precautions before starting his search, glancing at his wrist to check the time every minute or so. When he was done, he took a final look into the bathroom. There was a small shelf of paperback books over the radiator. He ran his finger along the row, stopping as his eye caught on something which seemed out of place, a nineteen sixty-nine Whitaker's Almanack.

Curious, he pulled it out and looked inside. His eyes goggled.

The Assassin went downstairs. He found Reynolds standing by the front window of the main reception room, watching the street from behind the gathered curtain - just as Brierly had watched Reynolds himself from that same spot all those weeks ago.

He opened the book in the middle and shone his flashlight on the photograph tucked inside.

'Who the hell is that?' The Assassin pointed to a grossly fat man, his face glistening with sweat. The man was dressed in a towelling bathrobe, the embroidered name of a hotel on the right breast partially obscured by a fold in the fabric. Over his knee was a naked child. The man's arm was raised, and his tongue was sticking out in concentration as he prepared to bring his hand down on the child's narrow buttocks. The photo was in black and white, but the welts from previous strikes were clear to see. The child seemed to be a girl, her face facing up towards the camera. The tracks of tears ran glistening down each cheek and her tousled hair was plastered against them. She looked very young.

Reynolds felt ashamed for even having seen the image. The girl's arms were stretched out ahead of her and she held something in her hand nearest the camera. Whatever it was, it drooped down and was mostly out of frame.

'Is that the only picture?' he asked.

The Assassin riffled through the book. Several other prints had been interleaved throughout the pages, showing other images of abuse by the fat man. Some were similar to the photo of the little girl. Others involving boys were much, much worse.

The Assassin returned to the picture of the man and the girl and looked one last time at her face. Fear and pain were to be seen there. The Assassin's cheek twitched.

'This is disgusting,' he said to Reynolds. 'You realise I found this in his bathroom? The guy is an utter hypocrite. He talked for weeks about trying to collect enough evidence to convict these people. Then he talked about how hard he resisted taking part in the abuse of children. And then I find this.'

He shook his head. 'I'm going to put this back where I found it. Wait for me here.' He left the room to tramp back upstairs again.

390

But when the Assassin returned, Reynolds was gone. He heard voices coming up from the basement and followed them down the narrow stairs. Reynolds was kneeling at the low table, poring over a book which had obviously come from inside the open safe.

'What do you have there?' asked the Assassin.

'Dynamite,' said the burglar. 'If I were you, I'd put this back where we found it, before it blows up in all our faces.'

The Assassin gave him icy look. 'I'll decide that. Let me see.' He crouched down beside Reynolds and started flicking through the contents for himself.

It wasn't a book, but rather a manila folder with labelled dividers which made a crude alphabetical index. Every institution of the Establishment was represented, with subdivisions for certain of their individual members. Sometimes the sections contained only a couple of items - a photo, a letter, a diagram - others were as thick as the Assassin's thumb.

He didn't know how compromising the file might turn out to be for some people, but he had a good idea. His other question, as he neared the end of the dossier, was whether this was Smythe's private copy of an official file held elsewhere. But it didn't give that impression. It had the quality of intelligence in its rawest form.

Reynolds had the same idea as to its potential value. 'I'm having that,' he said, once the Assassin was finally done.

The Assassin closed the folder and stood up, clasping it firmly to his chest. 'There's two of us and one of you,' he said, giving Reynolds a stern look 'You will get this, I promise. But not right now.' Still frowning, he pursed his lips to demand silence in front of the burglar.

'Well, make up your minds,' said their accomplice. 'If you want me to lock it back inside, I'll need five minutes. Did you find a key upstairs?'

The Assassin glanced at Reynolds who shook his head.

'Go ahead and relock the safe anyway,' said the Assassin to the cracksman. 'Your best job yet, so that no one would ever know it had been opened. I just need a minute here.'

The Assassin laid the folder on the floor and turned back to the section labelled 'Foreign intelligence agencies.'

'Move over,' he said to Reynolds. 'Give me space.' He snapped away at the pages until his camera ran out of film.

He turned to a section entitled 'Labour Party - Driberg' and pulled out a few pages which he handed to Reynolds. Police charge sheets and reports. From what Smythe had told him about the Labour MP and his exhibitionism, he doubted it contained any new secrets. The file with the rest of the contents he handed to the burglar.

'Take this back to Jimmy's place,' said the Assassin. 'Tell him not to let it out of his office. Ask him for double your money and tell him Pfeiffer said so.'

The burglar took the file gingerly.

'It's alright,' said the Assassin. 'We're the good guys. And Jimmy's not the only powerful friend I have.'

He turned to Reynolds. 'Okay. Time to go. You and I can keep a lookout in the garden.'

The Assassin and Reynolds waited in the shadow of the shrubbery, the Assassin listening for traffic in the street running along the side of the garden. Reynolds silently seethed with anger, almost as angry at himself as he was at the Assassin.

'What's your game?' he finally asked in a sibilant whisper, waving the pages on Driberg in his old flatmate's face.

'For God's sake, put those away,' said the Assassin. 'I wasn't lying. You will get the document, and in its entirety, as I promised.' As the Assassin had flipped through the folder he'd seen a section for the Conservative Party, but no subsection for Heath, not as far as he could establish at a quick glance. Maybe it had been removed.

'What will Masterson and I have to do in exchange?' asked Reynolds sourly.

'Quiet. I'll tell you on the way to his house. It's all part of Kramer's plan.'

A sullen silence descended again. The burglar was as good as his word and after another five or six minutes emerged with his tool bag, relocking the garden door behind him.

'Quick, over the wall,' said the Assassin.

'Bastard,' said Reynolds.

The burglar looked at the MI5 man strangely. 'You don't know what he is.'

The Assassin drove the burglar back to Stockwell station. There were no goodbyes - the rear passenger door banged shut, and he was gone.

'Now are you going to tell me what's going on?' demanded Reynolds.

'Do I need to? You saw the photographs for yourself.'

'I know. They're bad.'

'So we're agreed? You and Masterson are going to shut down Fryatt's network, as I asked?' said the Assassin.

'He has children too. He might be ambitious at work, but he's not a cold-blooded German.'

'Who said I was German?'

The Assassin swung the car around and took the South Lambeth Road, heading for Vauxhall Bridge. 'Before we get to Masterson's house, let me tell you what happens next.'

'Go on then.'

'Tomorrow night I'm taking one of the people we were meant to be smearing to Norfolk. When we get there, I believe Smythe is planning to kill him.'

'Why?'

'It's what I said to you and Masterson the other day in Seven Dials. The SDECE was brought over to undermine people who'd threatened to act against Heath. But at best, that was a convenient lie. Fryatt and Smythe wanted us to dispose of them, because their threats against Heath were also starting to become a problem for them directly. It's unlikely that they'll try anything against me in Norfolk, but in my mind's eye I'm seeing the current person of interest being taken off to a side room and then us hearing a pistol shot.'

'What do you mean, "us"?'

'That's my price for the dossier and for the real name of "Treasure." I want you and Masterson to follow me up to Norfolk and make sure that things don't get out of hand. I want Masterson to deliver a warning to Smythe that will get back to Fryatt. That their careers in entrapment are over and if they want the evidence of their own blackmail to stay hidden, it's on pain of their continued good behaviour.'

'And that's it?'

'At least we'll have shut down one network. Saved some children, perhaps. Give some thought to it while I drive. You know how to sell the idea to Masterson better than I do. Otherwise the dossier goes by diplomatic pouch to Paris tonight.'

In the passenger seat Reynolds leafed through the pages on Driberg one by one. As they neared Vauxhall, he turned to the Assassin. 'I've never read such filth. It says here that he consumes the... the... produced by teenagers because he believes it has rejuvenating properties.'

'Smythe told me that Driberg is under the protection of a Labour politician called Callaghan.'

'He was Wilson's Home Secretary for the last couple of years before the election,' said Reynolds.

'Well, Driberg is an MP who's never charged with any sexual crimes. He's been allowed to get away with it for so long, that the Establishment can't afford the scandal of his exposure. And I bet he's not the only one in the same position.'

Reynolds was bitter now. 'The more prominent the public figure, the better they're protected, in a perverse way.'

'Now do you understand why we have to do what I've asked?'

Reynolds didn't reply. He stuffed the pages on Driberg into his jacket pocket and sat in silence for the rest of the journey.

After another twenty-five minutes, the Assassin pulled up outside the address in Belsize Park which Reynolds had given him.

'Not here,' said Reynolds. He led them around the corner to another stuccoed house and gave a single soft knock on the front door.

A few seconds later, Masterson beckoned them inside, giving a swift look up and down the street as he did so.

'Keep your voices down,' he said. 'The twins have only just gone back to sleep again, the cunning little bastards.'

They sat round a plain wooden table in the kitchen.

'Well?' he asked.

Reynolds started his report. 'Smythe's certainly been watching the scene, there's page after page of proof of that. But there's evidence to believe he's gone further than anyone in the police hierarchy might ever have asked him to. Dirty photographs that we found hidden at his place.'

'And what's your conclusion after tonight?'

'On balance, I believe what Hofmann said to us earlier this week - about Smythe running his own abuse network, or at best a surveillance operation that's now indistinguishable from the real thing.'

He spread out the pages from the Driberg section of the dossier on the table. Masterson took a quick look at the prints attached to them.

'Christ. Put these away in case my wife walks in. What else makes you think Smythe's part of the problem?'

'Darkroom, copying machine for movie film. Many, many photographs of well-dressed people taken at parties,' said Reynolds, collecting the pages and putting them back inside his jacket.

'But it's more than that,' added the Assassin. 'He's kept some of the material for his own pleasure. Artistic black and white prints of children being abused. Those we found in his bathroom.'

'Is this all true, Reynolds?' asked his boss sharply.

Reynolds nodded silently.

'And Fryatt? Could he also have been drawn in to that extent?' asked Masterson.

'Well, we didn't find any photographs of him and Smythe having a go at children, if that's what you mean,' replied the Assassin. 'But it scarcely matters. They're both involved in running it.'

'I've only got your word for that. I agree that if Reynolds says you found this material at Smythe's house, then you've got something on him. But I asked you for proof that Fryatt was involved too.'

'You didn't ask, but as it happens, I've spoken with two people who've independently confirmed it. The dossier we found may well contain incriminating material on Fryatt that we haven't seen yet. There wasn't time to go through it properly at Smythe's house.'

'There's a moral question here,' said Reynolds. 'We have a duty to act.'

'It doesn't matter which service each of us works for,' added the Assassin. 'Fryatt and Smythe have to be stopped and stopped now. For our own self-esteem as men, as much as anything else.'

'You two have really hit it off, haven't you?' said Masterson sardonically. 'So where's the complete file?'

'Somewhere safe. I want something else from you before you get it, though.'

'Of course you do.'

'Fryatt and Smythe are getting impatient with one of the people that I came here to smear. They want to take things further.'

'How much further?'

'I warned you the other day that they wanted the SDECE to dispose of them permanently. Trick us into killing them because the targets' threats against Heath risked drawing attention to their operation.'

'So they're going to do it themselves now? With or without you?'

'I think I've persuaded Smythe not to do so. Instead we're taking one of the targets to an abandoned military airfield in Norfolk this Sunday. I've arranged a flight to France where we're going to bury him in the hidden depths of the French police state. And he would be buried, he'd never show his face in Britain again.'

'So go ahead then. I won't stop you.'

'All I'm asking is that you and Reynolds come along with me to Norfolk and provide some backup in case Smythe changes his mind.'

'You told me on the way here that you thought Smythe might shoot this person,' said Reynolds.

'I don't know for certain. But I do want your help to stop things getting that far. And I need someone with an official status in Britain to give him the message that it's all over for him and Fryatt and their child prostitution ring - on pain of the dossier being used against them.'

'You also suggested that we raised hell with MI6 over it,' said Masterson. 'You're expecting that document to be used for a lot of things.'

'After Monday morning, I don't care what you do with it, as long as you stop Smythe.'

'And how would either you or we prevent Smythe from shooting someone, if he does change his mind about letting the bird fly the nest?'

'I'll bring a gun. You should too.'

Masterson rolled his eyes to the ceiling 'This is in danger of turning into a Mad Hatter's Tea Party. We don't carry guns just like that. I'm not even sure how I'd go about getting one officially.'

The Assassin looked at him for a moment, a grim set to his mouth. 'Do you know how to handle a Browning?'

'We shot with them in the Officer Training Corps at university.'

'Okay. You can borrow mine,' he said, taking out a dull black automatic from inside his jacket and placing it with a solid clunk on the kitchen table. 'Bring this with you to Norfolk.'

'You had that in your pocket tonight?' asked Reynolds, stunned.

'Yes, but it wasn't meant for use earlier, if that's what you're worried about.'

'Is it loaded?' asked Masterson, a covetous look in his eye.

'Do you want it to be?' asked the Assassin.

'Of course.'

'Here.' The Assassin reached into his side pocket and placed a box of rounds on the table next to the gun. 'Don't shoot yourself because you've forgotten how to use it.'

For answer, Masterson ejected the magazine, cleared the weapon, then pointed it at the opposite wall and dry-fired it. Reynolds looked at him with a new respect.

'You see? University education wasn't entirely wasted on me. I used to be able to strip it down and reassemble it in under thirty seconds too.'

'Sorry Reynolds,' said the Assassin. 'I don't have a gun for you.'

His former flatmate shrugged.

'I take it this means you'll come with me to Norfolk then?' asked the Assassin. Without waiting for an answer, he passed over the atlas that Smythe had given him with the sketch map inside. 'Follow the instructions on the diagram. Join me in the hangar that's marked there by a quarter to four in the morning at the very latest.'

'I need that dossier,' said Masterson.

'We have to have it,' said Reynolds. 'We can't afford for it to fall into the hands of the other side.'

'Reynolds means MI6 as much as the KGB,' said Masterson.

'I guessed as much.'

Reynolds looked at the Assassin speculatively. 'What if you'd planted the file in Smythe's house to trick us into helping you? Gave it to the burglar beforehand, so he could pretend he'd found it?'

'There's no way I'd have used those pictures. I don't care how important the cause is.' The Assassin looked at each of them in turn. 'Would you?'

'No,' they replied, shaking their heads.

Chapter Thirty-Three

The Assassin spent his final night in England at the Dorchester. On Sunday morning, he got up early for breakfast and when he was finished eating, went to reception to check for messages. As he approached the counter, he saw a man standing there with his back to him, trilby in hand. Just as he was about to retrace his steps and head for his room the long way round, Brierly turned and looked him full in the eye. The Assassin returned his stare, equally coolly.

'I need to speak to you,' said Brierly in an icy voice.

'Are you on your own?' asked the Assassin.

'Of course,' replied the ex-SOE man.

'Let's go to the park.'

The Assassin led the way over the road to Hyde Park, back in through the Curzon Gate where he'd gone with Smythe. This time however, he turned north, walking until they found a bench.

'Sit, Hofmann.'

The Assassin took a swift look around to check no one was loitering, then did as he was ordered.

Brierly remained standing a few feet away, on the other side of the path. He looked darkly at the Assassin. 'It took a while, but Smythe eventually found out where you were staying.'

'Where's Selene?'

'Right now she's having a long think about whether she really wants a career in politics.'

'Where is she?' asked the Assassin even more icily.

'Back in Shropshire by now, I imagine. At her parents' place. They're still on holiday, I believe.'

'Where's she been the past few days then?' asked the Assassin, fixing Brierly with a stare. The Englishman broke first and glanced away.

'She's been telling us all your secrets.'

'I don't believe you. She's got an inner strength, a determination you underestimate at your peril.'

Brierly sat down on the bench opposite the Assassin. From his coat pocket he took out a briarwood pipe and a leather tobacco pouch. The Assassin watched as he packed the bowl, then struck a match and sucked a couple of times to get the pipe to draw.

'I have all Sunday morning to chat,' said Brierly. 'So let's talk.'

The Assassin watched him warily, fighting the temptation to scan up and down the path again in case an arrest team was lurking.

'What do you and your boss really think about what we're trying to achieve through the EEC, Hofmann?'

'How do you mean?' The Assassin frowned.

'Kramer and I go a long way back. He's an out-and-out French patriot of the old school. I can't believe he completely changed his outlook on life when he went to Brussels.'

'I told you once before. Read his speeches. Whatever views he might once have held, you don't get to the level he's reached by faking enthusiasm for the Project, no matter how good an actor you are.'

'Oh, but he is. Even today, Kramer is still one of the best there is in the game. He has that ability to be two completely different people at the same time, to live a lie so convincing he can deceive himself when necessary. I think he nurtures you because he sees something of himself in the person going by the name of Thomas Hofmann.'

'You're thinking too deeply about it, Brierly. Kramer and I were put on the same path by a chance event.'

'And I think you underestimate yourself. Thirty years ago Kramer had no choice but to become an expert in reading people. Because when he got it wrong and recruited someone who was unsuitable as an agent, almost invariably they or somebody else more valuable to the war effort ended up dead.'

'People with two personalities aren't that unusual. Within some of us there's a new self and the old imperfect nature struggling against it. I was told that at a talk I went to on Wednesday night with the Caribbean lady I've been lodging with.'

'What voodoo is that?'

'Chapter Seven in the *Römerbrief.*'

'Those old fairy tales.' Brierly shook his head. 'Stop avoiding my question. Are you with us or against us when it comes to the EEC?'

'You ask as if it's something I have a choice over. Like we're having an intellectual debate at one of your ancient universities. You British have no understanding of our country. None at all. As far as we're concerned, you might as well have atom bombed us in 'forty-five.'

'Go on. But don't imagine you have a monopoly on suffering.'

'Germany was smashed up by the war. Literally so, in the case of our cities, but also in terms of our national territory. We lost regions that had been German for three quarters of a millennium. Generations of toil and hardship to tame the land, to build towns and villages. To put down roots that the Russians ripped up in a mere few months.'

'You made your choices as a country. It was the price you paid.'

'Having to pay it didn't make it any less painful. You English with your upper-class KGB traitors and your play-acting at espionage. You have no conception of the reality of Communism. What the Red Army did twenty-five years ago when they burnt and raped their way through the eastern half of our country. What they still do today to their own dissidents.'

'You sound like a German nationalist.'

'Again. You misunderstand. You ask me what I think of the EEC? My answer is that we're betting everything on Brussels. How else will we recover the lands stolen from us?'

'And how do you think that's going to happen? Panzers rolling across the Oder?'

'Don't be facetious. Whatever attempts might be made to reunify Germany one day in the future won't be done in our name. But we could do it in the name of Europe. You have your dreams for what you want Europe to become, why can't we have ours?'

Brierly took a puff on his pipe.

'You think that desire is wrong, somehow?' asked the Assassin. 'What would Britain do if the same had happened to you?'

'But it did happen to us - in a different way. A generation back, we had dominions far more extensive than anything Germany ever laid claim to.'

'What? You're trying to tell me that the war ended worse for you than it did for us?'

'One of the war aims of the Americans was the destruction of the British Empire and they achieved it beyond their wildest imaginings. Oh, it wasn't said so explicitly at the time, and it didn't happen all at once, but the signs were there. Heath saw them when he went to America on his debating tour after university in 'thirty-nine. He saw the isolationism, the contentment of large sections of the American political establishment to let Europe tear itself apart, leaving the way open for them to claim a new global empire.'

'You accused me a minute ago of sounding like a Nazi. Now you sound the same way to me. A phobia of America is pure Hitler propaganda.'

'The Americans played a geopolitical game on us. And now we're going to turn the tables and do the same back to them. It's our grand adventure and we're going on it together with our West German and French friends.'

The Assassin shook his head. 'Your adventure isn't some kind of jolly hiking holiday in the Alps. No one challenges powerful nations without getting hurt along the way.'

Brierly pressed home his point. 'Heath wasn't a full minister with a portfolio during Suez fifteen years ago. He was still Chief Whip. But he attended Cabinet meetings and had a ringside seat as the Americans stabbed us in the back. Why else do you think he wants Europe to become a world power in its own right?'

'None of this is new to the rest of us in the EEC. De Gaulle preached "*France fort*" for years. That's why we developed our own nuclear weapons while you made do with crumbs from the American table.'

'Will you make up your mind about which nationality you're meant to be? God, you bloody modern Germans are so infuriating. Listen to me, will you. Heath is the leader that Europe needs right now. He's prepared to go all the way on federation, and for Britain to make a political break with the US. That ought to be of interest to the Quai d'Orsay and anyone else who calls themself a European patriot, as you seem to be claiming for yourself.'

'What do you mean by "make a break"?'

'When he met Pompidou at the summit in May he agreed to end our special relationship with America and to abandon sterling as a reserve currency.'

'So what exactly did Heath promise the French President? To give up Polaris? Kick the US Air Force out of their bases in Britain?'

'The break with America was only described in general terms. A grand geopolitical reorientation towards Europe and away from our old alliances around the world.'

'How will he kill off sterling?'

'Sell off our balances so that it's no longer a global reserve currency. There'll be no way for any future government to turn back the clock. Which means they'll be unable to resist joining a new European monetary system.'

'And what does Nixon think about all this?'

'He imagines Heath is still an ally. The Americans are supportive of British accession. In their minds, Britain will act as their agent inside the EEC to corral the waverers on the Continent under the Western banner.'

'When Washington realises what Heath's long-term intentions are, what do you think the CIA will do then?'

Brierly shifted uneasily on the bench for a passing moment. 'They'll do what every intelligence agency always does. They'll reinterpret the facts to fit the message they believe their political bosses want to hear.'

The Assassin didn't reply. Brierly tamped down the tobacco in his pipe and drew on it again.

'Well? What do you think?' he said. 'I've explained to you just how far Heath is prepared to go in the name of the Project. But I don't see much evidence that either you or Kramer are reciprocating the sentiment.'

Now Brierly set down his pipe on the wooden slats of the bench beside him and pursed his lips. The Assassin sensed what was coming next.

'I heard some chatter about your yachting trip with Selene Warrington-Williams last weekend. Apparently, you met Heath down Hayling Island way. Correct? One evening in Bosham?'

'She recognised his yacht, *Morning Cloud*. Heath was sailing on the Solent that day - selection races for the America's Cup team, she said. Then we happened to end up at the same place on Saturday evening, an out-of-the-way hotel that we chose because we thought no one would recognise us there.'

'And that's where you met Heath? In the bar, I was told?'

'Yes. What of it? She introduced me as an Italian friend of hers. I wanted to maintain my cover.'

'How long did you speak to him for?' asked Brierly.

'Not long. A few words of small talk. He showed no interest in a conversation, but I suppose he likes his privacy.'

Brierly looked sceptical. 'It scarcely seems possible that you just happened to end up at the same hotel.'

'There's not much choice in these small places.'

'Did you have a photograph taken with him,' asked Brierly with narrowed eyes.

The Assassin looked back at him equally coolly and replied in a neutral voice. 'Yes, a souvenir. Selene took it on my camera.'

'I need the film. And any prints or copies of the negatives that you might have made.'

'It's a harmless snapshot.'

'I don't think it is. Do you?'

The Assassin shrugged.

Brierly gave a weary sigh. 'Did you play a prank on Heath in any way when the photo was taken?'

'What's a prank?'

'A joke. *Ein Scherz. Haben Sie ihn geküsst?*'

The Assassin frowned.

'I need the film,' said Brierly. 'We need the film.'

'That's not happening. Don't insult me.'

Brierly looked at him coldly. He pursed his lips once more.

'Was she worth it last weekend? I've heard that she's an enthusiastic screw. A real goer.'

The Assassin took a sharp intake of breath and the temperature in the park dropped by a couple of degrees.

'Oh, like that is it?' said Brierly. 'You have female friends, but you don't take them as lovers because you satisfy that need another way?'

'It's none of your business what I do or don't do,' said the Assassin angrily.

Brierly looked at him speculatively. 'I don't think you understand how far I'm prepared to go to get that film off you.'

'Where did this *Wahnsinn* story come from in the first place? Who suggested it to you?'

Brierly's eyes narrowed for an instant. He picked up his pipe and puffed on it a couple of times.

'I have other people in Number Ten. Ones whom your *femme fatale* accomplice knows nothing about. There was some office gossip about how she'd behaved abominably at the weekend.'

'So you sent her home in disgrace?'

'The amount of trouble she's in will partly depend on how fast Heath forgets what happened.'

'What if he doesn't?'

'Whatever happens or has happened to Selene Warrington-Williams is entirely her own fault. She asked for it by conspiring with you. But you'll have been responsible too. You should have thought of that before you did what you did.'

'What has happened to her then?'

'Nothing yet,' said Brierly quickly. 'She's been given an opportunity to think about it.'

'By whom? Who do you have access to for putting pressure on people?'

'I have means at my disposal.'

'That's what Smythe told me once about Fryatt. That he knew people who could get things done, which was why he'd called on you. Maybe Fryatt's returning the favour right now?'

Brierly said nothing.

'Do you know who Fryatt really is?' asked the Assassin.

Brierly looked at the Assassin shrewdly. 'His interests are aligned to mine.'

'I get the impression he only works for himself.'

'He's got more than one iron in the fire.'

The Assassin shook his head. 'Maybe you have several irons in the fire too? Are you using Fryatt and Smythe to put the screws on MPs who might oppose ratifying the accession treaty? I assume you perform the real dirty work for the Conservative Whips, don't you? A deniable department, completely off the books, which calls in specialists as needed. Just as you did with Kramer and me.'

Brierly kept silent.

'When Selene meets her married lover in the Whips' Office, does she pass on hints about who Smythe should photograph in bed with her next?' asked the Assassin. 'Because according to you, she's shameless in that department, isn't she? She literally doesn't care who she does it with.'

'Now you're fantasising. Take that back,' said Brierly sharply.

The Assassin shrugged noncommittally.

Brierly continued. 'You're also mistaken about Fryatt. He really is with the Foreign Office, and he really did spend three years in the Gulf.'

'Then why is he back here now running a child prostitution ring?'

'Hold your tongue. Don't make allegations about things you know nothing about.'

The Assassin ignored him. 'Why isn't Fryatt afraid of the organised criminals and policemen who run that kind of thing already? They make a lot of money each week. A hundred thousand pounds, I was told. They've got a lot to lose.'

'What's your theory then, given that you're clearly desperate to tell me?' asked Brierly sarcastically.

'He's dropped the hint that he's connected to MI6. Maybe even that he's part of it. The pimps and porn kings of Soho know that a link to the intelligence world means he's too dangerous to touch. And in any case, he's not going after the same market as them, is he?'

'Both of us have only ever looked out for Britain's interests.'

The Assassin thought back to the range of nationalities on display in the foyer of the Dorchester and nodded to himself. 'I'm sure the mobsters of Soho are attracted to the idea of blackmailing Arab oil sheikhs and Japanese businessmen. But they know it's not easy without personal access to that world. And they also know that it's potentially political. No criminal wants that kind of attention from the authorities.'

'Why are you so focussed on Fryatt?' asked Brierly.

'The first two Marks are out of the picture. Smythe and I are dealing with the third one tomorrow. I like to know who I'm working for.'

'And who's the person sitting across the path from me? The man who supposedly works for Kramer? You might have charmed Masterson, but Reynolds isn't so sure about you. Even now he thinks you're closer to the East German Foreign Trade Office than you've let on.'

'And he's right. I do know their foreign trade office. But in Brussels. Because my job involves watching the trade delegations of other countries. But I didn't know any of the East German trade officials in London before I arrived here, and I don't know where he got the idea that I did.'

'He tells me you've been spotted going there more than a few times. In recent days too.'

'It's where I meet my contact. I have to maintain the fiction of our interest in their trade promotion activities. After all, I might need to play this role again.'

'That I doubt.'

The Assassin was silent.

'This is your last chance,' said Brierly. 'Did you ask Selene to take a photograph of you being over-familiar with Heath?'

The Assassin shook his head in disappointment. 'If we're talking last chances then this is the last time that Kramer will help you,' he replied. 'What more could you possibly want from him than he's already done? Not that you've shown much gratitude so far.'

Brierly looked at the Assassin strangely. But it was an expression that the Assassin would have said was one of hurt more than anything else.

'He can give me the film that I know you have.'

'I know when to stop digging,' said the Assassin to the Englishman. 'Do you?'

Brierly was silent, he put his pipe in his mouth and slowly puffed away.

'Well. Goodbye then,' said the Assassin. 'I have places to be.'

–

He left Brierly sitting there and made his way out of the park. Just before he turned the corner of the path, he glanced back. Kramer's wartime colleague still hadn't moved. Blue smoke continued to curl up from his pipe into the morning air.

Crossing over Park Lane, he went back to the Dorchester. From the public phone booth in the foyer he called Club Trèfle to say he was coming to collect his equipment. Then with another quick glance around the lobby, he left and made his way to the club with the same care that he'd taken on his very first visit there in March.

The nightclub owner was sitting at the bar downstairs with another man whom the Assassin hadn't seen before. They were speaking French but stopped as soon as the Assassin drew near. The new man gave him a wary look.

'Can we speak?' the Assassin asked Jimmy.

Jimmy glanced at the other man.

'*Vas-y.*'

'Where's Matteu,' asked the Assassin.

'He's getting some sleep. He'll leave London early this evening to get up there in good time. How about you? You want a tablet?'

'I've come for my things.'

Jimmy got off his high stool and went around to the back of the bar. He bent down and lifted the green holdall up onto the counter. The other man peered at the end of the bag where 'Hofmann' was written in block letters and gave the Assassin another searching look.

'And the other thing that was brought here last night?'

Jimmy bent down again and placed a briefcase on the counter next to the holdall. 'The combination is "777."'

The Assassin flipped the catches. Shielded by the lid, he pulled out a couple of pages at random to check the contents.

'*Merci pour tout*, Jimmy. I'll tell my boss.'

Jimmy gave him a half smile. 'Get going then. *Bonne chance.*' They shook hands.

With a final glance at the new man, the Assassin picked up the briefcase. Swinging the green holdall over his shoulder, he left the club, heading south and west, away from Soho and Mayfair.

When he eventually got back to the hotel, he unzipped the bag and laid out his gear, checking batteries and going through equipment drills for the last time. He thought about forcing sleep with a tablet, as Jimmy had suggested, but decided he'd prefer a head free from chemicals during the next twenty-four hours. Instead, he ordered a steak from room service and dozed with the curtains drawn until it was time to go.

As he left the room, he took a final look at the telephone on the desk. Despite all the conversations he'd had with people over the past week, there was one call he still hadn't made. He closed the door behind him and stood outside in the corridor, irresolute, his conscience pricking him.

With a sigh, he unlocked the door again and strode over to the phone to dial the number in Brussels before he could change his mind. The phone at the other end rang and rang. He waited, hanging on the line for a full minute, but there was no reply. With a solemn face he replaced the receiver and left.

--

The Assassin parked on a deserted Liverpool Street at a quarter to eight and waited outside Broad Street Station, as agreed with Grieves. It wasn't particularly private, but the Assassin had no reason to suspect any funny business - not before the morning at least.

After a few minutes, the businessman emerged down the stairs at the side of the terminus carrying a small suitcase and a coat folded over his arm. The Assassin got out and waved him over.

'Ready?' he asked Grieves.

'As I'll ever be,' replied the other man flatly.

The Assassin took Grieves' suitcase and went round to the boot, stowing it next to his green holdall. Grieves got into the front. The Assassin closed the boot lid and joined him, glancing briefly across to the passenger seat. The Englishman sat there subdued, staring straight ahead of him.

'*Auf gehts!* Let's go.'

They were on the road for five hours in all, stopping only once, at an all-night transport cafe on the A12 for a late dinner of steak and kidney pie with chips.

After some desultory, inconsequential conversation about the weather as they left London, Grieves clearly didn't want to talk further. The Assassin switched on the radio, happy for the excuse of having to concentrate on the driving. Grieves fiddled with the dial and settled on Radio Four, which by that time of the evening was broadcasting classical music, though nothing which the Assassin recognised.

They reached Norwich at midnight. Once the city was behind them, the roads soon became narrower and the countryside darker. Just like Devon, thought the Assassin, but more desolate somehow, perhaps because of the emptiness of the flat land. What sort of people lived up here, he wondered? Only a few short hours away from the bright lights of London and it felt like they were at the very edge of human habitation. How he imagined East Prussia must once have been. Isolated villages amidst lonely forests and lakes at the far end of the German Empire.

During the final stretch, the Assassin asked Grieves to help navigate, handing him the road atlas and a pocket flashlight, hoping the activity would stop his passenger from thinking about the long night ahead of them.

His precaution paid off. Even though the Assassin had been up this way with Matteu on Friday, in the inky blackness he took a wrong turn which confused Grieves as well, despite him having the atlas open on his lap. After five or six minutes attempting to deny he'd made a mistake, he stopped so they could consult the large-scale Ordnance Survey map by flashlight, spread over the bonnet of the car.

At least the setback had stirred Grieves back into life. But it was an unquiet spirit which animated him as they drove the long way round to get back onto the right road. Anxiety was what the Assassin sensed most of in the other man. It unsettled him too.

At one in the morning, five hours after leaving London, the Assassin finally found the old emergency entrance to the airfield again, having already driven straight past it once in the dark. He turned off the tarmac of the public road onto ridged concrete and doused the car's headlights. The moon had risen, and he decided they could manage by its light alone.

'This is it,' he said to Grieves. 'I'll deal with the gate. You come and take the wheel.'

The Assassin went to the boot to fetch the bolt cutters he'd bought on Saturday afternoon, while Grieves went around the front of the car to the driver's seat. With a single rapid motion, the Assassin sheared through the rusted padlock of the steel gate. He wrenched once, twice, and dragged it open over the long grass and brambles that had grown up over the years.

Grieves was sitting white-faced in the moonlight, gripping the top of the steering wheel with both hands. The Assassin waved him through, pulled the gate shut again, then got back in.

'Drive on.'

The businessman did as he was told, heading around the perimeter track until they came to the end of a runway, vast and wide in the gloom.

'Turn here. Drive up to the hangar over there on the skyline.'

Slowly they approached the towering bulk, silhouetted against a blaze of stars. They bumped along until they came to an intersection with another runway.

'Stop for a moment.'

The Assassin twisted in his seat to look at something. 'Drive up that way,' he said, pointing to the left.

Grieves did as the Assassin asked. This runway's surface was in much better condition than the first. The sections of concrete were still level with one another, and they drove along without any of the jarring jolts from before. But after a few short seconds, the Assassin leaned forward into the windscreen as a paler mass emerged from the darkness, blocking the way ahead.

'Stop here.'

He got out and walked slowly forward. It was a stack of hay bales, laid right across the width of the runway. He pursed his lips, then returned to the car.

'Back the way we came.'

Eventually, they reached the hangar. As instructed by Smythe, they parked by the western side, the one furthest from the farmhouse. Getting out of the car, the Assassin sniffed the air.

'You smell that?' he asked Grieves.

'Pigs, maybe. The farmers sometimes put these old wartime buildings to agricultural use.' It was the longest sentence that Grieves had spoken since leaving London.

'Let's go inside,' said the Assassin. 'There might be an old office or something where we can wait. It'll get cold in the car.'

The side door opened easily. The two men stepped over the threshold to be met by an even stronger smell from the animals. Taking his torch from his pocket, the Assassin flashed the light around the cavernous interior - empty apart from a trailer with a flat tyre, a row of sacks of animal feed, and some other agricultural detritus, indeterminate in the gloom. Up against the side of the hangar, about halfway along to the full-width main doors at the other end, he saw the square bulk of the office which Smythe had mentioned.

As he quartered the hangar for a final time with the torch, he caught sight of something on the back wall. He played the light back and forth over it, despite the risk of drawing attention to themselves.

'What do you see?' asked Grieves, showing more interest in proceedings again.

'Look,' said the Assassin. 'I think it's a map of Germany. All of Germany.'

With the beam of the torch he followed the white-painted outline of the Reich, all the way from Strasbourg in Elsaß in the west, right across to Königsberg and Memel in the far corner.

'I wonder when this was made?' he asked out loud.

'Probably mid-war,' said Grieves. 'And then they kept adding to it until the end.'

Red flame symbols had been painted beside several of the cities. Some places had three or four tongues of fire next to them.

'They bombed the same targets more than once,' said Grieves. 'It's a record of the raids by the squadrons based here, I'm almost certain of it.'

The Assassin snapped off the torch. 'How can you be sure?' he asked.

'I was a cook in the RAF during my National Service. I heard a few stories from the sergeants and warrant officers who'd been in the war. I was only a boy back then myself, but I used to watch the bomber formations assembling from the field behind our house.'

'My grandfather was killed in an air raid. He was a worker at the Focke-Wulf factory outside Danzig.'

'Gdansk these days, I believe.'

'I know.'

'It was an unreal experience, watching the squadrons of Flying Fortresses and Liberators form up with their fighter escorts, circling higher and higher until they were almost out of sight. Then they'd head off for Europe, streams of contrails silently filling the sky, as if cast by some unholy god.'

The Assassin turned to look at Grieves. He wouldn't have taken him for a poet. 'Unholy is the right word. The war was a catastrophe for Germany, at all levels,' he said.

A bat flitted across the corner of the hangar and out through a gap in the corrugated iron exterior. The Assassin flashed the light again to take a better look at the office, or perhaps workshop. Blank windows pierced its wooden sides, some of them still with cracked glass in their frames. The room had two doors, one in its long side, parallel to the hangar wall and one in the end directly facing them. The nearest door hung askew from a single hinge.

They went inside. There was a wooden workbench along the back wall with burn marks on its surface and a rusted vice clamped onto one of its ends. In front of the bench stood a row of oil drums, and in the corner, some other clutter - broken chairs and an old tea urn.

The Assassin placed his green holdall on top of the bench. He and Grieves both tried sitting on the drums, which looked to be the more solid option, but they soon ended up rolling them away to reach the workbench and sit there instead. They perched side by side, the silence only broken by the scrabbling of rats.

'It's going to be a long wait,' said the Assassin. 'You want a drink?'

He offered Grieves the flask of tea he'd refilled at the transport cafe, pouring the businessman a full mug. Grieves cupped it for warmth. 'There was a lot of hanging around in the RAF,' he said. 'It's probably why I'm so impatient today.'

The minutes dragged on. They both knew they were avoiding the question of what was really going to happen in the morning. The Assassin switched off his torch to conserve the battery and spoke into the gloomy silence.

'Back at Saint Katharine's Dock you mentioned the parties you went to but shouldn't have,' he said, trying to see how far he could get without breaking the illusion.

There was a pause from Grieves. 'What do you want to know?'

'Do you ever wish things could have been different?'

'I wish I'd never heard about the parties, if that's what you mean. But once I'd started going, I couldn't stop. Once I'd tried it, I mean,' said Grieves. He didn't explain what "it" was. He seemed to have forgotten that he'd never actually told the Assassin what went on at the events laid on by Voaden, despite the Assassin's repeated questions that day by the dock.

'So how did you first get involved?'

There was another short pause. 'I was stupid. I let myself be persuaded to go to a sleazy country house party. I told myself it would be good for business. I was right, but it was the wrong thing to do.'

'Who invited you?'

By the faint moonlight leaking into the workshop, the Assassin could sense Grieves giving him a look, rather than seeing any narrowing of the eyes.

'An ex-policeman called Smythe who'd been thrown out of the police for taking bribes. At least, that's how the story went. Ever come across him?'

'Why? Should I have?'

Silence descended again for a second, a heavier silence than before.

'What was it like going to the very first party?' asked the Assassin.

Grieves tutted to himself under his breath. 'Like anything illegal which you try for the first time. Exciting. A sense of danger. There's something liberating when you can't see any faces.'

'What do you mean?'

'Everyone that night wore masks. Like at a masquerade ball.'

'Who was the ringmaster? The man who invited you, Smythe?'

'No. Someone else, someone who dropped out of the scene a year or two later.'

The Assassin held his breath, waiting to see where Grieves' mood would take him. 'How long was it before you went to the second party?' he prompted.

'Three or four weeks. I could hardly wait.'

'And you don't like waiting.'

'I'm used to getting what I want. I've been successful in business. I own companies all over the country.' The Assassin could feel the draught of air made by Grieves waving an unseen hand around the room. 'So I had an excuse to travel to all four corners of England and join in with everything they laid on. Wherever it took place, whoever with. No matter how wrong it was.'

'Who were "they"?'

If Grieves was trying to sustain a story on Smythe's behalf, it wasn't as important to him as his need to talk. Or confess.

'The ringmaster at that first party, as you called him, was a man called Voaden. A charismatic man. One of those characters you come across in life from time to time.'

'How do you mean?'

'It was like he had an animal magnetism. Uncanny it was. From the very start it was as if he could read my mind, or rather my soul. I was an open book to him. He had an instinct for knowing the experiences I would become addicted to next, before I even knew myself.'

'And what did you like?'

Now the words began to pour out of Grieves without check. 'It was wrong, you know. What we did to those kids. I did try to stop. Every few months I'd make an effort to wean myself off it. I tried all kinds of things as a distraction: a mistress in Mayfair who was into rough play, sailing holidays on the Cote d'Azur with a boatload of prostitutes, drugs in a hippy commune one summer in Copenhagen.'

The Assassin nodded grimly.

'I tried psychiatric therapy from a shrink in Harley Street. One day I even walked into the Irish Catholic church on Soho Square, intending to speak to a priest. I thought they might be able to give me some kind of exorcism.'

'But that feeling of power you got from hurting the children made it too difficult to let go?'

In the darkness, the Assassin just about made out Grieves hanging his head.

'Let's have some light,' he said to the businessman. He switched the torch on again and set it on the bench, angling the beam into the corner, so as not to shine into their eyes.

The Assassin pursed his lips and chose his next words carefully. 'So when did it start to really go wrong for you? Was it the party you told me about at the dock? When your friend saw some things he shouldn't have?'

Grieves folded his arms, confession suddenly at an end. 'And where do you fit into all of this?' he asked.

'What do you mean?' replied the Assassin warily.

'I don't know. Give me some more details about how you plan to get me out of here.'

The Assassin reached into his holdall. He took out an olive-green aircrew survival radio and set it on the bench between them.

'At first light I'll activate this beacon. It's used by air force pilots to call for rescue if they get shot down. My people will land to pick us up.' He reached back into the bag for the envelope of aerial photographs Kramer had sent him and tossed the print of the airfield on the bench next to the radio. 'Look. They've even done some reconnaissance.'

Grieves picked up the photo and used the torch to inspect the typewritten code in the corner of the print.

'All this is for real? You really are working with the French?'

'Tell me about the party that went wrong.'

Grieves set the torch down again. 'A girl died. Afterwards Voaden, the ringmaster, dropped out of sight. There were lurid rumours about what had happened to him.'

'And that's when you decided to broadcast your own rumours about Heath and the material you had on him?'

'We were worried about being tainted by association with Voaden, so we took the precautions I described to you back at Saint Katharine's Dock. But we weren't fearful, not at that stage.'

The Assassin frowned. 'So what changed?'

'Because later, my partners and I began to suspect foul play with the girl who overdosed.'

'Isn't an overdose already a case of foul play?'

Grieves sighed. 'Voaden left the scene under a cloud. Smythe went silent as the grave for a few weeks too. But then he came back into the picture. And this time there was someone else running the show alongside him. Someone who'd only ever been in the background before.'

'Who?'

'He was at the very first party I went to, the masked ball. He was giving one of the tarts a beating. Really laying into her with a riding crop. Went as far as drawing blood.'

The Assassin was certain it was Fryatt, but wanted Grieves to give him the confirmation himself.

'What do you mean by "my partners and I"?' he asked. 'Wasn't Smythe your partner? Or this other man?'

'Why do you want to know?' asked Grieves. 'I suppose it doesn't matter anymore.'

He held out his mug for more tea. The Assassin poured from the Thermos and added a slug of brandy from a hip flask.

'No,' Grieves continued. 'Not business partners. Not the usual sort anyway. It was myself and two other regular guests. But after a few months we'd become more like collaborators with Smythe, rather than his and Voaden's customers.'

The Assassin raised an eyebrow. 'What did you collaborate with Smythe on?'

'Developing Voaden's party network into something more ambitious. Some of us who go along to these events also end up helping to run them in different ways.'

The Assassin thought of Smythe's tale of how he'd been asked to act as security at the party in Devon. Maybe there was a grain of truth there. Maybe that was how his involvement had originally started.

'So what did your two fellow party-goers contribute to the operation?'

'One of them was a networker in his own right, he invited society guests. The other had access to children.'

'And you?'

'Business acumen. Smythe has collected lots of photographs over the years, worth a lot of money to interested buyers.'

'Blackmail?'

'Not directly. Not against the subjects of the photographs. Too crude.'

'Why?'

'It takes too long to work, and in any case, people react in unpredictable ways to that kind of pressure. His idea was, still is, to get into publishing. Magazines and personalised collections of high-quality prints. He thinks he can make more money that way than from running parties and supplying kids to individuals. No one in the photographs will be suing us for defamation, even if they could trace the source. We planned to crop the photos or else blur the faces of the adults. Of course, any adults who did recognise themselves and came to us to complain could have been blackmailed on the side anyway.'

'Why did you agree to help him? You didn't need the money.'

'I was in too deep by that stage to say "no." And it wasn't just Smythe pushing the idea. Even before Voaden dropped out of sight, that other man, the one who whipped the tart, he began to make noises too. One day maybe eighteen months ago, he came to me out of the blue and suggested I work with Smythe. He said he'd make it worth my while.'

'What was the other man's day job?'

'I've never been exactly sure. From what I've picked up, he's spent time in the diplomatic service.'

'Who was this man? Paris will need a name,' asked the Assassin.

Grieves hesitated. 'I suppose it doesn't matter. Not if we're leaving tomorrow.' There was a brief pause. 'He's called Fryatt.'

The Assassin composed his face. 'Was he pulling Smythe's strings from behind the scenes?'

'I don't know. They had a joint plan, but parts of it were on a much grander scale than anything Smythe could ever have come up with on his own.'

The Assassin waited for a moment or two, not wishing to appear over eager. 'Go on then. The more details, the more credible you'll be in Paris.'

Grieves looked askance at the Assassin for a second, but told him anyway.

'The way Fryatt described it to me last year, he wanted us to cast a wide net with the published material. Even the lists of subscribers alone would be highly valuable. He became quite megalomaniac about it all. He imagined us at the centre of a web controlling the whole of the British Establishment: MPs and ministers, civil servants, police, the military. Anyone we wanted removed, any business contract we wanted awarded, he had visions of looking up his address book and getting Smythe to make a discreet call.'

'Why did he want that power?'

'Why does anyone ever want it? Maybe he thought he could run the country better than the elected politicians.'

'How did he think he was going to push aside the real professionals? The gangsters who run Soho and the corrupt policemen who protect them?'

'Fryatt said we'd be untouchable. He was going to start by bringing in some new partners that only he had access to. Arabs from the Gulf. And he also said that a real police crackdown would be coming down on the porn barons soon, not the half-hearted attempt from two years ago.'

'Really?' asked the Assassin.

'That's why in 'sixty-eight, the Home Secretary at the time put in place a plan for an outsider to become the next Commissioner of the Met. Someone who the politicians can trust to work for them and not for the crooks. It will happen in the next year or two. That's the story Fryatt told me.'

'Which Home Secretary? Callaghan?'

Grieves nodded. 'Fryatt gave me the hard sell. He said he had protectors high up within MI6. People who couldn't afford to expose him because he knew their secrets. But he wanted us to be independent of any intelligence service funding. For the long term, our operation had to be self-financing.'

The Assassin looked at him in momentary confusion. What if the story he'd spun about Maurice Oldfield backing Fryatt had been right all along, without him realising it? Or what if there were others within the higher echelons of MI6 with even more awkward secrets than the Director of Counter-Intelligence? 'What exactly was your role to be in this arrangement?' he asked.

Grieves hung his head again. 'He wanted me to have the obscene material printed in secret and for us to distribute it through intermediaries. We were going to start with production, muscle in on distribution later. As extra cover, we even discussed setting up a civil rights group for pederasts which would act as a publishing arm. All heavily disguised, of course.'

'And all these plans were being discussed while Voaden was still on the scene?'

'Neither Fryatt nor Smythe said he'd be pushed out. We assumed he was in on it too.'

'But you told me that Smythe also dropped off the radar after the fatal party? Did Fryatt disappear at that time too? Is that what spooked you into making the threats against Heath?'

'It didn't seem so foolish at the time. We assumed someone had taken all three of them out of the picture. But when Fryatt and Smythe resurfaced, they didn't mention the rumours about Heath that we'd started in the meantime. So we assumed they'd been forgotten about or had never been taken seriously in the first place. The parties started up again and we carried on going to them as if nothing had changed. Smythe's business venture went on the back burner though.'

'But then several months later, someone does receive a call and here we are all together now.'

Grieves nodded slowly. 'It was ten days ago. The networker rang me up out of the blue and said we were being targeted by someone.'

'Did he say who was doing the targeting?'

Grieves looked straight ahead into the gloom. 'No. Just that there had been talk.'

'And what did Fryatt and Smythe say when you told them? What did you agree to do for them this time, in exchange for their protection?'

Grieves glanced away from the Assassin for a moment. Then he ran his hands through his hair and casually slid down off the bench, as if to stretch his legs. But he kept his back to the Assassin. There was a noise as the Assassin landed on the concrete floor too.

Grieves turned around to see the Assassin pointing a gun at him.

'What's this?' he asked in a quiet voice.

'I will fly you out of here,' replied the Assassin. 'But I need to know that you'll do what I say between now and the morning.' Then, in a sharper voice, 'On your knees, face towards me.'

'Fuck. What have I ever done to you?' said Grieves, his voice strained now.

The Assassin made no answer, but simply waggled his gun. With a bitter look, Grieves slowly sank to the floor. Keeping his eyes on the Englishman, the Assassin felt inside the holdall to find a set of handcuffs and tossed them to the ground in front of Grieves.

'Put them on, wrists in front of you.'

Grieves did so. The Assassin reached round to tuck the pistol behind his back and came over to make sure the cuffs were tight.

'What's all this about?' asked Grieves in an aggrieved tone. 'Don't you trust me?'

'It wasn't Annersley who phoned to say that Barker had been killed, was it? It was Smythe. If it really was Annersley who'd called you, you'd have been long gone from England by now.'

Grieves' mouth dropped open, aghast at the mention of the other two Marks' names. 'What's going on?' he asked. 'So you do know Smythe after all?' The pretence was finally over.

'Yes.'

'Are you working with him or against him?' demanded Grieves.

'That's Smythe's decision to make in the morning.'

'No honour amongst thieves, is there? Or do you lurk in the shadows of the intelligence world too, like Fryatt,' asked Grieves in a cynical voice.

'I've never spied on anyone in my life. I just get things done for people. Did you have any idea of the wheels you set in motion when you threatened Heath?'

Grieves shook his head, but it seemed to the Assassin, more in disgust at himself. 'We knew we'd be taken seriously. Heath is wide open to those kinds of insinuations. But then he only has himself to blame for that.'

'But he's not just another easily replaceable leader, is he? He's the current champion, the driving force of the UK's accession to the

EEC. Without him, it might not happen for another ten years. And there's far too much money at stake.'

'What money? People always say it's about the money. Or are you spilling some beans yourself now?'

'You're a businessman. You know the way the world works.'

'So?'

'The EEC spends as much on agricultural subsidies each year as the Americans do on their space programme, and it's just as ruinous. The Six are greedy for England's money. In fact, not greedy, desperate. The CAP will be bankrupt within a couple of years without your country's contributions. Not that your leaders have thought that far ahead.'

'That's not how it's been sold to us,' said Grieves indignantly.

'Now do you begin to understand what you did when you threatened Heath? You jeopardised the transfer of hundreds of millions of pounds from British taxpayers to the French treasury by way of EEC farm subsidies.'

'Smythe said you were lying when you told me that people in France would be eager for material to attack Heath with.'

'Not to attack him with. To own him.' The Assassin shook his head. 'You still trust Smythe, even now? 'Didn't you think it strange at all, when he and Fryatt did a deal with you to be the bait for the little scene being played out tomorrow morning. Or did you think you'd be able to work both sides, see who gave you the better offer?'

'They said the French had sent you here to act out the part of an East German agent, but that you might be here under false pretences.'

'In what way?'

'They didn't say. Maybe you're here to secretly undermine Heath on someone else's behalf. Maybe you really do work for East Germany, as was suggested to me. After all, you claimed to me that you met their trade minister.'

'Did you believe them?'

'They didn't give me a choice, not once they'd confronted me with what happened to Barker. And by the way, how do you know that it was him specifically who died?' he asked suspiciously.

'I didn't say that he died. I said that Smythe called you up to say he'd been killed. Almost everything that I've said to you is true. Even my meeting with Schalck-Golodkowski in Luxembourg. But just because I know a person, it doesn't mean I work for them.'

'So what doesn't Smythe understand about you?'

'Because he's starting from the wrong premise. He's become distracted by his own East German deception play. He doesn't understand how desperately France wants England to join the EEC. Of course Paris is interested in what you have to say about the Prime Minister.'

'And how do you know Smythe?'

'Through the man known as Brierly, who set up my meeting with your lawyer. They were correct in what they said. I was sent over by the French to act out the part of an East German agent. You were a person of interest. But then I began to realise why Smythe had marked you out.'

'Why do you think that was?'

'Threatening Heath might have seemed clever a year ago. But those threats were eventually heard in Paris and Brussels too. Just as Fryatt and Smythe had successfully got rid of Voaden, and people had begun to forget about that fatal party, you risked drawing attention to their vice ring again. You needed to be dealt with.'

'So why have they turned against you? Is it because you're going to help me escape them so I can tell the French what I know about Heath?'

'What did Smythe say would happen tomorrow morning?' asked the Assassin.

'That they'd arrest you, have you interrogated about whatever it is you're meant to have done wrong and deport you.'

'I think Smythe is still in two minds about tomorrow. I think he's preparing for more than one outcome. But I do think there's a chance he's brought us here to get rid of us both.'

'Fuck,' said Grieves. 'Part of me always knew it.'

'I guessed you did, at heart. But don't worry, we will get you out of here - away from them and the things they tempt you to get up to with the children.'

'Are you ready for whatever he's preparing for the morning?'

The Assassin shrugged.

'Why don't you trust me?' asked Grieves, rattling the handcuffs. 'What am I going to do? Hit you over the head while your back is turned and run away?'

Grieves leaned forward as he said this, shuffling his left foot as if getting ready to spring there and then. The pistol reappeared in the Assassin's hand.

'Right now I have some different questions for you. Sit.' The Assassin waved the gun, motioning Grieves back into the centre of the room.

The fight had gone out of the other man. He perched himself awkwardly on an oil drum.

'How much of the material that Fryatt and Smythe wanted you to print did you get to see?' asked the Assassin, as he tucked the pistol into his waistband, behind his back.

'Some of it.'

'I believe I saw some of it too, only last night. Don't ask me how.' The Assassin cleared his throat. 'I want to ask you about an abuser I saw in one of the photographs. A seriously, grossly fat man.'

Grieves' shoulders slumped. 'I think I know who you mean. There's only one person it could be.'

'Who?'

'Someone called Cyril Smith. He was mayor of Rochdale a couple of years back. Up and coming local Liberal politician, waiting for his big break to get onto the national stage.'

'The name means nothing to me. In the picture which I saw, he was beating a child over his knee. A girl, I think.'

Grieves looked down at his feet. 'I might have been there when that photo was taken. It was meant to be a sample of the material they wanted me to print.'

'You actually watched him beat her?' asked the Assassin coldly. 'For how long?'

Grieves' face twitched. He tucked his face into his shoulder, whether from shame or to rub an itch, the Assassin couldn't tell. 'At least a quarter of an hour, I think,' he said quietly.

'That would have made her sore.' The Assassin's tone was acidic.

Grieves nodded dumbly. The stream of confessions started flowing again.

'He must have done it to other children, lots of times before. He has a technique. He's a large man - in every way. Tall too. I imagine they assume there's no point in struggling. And he can hit hard. She was frantic by the end, could hardly breathe for sobbing. Afterwards, he sat her up on his knee and stroked her back as he kept telling her: "It had to be done, lass. It had to be done."'

The Assassin's cheek spasmed, the line of his scar whitening. 'Was that all he did to her?'

'He only does it with boys.'

The Assassin shook his head grimly.

'I'm sorry for what happened to the children,' said Grieves. 'For what we did to them,' he said in a scarcely audible voice.

'And what did happen that night, after Smith had finished beating her?'

Grieves whispered something the Assassin couldn't catch. 'Again,' he snapped.

'Afternoon. It wasn't the night, it was late afternoon. When he was finished, we carried on with her for the rest of the day, all the way until the evening. She came into the room a virgin.'

The Assassin stepped away from the bench. His hand started to reach round behind his back. 'What was in the girl's hand as she lay bent over Smith's knee?' he asked icily. 'There was something dangling down that I couldn't make out.'

Now Grieves' head sank onto his chest. It heaved once, twice, and then came a great sob of sorrow. Tears started to roll down his cheeks.

'What was in her hand?' demanded the Assassin more loudly.

'Her rag doll, for God's sake. Her fucking toy. And do you know the worst of it? After Smith left us alone with her, as she was in pain, all she could repeat was "Don't hurt my dolly, don't hurt my dolly." And we laughed at her.'

'Jesus Christ.'

There was silence for several seconds. The Assassin flushed alternately red and white. Step by step, he left the workshop, forcing one foot past the other. Grieves could hear him pacing the length of the hangar, his footsteps fading then growing louder again.

When the Assassin returned, he ignored the businessman. Instead, he went straight over to the bench and took out a pair of black overalls from his holdall which he proceeded to put on. He reached back into the bag for the tactical radio he'd shown to Matteu in Club Trèfle and clipped it to his belt. Then he walked over to the corner of the room and yanked out a broken chair from the pile of junk there.

'Lie down on the bench and don't speak to me again,' he said to Grieves. 'I'm going to sit here and wait.'

*

The grey pre-dawn light crept into the hangar through the narrow gap between the main doors where they hadn't been fully closed. The Assassin checked his watch and stood up. Going over to where his green holdall was lying on the workbench, at the end furthest from the dozing Grieves, he unzipped the bag and checked something inside.

Grieves stirred at the sound. He was curled up, finally at rest after a night of constantly turning back and forth. The Assassin didn't think the other man had slept a wink. The sign of a guilty conscience. A sign he recognised in himself.

A couple more minutes passed. Grieves sat up and shook himself to try to get warm.

Suddenly, there was a crackle from the radio hanging on the Assassin's belt, the static cutting harshly into the room.

'*Ça bouge. Ça bouge. Deux mecs*'

A half-smile of expectation played across the Assassin's face as the sun finally rose above the horizon. Through the dusty glass of the workshop's window he saw its rays strike the back wall of the hangar. The light played across the faded map of Germany. A whole Germany, united once more. The Assassin glanced at it one last time, his face expressionless again.

'What time is it?' asked Grieves.

'A new day. Get up and come over here.'

Grieves did as he was commanded, moving stiffly down the length of the bench, his hands still bound before him. The Assassin reached out to grab the businessman's collar and pulled him into position, to the right of the Assassin and slightly in front. Next, he reached into the green holdall, which was still lying on the bench, and pulled out an AK assault rifle with the stock folded up underneath. Slinging the strap over his head, he cocked the weapon and let it hang down by his side, concealed by Grieves' body from anyone standing in the doorway.

Just at that moment, a shadow was cast against the map on the back wall and Berlin sank back into darkness again. The shapes of two men could be seen coming in through the gap in the hangar doors, walking over the oil-stained concrete, past the places where engines had once been changed and bullet holes patched. As he approached,

Smythe began to shout out 'Hofmann, you bastard,' over and over again.

Grieves looked across fearfully at the Assassin. 'Save me,' he said in a whisper. 'Even though I don't deserve it.'

'None of us do.' Then the Assassin seemed to relent. 'But it's not me who can save you.'

He called out to Smythe. 'Over here.'

Fryatt and Smythe bundled in through the main door to the workshop. The Foreign Office man was apoplectic with rage, opening and closing his mouth like a stranded fish. Smythe simply drew a Smith & Wesson revolver from inside his jacket.

'Hand it over,' he said.

'What?'

'The negative of you and Heath in the pub in Bosham. And my file.'

Grieves looked nervously between the other three. Fryatt's contemptuous sneer broadened. 'Do it now,' he screamed.

For answer, the Assassin pulled Grieves in close to him as a shield. In the same smooth action, he raised the concealed AK, resting its barrel on Grieves' shoulder and pointed it at Smythe from behind the cover of the businessman's torso.

'What's going on?' came a new voice from outside the workshop. Masterson now appeared in the frame of the end door, Reynolds following close behind as they entered the room together.

Fryatt and Smythe whipped round to look at the newcomers. Masterson continued to advance, holding the borrowed Browning up in front of him in a double-handed grip, ready to fire. Reynolds had moved to one side, but still hung back slightly. Now Fryatt reached into his jacket and brought out a snub-nosed revolver, but a small one, more of a lady's handbag gun.

Fryatt pointed his weapon at the MI5 men and Smythe swung back to continue covering the Assassin.

'What the hell's happening?' Masterson shouted at Fryatt and Smythe. 'You stupid bloody fools. You've gone too far. We know what's been going on.'

'No you don't,' Fryatt shouted back. 'We've uncovered a Communist plot to smear the Prime Minister. These people are under arrest.'

'They don't look like they're under arrest to me,' said Masterson. 'Put your guns down, all of you. Look.' He lowered his own weapon to his side. The Assassin risked a quick glance in his direction. Hovering uncertainly behind Masterson, Reynolds' face wore a tortured expression.

Now the Assassin spoke up. 'They've come to kill Grieves,' he said to the newcomers, speaking out of the side of his mouth whilst he kept his eye on Smythe. 'Just like I said they would. I'm stopping them from committing a crime.'

'We have proof of the German's complicity,' Fryatt shot back. 'He took a compromising photograph of the Prime Minister and gave it to someone at the East German Foreign Trade Office. He's a Stasi agent.'

The Assassin frowned as Smythe fumbled in his jacket and held up a metal film canister. 'Look.'

'It's a roll of film. Here and now it tells us nothing,' said Masterson. 'Lower your guns and we'll find a way to make sure everyone gets what they want.'

'You're bluffing,' said the Assassin to Fryatt and Smythe. He shifted the barrel of the AK to remind them it was still there.

Fryatt gave him a sly, evil look. 'Brierly didn't buy your story about Bosham. He asked us to find out from Selene what really went on.'

The Assassin's eyes narrowed further. 'I said you're bluffing. She hasn't been in London since Tuesday.'

'She wasn't bluffing, or even blubbing as Smythe bent her over the back of the sofa in her lounge and made up for all the free nookie he's missed out on recently. The Honourable Selene Warrington-Williams wasn't very honourable after Smythe had finished with her.'

All remaining emotion drained from the Assassin's face, and his eyes seemed to depart to somewhere deep inside.

Smythe sniggered. 'But she didn't betray you. She just bit down on the gag. It didn't matter though. We found her copy of the negative anyway.'

A second passed. Almost imperceptibly, the Assassin took on a new, almost beatific expression.

'I'm leaving,' he said. He kneed Grieves in the back of the leg and prodded him into motion.

Smythe opened fire, hitting Grieves in the chest. The Assassin fired back four times. Single high velocity rounds - two for Smythe and two for Fryatt. An instant after Smythe pulled the trigger, Masterson whipped up his gun hand and shot in their general direction too, even though the policeman was already tumbling backwards.

The entire exchange of fire had taken three or four seconds at most.

Reynolds was frozen to the spot. The Assassin thrust Grieves forward with the heel of his hand and he sank to the ground, slowly collapsing forward over Smythe's legs.

'Fuck, fuck, fuck,' said Masterson. He looked at the Assassin. The German gave him a cool look in return, then let the AK drop to his side and hang by its strap again.

'What do we do now?' demanded Masterson.

Reynolds stood there stunned, transfixed by the runnels of blood finding their way along the cracks in the floor. 'This one's still alive,' he said quietly, pointing at Smythe with his foot.

Smythe stirred where he lay, one hand held weakly over his torn chest. He was twitching his feet, as if trying to free himself from under Grieves' bleeding body.

The Assassin slung his rifle round behind his back. He walked up to Smythe, picked up the policeman's Smith & Wesson, and drew back the hammer. Reynolds watched without comprehension as the German bent down and fired once into the centre of Smythe's forehead.

'Not anymore he's not,' he said.

The Assassin turned round to Grieves, who was also still moving feebly, and fired a second shot from Smythe's gun.

'This one's dead too.'

He checked Fryatt, but he'd been hit in the heart and had already bled out.

Reynolds was in the first stages of shock, mouthing silent words over and over to himself.

'You saw them shoot Grieves,' the Assassin said to Masterson. 'They've caused an international incident between allies. That's how everyone else will describe it, if they ever find out.'

'What do we do now? They're lying there on the floor and the problem's not going away.'

The Assassin unhooked the radio from his belt and spoke into it.

'*Ici Pfeiffer. Vas-y, vas-y.*'

'*Bien reçu*,' came the disembodied reply, accompanied by another hiss of static.

'We need to dispose of the bodies, obviously,' said the Assassin. 'We'll get away with it if we're careful. Smythe is in the police, but he's compromised. Fryatt isn't officially part of MI6. They'll be happy for things to stay that way. We make both of them vanish, and people's first conclusion will be that they left the country together. Maybe they'll think of Burgess and Maclean. Or even a gangland killing. They were muscling in on a lucrative business.'

Masterson pursed his lips at the mention of the first two traitors in the Cambridge spy ring.

'It's either that or explain why you were adding a fake East German spy into MI5's file of suspects,' said the Assassin coldly. 'And you know how much MI6 will enjoy telling that tale to your political masters.'

'Fuck,' said Masterson. 'They'll have a field day.'

'How are you going to get rid of the bodies?' asked Reynolds as he returned to the land of the living.

'This is a pig farm, right? You can smell it in the air,' asked the Assassin.

'There's a new shed built hard up against the other side of this hangar,' said Masterson. 'We saw it as we came in.'

'I have some people arriving in a couple of minutes. They've been here before. They told me when I came up here on Friday to scout the place out, that there's a meat rendering plant in the shed next door. It's how they dispose of the carcasses of sick or unwanted animals. The remains get fed back to the other pigs.'

Reynolds was sick on the floor.

The Assassin gave him a glance. 'Reynolds. I need you to go and wait by the main hangar door. Shout out when you see a green Land Rover coming. In fact, start opening the doors wide enough for them to drive straight in. There'll be a winding handle off to one side somewhere.'

'Who's arriving?' asked Masterson.

'French friends. Soho crooks who know how to take care of things. They'll drive my car and Smythe's back down to London and get rid of them there. Smythe will have paid the farmer to stay away until noon at least, but my guys will be finished long before then.'

'What are you going to do?' asked Masterson.

'I'm going home.'

The Assassin reached into the holdall and took out the olive-green survival radio. The others watched as he unclipped a small, folded-over whip aerial on one side, which immediately sprung upright. Rotating the function selector on the other side, he spoke into the radio's microphone with a controlled urgency. '*Pfeiffer, Pfeiffer, Pfeiffer.*'

There was no reply that Reynolds could hear. The Assassin turned the dial back to the beacon setting, then unhooked the tactical radio from his belt and attached the survival radio there instead using its carrying loop.

'You still need to give me the name of Treasure,' said Masterson in a gravelly voice.

'I want my gun back first.'

'Of sentimental value, is it? Did you use it to kill your first man?'

'No. My second.'

Masterson reversed the Browning and handed it to the Assassin butt-first.

The Assassin took out his black pocketbook and found a blank page. He wrote something, then passed the book over to Masterson. He peered at the name written there.

'Of course,' he said. 'It makes sense.'

'Now you know,' said the Assassin.

'You called him "Treasure" before. Is his codename "Schatz" inside another organisation elsewhere in Europe? *Mein Schatz...* "my treasure"... "my darling"? Some kind of private joke, is it?' He gave the Assassin a grim smile.

'I have something else for you,' said the Assassin, ignoring him. He reached into the holdall and took out Smythe's dossier. 'It's all yours. Use it well. Don't forget, you're a father too.'

'Don't patronise me,' said Masterson. 'I need to ask you something else.'

'No, first you and I need to help my guys get rid of these people.'

The Assassin went over to Smythe's body and stood looking at it for a second. He spat in Smythe's face and kicked the dead man's ribs. Without further ado, he grabbed the policeman by the ankles and started to drag him backwards out of the workshop and across the floor of the hangar. At some point, the film canister had rolled from Smythe's outstretched hand all the way over to the wall, but the Assassin ignored it for now.

'Take Fryatt. Quick,' he said to Masterson.

They dragged the two bodies across the width of the hangar and through a door in its far side - another post-war alteration to the building.

The door connected directly with the new shed, which was also in gloom. At the back they made out the movement of animals in their pens and heard them too, unsettled by the noise of humans, perhaps by the prospect of food. Where they entered the shed was an open space for the preparation of feed with rows of troughs and plastic buckets stacked up beside them. They dropped the corpses on a tarpaulin which someone had already laid out in front of an industrial machine made of stainless steel with a wide top feed hopper.

'You see?' said the Assassin, tapping his foot on the rubber-backed fabric. 'They'd already made their preparations to get rid of Grieves and me.'

Reynolds gave a shout from his sentry post by the main door to the hangar.

The Assassin and Masterson went to join him, just as Matteu drove in and came to a halt by the old broken-down trailer.

'Slide the doors back across,' shouted the Assassin to Reynolds. His old flatmate jumped to it and began vigorously turning a crank handle to one side, just where the Assassin had guessed it might be.

Matteu jumped out and gave the Assassin a nod. His two companions followed. '*Où sont-ils?*'

The Assassin indicated the shed with a jerk of his head. '*Moment.*' He set off back to the workshop.

Matteu and his companions went the other way, across to the animal shed and the task that awaited them there. Masterson and Reynolds looked at each other.

After a couple of minutes, the Assassin came back into the hangar, dragging the dead weight of Grieves behind him. As if compelled, Reynolds followed him to the animal shed and watched him lay out the body on the tarpaulin next to the other two. They were already naked. Matteu's men had stripped them, piling their clothes up in a heap at one corner of the sheet.

'*Vous savez comment ça marche?*' the Assassin asked Matteu, nodding at the rendering machine.

The Corsican gave him a sharp nod, then waved his hand to indicate they all should leave.

'Let's get out of here,' said the Assassin to the others. 'Unless you want to watch?'

Reynolds had no intention of staying a second longer. Behind him, Matteu's companions had already heaved Fryatt's body up level with the hopper, ready to feed into the machine. His black and silver hair hung down unkempt behind him. He'd made his last visit to the barbers of Jermyn Street.

Just as they left the shed, the Assassin stopped and cocked an ear. 'I've got to go.'

He ran back into the workshop for his holdall, then marched down the length of the hangar and stepped out through the wicket gate set into the large sliding main door. Masterson and Reynolds followed along behind.

From that point on, time seemed to slow down for Reynolds, as he and the Assassin approached the end of their journey together. The Assassin strode across the broken concrete apron in front of the hangar, holdall over his shoulder, the survival radio dangling from his belt. From somewhere in the distance came the sound of rotor blades carried in on the wind.

The Assassin unhooked the radio. He twisted the function selector dial and held the handset up to his mouth. *'Fumée verte. Je répète, fumée verte.'*

He placed the bag on the ground and took out what looked to Reynolds like a grenade. The sound of the helicopter grew louder. Suddenly, it popped up over the horizon and started to make a wide circuit of the airfield at a height of a couple hundred feet.

The Assassin pulled a ring on the top of the grenade and tossed the canister to one side. After several seconds, green smoke began to pour out of it, making a pillar of cloud which drifted across the face of the morning sun. Even higher still, untainted by the smoke, the moon sailed serenely above them all.

As the machine circled, for a moment Reynolds thought he was looking at the distinctive hump-backed shape of a RAF Wessex and wondered if there had been some deep British double-plot all along. But when the aircraft turned for its final approach, he saw the French naval roundel with its inverted order of colours, defaced by a black anchor.

The note of the helicopter's blades changed as it flared down into a landing, the undercarriage struts compressing as they absorbed the impact. Slightly crouched, the Assassin walked up to the machine, its rotors still spinning at full revolutions, ready for an immediate takeoff. He threw the holdall into the cabin through the open sliding door and was helped up inside by a crewman. Reynolds saw the Assassin slump down onto the floor, his back against the side of the fuselage. Someone slid the door across and the German vanished from sight.

The helicopter sat there for three or four seconds longer in which time Reynolds wondered if there had been a change of plan. But then the pitch of its engine increased and the ungainly machine lifted from the ground. It turned, disappearing slowly below the horizon. Silence fell over the apron. And just like that, the Assassin was gone.

Epilogue

The ugly piston-engined Sikorsky settled at the rear of the long flight deck of the cruiser pushing its way through the chops of the grey North Sea.

The aircraft handlers ran out to secure the machine to the lashing points and eventually the cabin crewman gave me the all-clear to jump down. I dragged the holdall down after me, then followed him past an Alouette of the same type that I'd flown in from Donegal back to Dublin last year, and then down again via a ladder onto the open gun deck at the stern of the ship.

Kramer was waiting for me at the bottom, wearing a naval officer's uniform. I'd forgotten how much he liked to dress up. This particular costume had five stripes on each shoulder tab, presumably to make sure that no one under an admiral dared speak with him and expose him for the fraud that he was.

I tagged along as he made his way forward through the ship, stepping over the thresholds of watertight doors, and once out along an open-air side gallery, before going back into the superstructure. Just inside the final door a gaggle of young sailors lined the passageway, waiting for us to go past, perhaps puzzled why the Navy's equivalent of a colonel had an adjutant who looked like they'd just spent a long shift in the engine room.

We climbed up a couple of decks and he took me into a well-appointed cabin, more like an office really. I knew I was getting the special treatment because of the armed sentry he'd laid on outside the door.

In the corner of the compartment was a conference table bolted to the deck with cushioned benches running along the bulkheads and an ashtray in its centre. He took a seat and mentioned me to sit across the corner from him.

433

'Well?'

'Fryatt and Smythe are dead, so is Grieves.'

He raised his eyebrows.

'They died this morning in a shootout at the place I was picked up from. Less than an hour ago. They died for no real reason related to the task you set me,' I said in a brittle voice. 'They died because they lost trust in their accomplices, and then they tried to be clever and trick you and Brierly into doing the dirty work of getting rid of them.'

'What happened?'

'This morning, Fryatt and Smythe turned up at the airfield. I'll never know for sure if they only meant to finish off Grieves.'

'What happened next?'

'They asked me for the negative of Heath. When I tried to leave and push past them, they opened fire so I shot back. Grieves died in the crossfire.'

'Who's taking care of the bodies?'

'Some nephews of Jimmy. A farmer uses the old buildings on the airfield these days. It's also occasionally used by certain London criminal gangs as a place where they dispose of the corpses of rivals. The farmer takes money to turn a blind eye to what goes on in the animal shed. But unfortunately for Smythe, Jimmy's people had been there before, so we knew what to expect.'

'How do they get rid of the bodies?'

I gave him a dark look. 'How do you think? They grind them up and feed them to the animals. For the three people who died this morning, it was no more than they deserved.'

Kramer looked at me solemnly, but the effect was ruined by his ridiculous disguise.

'Were you ever in the Navy for real?' I asked distractedly.

'No. Of course not.'

'You never really moved on from the war, did you?' I said more angrily now. 'Brierly left it behind, but you wanted to cling on. Why? Because you didn't see any real shooting action and you've been trying to make up for it ever since?'

I stopped speaking to massage my temple. 'But now I'm the one who has to act out your fantasies. Getting the Air Force to fly me over the Channel in March, just like you did with your wartime agents. This whole performance with the Navy. Your direct line to the SDECE, your access to secret intelligence, drugs, and other men with guns. The way you play your games with the Stasi through me, pretending to yourself that you're running a double agent.'

'Are you unhappy with your life then? The life that you only enjoy outside of prison, thanks to me?'

'I've done a lot of shit for you in the past two years, Kramer. I'm weary. A lot of people have died.'

'Brierly still wants the negative of you together with Heath.'

'Do you know what he had done to the liaison girl to make her give up her copy?' I asked.

'I don't care. If Brierly wants the film, he'll get it.'

'Is that why there's a guard outside? To make sure he does?'

'I have something for you,' said Kramer.

He reached into his briefcase and took out a brown envelope which he laid between us. He opened it and fanned out a set of black and white photographs of my wife, sitting at a table under an awning with another woman whose face appeared in some of the snaps. By the look of things, they were outside at one of the cafes on the Grand Place.

'There's other photographs. More incriminating.'

I sighed and pulled the prints towards me for a better look.

'There's nothing here. They're holding hands across a table.'

Kramer looked disappointed. 'And kissing in other ones too.'

I shrugged. '"Kissing" or "exchanging kisses"? You know who this other woman is, don't you?' I asked.

He didn't reply.

'It's the sister of her ex-boyfriend. The one she's pregnant by.'

'She's not pregnant anymore.'

'How do you mean?' I asked sharply. A nameless fear clutched at my throat.

'She gave birth two days ago.'

'Then it's definitely not mine. She must have got her dates wrong - again.'

'I'm sorry,' said Kramer.

'Sorry for what? For spying on her?'

'The negatives of these prints in exchange for yours of Heath.'

I shook my head in despair. 'And you were the one who told me not to overplan things.'

From the pocket of my overalls I took out the film canister and set it on the table. I'd picked it up when I'd gone back into the office, still stinking of cordite, to drag out Grieves' body. It was greasy with someone's blood.

'Take it,' I said.

Kramer slid across a different envelope with the negatives. I shook them out and without looking at what they showed, burnt them one by one in the ashtray in the middle of the table. I didn't know if the ship was fitted with smoke or heat detectors, but I no longer cared. There were red pipes for sprinklers attached to the deckhead, but Kramer didn't object when I got out my lighter.

'You're determined to maintain your own version of reality, aren't you Oskar?'

'What's my alternative?' Right now, not having slept properly for almost twenty-four hours I was in no mood for debate. I wasn't regretting my final trip to Belgrave Square with Smythe's dossier late on Sunday morning either.

'Is that it now? Are we done? When can I go and see my wife and her child?'

'Bad temper doesn't become you, Oskar.'

'Bad temper?'

'I said do a good job for me in England and you'd get that directorship.'

I had done a good job for someone though. A great job in fact for Major Johannes at the Normannenstrasse. Possessor of his very own copy of a dossier of potential blackmail material on influential figures within the British Establishment. Plus the compromising photo of Heath which the Czechs had tried and failed to get. Whether the Ministry ever chose to use it was another matter - unless perhaps to rub it in the noses of the ŠtB.

But over and above all that, we'd seeded doubts as to whether MI6's head of counter-intelligence had lied to his own spy catchers about being *schwul*. If Johannes was really lucky, one day in the future he might be able to claim he'd triggered a new witch hunt within the British intelligence services. Ripping themselves apart from the inside out once again - just as they'd done over the former head of MI5, Roger Hollis.

'And have I got it? The job?'

'Who else would I give it to? Who else has the same personal obligation to me? And the necessary ruthlessness?'

'So the job's mine if I want it? You know that I don't need to work? My wife's family is rich.'

'Ungratefulness doesn't become you either.'

'When you took me to the airbase in Paris in March, did you know what you were dropping me into? Did you know how slim the real risk to Heath was from the three Marks? I don't believe they ever had anything on him.'

Kramer said nothing.

'Did you or Brierly suspect that you'd been asked to solve a dispute within a gang of pornographers and abusers? Or was it the case that even if the risk to Heath was slight, you weren't going to take any chances?'

'France has been preparing the final act in this drama for the past ten years, ever since Macmillan first admitted England's defeat on the world stage and applied to join the Community. It's the best chance we'll ever get to put them permanently out of action.'

I no longer cared. If the British politicians didn't care about the cost to their country of joining the EEC, then why should I have an opinion either? Even if them joining did help France. Only on Sunday morning, Brierly had accused me in Hyde Park of being a German nationalist. Maybe I was. Maybe like Heath, I was something without realising it. Whenever I did my favours for Major Johannes, I was helping the Party prove its usefulness to Moscow, helping East Germany and its people, Communists and Christians, avoid any further crushing embraces from the Bear. After all, East Germany was still Germany.

'How am I getting back to Brussels? I presume that's where she had the baby?'

'Same way as you got here.'

Kramer walked over to the captain's desk, picked up the phone, and spoke briefly. 'They'll come and fetch you in ten minutes,' he said, replacing the receiver and coming to sit back down.

'You pulled some strings to arrange all this, Kramer.'

He tapped the film canister.

'If this is what you say it is, then it will have all been worth it. We have Heath's balls in a vice.'

'You're a lucky bastard, Kramer. You didn't plan any of this, it just fell into your lap. Four men died as a consequence.'

Kramer shrugged. 'I played the cards in my hand.'

'Heath won't care about any photograph you might possess. He's such a stubborn person that nothing puts him off once he's fixed on a course of action. Luckily for you, his determination to make his mark on history means he's stubborn in the cause of France.'

'But Brierly and the cabal he works for care very much about a potential scandal,' said Kramer. 'Heath's opponents in Parliament care for sure.' Kramer grinned to himself. 'But now we have you, our nuclear weapon planted directly under Whitehall, making sure they'll give us whatever we ask.'

I let him have his moment of triumph while I thought of the reaction in East Berlin when they received the courier package from Belgrave Square. I even started to smile myself. But then I sobered up.

'As long as you keep Heath in power, you'll never need to use it. He's the greatest Frenchman of the late twentieth century. That's a special kind of treachery.'

FINIS

Afterword

'We must be clear about this: it does mean, if this is the idea, the end of Britain as an independent European state. I make no apology for repeating it. It means the end of a thousand years of history. You may say "Let it end" but, my goodness, it is a decision that needs a little care and thought.'

Hugh Gaitskell, 3 October 1962

In 2003 Dr. Richard North and Christopher Booker published the first edition of their book, *The Great Deception*, the definitive account of the development of the EU and the UK's waxing and waning relationship with that organisation. It is a reference I have turned to throughout the writing of the Charlemagne Series.

In North's conclusion to the 2021 edition, he writes from the perspective of someone who has lived through the UK's entire 47-year membership. His interpretation of the rationale for joining is expressed below:

'In the first instance, membership was seen as the (or an) answer to Britain's structural problems and, more importantly, defining for the political classes a role which could fill the political vacuum caused by loss of Empire. At the other end, there were those who would attribute most or many of Britain's structural problems to membership of the EU, whence leaving was seen as the solution. In neither case were the protagonists correct. Joining the EEC was no more a cure for Britain's problems than was leaving the EU.'

'Having lost an empire and failed to find a role, as Dean Acheson had so perceptively put it, it had taken refuge in the then EEC as a means of avoiding having to confront its new status. It is significant, therefore, that when it came to the campaign to leave the EU… what was hardly explored was that, once out of the EU, Britain would have to confront that self-same issue which it had been

avoiding for so long… To that extent, Brexit was never an answer to anything. It is simply the precursor to something bigger and more important, creating an opportunity better to define ourselves.'

The motivations of governments and political parties are the motivations of the individuals who make them up. They are as varied as the viewpoints I have tried to capture in this novel, and then more varied again.

But whatever the exact intent of the historical players mentioned in the narrative, avoiding the fundamental national questions outlined by North had grave repercussions for the presentation of the Project. It was this deception which ultimately doomed its acceptance by the British public, as over time, the true nature of what Heath had signed Britain up to became better understood.

'Thus, brick by brick, would the great supranational structure be assembled. Above all it would be vital never to define too clearly the ultimate goal, for fear this would arouse countervailing forces. In this sense, an intention to obscure and to deceive was implicit in the nature of the "project" from the moment it was launched. This habit of concealment was to become a defining characteristic. Despite that, there are those who argue that, if there was deception, it was easily penetrated. The intentions of the founding fathers of the EEC, and their successors, were either openly declared or otherwise accessible to anyone who took the trouble to seek them out.

This claim probably had its greatest force when applied to the outcome of the 1975 referendum, but the arguments tend to ignore the very different political and social environments of the time. In that pre-internet age, information was not always easily accessible. During the campaign, this current author (RN) sought to obtain a copy of the Treaty of Rome. It could only be bought from a very limited number of HMSO shops, necessitating a visit to High Holborn in central London to obtain one. But it could be bought and, reading for myself that the parties were "determined to lay the foundations of an ever closer union among the peoples of Europe", I voted "no" in the referendum.'

(North, 2021, *The Great Deception: The Secret History of the European Union*)

One detail I came across during my research puzzled me when trying to understand the motivations of the rank and file - why did the May 1971 Conservative Women's conference finish with the playing of

'Land of Hope and Glory,' as they cheered Heath on his way to the summit with Pompidou?

Heath had just told the conference attendees that the EEC would achieve what Hitler and Napoleon had failed to do. How could they hear these words, and then play the tune to a patriotic song containing the following lyrics?

> *'Wider still and wider*
> *Shall thy bounds be set*
> *God who made thee mighty*
> *Make thee mightier yet'*

Setting aside the power of leader cults within political parties, perhaps they imagined that Heath was going to lead 'Europe', like a kind of latter-day liberal Napoleon - after all, he said 'we' would achieve the Corsican dictator's dream. Maybe they believed that membership of the EEC would represent a second British imperial age, compensation for the ending of an earlier one.

But if these were the reasons for their cheers, as the UK was about to find out over the coming 45 years, they were delusions which existed in their heads only.

-

The quote from Gaitskell at the start of this Afterword shows that some people at least weren't taken in by the soothing description of the EEC as a 'Common Market.'

But in fact, it wasn't only some people, but the majority of voters who were opposed to joining. For all the accusations directed at pro-EEC political figures over their use of slippery words to sell the Project, in one sense their lies didn't matter, because they weren't believed by most of the electorate. The political establishment's justification for taking Britain into the EEC, regardless of what the people wanted, relied on the fig leaf of their various parties' 1970 manifesto statements and the principle of representative democracy.

On 4 May 1971, The Times carried a report of an event where Geoffrey Rippon (the Minister responsible for accession negotiations) firmly rejected the notion that any kind of EEC referendum would be considered. David Spanier, The Time's European economics journalist provided additional comment to the report, which quoted the results of the latest opinion poll on membership:

'Mr. Rippon's comment that "the decision whether or not to join cannot be based on public opinion polls" can be seen as a retort to critics of the Government's approach. It has an added point in the light of the latest poll published in The Sunday Times, which showed that 65 per cent were opposed to entry, and only 20 per cent for it, with 15 per cent undecided.

Privately, the Government are concerned at the unenthusiastic. not to say hostile, attitude of the public to Europe, as shown by the polls.

Publicly, however, they have given no sign of being alarmed by opinion polls. What ministers have done is to try to raise the public's sights on Europe, by showing enthusiasm for its political importance to Britain, and relegating the bread and butter issues as of secondary significance.

Still, if there is progress in Brussels at the crucial ministerial meeting next week, the Government will be extremely relieved.'

Whether Spanier intended it to be read that way or not, his last sentence is damning. On one hand, Heath and his cabinet assured the public throughout the accession process that EEC membership would result in 'no erosion of essential national sovereignty' (as promised in the July 1971 White Paper) - on the other hand they refused to allow this assertion to be tested by the public in a free vote.

Rippon called upon a higher principle to avoid taking the decision to the people. As reported in the same Times article, he claimed:

'Britain had founded her liberties on the representative principle. This was parliamentary democracy, and other democracies, though according great importance to Parliaments, might have alternative traditions.

He gave a warning that in Britain any departure from the doctrine of parliamentary responsibility in deciding national policy would set a precedent which all would live to regret. "The holding of a referendum on this issue would thus be unthinkable in this country."'

But a system of parliamentary democracy where the different representatives can offer no alternative choices to the question on whether that democracy should continue to exist, is clearly in an exceptional situation - one where the intended logic of the system has broken down. And at the last General Election prior to entry, this was precisely the case. The relevant paragraphs from the three manifestos are reproduced below.

Conservative Party:

Right at the end of the 1970 Conservative manifesto came a paragraph entitled 'Britain and the World.' Along with the 217-word text on the EEC, reproduced in its entirety below, were sections on defence alliances (350 words) and Rhodesian independence (122 words). The entire manifesto was 10,6867 words long, of which the intent to join the EEC took up 2%.

'If we can negotiate the right terms, we believe that it would be in the long-term interest of the British people for Britain to join the European Economic Community, and that it would make a major contribution to both the prosperity and the security of our country. The opportunities are immense. Economic growth and a higher standard of living would result from having a larger market.

But we must also recognise the obstacles. There would be short-term disadvantages in Britain going into the European Economic Community which must be weighed against the long-term benefits. Obviously there is a price we would not be prepared to pay. Only when we negotiate will it be possible to determine whether the balance is a fair one, and in the interests of Britain.

Our sole commitment is to negotiate; no more, no less. As the negotiations proceed we will report regularly through Parliament to the country.

A Conservative Government would not be prepared to recommend to Parliament, nor would Members of Parliament approve, a settlement which was unequal or unfair. In making this judgement, Ministers and Members will listen to the views of their constituents and have in mind, as is natural and legitimate, primarily the effect of entry upon the standard of living of the individual citizens whom they represent.'

(The Conservative Party, 1970, *A Better Tomorrow*)

The reader can decide for themselves if any of these promises were kept. Certainly, Heath had no intention to merely 'negotiate; no more, no less' - he had already decided to join, regardless of the cost to the UK, and regardless of his claim that 'there is a price we would not be prepared to pay.' Unless Heath was prepared to define that price for the electorate, his words were sheer sophistry.

Labour Party:

We have applied for membership of the European Economic Community and negotiations are due to start in a few weeks' time. These will be pressed with determination with the purpose of joining an enlarged community provided that British and essential Commonwealth interests can be safeguarded.

This year, unlike 1961-1963, Britain will be negotiating from a position of economic strength. Britain's strength means that we shall be able to meet the challenges and realise the opportunities of joining an enlarged Community. But it means, too, that if satisfactory terms cannot be secured in the negotiations Britain will be able to stand on her own feet outside the Community.

Unlike the Conservatives, a Labour Government will not be prepared to pay part of the price of entry in advance of entry and irrespective of entry by accepting the policies, on which the Conservative Party are insisting, for levies on food prices, the scrapping of our food subsidies and the introduction of the Value-Added Tax.'

(The Labour Party, 1970, *Now Britain's Strong - Let's Make it Great to Live In*)

And finally, from the Liberal Party of Jeremy Thorpe:

'In Western Europe we want the closest possible political unity. We see Britain's joining the Common Market as a part of this unity. The Common Market is an exciting experiment in the pooling of national sovereignty in the economic sphere. It can be the forerunner of a similar unity in foreign policy and defence. Liberals advocated Britain's applying to join at a time when it would have been very much easier than now. The Labour and Conservative Parties would not listen though they both subsequently came round to this point of view when in office. Liberals continue to believe that satisfactory terms can be obtained for British entry. In any event we wish to see the breaking down of barriers to international trade.'

(The Liberal Party, 1970, *Liberal Party General Election Manifesto*)

A test of the consent of the people to joining the EEC and changing the nature of their representative democracy did not occur on 18 June 1970, given the dominance - both then and now - of the three main parties. A special vote to gain this clear consent would appear to have been entirely reasonable, and four years later, the 'departure from the doctrine of parliamentary responsibility' which left Rippon so aghast did indeed take place.

But as for Rippon's assertion that a referendum before joining on 1 January 1973 would have 'set a precedent which all would live to regret' - let history be the judge.

Miscellany

Firstly, my heartfelt thanks in particular to Stephen McKittrick, Stephen Philips, and Jim Perkins for their support and generous advice, not only over the past 18 months but also since the early days of the Charlemagne series.

In the interests of space, the paperback edition of the Miscellany contains a reduced set of 16 notes on the following key areas listed below. The full Miscellany with 109 notes is available in the ebook edition (ISBN 978-1-00577-911-5), available on Amazon and other online stores.

Chapter 1   - the Czech honeytrap plot to target Heath
Chapter 6   - national sovereignty in the context of the EEC
             - the speed of unification and its end state
             - Heath's claims on British control over unification
             - Heath's relationship with the truth
             - opinion polls in 1971 on EEC membership
             - Heath's intelligence gathering on MPs as a Whip
             - Heath's stinginess with money
             - the campaign to sway MPs in favour of the EEC
Chapter 11   - Britain's new role in the world as part of the EEC
Chapter 13   - the French President's view on Britain's
               geopolitical destiny
             - Danczuk's view on why Cyril Smith escaped
               justice
Chapter 14   - Heath's claim he would succeed where Napoleon
               failed
Chapter 19   - Jeremy Norman's view on Heath's sexuality
Chapter 27   - the Dickens dossier
Chapter 33   - Heath's anti-Americanism

The key sources quoted below are:
- Rupert Allason's and Philip Ziegler's biographies of Heath (2010 and 2019 respectively),
- Simon Danczuk's 2014 biography of the Liberal Democrat MP Cyril Smith,
- Jeremy Norman's 2013 autobiography, and
- The Times archive.

Note: References to Books 1, 2 and 3 are to earlier Charlemagne series novels.

- Chapter 1 -

9. *What I can tell you is that back in 'sixty-nine no one in Whitehall took seriously the suggestion that Heath was at risk of blackmail from homosexual Communists.'*

The Czech attempt to honeytrap Heath is described in detail by Rupert Allason's in his 2019 biography, where he implies that Frolik wasn't the only source of the story. According to Allason, the plot was hatched by Jan Mrazek, the ŠtB Rezident (head of station) in London, and the organist in question was the bisexual Professor Jaroslav Reinberger.

By way of credentials, Allason has a long familiarity with the intelligence world, writing books on espionage under the pen name 'Nigel West.' He is also a former Conservative MP, and as explained at length in the introduction to his book, is an admirer of Heath - a long-term friend of the Allason family.

The Heath entrapment story was first disclosed to the public in Frolik's 1975 autobiography (he died in 1989). The BBC researched the claim in 2012 and concluded that Frolik's story was most likely a smear against Heath by his opponents in the Conservative Party (the leadership election he lost also took place that year). But this explanation doesn't account for the fact that the story had already been circulating in Whitehall since 1970. From the BBC correspondent's own article:

The book only came out in 1975 but rumours had been swirling for years before. "I first heard about it not long after I became Mr Heath's principal private secretary at Number Ten in 1970, just shortly after he became prime minister," recalls Robert, now Lord Armstrong.'

The BBC article also fails to mention that Heath himself referred to such a plot in his own autobiography. Like other episodes he relates, it is curiously different to other accounts. Heath claims he was warned by the head of MI5 of a plot involving an organist in 1970, not 1967, and that the agent was from Poland, not Czechoslovakia. From Heath's book:

'His people had heard that a church organist was being sent from Poland to London to give a recital, to which I would be invited, in the hope that he could have an interview in order to obtain the latest political information from me. As I had never heard of the organist, nobody else was able to identify him and there was no evidence whatsoever of any such organ recital in London, this kind of nonsense hardly seemed to represent a fruitful way of occupying either my time or that of MI5.'

Of course, another possibility that there was a genuine blackmail plot by a Warsaw Pact country in the late '60s, one which was recycled as a domestic smear five years later. Whatever the actual facts, what is known, is that a story of this nature was in circulation in 1971.

(Allason, *Ted Heath*, Ch.10; Corera, 25 June 2012, *Heath Caper*; Heath, *The Course of My Life*, Ch.17, p.462)

- Chapter 6 -

7. *'An EEC of ten rather than six will be able to promote our national interests better than we currently do on our own. British sovereignty won't be eroded or diluted in any way by joining the EEC.'*

This claim was often repeated in different forms over the period 1971-3. From the Heath government's own July 1971 White Paper:

'There is no question of any erosion of essential national sovereignty; what is proposed is a sharing and an enlargement of individual national sovereignties in the general interest.'

(Command Paper 4715 *The United Kingdom and the European Communities*, p.8)

Ziegler refers to discussions in Cabinet on the issue, where some members felt that the inevitable loss of independence was being glossed over in the drafting of the White Paper. Ziegler's comments that:

> *'It was not dishonest but it was disingenuous. Heath did not lie about his intentions but, so far as some of [the Cabinet] were concerned, he felt that the less that was said, the better it would be. Any possible surrender of sovereignty was hypothetical and lay in the relatively distant future; why therefore stir up fear and suspicion by discussing it now?'*

(Ziegler, *Edward Heath: The Authorised Biography*, Ch.14, p.290)

Allason confronts the same issue, when he writes about how Heath tried to backtrack in later years on the sovereignty question:

> *'...there are plenty of examples where he gave personal assurances that Britain's sovereignty would not be undermined by joining the EEC. In reality, what he meant was that in his view, Britain's interests were not compromised by accession, although a loss of sovereignty, by pooling it with other member states, was quite obvious. Yet for Heath, it was simply the achievement of joining that meant everything.'*

(Allason, *Ted Heath*, Ch.8)

13. *The line that Heath and the Foreign Secretary are taking with the press is that any new supranational political institutions will only evolve gradually over a long period of time. And by the way, he never explains the meaning of the term "supranational" either, let alone use it'*

The Cabinet was in on the deception too. Alec Douglas-Home, the former Conservative Party leader who served as a minister under Heath, spoke at Heriot-Watt University, February 12, 1971. His words were reported in The Times the following day:

> *'In a continent where the nation-state has played so large a part, I forecast that new political machinery will evolve slowly and that new institutions will be limited to those where there is a practical job to be done.'*

This was an assertion by a man who knew full well the contents of the Werner Plan and its plans for full economic and monetary union by 1980.

Heath had a vision for a Europe as a new Great Power (if not an actual superpower). Speaking after a trip to Bonn in May 1970, he said in the context of the Middle East:

'We do not want Soviet encroachment in the Mediterranean, nor a clash between the big powers. If in four-power talks on the Middle East Britain and France spoke with the weight of a united Europe behind them, much could be achieved. The Common Market must be more than haggling over butter and coal.'

(The Times, May 9, 1970)

Heath and 'supranational' scarcely appear together in the same article in The Times archives. Wilson got himself much more tied up by the term 'supranational', perhaps because of the legacy of his predecessor, Gaitskell. In 1969 at the Guildhall dinner referred to above he quoted Gaitskell's words:

'Whatever the future may hold, the creation of supranational, federal, political or defence institutions is not a reality in 10 or 20 years.'

(The Times, July 30, 1969)

Heath was even more cryptic. Interviewed by Die Welt in 1966, and reported The Times, his response to their correspondent's question speaks for itself:

'Die Welt: Britain always appeared to be an opponent of supranationality. Would you, Mr Heath, as the politician in charge of the 1962 negotiations and as prospective leader of a Conservative government, clarify the position of the Conservative Party in this respect?'

'Heath: When I opened negotiations with the community in Paris in 1961 the Conservative Government accepted the Treaty of Rome and the supranationality it contains. That remains the position of the Conservative Party.'

(The Times, October 28, 1966)

14. *'And he's told people that he'll veto any further progression towards a federal state if he disagrees with it.'*

Allason's view is that Heath was making 'extravagant assurances concerning... political sovereignty,' based on a belief that a British veto would always be in place to block any policies deemed to be 'unacceptable politically.'

(Allason, *Ted Heath.* Ch. 5)

This point is amplified by Ziegler in reference to that key phrase in the White Paper of there being: 'no question of any erosion of essential national sovereignty.' He notes that the definition of the word 'essential' depended very much on the viewpoint of the reader and wasn't one on which Heath had 'any inclination to enlarge.'

Ziegler too, mentions the fig leaf of veto, or as the Government claimed in the White Paper:

> '*On a question where a Government considers that vital national interests are involved, it is established that the decision should be unanimous.*'

This, however, was another lie. The Luxembourg Compromise was a gentleman's agreement without legal status - as Britain was to be the first to find out in 1982, when it tried to invoke the Compromise over agricultural price increases and was subsequently struck down (see Book 1: 'At the Court of Charlemagne').

(Ziegler, Edward Heath: The Authorised Biography, Ch.14, p.286; Command Paper 4715 *The United Kingdom and the European Communities*, p.8)

20. *'He claims a lot of things… Not all of them true.'*

Heath has form when it comes to stretching the facts. On top of his alternative version of the Czech homosexual entrapment story, where the year and the country were changed, he also claimed he'd commanded a firing squad in occupied Germany in September 1945 which had executed a soldier 'of Polish extraction' who was guilty of murder and rape.

Allason completely pulls this claim apart: at the time in question, capital punishment was by hanging; only one British soldier (a H.N. Yarlett) in the whole of the North-West European theatre of operations was convicted of murder in the period (with a recommendation for clemency); the condemned man wasn't wearing uniform and someone of Heath's acting-colonel rank wouldn't have commanded a firing squad. There's no mention of the event in the regimental war diary (signed by Heath) and the story didn't appear in the first draft of his 1998 autobiography (it appeared later, without explanation to the publisher).

Ziegler simply cannot believe Heath would have lied to that extent and suggests the story must relate to a Polish national who was executed in Hanover at that time. As regards a reason for Heath to embellish, Allason too is at a loss. The most obvious explanation would be a desire by Heath to polish his liberal credentials. He was a life-long opponent of capital punishment, claiming his stance was triggered by this very event - for which there is no historical record. But why wait until 1998 to add this detail? And why in his long history of public speaking and public life had he never mentioned it before?

(Allason, *Ted Heath*, Ch.2; Ziegler, *Edward Heath: The Authorised Biography*, Ch.3, p.46)

26. *'Before the election last year, Gallup reported sixty percent. It's hardly changed since then. In fact, there's a poll coming out in tomorrow's Sunday Times which says that sixty-five percent are opposed. On the other hand, Fleet Street is unanimous in its support for the Common Market.'*

The Gallup poll from April 1970 is quoted by North. The results of the poll reported in The Times, May 4, 1971, were 65% against. 20% in favour with 10% undecided. Excluding the 'Don't Knows' the opposition to joining was 72% - not far off the 75% figure claimed in that same month by the 'Common Market Safeguards Campaign,' a eurosceptic lobby group (at the time they were called 'anti-marketeers').

29. *'He loved all the secrecy as a Whip… He even started a card index on the MPs in which he recorded their psychological strengths and weaknesses.'*

According to Ziegler, Heath as Chief Whip really did maintain a card index of Tory MPs (the database of the pre- computer age) and their psychological strengths, weaknesses and foibles:

> *The Whips, if only to be alert to incipient scandal, had always felt it necessary to know a lot about the private lives of the individual members; under Heath procedures were regularised, card-indexes established, the psychological strengths and weaknesses of each member analysed and recorded.'*

(Ziegler, *Edward Heath: The Authorised Biography*, Ch.5, p.76)

30. *'There's a Westminster story about a black book, where the Whips record the sexual misdemeanours of MPs…'*

Allason, the espionage writer, has much to say about the intelligence gathering activities of the Whips:

> *Whips were, and are, the repositories of indiscretions, embarrassments and infidelities which are governed by a Mafia-like code of omerta. Of course, such*

knowledge can be construed as useful capital to be drawn against should the opportunity arise...'

Later in the same chapter, he writes:

'Whips often joke that they need to know about the private lives of their colleagues so they can be contacted a short notice, and to prevent them from embarrassing wives when telephoning round to gather in the troops for a division. Most of the time such information remains inside the Whips' Office.'

(Allason, *Ted Heath*, Ch.5)

31. *'Heath never pays for any of his professional expenses if he can help it. And that's despite his backers making him a Name at Lloyds.'*

According to Ziegler, Heath was not a mean man - but everything else in his official biography gives the opposite impression. Maybe Heath's notorious stinginess was down to social ineptness, but maybe even that is being too kind.

'The money he thus earned he guarded assiduously. He was not mean – he was capable of surprising generosity and when he entertained he liked to do so in style – but he much preferred other people to pay for things. There are innumerable anecdotes of people who thought that they were being treated to a drink or meal and ended up paying the bill themselves. Every expense was carefully considered and often begrudged.'

(Ziegler, *Edward Heath: The Authorised Biography*, Ch.8, p.137)

'Though he was determined that everything in Albany should be of the highest quality – whether in the vintage of the wines or the elegance of the furnishings – he never missed a chance to economise. His old friend and commanding officer, George Chadd, was now dealing in carpets: Heath expected him to provide the best for his new flat, but only at a substantial discount.'

(Ziegler, *Edward Heath: The Authorised Biography*, Ch. 8, p. 142)

Intriguingly, Ziegler makes no mention of Heath joining that lucrative club known as becoming a Lloyds Name, but Allason does. He believes Heath's membership dated from 1964 when Labour won the election, and he lost his Minister's salary after banishment to the Opposition benches.

'It seems likely that this was also the moment that a group of wealthy businessmen, led by the builder Maurice Laing, decided that Heath needed some financial independence. Precisely who participated in the syndicate, and what the terms

were of the trust or arrangement that was created for his benefit have never been disclosed, but it gave Heath security that he would never be able to achieve on the pay of an MP. It also provided him with sufficient capital to join Lloyds as an underwriting member, thereby gaining a second income from the original capital.'

(Allason, *Ted Heath*, Ch.5)

32. *'...the split is four-fifths in favour of joining. But that still leaves over sixty potential rebels and the Party's majority is only thirty. They're talking about a "fierce campaign of conversion" for the doubters.'*

Ziegler records the state of play at the start of 1971, as reported to Heath by the Chief Whip. Among the incentives offered to waverers during the 'fierce campaign of conversion' were: 'seminars, visits to Paris and Brussels and dinners organised by the Conservative Group for Europe.'

(Ziegler, *Edward Heath: The Authorised Biography*, Ch.14, p.278)

- Chapter 11 -

1. *'He told us that that once Europe is united, we can get back properly into the geopolitical great game.'*

Heath expounded his view of a multipolar world in a BBC Panorama programme broadcast on 24 January 1972, reported in The Times the following day:

'Asked if he saw Europe as a "third force" Mr Heath replied, "Well, you see, third force has got this unfortunate connotation of being a neutralist, wet sort of gathering which is going to give everything away. I don't see Europe in that way at all. That may have been the case when you had two super powers, the United States and the Soviet Union. Now you've got China emerging; it's in the United Nations, building up its power. And we in Europe. I believe, can be a force on our own which stands for the things which Europe believes are important." While Mr Heath was clearly fired with great enthusiasm for the grand design of a United Europe, he was also aware of the real problems facing the Community "as a whole and Britain in particular."'

(The Times, January 25, 1972)

2. *'We're going to be a force in the world again. In Africa we'll put all the colonial baggage behind us and have a fresh start there too'*

Ziegler reports a dinner attended by Tony Benn at Number 10 in June 1972:

> *'After dinner, Heath made "a mad, impassioned speech about Europe and Africa and how, now the imperial period was over, Europe was united and it would work with Africa to be an influence in the world. It was nineteenth century imperialism reborn in his mind through status within the Common Market."'*

(Ziegler, *Edward Heath: The Authorised Biography*, Ch.18, p.400)

Ziegler goes on to say, that in fairness to Heath, this was an extreme interpretation of his genuine concerns for the developing world. This interest comes through in many of his speeches leading up to accession. One of these from October 1972, sounds familiar to modern ears, even over 50 years later:

> *'For the first time the countries of Western Europe have not only the responsibility which their privileges impose upon them, but also the opportunity and means to. apply their energies together in a concerted manner. There is room for many views about how this responsibility can best be fulfilled.*
>
> *We have suggested as one possible means that in certain cases we should be prepared to lighten the burden of indebtedness by a waiver of interest on aid loans to those countries who face the greatest problems. Another possibility is that we should re-examine the terms and conditions of our aid, so as to make sure that it benefits the developing nations to the greatest degree possible...*
>
> *We can all agree that the problem of bridging the gap between rich and poor countries is likely to prove one of the greatest challenges of all to our imagination and statesmanship in Europe.'*

(The Times, October 20, 1972)

- Chapter 13 -

2. *The French president had been insistent with the presenter that Britain's only geopolitical option was 'Europe.' The 'open sea' belonged to the past.'*

In May 1971, Pompidou recorded an interview in France for Panorama which was well-received by the pro-EEC faction within the Conservative Party.

In the interview he slips in a few lies of his own, such that the only form of government for Europe would be 'confederal' (i.e. intergovernmental) and rejected the notion of a 'technocratic or administrative power which imposed itself on several states' - which of course is exactly what the supranational EU Commission was designed from the start to do.

But Pompidou would have left the BBC viewers in no doubt as to the change of identity that the British government was being asked to make (not the British voters, though):

'But obviously it is a very big decision that has to be taken by the Prime Minister and the British Government. Because as Sir Winston Churchill said: "If you ask me to choose between Europe and the open sea, I choose the open sea."

And today I think the question for Britain is to choose Europe. I, for one, wish the choice to be made sincerely and deeply while, of course, assessing all the changes it will bring about in the life of the British, in their very conception of it and in their relations with the outside world.'

(The Times, 18 May 1971)

5. *'If the Establishment is never forced to confront child abuse within its ranks, then who knows how far it will eventually spread throughout society?'*

As Danczuk's biography of Cyril Smith progresses, and he reports even more examples of the official blind eye shown to Smith's blatant abuse, he becomes ever more despairing - and puzzled.

One of the most extreme stories of Smith's invisibility to the law is an account of a CID training seminar in the early '80s. At one point, CCTV footage from Euston Station was shown to the attendees, which unmistakably showed Cyril Smith propositioning a boy. Everyone present knew exactly who it was, but the attendee interviewed by Danczuk (and presumably his colleagues on the course) naively assumed that the British Transport Police must already have been on the case.

The rationale for this blindness, as offered by Danczuk, comes from another police officer. The explanation is fantastical, but might well be true:

'One caller, a former dog-handler with the Metropolitan Police, said Special Branch officers had long shared the police's irritation at Cyril being able to avoid prosecution, but there was a simple explanation. The DPP was worried that Cyril might be able to do something remarkable if he went to trial. He might have been able to win public sympathy for paedophilia.

This sounds incredible now but the former police officer went on. 'They knew how popular he was in Rochdale and thought it might backfire. They thought ladies in Rochdale would be offering their children up in a show of support.'

My head was spinning at the thought. It sounded complete lunacy. But if you followed this thinking down the rabbit hole into 1970s Wonderland you quickly had to acknowledge there were more than a few advocates for paedophilia.'

(Danczuk, *Smile for the Camera*, Ch.9)

- Chapter 14 -

1. *'He told them he was going to achieve through negotiation what Hitler and Napoleon had failed to achieve through conquest.'*

Of all the lines uttered by Heath on the topic of joining the EEC, this is perhaps the most egregious one, in terms of laying out his imperial ambitions for the EEC - and his own imperial role within it. Where Napoleon had failed, Heath would succeed:

"'We in Britain. and our friends in Europe. face at this moment of history a momentous test of will. Do we have the courage to forget the dissensions and the suspicions that have divided us, and to learn to work together for lasting peace and prosperity, not just for our country but for a continent?" Mr. Heath asked. "Do we have the wisdom to achieve by construction and cooperation what Napoleon and Hitler failed to achieve by destruction and by conquest?" There were, he admitted, people who deeply and sincerely opposed Britain's entry on any terms. The issue was complex but the opportunities were too great to be missed. "Let us all recognize the opportunity that is now presented to us for what it is: the chance to unite Western Europe."'

(The Times, May 20, 1971)

Egregious and imperialistic or not, it was what the Conservative women wanted to hear. Maybe they thought Britain was about to bring Europe to heel in the way that Napoleon had. How else to explain the playing of 'Land of Hope and Glory' on the organ of Central Hall?

'Mr. Heath was clapped to his feet twice by the conferences when he finished speaking. His vision of a united Europe had brought a tear to the eyes of several of the senior lady Conservatives sitting beside him. And as the huge organ of the Central Hall thundered out "Land of Hope and Glory" behind him, Mr. Heath left for what he clearly saw as an appointment with history.'

There were two party-poopers though, claiming that Heath the European emperor was wearing no clothes.

'Mr. Heath missed the discussion on British entry in the morning session when Mrs. Joan Martin, of Banbury, gave warning that if Mr. Heath took Britain into the Common Market "he will split the Conservative Party from top to bottom and we shall then be open to a new Labour Government which will last for a very long time indeed." Mrs. Sheila Leach, of Rugby. was also worried about Britain's future once she was in the Common Market. A Conservative Government would not go on for ever, she said, and a Labour Government. dedicated to international socialism. might lose Britain in political unity with a Europe already increasingly at the mercy of communist groups.'

But ultimately, Comrade Napoleon was always right and opposing him was 'heresy.'

'The other 12 speakers from the floor all supported entry, although their more reasoned arguments evoked a less emotional response. Only when two of them pointed out that to question entering the E.E.C. was to question Mr. Heath's judgment did the conference realize the possible magnitude of its heresy. It was left to Mr. James Prior, Minister of Agriculture and Fisheries, to bring the emotion back into the pro-Market lobby. How ironic it would be. he said, if we British, whose ancestors had formed the greatest nation on earth, lacked the courage and vision to ensure that we remained a great nation now.'

- Chapter 19 -

1. *'Redecorated Number Ten with white and silver patterned wallpaper and gold moiré curtains. Artistic after a fashion with his music. Enjoys the manly rough and tumble of life under sail and his mother is the only woman he ever loved.'*

In an article written for The Times in 2014, Jeremy Norman sets out his thesis that Heath was a closet homosexual.

'How did we know Ted was gay? It's called "gaydar", the sixth sense that's made up of gesture, looks and a list of characteristics common in gay men but, above all, by getting to know him. We had all learnt the hard way to disguise our natures, so it made us experts in recognising others in hiding. We sensed that he was reaching out to us because we were a gay couple…

Ted was always entertaining but never intimate. He had so schooled himself to suppress and hide his nature that it made him too guarded to become close. At times the strain must have been unbearable and at those moments he turned to the solace of music.

There was an emptiness in his life that is often found in those who have never known requited love. He wanted to connect with us but had no idea how to do so'

(The Times, 14 September 2014)

In Norman's autobiography, he writes that Heath had a 'long-buried gay designer gene' - based on the interest Heath that took in the redecoration work at Arundells, his 'magnificent Queen Anne house' in the close of Salisbury Cathedral. But Barbara Castle wasn't so sure:

> 'In his biography of Heath John Campbell described the new décor as being painted with "strong masculine colours" that reflected both his personal taste and his view of what a modern prime minister's residence should look like. Heath scrawled an indignant "Nonsense!" in the margin. Barbara Castle, on the other hand, found that "someone with appalling taste had had it tarted up: white and silver patterned wallpaper, gold moiré curtains of distressing vulgarity...It looked like a boudoir."'

(Ziegler, *Edward Heath: The Authorised Biography*, Ch.12, p.252)

Heath took his sailing seriously, which given the amount someone or some people invested into his hobby ought not to be surprising. Maybe it was a passion more than a hobby, though.

> 'Heath took the point, Hurd replied, but there was nothing in the least aristocratic or leisurely about life on Morning Cloud and "anyone sipping a Martini aboard would quickly cease to be a member of the crew."'

(Ziegler, *Edward Heath: The Authorised Biography*, Ch.11. p.222)

Despite Norman's insistence that Heath was a closet non-practicing homosexual, he still has no direct evidence for his assertion. If Heath had gone to Harrow, as Norman did, then based on Norman's accounts of his schooldays, he could hardly have avoided exposure to homosexual activity. But exposure alone wouldn't be proof. The conclusion of most commentators is more mundane - that Heath was asexual, uninterested in the topic. But whether Heath was interested or not, other people were, and he was subject to lifelong speculation, and indeed the blackmail attempt by the Czech ŠtB in 1967, as related by Josef Frolik.

> 'His love of the organ (or so an organist told me), his exaggerated affection for his mother, his great artistic sensibilities and his bachelor, almost monastic, life lead me to the conclusion that if he had a sexuality, as everyone must, he had to be inclined towards men. That impression was reinforced by his monosyllabic answers to questions about his love life and his one close women friend: he clearly had something to hide. Sir Edward was a master at monosyllabic equivocation and evasion. "Yes, that's right."

Was all he would reply to the question, "Were you sad when she married someone else?"

(Norman, *No Make-Up*)

- Chapter 27 -

2. *'There's Westminster rumours of a kind of black book, just like the one the Whips maintain on the MPs. But this one supposedly contains the secrets of the entire Establishment, all the way from the top to the bottom.'*

Over the winter of 1983-4 the Conservative MP, Geoffrey Dickens, passed two dossiers of allegations of child abuse by Establishment figures to Leon Brittan, the Home Secretary at the time. In an 1983 interview with the Daily Express, he also threatened to name eight prominent figures under Parliamentary privilege if no subsequent action was taken.

Dickens was convinced his material was explosive - it would 'blow the lid off' the lives of powerful and famous child abusers, according to his son in a 2014 interview with the BBC. Needless to say, nothing of the sort took place, leading to several theories about what happened next. Marking their own homework, a Home Office report in 2013, claimed that the 'credible' elements of the dossier had been were sent to police - and what they deemed not credible had been 'not retained.'

Dickens did claim one prominent scalp during his career - that of Peter Hayman: diplomat, MI6 officer, and member of the notorious Paedophile Information Exchange. In 1978, Hayman inadvertently left behind a package of compromising material on a bus which led to him being caught by the police - before being released with a warning not to send any more porn through the post.

The story broke in Private Eye in 1980, and in 1981 Dickens did indeed name Hayman in Parliament.

- Chapter 33 -

1. *'Heath wasn't a full minister with a portfolio during Suez fifteen years ago. He was still Chief Whip. But he attended Cabinet meetings and had a ringside seat as the Americans stabbed us in the back.'*

Heath's anti-Americanism may have started any time. In 1939 he went on a universities' debating tour to an isolationist USA. From 1944, he served in an Anglo-American army in north west Europe, one which became increasingly American and less Anglo with every passing month after D-Day.

From 1961, as negotiator of Britain's first application to the join the EEC, he moved in Gaullist circles and just like the General, Heath's friend Jobert was a strong believer in French foreign policy being independent of the US.

Allason claims that Heath's involvement in the decision-making around the fateful 1956 intervention in Suez was closer than generally realised:

> '...while it has been well-known that Heath attended the Cabinets held on 25 and 30 October, few knew that in fact he had been brought into Eden's inner circle rather earlier, at Chequers on 21 October, when the controversial decisions were made to participate in a clandestine plan hatched by the Israelis and the French to invade Egypt.

(Allason, *Ted Heath*, Ch.4)

During two further trips to Paris following the May 1971 summit with Pompidou, Britain's new world order began to take shape:

> 'Heath allegedly gave a firm commitment to abandoning Sterling and joining a single European currency, monetary union having been agreed by the six in March, and... an assurance that the 'special relationship' with America would be abandoned in favour of a tilt towards a European axis. As Heath later described it... "Our purpose was to see a strong Europe, which could speak with one voice after a full discussion of the world problems affecting it, and could then exert effective influence in different parts of the globe."'

(Allason, Ted Heath, Ch.8)

2. *'And what does Nixon think about all this?... He imagines Heath is still an ally.'*

According to Henry Kissinger, the personal chemistry between Nixon and Heath would never have worked, even if they'd been on the same page politically:

> 'Heath shared too many personality traits with Nixon for those two quintessential loners ever to establish a personal tie. Like Nixon, Heath was uncomfortable in personal relations and felt more at home in carefully planned, set-piece intellectual encounters. Less suspicious than Nixon, Heath was not any more trusting.

Charm would alternate with icy aloofness, and the change in his moods could be perilously unpredictable. After talking with Heath, Nixon always felt somehow rejected and came to consider the Prime Minister's attitude toward him as verging on condescension.'

(Allason, *Ted Heath*, Ch.7)

The misapprehension, misunderstanding and meddling of the US government in the politics of European unification deserves its own study. Monnet's links with George Ball are referred to in the notes to Chapter 6 and North notes another connection:

'From [1948], as recent academic research has established, the [American Committee on United Europe] was used as a conduit to provide covert CIA funds, augmented by contributions from private foundations such as the Ford Foundation and the Rockefeller Institute, to promote the State Department's obsession with a united Europe, in what one historian has called a 'liberal conspiracy'.

(Booker & North, *The Great Deception*, Ch.3, p.111)

The American desire was to have Britain inside the EEC, pulling the strings on their behalf. It didn't always work out like that. As regards Nixon and Heath's specific asks at the time:

'...their first real discussions had taken place shortly before Christmas [1970] when Heath stayed at Blair House as an official guest. On that occasion Nixon gave his approval to Britain's imminent accession to the EEC, in the belief that this would bolster NATO's strength, and Heath sought American support on Rhodesia and South Africa.'

(Allason, *Ted Heath*, Ch.9)

Short Bibliography

Rupert Allason, 2019: *Ted Heath*

Thomas Allen & Norman Polmar, 2004: *The Spy Book*

Christopher Andrew, 2010: *The Defence of the Realm*

Christopher Andrew & Vasili Mitrokhin, 1999 & 2015: *The Mitrokhin Archive: The KGB in Europe and the West*

Stefan Berger & Norman LaPorte, 2010: *Friendly Enemies*

Christopher Booker & Richard North, 2005 & 2016: *The Great Deception: The Secret History of the European Union*

Maud Bracke, 2013: *Which Socialism, Whose Détente?*

Alfred McCoy, 1972, 2003: *The Politics of Heroin*

Anthony Daly, 2018: *Playland*

Simon Danczuk, 2014: *Smile for the Camera*

Anthony Glees, 2003: *The Stasi Files*

David Hannay, 2000: *Britain's Entry into the European Community*

Hermann Hartfeld, 1980: *Faith Despite the KGB*

Edward Heath, 1998: *The Course of My Life*

Dick Kirby, 2020: *The Sweeney*

James Morton, 2012: *Gangland Soho*

Jeremy Norman, 2013: *No Make-Up*

Mariella Novotny, 1971: *King's Road*

Martin Pearce, 2017: *Spymaster*

Lilian Pizzichini, 2021: *The Novotny Papers*

John Preston, 2016: *A Very English Scandal*

John Preston, 2021: *Fall: The Mystery of Robert Maxwell*

Neil Root, 2019: *Crossing the Line of Duty*

David Teale, 2021: *Surviving the Krays*

Markus Wolf, 1998: *Memoirs of a Spymaster*

Philip Ziegler, 2010: *Edward Heath*

Printed in Great Britain
by Amazon